The World in Pancho's Eye

THE WORLD IN PANCHO's EYE

J. P. S. BROWN

UNIVERSITY OF NEW MEXICO PRESS
ALBUQUERQUE

13 12 11 10 09 08 07   1 2 3 4 5 6 7

Library of Congress Cataloging-in-Publication Data

Brown, J. P. S.
  The world in Pancho's eye / J.P.S. Brown.
      p. cm.
  ISBN 978-0-8263-4190-7 (cloth : alk. paper)
  1. Arizona—History—1912–1950—Fiction. 2. Mexican-American
Border Region—Fiction. 3. Mexico—History—1912–1950—Fiction.
I. Title.
  PS3552.R6856W67 2007
  813'.54—dc22

                              2007015700

Book design and composition by Damien Shay
Body type is Palatino 10.5/14
Display is Palatino Bold and Mesquite

For
GEORGE and **PATSY MCCULLOUGH**,
gracious friends in Pancho's eye.

ACKNOWLEDGMENTS

I started writing this book in longhand in 1995 and finally sold it ten years later. I finished a 960-page first draft in 2000. I had not published anything since 1994, so I was not confident that I'd done anything good. I asked partners Chuck Bowden and Mary Martha Miles of Tucson to give me their opinion of it. They are good writers and everybody knows it. Mary Martha told me she liked it. Chuck liked it because it's not sentimental.

Twelve agents showed no interest in subsequent drafts of *Pancho*. I found out that Al Hart, who had been my publisher at Dial Press in New York for my first three books, now ran the Fox Chase Literary Agency in Pennsylvania. I contacted him and he said he was not taking on new clients, but would represent *Pancho* if he liked it. He liked the first draft enough to tell me it was too long and I needed to cut it.

I cut it to about six hundred pages, sent it back to Al, and kept only the small remnant that remained of my heart. He said, "It's too long; cut it."

Although I trusted Al's opinion, I could not cut another word. I sat on it a while, read it again, and still could not cut it. I only knew one person on whom I might impose the job, but she is a former wife. Jo Baeza of Pinetop, Arizona, and I were sweethearts as kids, then married nine years, then divorced. We barely spoke, but she had coached and loved me through the publication of my first three books. She would be honest, maybe have pity on me and assume the task, and she would defend my precious words.

When I asked if she would do it, she said, "Of course." "Please be gentle," I said. She said, "Prepare to die." Then she cut it to its present form and I didn't die.

Jo left me with a lot of stories I can still use. I like the lean *Pancho* as much as I liked the fat one, maybe more. After Max Evans read and recommended it, the lean version sold to the best publisher of Western Americana in the world, Luther Wilson of the University of New Mexico Press. So there you are. I have these five people to thank for the good time you will have with this book, so I guess you do too.

ONE

La Potranca

A potranca *is a filly. To a horseman the term recalls more than only the picture of a young, female horse. At the sound of the word, he recalls the leggy, lithe, headstrong traits of great mares he knew when they were young. It recalls the deeply tender looks they gave. It recalls the unconscious grace of princesses and their regal acceptance of homage.*

Michael Paul Summers was born into a family of cattlemen in August of 1930 as the Great Depression and drought choked Arizona ranches. His mother was Maggie Summers, daughter of Bert and Maude Jane Sorrells. From 1890 until 1918 Bert and his brothers Roy and Ray controlled more than one million acres of cattle country and ran thirty thousand mother cows in southern Arizona and northern Sonora. Bert died in the flu epidemic of 1918 and by 1930 his three sons and Michael Paul's father, Paul Summers, were about to waste the last of his legacy on whiskey. Maggie knew they were doing wrong, but she was too wild and volatile to stop it.

People in Santa Cruz County said that Maggie did not arrive on earth the way other people did. They said she hit the ground running. The cattle people called her *La Potranca*. They admired her as they would a racehorse, but she was bronky and did not allow reason to curb her actions. She was quick to love, but also quick to start a fight. She loved contention as much as peace. She liked to run and play, was decent with a fine moral sense, could do hard work as though tapping for a dance, but she could be as mean and ungovernably ill-tempered as she was decent and good.

Paul Summers was a cowboy who had worked for Bert and Maudy Jane and was best friends with Maggie's brothers. He loved to cowboy, ride broncs, get drunk with his friends, and be Maggie's husband as long as it was fun, but he tried not to get serious about any of it. When Maggie reminded him that he would have to stop running and playing and be a responsible man, he only grinned.

The women in Mikey's family should have worried about the amount of alcohol their men used, because the very atmosphere they breathed was permeated with the fumes. However, when they were young they seemed to think that drinking was only entertaining, insignificant, family mischief.

The failures of the men were blamed on the recklessness and love of fun with which the women thought they had been born. Nobody thought their lives might be better if they stayed sober.

Drinking was not frowned upon by most border people as much as it was by most people who lived north of Tucson. The border between Mexico and the U.S. was called "the line." Americans were not permitted to buy whiskey in the stores in 1930 because the U.S. government enforced Prohibition, but people in Nogales could go across the line and drink all they wanted in full view of federal lawmen. Customs inspectors on the line massed no attack on the influx of booze into Arizona, either. If a rancher wanted mezcal, he could intercept one of the burro trains that passed regularly through his ranch. He could buy his booze cheap from a smuggler by the *barrica*, the twenty-liter keg. The smugglers were so confident in their business that they figured even burros could outrun the kind of pursuit the feds might send after them.

Cowboys were notorious for getting drunk when they went to town. A cowboy worked for months out in the country with no whiskey, no music, no companions, and nobody but an old cow or a mean horse to hear him howl when something distressed him. He and everybody else figured he ought to get drunk when he was in town. At least, nobody blamed him if he did.

About the time the Sorrells women came to realize the deadliness of the sickness in their men, cowboy recklessness had cost five fortunes and their families had split and scattered. If the livers and stomachs of the men had not been so hardy, their heads not so thick, perhaps they could have died of alcoholism early and saved a lot of money and grief. As it was, they drank on healthily until their entire quota of whiskey was gone and then they drank everybody else's, too. Nobody ever worried they would die that way. As men who did cowboy work, they rode in acres of accidents all the time. Drunk, they survived wrecks most horrible. They did not die of their accidents or the effects of alcoholism until after they sobered up.

On the night Mikey was born, Paul and his cohorts arrived at the railroad cattle pens on the outskirts of Nogales, Sonora, with a herd of two thousand cattle they had driven up from Magdalena. As soon as the cattle were penned, they rode the *cacharpa* bus to the International Bar on the Mexican side of the line to drink tequila with lemon and salt. The cacharpa was an early 1920s model truck with a canvas cover and passenger benches bolted down in the back.

Paul did not think to call his mother-in-law's house to ask about Maggie, even though he knew it was time she gave birth to their first child. He could not easily break away from his cronies to find a phone on the line. In the summer, the International Bar's doors were left wide open twenty-four hours a day so people only had to take one step in off the street to have a drink, but the place had no phone. Paul and his cronies had too much of a thirst to think of anything else for a while.

At eleven o'clock, Bill Shane, who lived next door to Maudy Jane, Maggie's mother, came to work as a customs service inspector at the Morley Avenue *garita*, the station house on the line. He saw Paul in the International Bar and walked over and told him that Dr. Gustetter was with Maggie and his child was about to be born. Paul and his cohorts commandeered another Mexican cacharpa and arrived at Maudy Jane's just before Michael Paul was born. They did not stay long. Maggie was in no mood for a visit with a bunch of cowboys. She said that Paul and his partners smelled as bad as coyotes who had spent the night with their heads inside an old dead carcass, and that made her afraid to even have them in the house. Paul's cronies tried to make him stay home, but as soon as Michael Paul was born and Dr. Gustetter said that mother and son were well, Paul fled. He knew his wife. No one could get along with a catamount who had just given birth.

He returned with his cohorts to stand at the International Bar for the rest of the night. At dawn, they took the cacharpa back to the cattle pens, caught and saddled their horses, and drove the herd down the Nogales Arroyo to the line. They were about to sober up when they reached the border at sunup, which made them gaze toward the International Bar like barn-soured horses.

Paul was the only one undisciplined enough in his drinking to break ranks. He made a dash for the International and bought two bottles of tequila. After he gave everyone a swallow, he stashed the bottles in Herb Cunningham's saddlebags to be smuggled across the line. Herb also worked as a line rider for the customs service, except when he worked as a cattle buyer and trader with Paul, and his brother customs officers would never inspect his saddlebags for liquor.

After crossing to the American side, the herd was driven through the middle of town and then out on the Tucson highway. The cowboys worked hard to keep cattle off people's yards. The steers were inclined to eat everything in sight and the front yard lawns and flowers would have been a banquet for them. The Tucson road was paved in sections, and bars of thick tar connected the sections. The tar softened as the day warmed and the cattle tracked through it and spread it around. The road was shaded by tall cottonwood, mesquite, poplar, evergreen, and willow trees that grew on the edges of the front yards and buzzed with locusts. The day was still and new thunderheads appeared and began to climb, pile, and roil toward their highest perches in the sky.

When the steers reached Maudy Jane's house, she helped Maggie out to sit on the front porch with Mikey, then stood in her front yard with a broom to protect her grass and flowers from the steers. The hoodlum cowboys straightened in their saddles so Maggie and Maudy Jane would not see how drunk they were.

Maggie wanted Mikey to watch the cattle and horses go by. People not raised around cattle seldom take pleasure in the way they look. City people wonder what cattle people see in cattle, and cattle certainly do not consider people to be much good. Mikey's family liked the way they moved, the way they were made, their sounds and odors, and his parents wanted to know what his first impression of them would be.

The sound of cattle, from the click of their hooves to the rattle of their horns when they are close together, even their bellowing, called "bellering," is good to cattle people. They love to hear their cattle bawl, as they love the voices of their children. Cattle are their work, play, and subsistence. People are grateful to cattle because they give up their lives to preserve families.

Cattle people love the look in the eyes of cattle and the way they perk their ears. They laugh at their comical ways and feel sorry when they have to be shipped away to market. They see grace and cleverness in them. They have peaceful, happy dreams about cattle and dreams that make them sad. They are able to grow close to cattle because cattle teach them new lessons every day. Cow and horse manure is inoffensive to them. Cattle people like the smell of manure and do not feel dirty when they get it on them. When cattle show great heart and courage, which is often, they justify the dedication of the people who care for them.

Paul was anxious to see if his son would enjoy cattle as much as he did and he was happy to parade a herd by Mikey so soon after he was born. He was happy to imagine that Mikey liked what he saw. Who knew what he saw? A cowman's infant might see, hear, and enjoy more than anybody could guess. At least he was being exposed to what Paul believed was best about the world on the first day of his life.

Maggie liked cattle too, but would not admit it. Her parents never told her to love livestock in so many words, so the nuns of St. Joseph's Academy in Tucson had tried to teach her that good people should love music, cleanliness, religion, culture, and humanity a whole lot, but that cows only gave milk and provided staple ingredients for soup. A lady could get cattle on her person and that could be malodorous and painful. A Catholic girl should carefully avoid closeness with beasts. The soul of any girl who gave the impression that she could be in concert with cows was lost. In spite of what the nuns taught, Maggie was glad to hold her son close to a herd of two thousand steers as it rumbled by only thirty yards away, even though he could barely open his eyes to the glare of the day.

Paul's laugh made other people happy, but Maggie seldom laughed with him when she wanted him to behave. She could see that he was about to act silly, so she did not smile.

Paul was a showoff and wilder than a wolf. Encouraged by a smile from Maggie, he might try to jump his horse over the house. He figured that everybody is a showoff, but it's no good unless the showoff has a lot of style. No matter how much of a flash a man could be, he would look bad if his horse's tail was too long or too short because he is no horseman if he does not know how to groom his horse's tail to its proper hock-high length.

Paul did not ride peacefully up and down the herd as it passed by his wife and son that day. He spurred his horse into a run to turn miscreant cattle back into the herd, reined him into a long slide to stop him, then spun him on his hind legs toward the cattle to show him off.

The horse was a wiry, brown gelding with a diamond on his forehead. Paul called him Ice because of the diamond. He had been a green bronc when Paul took him down to Mexico. Now he turned back through his own tail to stay ahead of cattle.

When the herd was so intimidated by Paul and Ice that it streamed by Maudy Jane's house without even looking at the lawn, Paul showed the horse some flat stepping stones that crossed the lawn to the front door. "Hold Mikey up so he can watch this, Honey," he said. He touched Ice with his spurs and checked him softly with his rein at the first stepping-stone. Ice would have climbed Granny's chimney if Paul wanted him to. When he tried to take a step, Paul checked him and did not let him put his foot down unless it stepped on a stone. When he figured out what Paul wanted, Ice dropped his nose to the ground and walked carefully across the stones to the front porch where Maggie stood.

"Ha, ha, ha," Paul said. "How do you like that, Honey?"

Maggie did not look at him. "Slick trick for a worthless pair like you and that horse. Is that all you've had to do while you've been gone, teach a darned old bronc to walk on rocks?"

"Ha, ha, ha," Paul said. "Well, have to go. *Adios.*" Divots of turf flew off Ice's hooves as Paul backed him off the lawn.

"Paul, you've *ruined* mama's lawn," Maggie shouted, but Paul raced down the road to turn the leaders of the herd away from the Shanes' lawn.

After the herd passed the Dalton Dairy on the open highway, Paul and Buster, Maggie's brother, pushed their *remuda* of saddle-horses ahead to the Rock Corral Ranch that belonged to Maggie and Paul. Buster went in the house to cook dinner. Paul wrangled Maggie's Little Buck out of the horse pasture, saddled him, and turned Ice loose. Little Buck was a four-year-old Steeldust-bred Buckskin. His yellow hide was dappled, and a black line covered his spine. In the summer when the sun caught the clear highlights on his coat, it turned the color of dappled gold. The hair of his mane and tail was as black and glossy as an Apache girl's. When Paul broke him, he did not buck a jump and he took to cattle like a bulldog takes to cats.

Bud Parker had given Maggie the horse. Bud and his brother Dink raised Steeldust horses long before anyone but cowmen knew their worth, long before anyone called them "Quarter Horses."

Paul spent two years making Little Buck into a cow horse. Now that he was a made horse, Paul was forbidden by Maggie to ride him. The horse was smart enough and snooty enough about himself to know he was Maggie's pet. Paul might be in charge of the work, but Maggie supervised all the petting on the ranch and Little Buck knew he was Maggie's main patty pet. Maggie was not there that day to stop it, so Paul was glad for a chance to saddle him and put him to work. He was a luxury of smoothness to ride. A few hours of discipline could only do him good. As long as Maggie stayed in Nogales to recuperate from Mikey's birth, Paul was almost sure that she would not find out that he defiled Little Buck with toil.

Paul left the horse to soak under the saddle and went to the house to see if Buster had fixed any chuck. He found a pan of hot biscuits and a fried steak on the oven lid. Buster was asleep on a cot out on the screened Arizona room with a nice breeze on his whiskers. Paul ate the steak with a biscuit, saw that two hours of light remained in the day, and went out to ride circle on his cows.

Paul kept his cattle gentle. No cow was ever allowed to trot away at the sight of him. He always rode around to the front of her and stopped her, held her a while, then turned her back the way she had come before he went on. Out in the open he put miles on the horses he trained and made sure he saw every one of his cows at least once a week. If he missed one, he tracked her down to make sure she was all right.

Paul said he did not worry that he would go to hell because he was a good cowboy. Being a good cowboy was his religion. The closest he had ever come to his grandmother's Catholic faith was the time he saw a rosary in her cedar chest when he was a child. His folks in Pecos, Texas, where he was born had not thought enough of him to teach him about prayer, so he never learned what the beads were for. When he was twelve, his uncle Billy Coyle shipped a herd of cows to Quince Leatherman, whose ranch was outside Nogales. Paul left Texas on the train with the cattle and never looked back.

He had stepped up on that train with a smile and a wave for his friends and relatives who happened to be at the shipping pens, and he stepped off in Nogales with a smile and a handshake for Quince Leatherman. Quince hired him without asking why such a little button had come so far away from home to look for work, and Paul said nothing about tribulations in Pecos. He seldom said anything about his life in Texas. Maggie only found out he was not an orphan when she and Paul applied for their marriage license and he stated that his mother and father were still alive.

A good rain had fallen on the Rock Corral Ranch. The washes had run. Paul's native Mexican *corriente* cattle had held their own in his absence. He was not a worrier and he enjoyed doing everything God gave him to do, work or play. He did not doubt that rain would fall on his ranch again. He believed any amount of rain that fell would be enough. He was happy that he and his partners would turn their Mexican steers out on a place that had been favored with its first summer rain. The market had been down so long, it would have to go up pretty soon. Smart steer traders bought on a down market and sold on a high one, so Paul believed he and his partners were about to do well. Surely the market was as down as it would ever be.

Paul headed out to check a watergap in the fence that crossed the ranch's biggest arroyo. He was not surprised to find that a flood of rainwater had broken the fence that was supposed to span the channel. The wire had broken in the middle and lay along both banks of the arroyo. He saw the tracks of a bovine that had slipped through the gap into Big Nose Blythe's pasture. Big Nose was a voracious man and liable to eat any neighbor's animal that trespassed on his place. Big Nose espoused the belief that it was bad for a body to eat his own beef. This was not an uncommon belief. Fat strays were not safe anywhere they might wander in the West.

Big Nose was a Texan who had come to Arizona with his pockets full of money. He shipped trainloads of Sonora steers to various parts of the nation, even in those hard times. He put every cent he made into range, water, and mother cows. He was so cold-blooded that Paul and Buster left him alone. Paul knew he was not smart enough to associate with Big Nose without being done out of his chaps buckles. He also knew one of his bovines could not stray to Big Nose's ranch without disappearing hide, hair, horns, tracks, and all.

Paul followed the tracks and caught up to one of his steers in sight of Big Nose's camp. Big Nose's headquarters office was under a canvas fly that stretched between a tent and a chuck wagon; he was too stingy to spend money on permanent shelter, or on wages for a cook. He cooked good meals for himself and camped alone, but was not too stingy to invite a neighbor to eat with him. He was not too stingy to stay clean, either, and when he went to town he bathed and shaved in a room he kept in the Bowman Hotel, and before he went out on the street he put on a fine 7X Stetson hat and a sharply creased three-piece suit and necktie.

Paul drove his steer home. At the watergap, instead of heading into the pasture where he belonged, the steer sidled into a thicket on Big Nose's side. Paul burst through the thicket to get around him, then headed him toward the watergap and stayed close behind him so he would not double back or stop and hide in the thicket. When the steer reached the steep bank of the arroyo, he shied at something on the ground, jumped high off the bank, twisted in the air to look back at his tracks, landed in the wash, and bucked into the pasture where he belonged.

When Little Buck reached the edge of the wash, he shied and sprang off the bank into space the same way the steer did. Paul looked down in time to see that the horse had stepped on a coyote. Paul stopped Little Buck in the bottom of the arroyo and looked back. The coyote was not a bit excited. He sauntered into the arroyo with his head down, climbed the opposite bank, stopped, and looked away. Paul spurred Little Buck up the bank after him and drew his pistol.

A cow with coyotes to contend with was a protective mother. A faraway coyote's howl warned a cow that she had better stay close to her calf. Coyotes did not normally prey on cattle. If they were seen near cows, it was probably because they wanted the protein they could get from fresh cow manure. Wolves were different. Sometimes wolves killed cattle for fun and left the meat for the buzzards.

Paul ordinarily did not shoot coyotes. He liked them, but Paul thought this coyote might be rabid because he was too unconcerned about being stepped on. He cocked his pistol. Little Buck danced sideways and rolled an eye at the weapon. Paul knew the horse was afraid of firearms, but he fired at the coyote anyway, and the horse threw an absolute fit. The bullet only dusted the ground under the coyote's belly. Paul kept Little Buck from bucking, but the horse would not stand still. Paul fired four shots in the coyote's direction and missed them all. The coyote was only twenty yards away but had not been made to believe this was an unsafe distance, so he did not even quicken his step.

Paul charged up the bank behind the coyote, pointed his pistol right down between Little Buck's ears, and fired at a range of ten yards. This was more than any horse could stand. Little Buck downed his shaking head, bucked to the fence, turned sharply along its side, and flew off the high bank. He landed hard in the sand of the arroyo beside an upright steel stake and his knees buckled. The sharp top of the stake gouged through Paul's left arm all the way to the bone. Paul could see his brush jacket was torn, and knew he was badly hurt and bleeding, but he only stuffed his neckerchief into the wound under the tear and headed for home.

Maggie and Maudy Jane listened to Paul's car roll into the driveway, the car doors slam, and booted feet come through the back door. Maggie liked to hear the hardy scuff of a cowboy's boots when they came in a house.

Her brother Buster was the first one through the door. He put on his face of sorrow and shame and went to Maudy Jane, his mama, for a kiss. He was merry all the time, except in front of his mama. His sorrow and shame face let his mama know how repentant he was for doing things that made him merry. When he put on that face Maudy Jane did not feel she had to scold him, he did not have to make excuses, and they both could believe he would try to behave.

Maggie could smell mezcal on Buster and Paul when they came in. Paul seemed so tired and sick by what she thought was the drink that she did not want to look at him. He would have to clean up and rest a month before she would be nice to him again. "Here you come, worse off than ever," she said. "And why in the world do you think you have to grin at me like a Cheshire cat?"

"That's just your way, isn't it, Paul?" Maudy said.

Paul hugged Maudy and called her Granny, then went to kiss Maggie without a grin. After that day he always called her Granny and gradually the whole family called her that.

"No, don't kiss me," Maggie said. Paul leaned over her and slid his good arm under Mikey and picked him up. "And don't kiss Mikey. He doesn't want germs."

"Aw, I bet he can stand a kiss from his old dad." Paul kissed Mikey's forehead and laughed softly. "How's he doing? Did he get any tittie?"

"There's something really wrong with him. He won't nurse."

"Believe me, I know why that is. You first have to give it to him, then hold still for him so he can suck. Otherwise, he won't be any better at it than his daddy."

"That's not it. I've offered it to him a hundred times. At first he tried to eat me alive. Now he just gives me dirty looks."

"Well, he's his father's son. He don't like iced tittie."

"Shut up. Just shut up, Paul. You think I'm cold and ornery? Well, I have a right to be. You never do *anything* right. Why don't you just go away and grin for Little Old Lupe on Canal Street?"

"Now, sis, Paul can't go anywhere," Buster said. "He's hurt."

"Now what has he done to himself?"

"He got bucked off onto a steel post."

"So that darned Ice finally bucked him off? I knew it would happen. Every time he starts showing off on one of those orang-utans he rides I can expect to hear that his head's been driven into the ground."

"The bronc didn't do it. Little Buck did."

"Paul doesn't ride Little Buck."

"I'm telling you, Little Buck ruined his arm and we're wasting time. You ought to doctor his arm instead of bawling him out."

"Well, it serves him right. Who told him to ride my horse?"

"Little Buck needs to work once in a while the same as everybody else," Paul said. "No one has ridden him for three months."

"And what did you do to Little Buck?"

"Nothing at all."

"You deserve what you got for riding my horse without permission."

"Yeah, that's what I get for topping him off for you."

"I can top off my own horse."

"We have to call the doctor for Paul. He's really hurt," Buster said.

Granny sat Paul on a kitchen stool to look at the wound. Buster had made a compress of a dishtowel and pressed it against the wound under the brush jacket, then tied another dishtowel tightly around the arm before he loaded Paul in the ranch truck and ran for Granny's.

"Couldn't you at least have found clean towels?" Granny asked. "These must have been draped over the wood box."

The shirt was stuck in the wound. Granny soaked the arm with warm water and peeled it off. The wound started to bleed. She brought out her own stash of two-hundred-proof pure spirit of mezcal and bathed the wound. The fumes that issued from the uncorked bottle made Buster lick his lips.

Maggie hated that a cowboy's wife was expected to be a nurse for every hurt carcass that came along. She did not like to touch infirm bodies or attend to wounds and sores, especially if they were nasty with blood or pus. Granny ministered to Paul's wound quickly and efficiently, but Maggie did not even look at it. Then Granny, Buster, and Paul fell gravely silent. At the sound of a murmur, Maggie turned to look at Paul, went pale, and grabbed a better hold on Mikey so he would not fall off her lap if she fainted. Paul's shoulder had been impaled, gouged, sliced, and torn from the bottom of the bicep up through the top of the shoulder. He slumped in the chair and Granny braced him with mezcal. Buster groped his way to another chair.

Granny washed her hands with Ivory soap, dressed and bandaged the wound, washed again, and took Mikey away from Maggie. "Well, Michael Paul, I guess you and I are the only ones still fit enough to make a hand in this lash-up," she said.

Maggie recovered, helped Paul to the bedroom, undressed him, and started bathing him. He told her how good a bath he had taken in the stock water tank at Cibuta only a few days ago on the trail. She told him the best he had done was make a hard adobe crust for her to wash.

"I'm sorry I don't bathe to suit you," Paul said. "I get out of practice."

"Oh, you don't do so bad when you're home. Your feet are always clean."

"That's one good thing about me—you don't mind my feet in your bed."

"I like your feet. Mikey's are just like them."

"I guess I'll just have to work harder so you'll like me again."

"You don't have far to go. You're not afraid of work, but you have to stay sober."

"Then, by God, I'll do that."

"Don't make brags you can't back up."

"Well, I'm a cowpuncher, not a professor of the dance."

"How about you just grow up? You have a son and you've got the last of our money. How about you do right for a change?"

Paul laughed as he always did at Maggie's statements of unswerving resolve. "Would that mean I couldn't have fun with Buster anymore?"

"Don't be a dope. It means you're a good man, so it's time you grew up and stopped spurring hell out of everything that comes along just so you can see what will come apart."

Granny and Buster came in with Dr. Noon. The doctor undressed the wound and sewed some of the muscle back together, but he said that most of the tear was too ragged for a doctor to repair. Paul would have to repair it after it healed by using it as much as he could.

Buster gave Maggie an accusing look. "See there, Maggie? Your poor man is hurt bad."

"How did you do this, Paul?" Dr. Noon asked. "I didn't know you had a river on the Rock Corral."

"We don't have any river. We've only got wells, tanks, springs, and windmills."

"No swamps or marshes, either?"

"Got the Santa Cruz River nearby, but it's dry as bonemeal."

"How do you explain that awful wound, then?"

"Doc, Maggie's horse stumbled with me and I stuck a fence post through it. What's that got to do with waterholes?"

"Looks like a crocodile got you. Any such thing as a dry land croc?"

Paul laughed.

"Because it's hard to believe a fence post did that. That wound is so ragged and deep, it looks like some old bull crocodile from the Belgian Congo tried to feed on you."

"Maybe a crocodile did do it, Doc. I've always said I leave crocodiles in the toilet when I go to the bathroom drunk, and I've darned sure been drunk."

"Paul!" Maggie scolded.

"He does," Buster said. "He tells everybody that he drops crocodiles when he's drunk."

"Now I've heard everything," Maggie said.

"Anything can happen when we're drunk," Buster said.

"My gosh," Maggie said.

Dr. Noon closed his bag and stepped out of the room with Granny. "That's an awful gash, Maude," he said. "There wasn't much I could do for it. I think, between us, we did get it clean."

"I think we better keep him in for a while," Granny said.

"The wound doesn't smell good and may already be septic. The man has to rest and stay sober. I'd hate to lose old Paul to the whiskey."

"He won't keep still if we take away his whiskey," Granny said.

Maggie joined them. "What's this about the whiskey?"

"He can have whiskey, Maggie," Dr. Noon said, "but only enough to keep him quiet. I don't want him getting drunk."

"I'll not let him have any darned old whiskey."

"He ought to be able to have a little drop to keep him home," Granny said. "You can't just take a man's whiskey away when he's been living on it as much as Paul has."

"I'll pour all he wants on the gash," Maggie said. "He won't get a drop down his gullet."

Dr. Noon smiled reservedly and started toward the door, then stopped and turned back. "Dr. Gustetter was with me at the hospital when you called. He wants to know how your baby's doing."

"Not good," Maggie said. "Not good in any shape or form."

"Why not?"

"He won't nurse."

"You mean he hasn't nursed at all?"

"At first he chewed on me like one of those crocodiles you talk about, then he lost interest."

"Why haven't you called your doctor?"

"I thought he would nurse if he got hungry enough, but now I'm worried."

"Let's have a look at him."

Maggie led the way to Mikey's crib.

"So this is the outfit's new cowboy," Dr. Noon said. After his examination he said, "His color's good, but his belly's too lanky."

Mikey started to bawl for Dr. Noon.

"Can you tell what's wrong with him?" she asked.

"I'm like you. I bet he's just hungry."

Maggie wailed. "I know it, but he still won't have me."

"Tell Buster to come in here," Dr. Noon said.

"Here I am," Buster said from the door.

"Buster, we're both cowmen. What do you think could be the matter with a healthy, newborn kid from strong stock who won't suck?"

"If Maggie don't look out, he'll leppy."

"Which means?"

"If he don't get some ninny soon, he won't ever want it, and he'll be a runt."

"Why isn't he getting his ninny if he's healthy?"

"He might be healthy, but he ain't quick enough. His mama needs to stand still so he can suck. Maggie's too wild and Mikey's too little to keep up with her."

"Now, wait a minute," Maggie said. "It's not my fault. I haven't gone off and left my baby alone for one minute."

"Maggie, I'm sorry, but you're too mean about giving your tittie," Buster said.

"I haven't been mean to my own baby."

"Buster, go out and catch the first wet cow you can find and milk this child a bottle of sweet old cow's milk," Dr. Noon said.

That was the way Mikey's parents got along when he was born. Maggie kept everyone in contention and did not exclude her newborn son. Contention gave her a reason to run out of control and she seemed to like that. She searched for ways to try people's patience until someone opposed her, then she threatened to throw a fit until everybody backed off. She never physically hurt anyone when she had a fit, but the embarrassment she caused was widespread.

Paul had a terrible time with his arm. He was in a high fever when Dr. Noon came to see him the next day. The doctor said he might have to amputate the arm.

Paul said, "Ain't that something. Where would you start hacking, at my neck?"

Dr. Noon said the fever was a sign that Paul might have blood poisoning. It would spread and Paul would die. Paul said it was not the poison in his arm that caused the fever; it was because Maggie had deprived him of the Old Poison. Dr. Noon said that he would not prescribe whiskey for blood poisoning. Paul had better try to remember his prayers if whiskey was the only medicine he would take.

The patient did not suffer much longer. When Dr. Noon prescribed amputation, the arm got better fast. Buster cured the fever and delirium by smuggling Paul a bottle of Waterfill Frazier when Maggie was asleep. He took care of the rest of Paul's ailments with herbs. He put the *yerba el pasimo* on the wound to draw off the poison and hid a sack of mint leaves under the bed for them both to chew for the whiskey breath.

Maggie was hard to fool, but no two drunks in history ever stuck together more faithfully and cunningly than Paul Summers and Mikey's uncle Buster Sorrells. No two friends ever enjoyed each other more, or understood each other better than Buster and Paul.

Buster supplied vital spirits and laughter and Paul recovered. Later, the family laughed and admitted that probably nothing else in the world of medicine could have saved that particular patient.

Paul said that he was told by Dr. Noon that tuberculosis of the bone had infected his arm. Being told that would have been enough to scare anyone to death, but not Buster and Paul. No horror in all the world could have been worse for those two than being deprived of their whiskey.

TWO

PANCHO'S EYE

A cowboy is reckless. If he does not know how to risk his skin, he does not know how to make a hand. If he won't jump, he'll never land in the right place at the right time. A cowboy has to take chances if he is to put himself in the right place at the right time to stay ahead of his cows.

By the time he was three, Mikey spent all his waking hours outside and half of that time in the cottonwood, elderberry, and willow trees of his front yard. The only time he went in the house in the daytime was when Maggie called him back to Earth for noon *sopa* and *siesta*, the Sonorans' lunch of pasta soup and a nap. The tall cottonwood and willow trees were for adventure. The elderberry tree was for contemplation.

Mikey's horse Pancho could keep him out of the trees. Every evening the horse came out of a mesquite thicket in his pasture to be fed. Before his feed was put out, Mikey climbed up and sat on the top of a railroad tie that served as a corner post of the pasture fence to talk to him and pet him.

Pancho's inky, blue-black color came from feral Berber blood that the Spaniards brought to Mexico. His eyes were blue-black from a distance because they reflected his coat, but up close inside the clear globe, they were brown as wet dirt. When he came to the fence, Mikey talked to him and looked into his eye from a range of two inches. The clear, outer globe of his eye enclosed another complete and alive brown world composed of rained-on muddy mesas and fertile valleys.

Mikey thought the world in Pancho's eye was a model of the best spot on earth. A place on earth waited for Mikey that was the same as that world in Pancho's eye. It was a place of his own clay, a spot that God held only for him. Someday he would find it and live there.

As Mikey grew, he was given to understand that it would be his lot and privilege to use his life in the care of cows. That was the work for which he must prepare. Only until he had spent himself as a cowman could he be lowered into a grave of the sod that he saw in Pancho's eye.

Mikey's time with Pancho was his most peaceful time. He watched for everything and everyone he loved to become reflected in Pancho's eye. He liked to watch his father's, mother's, and dog's reflections appear in the eye when they came near. That was where they belonged, where they were most pure as themselves, side by side with him in Pancho's eye. He could see the cows in the hospital pen, too. The dirt and trees were the background and staples of the world he saw every day in Pancho's eye. The fathers, mothers, horses, dogs, and cows of his world were the most loved, but they were transient. The dirt and trees were constant and would never change. He hoped nothing and nobody of his and Pancho's private world would ever change and that thought gave sadness its chance to lurk into his happy heart.

Once, Mikey ventured to touch the clear globe of Pancho's eye. He only wanted to find out more about it because of all the purity and warmth that emanated from inside it. He thought Pancho liked to be petted everywhere. He wanted to caress the beautifully clear and fragile globe that covered the precious clay in the eye because it was so perfect and it reflected everything he loved and made the details of his dreamworld so clear. But he wanted to touch Pancho's eye mainly because it was the window of this brother creature that gazed back at him with such calm friendliness.

That was when he learned that he'd better not touch Pancho's eye if he wanted him to keep coming to the fence to visit. He found out he could not could get so proprietary as the owner of Pancho the horse that he thought he could touch him anywhere he wanted to, because Pancho the friend might go away and not come back.

Mikey was lucky Pancho was so noble that he did not stop liking him because Mikey had touched his eye. He flinched so quickly away that Mikey was afraid he had hurt him, but he came right back and settled his head as close as ever, so close that Mikey could feel his breath on his belly again and could watch his own breath fan Pancho's great whiskers and lashes.

Thus, Mikey became sufficiently awed by his horse early so that he had a chance to someday become a horseman. He hoped that Pancho loved him but he suspected that he was unworthy of the love of a being so pure. Pancho was good to him, but he might be too much of an aristocrat to reciprocate Mikey's deep affection. Pancho might only love other matchless horses, which was only right.

Mikey imagined that he found in Pancho's gaze everything that was good about fathers, mothers, horses, dirt, dogs, cows, trees, grass, bosom pals, and what he believed would be good about sweethearts, though a sweetheart never visited him in Pancho's eye. The movie star Jeannette MacDonald was the one he dreamed would visit him some day.

In those first days when Mikey came to realize that he had been planted alone in a small and helpless quantity of flesh upon the face of the earth, he found that dirt could be his for the time that it was under his feet. Dirt was free to be trod upon, manipulated, covered, used, sifted, dug, or tasted, especially the dirt around his Granny's house. However, when he was near other people's dirt, especially the dirt under the feet of crowds at events like rodeos and Mass at Sacred Heart Cathedral, he learned that he'd better mistrust the footing. When he was barefoot or in his boots, he could almost always get where he wanted to be. He wore his boots when he rode Pancho. In his bare feet, he was light, free, and difficult to hold. Barefoot, he could almost fly. He only wore his shoes when he went to town to be among the crowds and when he did, he knew if he did not look out he would be stepped on.

Baxter, Mikey's white dog whose tail curved over his back like a scorpion, marched along close to his side as long as he remained on his own turf. If Mikey left the yard, Baxter pulled up, panted with his head up, and let him go on alone. The reasons Mikey stayed home were so he could be with Baxter, climb his trees, visit with Pancho, take on adventure that visited him in his own yard, or sometimes Maggie would make him stay.

Mikey and Baxter knew, loved, and understood each other completely. When he was with Baxter...even when he was away from him and could only think of him, remember him...even after he grew up and Baxter was long gone, the dog lay warm and light and loving on his heart. *Eran únicos* was the Mexican saying that fit them. Baxter's spirit was one with Mikey's. That is why the boy hated so much knowing for certain a car would kill him someday. He saw so many dogs and cats, horses and cows and wild little animals killed by cars on the pavement of the Tucson road in front of his house that he knew it would happen to Baxter. He worried about it all the time. Dread of it would settle in his heart and cause him to stop and talk to Baxter about it. He believed that Baxter did not go out on the highway or leave his yard like other dogs because he knew it worried Mikey.

Mikey loved his home sod with his whole soul, heart, and mind because it was his headquarters for world adventure and his sure haven of rest and love, but he learned early that home cannot hold the natural man. Home was his rallying point, but most of all his sallying point. He could never feel good about staying in his rallying point if he did not sally forth and contest the world at every opportunity.

Maggie's strictest standing order was that Mikey stay at home, especially when she was not there. Consequently, she had to spank him every single day for "running off." When she was not home, Mikey's urge to venture away was unsupportable and he never once resisted it. When she was home he usually did not like to stay long in her company, nor did she want him to, but he found out later that if he went far enough away, to another county, or another state, he missed her more than anything or anybody.

Mikey walked away from home when Maggie was there, called away by attractions he could not resist. These attractions were so natural to him and irresistible that he did not realize he was being disobedient. He was not sneaky; he was drawn and held away by the absolute urgency of his commitment to adventure. Mikey liked Paul's, Granny's, Pancho's, Billy Shane's, Baxter's, and Nina's company the most and it was an adventure for him to be with them. His godmother Nina was Billy Shane's mother, and she lived two doors down the highway.

Mikey's trees were the stages, the sets in the theater upon which he played to become a man, his substitute for tallness until he grew up, the vantage from which he solved each deep, sore problem that came up, his haven from danger and from grown-ups who tried to make him into somebody he did not want to be.

In the trees he learned the advantage of having great style; that courage was better than cowardice; that real bravery could not be realized unless real fear was surmounted; that recklessness was admired and envied by all his people; and that height and space gave a special grace to a boy's play.

The highest, thinnest, leafiest branches that could sustain only the weight of his small carcass were Mikey's ideal perches. When he was in the trees nobody could intrude on him because he could hide unseen and untouched. In the trees, his life was as it ought to be because even the grown-ups admired that he could do something they could not do. Even when he returned to Earth to be with everybody else, he could do it in a style that was inimitable, a style heedless of the ordinary laws of gravity, balance and counterbalance, and of self-preservation, a style his elders would remember even when they used their power to control him on the ground.

Natalia Shane, whom he called Nina, the Mexican nickname for godmother, had been in the house when Mikey was born. Billy Shane, Nina's boy, was Mikey's first best friend. Billy was three and already full of adventure when Mikey was born and he could not wait for Mikey to grow up and run with him. He was the first to lead Mikey up into the high branches of a tree. He was wild and tough, but was a gentle boy who put all his heart into his endeavors and that suited Mikey. He never was one to play with toys or eat candy. By the time Mikey could run with him, Billy owned no toys. He could not sit still for long in any but a Tarzan movie, so he seldom went with Mikey to the picture show. Mikey never saw him completely enjoy anything but his own adventures. Mikey kept a teddy bear to sleep with until he was four, and Granny gave him lead soldiers and toy guns, but he never trotted them out when Billy was around.

Billy and Mikey did not have to work. They only ran and played with all their might from morning until night. By the time Mikey was three and Billy was six, Mikey began to try to fly to keep up with his friend. They had the big trees in front of their houses in which to climb and swing. They had the arroyo that ran by their houses for sand, and soft, high banks from which to let themselves fall. They had the steep, rocky hills behind their houses to climb and use for headlong downhill flight. They smoked elderberry roots in the arroyo and hugely enjoyed them. A thick, round elderberry stogie gave forth thick, white smoke, drew evenly, and did not make them drunk or sick.

The Horrells lived between Billy's house and Mikey's. Mr. Horrell was a customs officer who worked with Billy's father. Mikey called Billy's father "Uncle Bill." Mr. Horrell, Uncle Bill, and other customs service officers practice-fired their pistols and rifles in a vacant lot between their houses. Billy and Mikey would dig the slugs out of the hillside and lay them on the tracks for the train to flatten and polish when it whistled by.

Uncle Bill Shane kept a two-acre truck garden on his property and he grew and sold vegetables. He drew water from his own well with a gasoline engine that pumped it into a steel storage tank he had erected on the side of the steep hill behind his house. The tank was in a precarious spot and was secured by four guy wires that stretched from the brow of the tank to steel stakes in the ground.

Uncle Bill was a Texan like Paul, but he was settled and he loved to be with his family and work hard in his garden. As soon as he got home from his shift at the garita on the line, if any daylight remained, he changed into work rags, donned a floppy straw hat to protect his fair skin from the sun, and went out to sweat in his garden. He smoked crimp-cut Prince Albert tobacco that he rolled in white papers. Mikey knew he would smoke Prince Albert cigarettes rolled in white papers when he grew up to work as a cowboy, and he would revere Uncle Bill every time he lighted one. The thought that he might rise to Uncle Bill's stature and do anything Uncle Bill could do made him happy, for he believed the man was another of his fathers. Paul smoked Bull Durham in brown papers. Mikey liked brown papers better than white, but he knew that he would prefer Prince Albert and so would settle for white papers because Uncle Bill would never smoke the wrong kind.

Billy and Mikey did not get into much trouble for being mean, unless scaring their mothers could be called mean. They were spanked on their butts for scaring their mothers with their adventures, just as they would have been punished for playing with matches, breaking a window, or swiping something from a store. So they knew that scaring their mothers was a crime, though not one that made them feel guilty, nor one they could stop committing. Their mothers punished them for the scares even before Billy got a bicycle and Mikey started climbing trees and riding Pancho, but the boys' butts were so tough from spanking that their mothers had to stop being scared or perish from worry.

One day Maggie produced a pair of bib overalls and told Mikey he could wear them over his shorts and did not have to wear anything else: no socks, no shirt, no shoes. He and Billy went down the road to visit Skippy Swikert and the Anderson kids who lived by the Indian Springs store. They never bought anything at the store and Billy did not like Skippy or Charley Anderson or his sister Maureen. Mikey got along with them, especially Skippy, but though Mrs. Anderson was kind to Mikey, he suspected that she did not like him and he was dead certain she did not like Billy.

Indian Springs was down in a deep well behind the store. Mrs. Anderson warned Billy and Mikey to stay away from it because it was dangerous. Calling it that in an awesome tone ensured that Mikey would have to get as close to it as possible to see if anything would come apart.

A few boards had been laid across the open mouth of the well and covered with a few rusty sheets of tin weighted down by rocks. Billy and Mikey moved the tin to see into the dark well and it indeed appeared to be a dangerous place, though pleasantly cool and shady. Mikey figured the water would probably be cold and sweet if he fell in and had to drink a lot of it. Billy assured him that if he fell in, if the scare did not kill him, the fall would stun him so he would probably not float and the water was so deep he would drown.

Billy already knew how to swim, but Mikey did not have any idea how a person would save himself if he fell into that well and survived the fall. So, he had to get closer and closer to the fall while Skippy and the Andersons warned him to stay away. To show them how safe it was, he walked on the tin. When they shouted at him to stay over the boards he had to show them that the tin alone would support his weight. It might buckle for some ordinary kid, but not for Mikey. Was he not the one who could climb higher than any other kid into the smallest branches of the trees without falling? Then, just as he thought he had proven his immunity to the law of gravity, down through the tin he plunged, deep into the dark space, smack onto the hard, cold water. The shock of immersion stunned him, but he did not stiffen. He relaxed and thought he would never come up for another breath of air, even if he could have known which way was up. When he did come up, Billy had skinned down the well ladder into the water at the speed of falling and was yelling at him to grab his suspenders. Mikey grabbed them and Billy hauled him out. They climbed the ladder and hit for home as Skippy's and the Andersons' mothers scolded them to get home and scolded their own to get in the house.

Mikey's new overalls were so drenched that they poured, gushed, squished, and squirted water in all directions all the way home. Mikey's Nina was watering her flowers in the backyard when the boys arrived. In an instant she appraised their condition, read their anxious looks as boys who thought they had lost their last friends, and ruled that they would not find any in her yard, either. She jerked Billy around by one arm, began stripping him of his clothes, and ordered her godson banished to his home and out of her sight.

Mikey looked back once just as Nina bared Billy's butt. Billy, in despair because he was sure that he was about to die, cried out with a final statement: "All right, kill me, but I'll never save Michael Paul's life again."

With the *spitspitspit, spat, spat* of Nina's hand on Billy's butt, Mikey ducked his head and hurried on spraddle-legged in his wet overalls toward home. Maggie already knew that he must be coming under a cloud of disgrace because the whole neighborhood could hear the slap of Nina's hand on Billy's butt and his awful howls. Maggie was hungry for reprisal against her son even before she knew what he had done. As soon as he was in range she gathered him up, jerked down the overalls, and *spitspitspit, spat, spat, spat, splat...splat...splat* went her open palm upon his butt. And then, the hunger satisfied, Mikey was lifted by one arm, stood on his kicking feet, and released, and except for the telling, retelling, and the laughter over the story of the Indian Springs plunge, the adventure was at an end.

That evening Mikey's cowboy father came home from Mexico and Maggie told him about Mikey's tailspin into the well and how he had baptized his new bib overalls. Paul thought about it and puffed on his cigarette a moment, then said, "Well, what did you expect? Put a cowboy in a pair of bib overalls and he'll fall in a well and nearly drown every time."

The two mothers never measured the boys for their spankings or wound up and landed haymakers on them with murder on the mind or with premeditation. They found the range and *spitspitspit*. If they could have stopped after the first three whacks their sons would hardly have felt spanked, but they always warmed up to it and continued for another six or seven whacks in the plush before they quit. Five minutes after the last whack, the boys stopped hurting. Their butts were so tough the spanking hurt their mothers' hands more than they did the boys.

Once, Maggie, realizing this, took a new hairbrush to Mikey but shattered the handle before she even got started. With that, she broke down and cried. She had sacrificed a week's lunches at her job in the county assessor's office to buy that new brush and she did not have the money to buy another in that Depression. Mikey felt so bad about it, he begged her not to cry, then told her that a peach switch hurt a whole lot more anyway.

Mikey could never stand to see his women cry. Later, when he began having sweetheart trouble, he always knew it was over if he felt a secret glee when they cried. He thought Maggie was bawling because she had not been able to finish the job on his butt after she got in the pay dirt. He told her she could get in the plush real quick with a peach switch. That was how they knew they loved each other: they were always able to give away their secrets of self-preservation as consolation to each other if they found they had pushed too far.

Mikey and Billy did a lot of tearful bellering around that neighborhood, but mostly because they were sorry they had angered their mothers, not so much because the spankings hurt. Most of the time Maggie and Natalia would grab them just as though they were going to kill them, and then only succeed in raising a lot of dust out of the seat of their pants. The boys were always down in the dirt. The mothers had to strip them if they were to make an impression.

A mother who owns a boy who has been down in the dirt one minute and in the top of a tree the next finds that there is no end to the variety of foreign matter a whack can lift out of the seat of his pants. One time after dark when Mikey was long overdue at home because he was so busy playing fort in the dirt with Skippy and the Andersons, Maggie came out and tracked him down, slipped up behind him, and grabbed him. When she lifted him out of the pile of rocks that was his fort and delivered the first whack, she spanked a giant centipede off his pants that was eight inches long and three inches wide across the shoulders. The bruise her hand gave the monster made it squirm and roll on the ground in agony and it clacked his legs together with a sound that was like twenty women's knitting needles picking at each other. Billy squashed it with a rock before it could recover and attack anyone. That centipede scared Maggie so thoroughly, she even forgot that she had intended to spank Mikey in front of all the other mothers and kids.

Mikey got spanked daily and never could figure out why everything he loved to do—and therefore could not help doing—scared Maggie to death. He honest to God did not want to scare her. He might show off for her like his dad did because he was proud of what he could do, but she said the feats that gave him the most pleasure to perform scared the peewadding out of her. He never held his spankings against his mom because it was tit for tat that way, and he could pay for getting to do what he wanted and be his own man.

Mikey knew a lot of sorrow, though. He was a kid who knew how to give a lot of love and loyalty and he did not spare it. When someone he loved was in distress his own distress was terrible. Paul and Maggie could not get along. By the time Mikey became aware of them as individuals and himself as a person, he realized they fought as though they hated each other. Paul could do no right and he referred to Maggie as Madam Queen. Madam Queen wanted to rule and be paid homage. Paul wanted to run and play and be a happy, common man. Madam Queen allowed Paul to love her on Sundays when he was home, but he did not get to do it—better not even take off his hat—unless he first presented her with an apple and the Sunday funnies.

When Mikey's uncles and their families visited, everybody laughed at Paul's and Madam Queen's separate versions of their stories. However, when Paul and Maggie were alone, they insulted each other so terribly that their love fell away in pieces that they could not ever put back.

Mikey's father was not mean or violent. Drink only made him happy, so Maggie never suffered any black eyes, but he never spent an evening of quietude at home with his wife and son. The *vaqueros* had nicknamed him *Pablo Ligero*, Fast Paul, and it fit him. Mikey and Maggie worried every evening that Paul was so late that he might not come home because he was down under a broken-legged horse, then they were given to watch him come in drunk.

Gradually, Paul lost out being Mikey's father and Maggie's husband and he was no longer respected as such for a long time before he was finally and irrevocably banished. By the time Mikey's sister Maudy was born, Paul was off by himself on a high lonesome 99 percent of the time and already lost to his family.

When Paul had been home sober, though, he and his family enjoyed times of great happiness and fun. The gloom brought on by Paul and Maggie not getting along only lasted while they fought. Neither of them stayed swelled up long and neither held a grudge. Normally, the Summerses were prone to happiness. Seeing his parents kiss brought upon Mikey's face the kind of uncontrollable grin that made a kid's jaws ache.

When Mikey was able to sally forth and cowboy with his dad, his mother was happy, his Granny was happy, Baxter and Pancho were happy, and the boy found himself immersed in the most awful glory of his boyhood. His happiness was awful because he enjoyed an awesome, worshipful love for his dad and the work he did. Paul's capacity for doing Mikey good, whether it be to give him a lesson, something to eat, a puff of his Bull Durham cigarette, or just the way he turned his head, kept Mikey in awe and wonder for the adventure of it all.

Mikey did not remember when his dad first let him rein Pancho on his own to control the horse's starts and stops and pace at cattle work. He did not know when he first made a hand in the cow work, rode fence, branded, rode circle, and gathered outlaw cattle with his dad and uncles and other grown-up help.

Mikey was so hungry for the life that Paul could give him that he never asked how much farther they had to ride that day, or when they would get where they were going, or what they would have to do. He did not always know where he was going when he left the house with his dad. One minute after Paul's car started moving away from the house, he fell into a coma that lasted until the car stopped. He was headed out to do the work for which he had been sired and he needed to be fresh and rested so he could think straight and make a hand. He might wake up down in Magdalena in Sonora on a ranch owned by Cabezon Woodell or Del Mercer, or he might find a day's riding needed to be done on Uncle Buster's 61 Ranch, or his Leatherman Ranch, or he might have to make a circle alone somewhere on his dad's cattle. He learned early that he'd better be able to think before he jumped Pancho out after something, opened a gate, took down his rope, or opened his mouth.

At times, when Paul was off on a high lonesome of one kind or another, Uncle Buster would come and take Mikey and Pancho out to work cattle. Mikey was almost as crazy about Buster as he was his dad. Paul and Buster were so easygoing and good at cowboying that Mikey never learned that it was supposed to be work. Because of those two, cowboying was an adventure that included love, concern, and admiration for the animals and the cowboy companions on the job. Other elements of cowboying were fun, excitement, risk, and athleticism. Those were ordinary elements of cowboying, but Paul and Buster punctuated it all with the eye-watering abandon of headlong, downhill, brush-popping, open field horseback runs that other little kids did not ever experience in the company of their elders.

Whether Paul was home or not, the corral at Mikey's house served as a hospital where cattle and horses recovered from their ailments and injuries. Before he was able to handle and doctor the animals, Mikey's job was to watch them, keep them in the pen, and feed them. He did not think of his participation as work. The duties came as a natural function of a child like Mikey who was raised as a partner in the family livestock. It became fun from the first day that Mikey was asked if he was strong enough to help carry a full bucket.

Mikey learned to get on his horse by himself when he was three. For some time he had sensed that Paul did not appreciate having to lift him to the back of his horse when it was time to ride. Mikey believed this must be because he was Fast Paul and did not want any son of his to go through life having to be lifted onto his horse. Paul put up with doing it for Mikey while he was little, and though he never said anything about it, Mikey felt that he was expected to get himself on his own horse just as darned soon as he was able. He sensed that every time he asked Paul to boost him onto his horse he borrowed on a diminishing credit. If he waited too long to learn to get on by himself, Paul might someday decide he was too much trouble and leave him behind. Paul's mouth still smiled when he said, "Up you go, Mikey," but his hands never lingered to steady him, and his eyes said, "I have seen you climb into the tops of the trees where the limbs are so small a cat would fear the sway, so make me the same kind of hand horseback as soon as you can, or you will find yourself left at home with the kids and the women."

Mikey learned to get on his horse by himself the day he rode Pancho out to Sonoita Creek with Paul to bring in a band of mares. Paul rode a big four-year-old paint bronc that day. The horse had never been touched by human hands before he was four and Paul had only been riding him a month. However, when Paul Summers rode a bronc, he got rode and schooled every minute the sun shined. The paint was already smarter in the ways of a cowhorse than most old gentle horses of the region. He was being hackamore broke and he carried his head right and already knew how a cowboy needs a horse to stop and turn and keep a prize angle on a cow.

Paul and Mikey rode down the Tucson highway past Dalton's Dairy and Bill Knox the blacksmith's, across the Santa Cruz River, and on to Sonoita Creek. Paul cut for his mares' tracks along the creek, found them, and tracked them through tall cottonwood, willow, walnut, and mesquite groves. The stream was clear and full of minnows and after they had been on the tracks a while, they dismounted and lay down on their bellies on a sunny rock to have a drink. The horses made little sound in the dampness and shade and for the rest of Mikey's life, every time he rode beside a creek, he was reminded of that day with Paul by the feel of the horse under him, the smell of leaves underfoot, the brush of branches on his face, the sun on his back, and the cool shade of the trees.

In the beginning the boy's only responsibility when he rode with Paul was to keep him in sight. Paul did not expect him to turn a herd, or get in front of it and stop it, or even to keep it going in the drags, only to keep him in sight. No matter what his pace, Mikey was obliged to stay with him because Paul did not want to finish a sashay and then have to leave the work he had accomplished to look for a lost boy.

After a while the tracks lined out together in one direction and Paul straightened in his saddle and turned the paint loose in a high lope. When Granny wanted to say something good about Paul, she always said, "The man sat a horse straight as an Indian."

His back was straight over the horse and his body from the waist down became part of the horse.

Pancho knew what he and Mikey had to do. He sighted on the paint and kept up. If Mikey was about as hard to lose as a bobcat on his back, it was because the boy wanted to be with his dad so much he did not yet know what it was like to fall off. Nobody he knew ever just fell off. They got knocked off or bucked off, but by the time he was three, Mikey could go sound asleep on Pancho and not fall off.

The mares sensed the horsemen and loped away so they would not be caught standing still. Paul swung out in a half circle to get ahead and stop them. The brush was so thick, the band's dust could only be seen when they crossed sand or loam. The paint stretched into a run and Pancho sprinted to keep up. Pancho was gentle and quiet, but he was equal to any speed the paint could show.

All of a sudden, Mikey saw the band running hard through brush on his right. Paul skimmed by a tree and turned at a sharp angle around its other side. Pancho made the same turn. A big limb loomed in front of Mikey's eyes, sheared him out of the saddle, and dumped him on his head under the tree.

Mikey left the world for a place that was black and quiet for a while, then his ears suddenly opened with a bright ring that brought him back. A black shadow blocked the sky when he opened his eyes. Then he realized that Pancho was standing over him. The horse had been at a dead run and could not have stopped so suddenly. He had come back for the boy, for he was straddling him. To get going again, Mikey put a foot on a chestnut inside Pancho's leg, shinnied up and caught a saddle string, pulled himself up to the horn and into the saddle, and kicked Pancho into a lope.

Mikey was on the ground a long time because Paul had time to stop the mares and hold them until they quieted. When the mares were completely under control and Mikey still had not shown up, he rode back to look for him. The boy met him in the brush. Mikey was glad that his dad had not whistled or called for him. He did not ever want him to worry. Mikey was sure that he only got to ride with his dad because he did not require that the man act like a father all the time.

Paul drove the mares away from the creek and penned them at Bill Knox's where he could have a drink of moonshine whiskey. Even then, Mikey accepted that his father would rather pen his livestock before sundown with someone who was generous with his whiskey than drive on and reach home after dark.

Bill Knox was a World War I veteran who did all Paul's ironwork. He had been wounded and shell-shocked in France. He and Paul were close buddies, but most everyone else in the region gave Bill a lot of room because of his being shell-shocked. A picture of soldiers in their trenches in the very midst of battle hung over his forge. The picture was highlighted by the red fire of bursting shells as soldiers fell under the intense weight and storm of battle. Mikey understood being shell-shocked meant that when Bill looked at that picture of the mayhem of combat it made him happy. When he fired his forge and its heat swelled under the bellows, the glow rose into that picture and Mikey could see and feel the heat of battle and could not wait until he grew up to become a soldier so he could go off to war and come home shell-shocked like Bill Knox.

Bill Knox was tall and gaunt and his skin was ivory white. His blacksmith's hammer had caused spatterings of molten iron to pepper his skin. The spatterings were tiny and far apart and some were smudged and some were still fat little dots waiting to get wiped into smudges with his sweat. He wore a vestlike undershirt with a great gap torn out over the ivory page of his middle and the creases in his belly were lined with black iron residue. He wore an old fedora that looked heavy with the weight of dirt, sweat, and the powder of his iron.

Mikey looked down that day and saw that Bill Knox's long, fragile, white toes were bare against the black dirt floor of his shop. He handed his jug of corn whiskey to Paul and stretched his legs out before him and the boy saw to his delicious fascination that thick lines of black, moist, ironized clay sealed his toes uniformly together. Mikey looked up at his dad in time to watch him shape his mouth to fit the jug before the ceramic touched it, and with the shaping of his lips came a preparatory grimace that showed extreme respect for what he knew the drink was about to do to him.

Paul then asked his son to show Bill and his wife and daughters how he could get on Pancho by himself. He told them that Mikey always kept his dad in sight when they rode together and no matter what Paul needed to do, he had never been able to shake Mikey. That was why he had worried when he stopped the mares and looked back and the boy was not with him. Mikey had to tell how the limb knocked him off Pancho and how the horse was standing over him when he revived. He had to move aside the black foretop of his hair and show them the scraped lump on his forehead.

Every time Paul told that story he marveled at how Pancho had stayed with Mikey instead of running off. Mikey also decided that Pancho was marvelous for stopping and coming back, but when it had happened he did not think Pancho's faithfulness was anything out of the ordinary. He was used to having the horse stay with him. That was where he thought his horse was committed to be because he was Mikey's horse and Mikey was his boy.

Bill's three girls were towheaded and pretty. Lorraine, the oldest, was a year older than Mikey. She brought a tiny vial of Mercurochrome, which she called "monkey blood," to nurse the lump on his forehead. She stood very close to him and gently swabbed the scratches with a cotton ball soaked with the brilliant medicine. She stood with her face close to his and blew on his scratches to cool the medicine's sting. She looked down and stumbled into him, an eyelash grazed his cheek, and her smell and touch caused a deep, mysterious itch inside him. No one but his Nina, Granny, and Maggie ever touched him up close like that. Their touch was nice but left no effect after they quit. Lorraine's touch caused him to slip into a dazed paralysis.

Mikey had never been around a girl who handled him as she pleased. Lorraine just did as she wished with him right in front of everybody as though nothing was wrong with it. That moment with Lorraine sweetly slowed down Mikey's heart. He did not want to move even a corpuscle out of her way. He enjoyed it so much it worried him.

Paul fell under the power of Maggie's anger when he and Mikey returned home that evening. Mikey could not see that his dad had done anything wrong. The man had only enjoyed himself a little with Bill Knox and his whiskey at the finish of a good job. He had celebrated Pancho's nobility and Mikey's graduation from earthbound kid to horseman big enough to mount by himself. Poor old shell-shocked Bill enjoyed Paul, and even Mikey could see it was rare for him to have someone he liked stop to talk and drink with him.

Maggie's unreasoning anger made their home an awful place that evening. Mikey's heart sickened at the words she said to relieve the pain he saw in her eyes. The humble pain he saw in Paul's made him weep. Maggie seemed to need to instill hate in them both because of Paul's drinking, but this time Mikey had seen for himself that Paul had done nothing wrong. He could see how much trouble the drinking caused, but he did not see why his mother and father should hate each other over it.

Nobody in the family gave a darn what the kid felt. Maggie and Paul did not seem to think their fights would have a bad effect on Mikey. However, if anyone had asked the boy how much it hurt to see his mother and father fight, he would have said that he thought the pain his parents caused was deadlier than any childhood disease he could imagine. He knew kids who were real sick. He believed his pain made him more frail and sorrowful than the kid with a weak heart who could not go out and play. He was chronically unhappier than his friend who was crippled by polio. Mikey would have been happy to carry any kind of pain right to his death, if that would make his parents stop hurting each other.

Mikey worried that his parents would someday become so mean to each other that they would go away and leave him. He even worried about it during happy times when they forgot to fight. Nobody ever asked to help make his worry go away and it sure never occurred to him to ask anybody for that kind of help.

Nobody recommended a medicine that could alleviate that type of pain. Nobody patted the boy and told him they knew how it felt, or offered a cool rag, or a cool hand, or even a vaccination, to make him feel better. The pain that enveloped his heart when his mother and father tore at each other's feelings and took each other's hearts in a death grip choked his throat and filled him with tears.

Mikey's weeping would not turn his parents away from their fights, because if there was anything they considered more contemptible than the hurt they did to each other, it was to see Mikey cry about it. His heartbreak did not hurt anybody but him, so he had to take himself away from it. Luckily for him he could sit by Granny, his Nina, Pancho, and Baxter and get away quickly to run with Billy.

Mikey sometimes thought that it would be better if he let his heart break so he could die once and for all. Maybe that would make Paul and Maggie kiss and stop fighting. He realized it was more likely that they would not admit that they were the cause of his heartbreak and would say he died of some silly congestion. Then nobody would be left to care if they killed each other, or hope that they would show some love for each other, or give them one dim reason to stay together anymore.

Their anger always subsided before they killed each other or hurt each other's bodies. Renewed hope that they would touch each other gently, speak softly to one another, and smile at one another again, always eased the pain in their son's heart just before it killed him.

The love of his parents made him plenty happy sometimes. Maggie liked to teach her son everything that was of value to her and she was a generous and patient teacher. He was not a hard-headed learner. He liked almost all the things that she liked, especially reading. Billy Shane came home from first grade able to read the funnies and excluded Mikey from that new adventure for a while, so Mikey asked Maggie to teach him to read. He learned to read *Dick Tracy* as fast as she was able to help him absorb the rules of letters. That learning time was wonderful for Mikey because he had to sit very still with his mother's voice in his ear, in the very middle of her sweet breath, with her touch close and soft upon him.

During the first three years of Mikey's life, Maggie and Paul took him everywhere they went and he never thought they could go away and leave him. To be inside the embrace of his father and mother was all he wanted. After he was three, they stopped hugging him. Other kids took their inclusion in the love of their fathers and mothers as a matter of fact. Mikey looked for it, hoped and longed for it, but finally learned to do without it.

Mikey's sister Maudy Marie was born when Mikey was five, two years after Paul and Maggie's war had begun and only six months before they separated. Maudy never knew how good life could be when Paul and Maggie loved each other. The Summers kids loved their parents from birth because they depended on them for warmth, shelter, and food like other kids, but Maudy never knew what it was like for them to love her graciously. After Paul and Maggie quit loving each other they imposed conditions on all loving done with kids.

Paul would love his kids if he could drink and cowboy and be reckless and did not have to come home. Maggie loved Mikey as long as he realized that Paul would have to stop drinking, come home when he was supposed to, and not spend his paychecks recklessly. When she was mean to Mikey, it was because she was especially angry at Paul. She would allow her son to love her as long as he did not act like Paul and Paul did not act like Paul. She planned to see to it that Mikey became a man not like Paul, but like another kind that she would mold.

Drinking was blamed for the downfall of the Summers marriage, yet when Mikey thought of the good times, when the love of his parents had included him in its embrace, drinking had almost always been involved. When his family met at a branding, a general roundup, or any other kind of reunion, everybody drank beer or the hard stuff and all the things that had been done wrong became all right. The fights were told and retold for the humor in them. The times Maggie had wanted to kill Mikey for scaring the peewadding out of her became funny stories, adventures that had thrilled them both.

The first time Mikey remembered drinking beer was at Los Parados, a drive-in beer joint across the line in Nogales, Sonora. At that time the Summerses were all in love, and once in a while on Sundays Paul drove them to Los Parados where they sat in the car and were served beer on a tray attached to the windowsill. Paul poured Mikey his first beer in a shot glass there as soon as the boy was able to stand up in the seat.

Mikey loved beer from the start. It did not just lie there and wait to be consumed. It acted and was full of its own energy. He was fascinated by the life it demonstrated in the jewel-like bubbles it formed inside itself that rose amiably and busily in a straight line to the surface and joined in foamy celebration at the top. The tawny color and the gemlike bubbles held him. This was not food. This was the assimilation of the essence of the jewel without the hard, cold weight of the stone. This was true spirit for a person to taste and swallow.

In the beer Mikey saw the very spirit of his family when it was on good terms, in good times, when its love was full. Maggie and Paul were good at laughing. The three Summerses laughed a lot at Los Parados and at other, larger family gatherings with beer. One shot glass was all he was given at a time. Maggie insisted on that. Paul would ask if Mikey could have another, but he would never argue when Maggie said no. The boy learned to savor the friendship of the bubbles when they visited his tongue, the coolness of the swallow, and the warm glow it carried to his belly. He learned to pause happily with that glow inside him while his parents laughed and talked and to watch the late bubbles rise in the glass along the same paths to catch up with earlier, more hurried bubbles and to savor the good, strong smell of it. Each bubble was an individual glitter in a rich, clear jewel. Beer was one of Mikey's simple pleasures, but it seemed so complicated when he examined it that he did not think he would ever stop finding new wonders about it.

Mikey knew that his parents were having a tough time making a living. Maggie confessed to Mikey that they could not always be happy because they were "hard up" and this was not only the fault of the Depression. Certain people had taken advantage of them. All the young breadwinners of that time were hard up, but if Paul did not grow up and face their problem and take as deep a seat as he did when he climbed on a bronc, the bottom would fall out from under his family. The bottom did fall out.

When they stopped having fun together, Paul and Maggie lost one another.

Maggie could not understand how a man who loved the hard work of cowboying as much as Paul could not adapt to some other kind of hard work that paid better. Paul said that cowboying was the only work he could do. When he and Maggie first married, they had money, livestock, and credit. When that was gone, Paul's ability as a cowboy was not worth a nickel.

Paul told Maggie that if he could not cowboy he might as well be dead, because his life would be over. He did take other jobs. He went to work for the highway department long enough to learn to drive a Caterpillar and to take home a Caterpillar watch fob to show Mikey, but he ruined that by sparking a rancher's sister who lived near the camp where he stayed during the week. The rancher was an old friend of Paul and Maggie's. His ranch neighbored Buster's and it was only natural that he offer Paul his hospitality. Full of fun as Paul was, it was only natural that he and the rancher's sister, who also liked to have fun, got together.

Paul had cronies who drank, made, or smuggled whiskey everywhere in Santa Cruz County. If he was horseback when he saw a crony, he stopped and got off his horse to visit a while. If the crony had any whiskey, Paul drank with him. If Paul was riding a machine, he "shut her down," climbed down, and squatted in the shade to visit and drink. If the crony did not have whiskey, Paul knew where it could be found and was capable of walking his Caterpillar off the job and across country to go get it. No cowboy was capable of going afoot any farther than the nearest corral to get anything he wanted, even whiskey.

Paul's family saw little of him after he took the highway department job. He lost that job right away because he disappeared with his Caterpillar too often for reasons he was unable to explain. He told his son during one of his quick visits home that one day, when he was operating the Cat in the midst of impenetrable dust, pounding noise, and heat that bubbled the paint on the machine, he looked up into the cool reaches of a canyon in the Tumacacori Mountains on the Rock Corral Ranch and remembered how he had ridden horseback there looking after his own cows and doing the job for which he had been born. He became so sad that his cowboying days might be over that he wept. The tears made big adobes when they mixed with the dust caked on his face, which made him laugh. Not long after that he got fired, but he could not feel bad about it. Being a catskinner had not made him proud. He was only proud that he had never been fired as a cowboy.

After the highway department job, Paul went down to cowboy for Cabezon Woodell in Sonora and that was the end of his marriage. Mikey stopped cowboying. Uncle Buster stopped coming to see Mikey because Paul was never home anymore. The boy came to realize how happy he had been when his dad was making him into a cowboy, because now he could only dream of being one, like all the other kids.

THREE

SONORA GIRLS

*C*ows are not troubled by their calves. Mares are unperturbed in
their love for their foals. The smarter people become, the more their
kids bother them. What happens to simple sweetness? Who are the
dumb animals?

When Mikey was old enough to stand up in the seat of the car,
Maggie would dress him up, part his hair in the middle, slick it
back against his skull so he would look like his handsome uncles,
and take him to Nogales. She always parked the car on Morley
Avenue in front of the stores. She rolled down the windows to give
Mikey air, told him to stay put and watch the people go by, but not
to stare, and went away to the shops.

Mikey looked for a friend in each face that passed. He made
ready to smile when he looked into a face in case he found that he
knew the person. If he liked the face, he smiled whether he knew
the person or not. He and Paul were alike that way.

The first friend Mikey made on that street was an old black man named Joe. He came by almost every time Mikey was in town. Mikey became Black Joe's friend long before he was even noticed by him. He came by puffing his pipe with his eyes downcast the first day and Mikey liked his face so much he felt forced to stare: The face passed within a foot of the boy's. The man walked slowly, so the boy was given a long, close look. Black Joe wore a brown hat that seemed to be powdered all over with ashes. His face was deeply lined, and the lines looked as though they were full of light gray ash that also lay in the lines of his hands. He wore a dark suit vest with his tobacco can, a gold watch and chain, another pipe to smoke, matches, and a handkerchief all showing above the rims of the four breast pockets. His walk was a poised and graceful amble.

That was the day Mikey began to study the way men walked. He began to think that the pace of a real man's walk must always have a special style that suited him. Black Joe's walk was unconsciously dignified, stately, and had taken shape with the grace of the way he lived. He did not drag his feet and he did not limp. He coasted at one mile per hour, even down as slow as half a mile per hour. His feet never seemed to leave the pavement, yet they did not touch down between steps, the same way that heavyweight boxer Joe Louis's feet imperceptibly cleared the floor when he jumped rope. One day Black Joe raised his eyes and Mikey saw that they were as feral as Pancho's. Years later, Mikey became aware of what he saw in those eyes. They looked at the world as though they had been doing so since before 2000 BC and were still not tired enough to quit. They were the world's eyes, the ones the world used to watch what went on outside its heart. They had been much used but would never tire of what they saw or be surprised.

The third time Black Joe came by, Mikey murmured hello. He looked at Mikey and gave out a rumble so deep the boy could not understand the word for the sound. After that he would look into Mikey's eyes from farther down the street as he approached, then rumble something as he went by.

Maggie told Mikey that Black Joe had been a good friend and comrade in arms of Mikey's Granddaddy Bert. He owned the indoor shoeshine stand on the town plaza. Paul and Buster liked to stop and sit under a shade tree on the plaza with him from time to time and share a bottle of whiskey. He had been decorated for bravery as a Fort Huachuca cavalryman against Geronimo.

Mikey told Granny about him and she said he was Old Black Joe, hers and Granddaddy Bert's best friend of all time. Mikey asked why he was called Black Joe. Mikey felt a kinship with Black Joe because of the nickname. The grown-ups in Mikey's family called him "Black Man" because his hair was so black and he burned so black under the sun. Black Joe did not look very black to Mikey. He was not as black as little Chapo Valenzuela, Granny's gardener who walked over from across the line to tend her lawn and flowers every Saturday. Granny said that he was called Old Black Joe because a song was named after him. She sang the song to Mikey and taught it to him. The next time Black Joe came by on the street, Mikey said, "Hi, Joe."

He looked at the boy with the world's eyes and said, "Hi, Joe," and started on by.

Mikey was willing to be Joe if Black Joe wanted that, so he said, "Is my name Joe, too?"

He stopped and said, "What do you call yourself?"

He seemed to like Joe, so Mikey said, "Joe."

"What else?"

"Michael Paul Summers."

"You say Paul Summers?"

"Yes."

"Maggie's your mama and Paul is your daddy?"

Maggie returned to the car at that moment. She shook Joe's hand and said she was glad her boy had stopped him so she could visit with him. He had great, burnished gold teeth and some of his color had come off on them, but his tongue was pink as a flower. He told Maggie that he and Mikey had been friends a long time but they had not spoken until that day. He was glad to know that Mikey was Bert Sorrells's grandson.

After that, Black Joe spoke to Mikey every time he came by, but he only patted the boy's hand, rumbled at him cheerfully, and went on.

Mikey's uncle Joe Sorrells drove a Wells Fargo Express delivery truck every summer for college money. Mikey often saw him on the street. Uncle Joe and he could spot each other in any crowd, even if one of them tried to hide as a beggar wearing an aviator cap and goggles. Most of his pickups and deliveries were on Morley Avenue in three blocks of stores between the county courthouse and the Ville De Paris in front of the garita on the line.

Uncle Joe would drive up and double-park, then talk and laugh with the drivers of the cars that were stopped in the street by his truck while he loaded and unloaded packages. He could swing aboard the bed of his truck without touching it with anything but his hands and the soles of his feet, and then handle the packages as though they were feathers on the tips of his fingers. No one seemed to mind when Joe's truck blocked the way. He had been a great high school athlete and was making a good name as an athlete in college. He was handsome as a racehorse, and he was as good a grown-up friend as Mikey ever had. Everyone called Uncle Joe "Bronco."

"*Brrronco,*" the men would growl at him when his truck blocked the street and made them wait, and then they would smile.

Mikey made friends with pretty girls who were still childlike enough to try their new wooing powers on him. They suspected they were pretty and were learning modest ways to find out if it was true. They made eyes even at little boys like Mikey as they searched for somebody simpatico, someone else who might want to let them know they were good-looking and share his own goodness with them. They walked down the street with their hips swaying, their pretty eyes full of the pure joy of innocence, and with a power to lay men low that they did not understand. They gave Mikey as much attention as they did boys their own age. Most of them were from Sonora and did not have to worry about being pretty. Sonora girls had enjoyed a worldwide reputation for beauty since the time of Maximilian and Carlotta. These who passed by on Morley Avenue flirted broadly and believed no one would take it as anything but innocent fun.

The girls who stopped to talk to Mikey were not always the same girls, but they universally shared a desire to woo the world.

On the street they cast warm glances and watched for a chance to meet someone else's gaze. When their eyes met Mikey's they smiled and sometimes stopped to talk.

"*Ay, mira, que muchachito tan simpático.* Look at the handsome, friendly little boy," one might say. "*¿Cómo te llamas?* What do they call you? I'm Rosina and this other girl is Sparky."

"Miguel Pablo Veranos Sorreles," he would say. According to custom, he always included Maggie's maiden name. He was used to being told he was good-looking because all little boys were good-looking to them. He did not need to believe the girls were serious about wooing him, only that they wanted him to like it.

"*Ay,* Miguel, how beautiful you are," one of them might say.

"*¿Adónde van?*" Mikey would ask. "Where are you going?"

"*Ay,* we've been looking for you, Miguelito. Are you married?"

"I'm still too little."

"*Ojos de gato.* Where did you get those cat eyes?"

"From my mama and daddy."

"*Ay,* will you be our Miguelito?"

"I am called Mikey."

"Will you?"

"No."

That made them laugh. "Why not?"

"I belong to Maggie Summers."

"Ah, she's your mama, but when you grow up I want you for my sweetheart," Rosina might say.

"No, me," Sparky would say, and she would move closer to Mikey. Rosina would then try to crowd even closer.

"I like you both."

"Ah, nooo," Sparky would whine. "Are you only another *mujeriego,* a ladies man who will only cause me pain, a *milamores* who wants to have a thousand women?"

"If you want her you can't have me," Rosina, or Carmela, or Maria would say.

All this time they stood close to Mikey without touching him with anything but their sound, smell, breath, and gaze. They kept their arms decently at their sides. They were chaste girls, virgins while they stopped to talk to the boy, clean and decent as always, or clean and decent for a moment as they once had been. Abruptly they would leave, but they always looked back at least once before they went out of sight.

Mikey's favorite passerby girlfriend was Enriqueta, called Queta. She was small and *prieta*, dark complexioned, with delicate features and shiny black hair that curled around the heavy golden earrings she wore. She first stopped to talk to Mikey when he was three or four. That first day she acted as though she had known him all his life and immediately started up a serious conversation while her black eyes took stock of him with a completely proprietary gaze.

Every time Queta stopped after that she took stock of Mikey with that look and without asking questions about how he had been, or why he might have a bandage on his finger. Her gaze would inspect the changes that had taken place since she last saw him while she spoke of other things. The two could have been old lovers meeting after their affair was over and she did not want to ask him about the changes in his life for fear that he would want to start up feelings for her again.

She was so beautiful, even the most racist of men overlooked her dark complexion. She was famous along the border for her singing voice. She was a soloist at Sunday Mass for the Ave Maria, at the fiestas for *ranchera* country songs, and for love songs at suppertime in the best restaurants of Nogales, Sonora. Mikey hummed her songs to himself and remembered the gentle spirit with which she sang them. She was more company when he closed his eyes to go to sleep than even his guardian angel.

Sometimes Mikey would look up the street and see that she had already fixed him in her gaze and was bearing down on him. He would smile and when she reached him say, "*¿Qué hubo*, Queta? How have you been?"

She never smiled but would say something like, "*Where* have *you* been? I've been by here twenty times in ten days hoping to see you, but you have not been here. This has kept me *triste*, sad."

Sometimes, if Mikey saw her coming far enough away, and had time enough to think about it, he would play her game and look steadily at her and not smile.

Then she might say, "Why are you so serious? Is it because you missed me as much as I missed you? Now you know how I feel when I come by and you are not here."

One day when Mikey was five, he saw Queta on the street with a tall, blonde Anglo man. The street was crowded, but she stopped and spoke angrily to the man, as though to plant him in place so she could walk away from him. She turned to leave, but he grabbed her by the arm and fell in step with her. When they came abreast of Mikey, Queta raised her eyes to look at him but made no greeting.

Mikey saw that she might go on by and said, "Queta, it's me, Mikey," and stopped them both. She pulled away from the man and hurried into the backseat of Maggie's car. "I won't be able to talk much today because I have to meditate," she said to Mikey. "I've not been meditating enough."

The man grinned while Queta rolled up the window and shut him out.

"Enriqueta," the man said.

Queta would not look at him.

"What's this meditating you have to do, Queta?" Mikey asked.

She put her finger to her lips and said, "Shhh," then very softly said, "*necesito pensar*. I need to think."

After a while the man walked away. Queta stirred, sighed, and said, "That was a good meditation," then stepped out of the car and walked away.

All the everyday girls of Mikey's childhood were brown from the Sonora and Arizona sun. Queta's burnt-brown-to-the-edge-of-black prieta complexion probably came from down in some hot, Moorish blood of hers. Even Lorraine Knox was browner than other blonde girls who did not grow up in Arizona. Children played outdoors all the daylight hours. Mikey was made to come indoors only in bad weather, or at night, and then he was planted in one spot where Maggie or Granny could keep track of him. He was not allowed to run and play or raise his voice in the house. He got spanked for that even before he could run and talk. Mikey was Black Man and like all the men of his family, he belonged outside during the day.

Panfilo Gandara was another regular passerby. Mikey had been told that Panfilo did not own more than half a brain. He did not have any skull above his eyebrows, and his face was vulnerably pale. Panfilo was not witless. He pretended to make entries in a ledger he carried. His family kept a discreet watch over him. They were wealthy, and they kept Panfilo in the Montezuma Hotel. His servant, a man who had retired as *mayordomo* of a Gandara ranch, delivered meals regularly to his room and stayed to make sure he ate them.

He seldom looked anyone in the eye. He was quick and restless as a fly, would pause to absolute stillness for a breath if someone spoke to him, then turn his back and flit away. Often, when he came by Mikey, he would turn his head purposefully away, then violently swing it back to stare the boy full in the face. Mikey began to think that he was the only one who was stared at by Panfilo Gandara for more than one instant at a time and he did not like it.

Panfilo came out of the Montezuma every morning in clean, pressed clothes and so freshly bathed that droplets of water dripped from his sideburns. Except for not having a forehead, Panfilo was handsome of face and figure. He had one thick, black eyebrow across his face that bridged the space between his eyes. His eyes were a solid, glittering black that seemed to have no pupils. He always wore a look of intense concentration. Every once in a while he would scowl, jot a line or a circle in his ledger, and move on with great importance, as though his compilation of jots and circles was urgently needed for posterity.

Sometimes he was made to sit with his family for a snack at the lunch counter of the Owl Drugstore or Bracker's Department Store. On these occasions, he did not look at his food or seem to want it. He stared at everything else in the room until one of his relatives called him back to his food. He would then humbly redirect himself to his snack for a moment or two.

On the day that Queta had taken refuge in the back of Mikey's car, Panfilo came by, stopped, and stood with his pencil poised above the open page of the ledger, as though prepared to make an entry, and stared into the faces of people who passed. Mikey wanted to see inside the ledger, but when he spoke to Panfilo, the man stared blankly at him and then turned away unconcerned, the way an ape in a zoo might look and turn away from the millionth tourist who walked by.

The look of an ape on Panfilo's face made Mikey laugh. Panfilo went up the street and Mikey thought he was gone, but he stopped, turned around, and headed back. When he came abreast of Mikey's window, he turned and screamed with laughter in Mikey's face. He then stepped back, shaded his eyes with his hand, and gazed upon a mountain in Nogales, Sonora. Mikey thought that pose was funny, so he laughed again. Panfilo whirled and bawled in Mikey's face. Mikey recoiled, recovered, bawled back at him, and laughed again. Panfilo took hold of him in the big grip of one hand, shook him, and jerked him so close to his face that Mikey saw right down his throat when he bawled again. Getting hot breath and spit on his face angered Mikey. He braced his feet against the door and hauled the man's head and shoulders through the window.

All of a sudden, the fight went out of Panfilo. His mouth closed, he let Mikey go, and he backed away from the window. Black Joe had taken him by the back of the neck the way a hawk takes a rabbit. Panfilo mewed and flailed his arms. Joe pushed Panfilo's head down to his knees. Panfilo was tall and broad shouldered, young and muscular. People were afraid of him because of the animal way he moved and looked at them, but Joe's hand on the back of his neck made him want his mama. He dropped his ledger and pencil and tried to unlatch Joe's hand, but Joe opened the front door of the Montezuma, shoved him into the lobby headfirst, and deposited him in an easy chair.

The Gandara family manservant appeared, picked up the ledger and pencil, and turned to Mikey. "¿Te lastimó? Did he hurt you?" he asked.

Mikey shook his head. The servant opened the front door of the hotel for Joe, waited for him to come out, then went in and took Panfilo by the arm and walked him toward his room.

Mikey tried to keep a good eye out for old Panfilo after that. One day the *loco* walked by so close his sleeve brushed the car door. Mikey thought he might turn and bawl at him again, but he went on to accost some poor lady with his ledger. Mikey turned away for something better to look at. When he turned back, Panfilo's big teeth were grinning inside his window again.

Poor Panfilo. Uncle Joe had been teaching Mikey to box and had told him that the best defense any little boy could have against a mean grown-up, if he could not run, was to sock him hard on the end of his nose and yell for help. Mikey was not given time to aim for the end of Panfilo's nose, but he connected solidly with an eyeball. Panfilo covered his face and howled into his hands. The end of his nose showed between his hands, so Mikey followed Uncle Joe's orders and poked that, too. Panfilo cried, "Ay, ay, ay," and backed away to the middle of the sidewalk.

Mikey figured he was in for a big fight. He turned away for help and looked straight into the eyes of the Anglo who had bothered Queta. The man had watched the whole skirmish from five steps away, but he turned and sauntered away. The Gandara manservant led Panfilo away before he was able to look out from behind his hands.

In the year that Mikey was five and just before his parents separated, Maggie got pregnant with his little sister Maudy Marie. Paul went to Mexico to work for Cabezon and his visits home were infrequent, unscheduled, and never much appreciated. Maggie's temper was bad and everything Mikey did made her unhappy. She could not deal with her son without punishing him. Everything was a capital offense. At least once a day he got called in by Maggie, bawled out, jerked into the grasp, and executed on the nearest block over which he could be draped. Mikey became certain the woman would kill him. Thanks be to God, because Maggie always pulled up while he was still in good enough condition to go on, forget the fear of death, and resume his depredations.

Mikey was usually able to recover quickly, because when Maggie was angriest she grabbed up bludgeons that were too unwieldy for her to handle. She almost always had to throw them away and use her hand. The switch that she took to his legs when she had time to think about it really hurt, but that was his own fault. He had given her permission to use a peach switch.

However, he knew Maggie worried that sooner or later her son would kill her with exasperation, anger, and worry, or her hand would slip and she would deal him a lethal swat.

Mikey went too far the day he decided to amuse himself by pulling a trick on Maggie. He did not consider that she was going through a dangerous time. She hated being pregnant and her temper was shorter than the last click of a time bomb. Rules were more than strictly enforced. Justice was ignored. The plush spots on Mikey's butt got sore and stayed that way, and his spankings were coming with no more warning than lightning bolts. Foolishly, he did not think to postpone his mischief until a safer time. Instead he stepped up the pace. Then Satan took him over. He discovered a way to be clever and mean without violating Maggie's rules.

Mikey now rode the bus to and from kindergarten. The rule was that he come straight home from school on Mrs. Clark's Little Kids' Bus, change from his school clothes to his running clothes, and play in the yard with Baxter.

He could not violate the first rule because Mrs. Clark always made sure he caught the bus, even though she sometimes had to track him down and put him on the bus herself. Most of the time his having been away from his haunts all day made him feel an obligation to go right out on patrol as soon as he reached home. He would not remember that he should have changed clothes until he picked himself out of a mud puddle or tore a hole in a garment.

That was not all he did to get regular spankings, though. He left the yard for the slightest of reasons and he did not head home until he heard his mother call at dark, and he seldom heard the first call. If he was not home when Maggie came home, he got a spanking when he returned. Sometimes complaints from the neighbors about his activities in his own yard got him a spanking.

One day, he climbed into the topmost branches of his alamo tree and waited for Maggie to come home from work. She drove in, got out of the car, went in the house, and asked Bica for a report on him. Bica was the girl Maggie had hired to take care of him and keep their house. Even though Bica reported that she had not seen Mikey get off the bus, Maggie did not get excited until she called for him at dark and he did not answer. She went out on the highway, stopped directly beneath his tree, and called again. He forced himself not to answer. He let her march down the highway to Nina's to look for him. Nina told her that she had not seen him all day, either.

"Well, he's gone," Maggie said. "This time he's really done it." Then Maggie's worry caused a strange new situation that Mikey had not foreseen. Now his Nina was worried. When both his mothers went out and stood on the highway and called for him with a different kind of concern in their voices than he had ever heard, he knew that he was in the most fatal kind of trouble. That was not the end of it. Carmen Horrel, who lived in the house between Nina's and Maggie's, came out of her house and told Maggie she had not seen Mikey, either. Bica heard them calling and she went to the back door and started calling. Then Granny started calling. The Wingos on the other side of Granny's came out and told Granny that they had not seen him, and *they* started calling.

When Maggie passed underneath Mikey's tree again, he giggled out loud as a sign of surrender. The giggle was his white flag. A real giggle happened uncontrollably, but he wanted Maggie to take this one as the sound of innocent joy of a boy who had only been playing a harmless joke, not a disrespectful boy who waged war. The sound that actually came out was about the sourest, phoniest giggle any kid ever tried to fake in the history of kids.

Maggie looked up, found Mikey in the tree, and their eyes locked. She later told people that she was astounded by the terrible thought that came to her at that moment. She thought, "My God, I'm looking at myself in the mirror, and I'm a devil. I've given birth to my own, personal devil. There I am, my very own demon staring down at myself with my own green eyes."

Maggie's face did not cloud up and she did not yell for Mikey to come down out of that tree this instant, as she usually did. She turned pale and spoke in a quiet, measured tone that told her son that he was about to be treated as strangely as he had treated everyone else that day.

"Now, mama, I came home and changed my clothes and stayed in the yard, so I can't get a whipping," Mikey cried.

"I'm your mother, but you don't listen to me. I only try to keep you in the yard so you won't go off and get run over by a car or bitten by a rabid dog," Maggie said. "Instead of appreciating how I feel about you, you had to show me how ornery you really are. Without batting an eye, you just scared me out of ten years of my life and caused this whole neighborhood to be afraid that something awful had finally happened to you. Do not say one word. Just come down from there and get in the house."

Maggie usually ranted at him and kept his safety under scrutiny as he climbed down. This time she did not even watch him come down. Even though a slip or an error could cause him to fall and be maimed, Maggie was not in the mood to care. The realization that his proud show of verve and recklessness in the tree mattered not at all was more punishment than a whipping.

This time, Mikey's sorrow for having done wrong did not end with a good spanking when he touched down on the ground. He was told that he would not be absolved with a whipping. Maggie said that she was curious to see if he could find out what shame was.

"Frankly, I'm so ashamed of you, I don't know if I can live out the day," she said. "You're to blame for all the upheaval, but I'm the one who has to tell Granny, your Nina, Carmen, and the Wingos that I'm sorry, but my son hid in his own yard and gloated while all our friends and neighbors called for him. In another minute we would have notified the sheriff.

"Now, I don't care where you go with your face, but don't show it to me anymore today. Get in the house where you belong and don't let me see or hear from you until you discover how you can help me make up to everybody."

After a spanking, Mikey would have been himself again in ten minutes, but this new tack of Maggie's made him realize how mean he had been. She had tears in her eyes and her mouth trembled when she spoke to him. He went out to the porch to lie on his bed. He listened to his poor mother tell Bica that she was finally full of him. She was pregnant and did not want to deal with him anymore. He bawled for a while, then decided that he could still pay his debt to society, so he went to Maggie and apologized,

apologized to Bica, then went out to apologize to everybody else. The Wingos looked at him with no expression and only said that it was all right; they had only been worried about him. Carmen Horrell stood behind her screen door and told him that if he did not someday kill his mother with worry, he would kill himself, and she would die of sadness. His Nina only sat down when he came in, gave him a very brief hug when he said he was sorry, and told him to go home.

Maggie decided that Paul would have to take charge of Mikey for a while. That could not be easily arranged, because he was a full day's drive and a three-day ride over a horseshoe trail down in the Magdalena Mountains of Sonora. After a strenuous use of telephone and telegraph did not flush Paul out, Maggie told Buster to go down and get him.

Buster pointed out that it would require superhuman diligence to find Paul Summers and bring him home. Furthermore, Buster would have to leave bed, board, a formidable wife, livestock, and his ranch estate to do it. Before he agreed to go, he made Maggie acknowledge that this awful sacrifice was not his idea. Every respectable friend of Paul, Buster, and Maggie knew that he was the one who had to go because he was the only one in the world who would do it. Nobody else cared enough to brave the Mexican wilderness and its water holes. Maggie also knew that it was a shame, but Buster would enjoy every minute of the errand. He would like it down there with Paul so much that he might forget to come back.

This time a miracle happened. Buster made it out of Mexico with Paul in only three weeks. He sounded sober when he called Maggie from the Montezuma Hotel on the Arizona side of the line. Paul got on the phone and told Maggie to bring Mikey and they would have supper across the line at the Cavern Restaurant.

Maggie and Mikey bathed, dressed up, and drove to the hotel to meet Buster and Paul. They were not in the Montezuma lobby where they had promised to wait for Maggie, and they were not in the bar. They were not in the Owl Drugstore next door, either. Maggie and Mikey sat down in the lobby to wait.

At first Maggie was entertained by a parade of cowmen from both sides of the line, some of them with their wives and families, who stopped to visit with her. They stopped first on their way to supper and invited Maggie to go. Then they visited with her on their way back to their rooms after supper. After that Maggie and Mikey had nothing to do but watch the people go by on the street.

Roy Adams, Paul's cousin, strolled into the lobby with Vivian O'Brien and stopped to talk. Both of the cowmen were half tight with liquor, but they were gentlemanly and proper. They had been crossing cattle on the border all day, had been to supper at the Cavern, and were on their way to bed.

After a chat, Maggie asked if they had seen Paul and Buster. They looked away, stuttered, said "no" in too many ways, excused themselves, and left for their rooms.

Maggie said, "Come on, Mikey. I know where the sonsaguns are."

When Maggie headed for a fight in a hurry and Mikey was with her, she always grabbed him by the hand so she could make headway at her own pace without leaving him behind. He figured she also wanted to keep him close so he could be her witness later in the family fight at home. They covered the hundred yards from the Montezuma to the Cavern in about one minute, and that included negotiations at Mexican Customs and Immigration.

The Cavern had formerly been used as a dank, slimy dungeon where black scorpions and giant centipedes nested and feasted on convicts shackled to the walls. After it was vacated of its prisoners, the Kuriakis brothers bought it and turned it into a first-class restaurant. The scorpions and centipedes stayed to entertain the diners.

Every day at 11 AM the waiters and waitresses in black tuxedo uniforms began serving dinner in heavy chinaware on white tablecloths, with silver so soft a diner could leave his teeth marks on it. The mariachis strolled from table to table and played on request from opening until closing time. Other mariachis did the same in the Cavern's separate bar that never closed. The best foreign wines and cognacs were served there, as was the commonest Mexican beer and tequila. In the main cavern where everyone dined, the only light came from small lamps against rock walls that had been blasted by dynamite and hewn by iron tools, then polished smooth by squirming convicts.

Now, people arrived at the Cavern in the evenings dressed in their best with their pockets full of money, and left fed to the ears with good food and wine. A blind man could tell when he was within a block of the Cavern by the smell of *cahuama* turtle soup that cooked in big pots in the kitchen. The smell seemed to hang in a nutritious, steamy haze over the narrow Calle Elias in front of the place.

Maggie barged into the bar off the street. Paul and Buster, their hats on the backs of their heads, happy smiles on their faces, tequila shots in their fists, leaned against the bar. Girls leaned against their sides and smiled into their faces. The sight of Maggie with her kid in tow, so full of meanness that it showed like sparks coming out of her ears, put an end to that. The girls became fish that sounded for the depths of the sea. Paul and Buster's smiles disappeared.

The scene for which Mikey stayed was short. When she saw that Paul and Buster had crystallized in their tracks, Maggie turned Mikey loose, sailed in, slapped the hats off their heads and the drinks out of their hands, and stomped their toes with the high heels on her pumps.

Buster touched his toes in pain.

Paul said, "Honey, am I late already?"

Maggie could have pulled up and herded them home right then, but she wanted to castigate them. She needed to show how decent women deal with husbands and brothers who spend their time away from home with bartenders, mariachis, and whores.

When Paul did not bend over his foot to show that it had been damaged, Maggie spiked it again and then spiked the other foot. Paul grabbed her roughly by the shoulders to stop her from doing it again. She tried to kick him in the groin with both feet. She missed his most vital spot, but he read her vicious intent. He shoved her into a booth full of drunken students.

Ordinarily, this might have been fun for everyone, especially the young men in the booth upon whom Maggie landed, but Mikey, Paul, and Buster were afraid she would hurt her belly. Mikey had been warned many times by almost everybody in his family to be careful not to disturb the peace of Maggie's belly. Paul started toward her, so Mikey wrapped himself around a leg and hung on. He did not think his parents would kill each other if he could stay attached to his father's leg.

Paul only wanted to make sure that Maggie was not hurt. She was to blame for Mikey's fear that Paul would harm her. She had convinced Mikey that his father would probably beat her to death someday when he was too drunk to know what he did.

Paul hauled Mikey along on his leg while Maggie separated herself from the young Mexicans in the booth. Paul tried to shake Mikey off and said, "Madam, look what you made me step in." They both began to laugh and try to pry Mikey loose. They could not pry away even one of his fingers, so Maggie spoke angrily to him. That did not work, so she began to plead. Mikey did not turn loose until Uncle Buster tickled him, put his arm over his shoulders, and whispered, "Come on, Black Man, they're not mad anymore."

Maggie quit smiling, stalked away to the bar, and ordered a tequila *doble*. The bartender was quick to serve it. Maggie arched an eyebrow, turned to face Paul, and began insulting him. Paul did not know much about how to insult anybody. He only began to brag on the way the bar girls and whores had treated him.

Mikey backed away from them until he found himself out in the street, bawling. He walked miserably away from them. He did not realize how far he had wandered until he stumbled down the bank of the Nogales Arroyo, the same arroyo that ran in front of his house. He sat for a while in the sand in the bottom.

In those days the arroyo was a lot more crooked than it became after its path was engineered, directed, contained, and straightened by cement banks. Mikey started walking home but realized after a few moments that he was headed upstream, the wrong way. The arroyo ran downstream from Nogales to his house. He climbed out and found himself on Canal Street.

Mikey had been led off the main arroyo and up another dry wash by the music he heard from bars, nightclubs, and dancehalls. This was the Zone of Tolerance, the street set aside by the municipal government of Nogales, Sonora, for its bordellos. Mikey was only five and did not yet know bordellos.

He did know a familiar voice when he heard it. He could hear Queta singing. He went into a saloon and found her spotlighted on a stage singing "Quatro Vidas," "Four Lives," his favorite song. Nobody cared who came into that place at that hour. Mikey was so little nobody saw him at the door. The place was full of empty tables.

The spotlight was the only light in the place. The person who sang and accompanied herself on a guitar sounded like Queta but did not look like her. She was dressed in a colorfully brocaded and sequined *China Poblana* costume. Mikey knew how much work and good material went into a China Poblana. He had watched Mimita, his Nina's mother, sew, measure, and trim good cloth and bright thread for months to make a dress like that. Queta's China Poblana with its brocaded roses was just right for someone as classy as she, but if the voice had not been unmistakable, Mikey would never have known the singer was Queta. Her lips and cheeks were painted with thick swipes of red paste, and her eyebrow lines were thin, long, and drawn flat over her brows. The rest of her face, her neck, her bare shoulders, and her bosom were layered with white powder. Mikey knew only the eyes that peered wetly out of the powder and paint. Queta was only a specter inside it all.

Three women who were as heavily painted and powdered as Queta sat together at a table, not looking or talking to each other. They were overdressed in stiff, bright, homemade dresses. A man sat alone at a table near the front door. Another man sat with his back to Mikey at a table on the edge of the stage. Mikey climbed into a booth and fell asleep.

Someone screamed over Mikey's head. He looked up as a man and a woman wrestled against the booth. The man jerked the woman up onto her tiptoes in a bear hug, and then held her arms around his own head. She screamed in his face. The man's rumpled hair hung in his eyes. The woman was the one Mikey had thought was Queta, but now he could not see anything familiar about her. The man growled and twisted her arms behind her, bent her backward, and bit her on the mouth. She kicked at him and yipped angrily with the effort. He raised his fist overhead and struck her in the face. She slumped and he dropped her. Her face bounced on the floor. He kicked her in the side and stepped away. He went back to his table, pocketed his coins, and combed his hair.

Queta cried with her first breath as she regained consciousness. She lay with her face on the floor. Her arms were still behind her. One of the heels of her new red pumps was broken. The man looked at her. Then he turned away and Mikey recognized him as the Anglo man.

As soon as the Anglo left the saloon, the man who had been sitting by the door knelt beside Queta and called to the three women. Two of them were already on their way toward Queta and one in a blue dress hurried out of the room.

Queta whimpered and tried to raise her head. Her arms lay dead behind her. The toes of her pumps scratched feebly against the floor. The two women relaxed her arms by her sides and sat her up. Her head lolled on her chest. The women spoke kindly to her and called her name. The woman in blue came back with a bucket of ice water and a towel. She soaked the towel in the water, draped it around Queta's neck, and wiped her face, shoulders, and bosom with the ends and cleaned away some of the powder and paint.

The woman in blue looked at Mikey. "*¿Quién eres tú?* Who are you? Are you Forbes?" She pronounced it "Forrrvehs."

Mikey had no idea who Forrrvehs was. "No," he said.

All three women stared at him. "*¿Entonces, quién eres? ¿Cómo te llamas? ¿Qué estás haciendo aquí?* Who are you, then? What are you called? What are you doing here?"

"*Me llamo* Miguel Pablo Veranos Sorreles," Mikey said.

The woman in blue narrowed her eyes to examine him and said, "*¿Quienes son tus padres?* Who are your parents?"

"Pablo *y* Margarita Veranos. Paul and Marguerite Summers."

"*¿Eres hijo de Pol Somairs?* Are you Paul Summers's son?"

"*Sí.*"

"*¿Y, tus padres?* And your parents? Where are they?"

"*Allá están.*"

"*¿Adónde?* Where?"

"*En la Caverna.* In the Cavern."

"How did you get here?"

"I got lost walking."

"And now you find yourself here."

"Yes."

"Boy, I am not surprised. All your people find this place sooner or later. How old are you?"

"Five."

She looked at Mikey for a long moment. Then she said, "Five. That's a record, even for the men in your family. I am Maria Ester, a friend of your uncles. You stay right where you are. I'm going down the street to call the Cavern."

The iced towel helped Queta recover and the women walked her to the booth. Mikey stood back and watched. She did not look at him. She propped her face in her hands and gazed down at the table. Mikey could not see what the coward had done to her face. He thought Queta's, Nina's, Maggie's, and Granny's were the prettiest faces anyone had ever seen.

"Are you meditating, Queta?" Mikey asked.

She glanced at him, and then turned for a better look. "Is it you?"

"Yes."

"I am so *atarantada*, dizzy. You? I might have known you would come and save me."

"I got lost."

"What?" She was still confused.

"I got lost."

"I don't believe you. You came to save me like the other time at your car. That's why you're here, isn't it?" She laid a lovely, amused eye on him and a short gasp of pleasure escaped her. She cut it short because it hurt. Her lips were bloody.

"*Vente*. Come with me," she said.

She took Mikey's hand and led him to a private *sala*, a comfortably furnished living room lit by one kerosene lamp. She sat him on a couch, pulled off his shoes, and placed them side by side on the floor.

Mikey stared. This person of the powder, paint, and bloody lips exemplified the grotesque turn his life had taken the moment Maggie charged out of the Montezuma. He was not surprised to find himself in the private refuge of beaten, painted women in the middle of the night. He had always known something like this would happen if his parents did not stop fighting. Worse would happen. He would be this much separated from his folks forever. He always worried about that. This time he was truly lost from them and it was no dream.

Queta pushed him gently down, put a cushion under his head, dimmed the lamp, and sat nearby to rest. She dabbed at her face with the ends of the wet towel. He pretended to be asleep but watched her. That was no way to stay awake. He fell into the innocent sleep of a five-year-old and did not wake up until he found himself in his own bed the next morning.

FOUR

Sierra de San Juan

The Mexican horseman says, "Andando en el campo llano, como lo quiera el Cristiano; pero en subiendo la cuesta, como lo quiera la bestia. *Ride at your pace on the plain. Ride at your horse's pace on the mountain.*"

Paul loaded Cabezon's ranch truck with Mikey's bed and saddle, cases of canned food, spare truck wheels, and barrels of gasoline. He sat Mikey in the front seat beside him and left Nogales on a clear morning in October. They were headed for Cabezon Woodell's headquarters at El Carrizal, on the west side of the Magdalena Mountains in Sonora. Paul crossed the line at the port of entry of Sásabe in the Altar Valley. Sásabe was a pueblo south-west of Tucson at the end of seventy miles of dirt road.

Paul arrived at the line at noon. The garitas stood new and clean on a hill. The pueblo on the Mexican side lay in the dirt among the rocks of a canyon a quarter mile south of the line.

Customs and immigration officials on both sides of the line were on the alert. Two murderers were expected to try to cross somewhere along the border to escape the law. One had murdered his family in Mexico. The other had murdered while robbing a bank in Douglas, Arizona. The Mexican was expected to head into Arizona. The American was expected to try to hide in Sonora.

The American officials on the Arizona side were fresh, clean-cut young men. Paul wanted to ask them if they knew anything of the killers when he stopped for their inspection, but they only smiled and waved him on through the gate.

Paul and Mikey went inside the garita on the Mexican side for their truck permit from Mexican Customs. The customs official in the garita was an old, gray fellow who doubled as immigration officer. He sat at a typewriter in the front office. He wore Levi's with the cuffs turned up over the insteps of his boots, a short-sleeved civilian shirt, and his official cap cocked over one ear. He processed the visas for a man and a woman. He was a good typist using two fingers. His index fingers landed heavily and surely on the keys without his having to wonder where they struck. The doors and windows of his office were wide open. The office was spare and neat. Only a stack of blank visas, the typewriter, and an American fifty-cent piece were on the desk. When Paul and Mikey walked in, the American couple walked out and the officer pulled open a drawer and brushed the coin, like a big crumb, off the table into the drawer without looking at it.

Paul already had his visa for immigration and Mikey did not need one, so the officer took them into a separate office to issue the customs truck permit. Sásabe, Sonora, was in the region called La Pimería Alta. Almost everybody who passed there knew or were related to the few ranching families that lived inside that region, which covered several hundred square miles on both sides of the line. Everybody who stopped to be processed was headed for a place to sleep in Sonora that night.

"I must be getting old, Pol," the customs inspector said. "I did not know when you left Sonora last."

"I went out at Nogales, Cabo."

"And this boy with you, on which side does he belong?"

"He is my son and belongs to me."

"Ah, a little Pol."

"Shake hands with El Cabo, the corporal commander of this post, son."

Mikey shook his hand.

"This isn't a Yaqui you're trying to bring back to Mexico, is it, Pol?" the Cabo joked.

"No. He is *prietito*, but he's mine."

When the permit was complete, the inspector handed it to Paul, followed him out to the truck, and stood by for a moment to talk. "You know, the judicial police stand vigilant even up here in the north for that Nolasco who killed his wife and four children in Chiapas," he said.

"That's what we heard. And the Americans search for a gangster."

"Did the gangster kill his family, too?"

"No, he is only a bank robber."

"Ah, then, your criminal is a romantic bandit like El Chamaco Nelson, Baby Face Nelson, then?"

"Yes, only I think this one's name is Kelly."

"In these times, who would not think of becoming a bandit if he could be rich and famous like El Chamaco Nelson, no?"

"*Tienes mucha razón*, that's a very reasonable observation, Cabo."

"I started to tell you. The government mounted a nation-wide manhunt for that Nolasco with much publicity. He is an insane Indian who probably ran straight into the jungle after he killed his family. He did not have to go more than three meters to hide. Do you think the judicial police should stage a search on the Pimería Alta of Sonora and Arizona for a *guacho* who does not know his way out of a jungle thousands of leagues to the south?"

"It doesn't seem right, does it, Cabo?"

"Of course not, but last week, an army unit of our very same government slaughtered a family of Christians at Los Molinos with as much dispatch and facility as they would have cornered and killed a herd of *javalina*. This they did only ten leagues from here, with no fanfare, no newspaper account, and no radio announcement. The commander of the unit probably did not even consider those murders worthy of an entry in his log book."

"Who did they murder this time?" Paul said. "Did I know them?"

"I don't think so. They were Yaquis who had fled the reservation at Bácum. Someday this government for which I work will have to make an accounting to God for another dead father and another dead mother and three dead little children."

"*Que chingado*," Paul said.

El Cabo looked at Mikey, then at Paul. "Does the little Pol speak Spanish?"

"Better than me and as well as you," Paul said.

"Then let's talk about fiestas or something, not murder in President Calles's glorious revolution against Indians and Christians."

"When will they stop killing Yaquis and Catholics, Cabo?"

"Ah, the government's mothers and fathers have stopped them from killing Catholics. They won't stop killing Yaquis until they are all dead, or have flown to the United States."

"The way the government cavalry kills them where it catches them, it's a wonder a family got as far north as Los Molinos."

"They came down from the mountain route to hide and rest with the Caballero family at Los Molinos because you and El Cabezon were not in your mountain camp to receive them. Don Juan Caballero gave sanctuary to many of the people while you were gone, until someone informed on him."

"The poor people. What did the government do to don Juan?"

"Nothing. As you know, don Juan's skin is very white. I don't think he has a drop of Indian blood. They got all they wanted when they butchered the Yaqui family."

"Now what will the people do?"

The Cabo winked at Mikey. "I thought you might know, Pol. I think that is why you are here again."

"Ah, maybe good whites like you—Catholics—will help them, Cabo," Paul said.

The Cabo laughed and pointed at Paul. "*Tú*, Pol. You vaqueros who work and move in the mountains are the ones who can help them. I'm on the wrong side. They don't try to get out through my garita."

Paul laughed. "Me? How can I help anybody escape the government? Haven't you heard? I'm only good at helping Mexicans drink mezcal."

"Yoouu, Pol. You and Gato Cañez, Del Mercer, El Cabezon, and the Caballeros are the ones the Yaquis thank when they reach the United States. Why else would you come here in times like these? To work cattle? Nooo. Cattle are not worth anything in your country or mine right now."

"We are only here to build El Cabezon's herd, Cabo."

"That sounds good, but no one believes it."

"Believe it," Paul said.

"Tourists and cattlemen prefer to use the good international highway through Nogales, not this *garra de camino*, this trashy road in its ditch of rocks."

"Ah, but we have to use this wild road now because we're going to work the Sierra de San Juan for wild cattle."

"Sure. Pablo Ligero, the great Fast Paul, is only in Mexico to hide his light and catch wild cattle in the mountains. I believe it and hope it goes well."

"Thank you, Cabo. Here, take this for the cigarettes." Paul gave him a dollar. The Cabo stood back and held the bill loosely in his open hand as Paul and Mikey drove away.

Paul drove to the end of Sásabe's rocky street and stopped at the hotel next to Soony Jaquez's bar. Soony and Paul were friends. Paul registered for a room in the hotel, and then took Mikey out the back door, across the urine-soaked backyard of the bar, and through a tapia gate to Soony's patio. Soony's Saint's Day was being celebrated. A fifty-five-gallon barrel of mezcal with no lid stood in the middle of the patio. A long-handled dipper was hooked on the brim of the barrel. A band of mariachis with trumpet, violin, guitar, and *guitarrón*, a potbellied guitar, arrived.

Paul and Soony sat in the shade with a cup of mezcal between them, pushed their hats to the backs of their heads *a media cabeza*, laughed, and Mikey knew Paul was planted. Soony's wife led Mikey into her kitchen for supper with Soony's kids and Monche Cañez, Gato Cañez's son. Gato was Paul's partner on Cabezon Woodell's crew. After supper Monche and Mikey went out into the street to play *Mostrenco*, Mustang, with a gang of boys Monche's age. The boy who was "it" carried the *reata*, the lariat. The rest of the boys were mustangs. The boy who was "it" had to rope a mustang and lead him back to a corral where he became "it."

Mikey was the littlest kid, so he did not get roped. He would never have been able to catch the bigger boys. Everybody was barefoot, so he took off his new boots so he could run. He was fast for a five-year-old, but those boys were lightning.

About nine o'clock, Lina, Soony's pretty fourteen-year-old daughter, came out to the street. She wore a cotton dress over bare legs and feet. Her light brown hair was long and wetly combed. The boy who was "it" made a run at her and roped her. She did not complain about being surprised and blindsided. With no expression on her face, Lina swung a loop and ran at Mikey. Mikey whirled and ran with his head down to get away, but she reached out with a long throw and caught him. She reeled him in, gave away the reata, picked up his boots and socks, put her arm over his shoulder, and took him home. He was fed a pastry called *pan de huevo* with *café con leche*, coffee that was half hot milk and sweetened with wild honey. In the dark, lamplit room with the music and the warmth of the fire in Señora Jaquez's kitchen stove, he fell asleep before he thought to get out of his chair.

In the night he awoke in the hotel room to the sounds and smells of scorched bedbugs. Paul had overturned his cot so he could scorch the springs and the mattress with a torch of twisted newspaper. Bedbugs had gathered in clusters like elderberries on the underside of his bunk. The torch huffed hot wind. It roared and threw sparks as Paul wiped flames on the bugs. Some of the bugs popped when they sparked into flame, then became black spots on the mattress.

Bedbugs did not bother Mikey, so he turned his face to the wall to sleep. Paul's sleeping habits were Spartan. Before he climbed into any bed except Maggie's he sprinkled it with sand and gravel so he would not sleep too soundly. Mikey wondered why his dad went to so much bother to get rid of the bedbugs. They would probably have done a better job of keeping him from a sound sleep than the sand and gravel.

As they drove the next day, the road south across the desert crossed a hundred wide, sandy washes. Paul and Mikey stopped at the Arroyo del Sásabe and ate lunch under the shade of a Chino tree. The shade was so solid and cool, it seemed wet enough to drink.

In late afternoon, Paul turned off the main road and climbed east toward the mountains over a narrower road. They reached Rancho El Carrizal, Cabezon's base camp, an hour after dark. Mikey was in a dead coma.

He awoke in his bedroll on the kitchen floor the next morning. A young woman introduced herself as Balbaneda Valenzuela, the cook and housekeeper for El Carrizal. She kept her back turned while Mikey got out of bed and dressed, then she led him to a washstand, poured warm water into an enamel basin for him, and tested its temperature with her fingers. He washed his hands and face and dried with a towel that Maggie had packed in his bedroll with his clothes. Balbaneda gave him café con leche and he headed out to catch up with Paul at the corral.

Granny had given Mikey a black beaver hat that she bought by mail. The smooth, shiny beaver hair was still on it and a white band encircled the crown. That day was the first time he wore it.

Paul had taken Pancho with him when he joined Cabezon the previous fall. Mikey was anxious to see him again. The corrals were a hundred yards away on the downwind side of the house. A waterlot outside the corrals was full of cattle. Dust rose out of a pen full of horses and mules, and Mikey saw Paul toss a wide, overhand loop into a corner and catch a mule around the neck. In that way he roped all the horses and mules that would be used on the mountain. He caught the mules first and vaqueros led them away to be saddled with *patisales*, packsaddles. Mikey stayed outside the corral and kept quiet until all the *bestias*, the saddle horses, had been caught.

Mikey's saddle, blankets, and bridle were lying on the ground outside the corral beside Paul's and Gato Cañez's. Mikey could not see Pancho, but when he saw Paul pick up his bridle, he jumped into the corral and ran over to be ready to saddle his horse.

At first, Mikey did not recognize the horse that his father handed him. He was Pancho, but his black coat was full and slick from the green feed he had put away with the work he was doing. His coat was dappled now, and the lighter hair was bluish gray.

He also acted differently. He did not amble up to the corral to be caught the way he did at home. He did not stand with his ears lolling and his eyes drowsy. His ears worked back and forth on the alert, and he watched Mikey to be sure he was where he ought to be.

Before he had recognized Pancho in the bunch, Mikey had admired him as a quick and ready young tough who was wise to the trick of ducking his head when he heard the whistle of the reata. Now, the horse watched Mikey out of a wary eye the way a top horse should.

Mikey found himself a bench, put his saddle and blankets on it, then climbed up and saddled his horse. Pancho did not want to stand for it as he did at home, but a low word from Mikey fixed him in his tracks. Gato watched Mikey saddle his own horse and bragged on him to the rest of the crew. The boy knew he still would not be able to tighten his cinch enough. He was not strong enough to tighten it all the way, but as Pancho's belly shrank, he would draw out enough of the slack in his latigo. In this way he would keep his saddle in place and steady over the horse's good withers throughout the day.

The crew breakfasted and then packed beds, provisions, and camp gear on the mules with block salt for cattle and sacks of grain for the horses and mules. The remuda and the pack string were driven out of the waterlot and then the cattle were driven out. Two vaqueros drove the remuda and then two more drove the pack string with one man in the lead and one in the drag. The cattle were easy to handle and anxious to move. Paul, Gato, Del Mercer, and Manuel Valenzuela headed the herd into the mountains. Mikey rode in the drags. With Pancho under him he did not worry that he would make a hand no matter which way the cattle headed or if they tried to get away. Nobody on any cattle drive could ever expect that he would not have to turn the herd by himself at one time or another. Mikey was ready for his chance. He was finally at work with no immediate threat of having to return to town, and he would never have to worry about what to do with himself for as long as he lived.

Paul was riding a bronc he called Chamaco, Kid, a horse that bit, struck, kicked, and bucked, but who was a ground-pounding demon for travel. He was a horse about whom Gato said, *"Donde lo soltaban, allí se metía,"* which meant that he dove suicidally head-long into any task for which he was loosed. The best thing about him was that he ate cattle. The worst thing about him was that he ate people.

The herd was driven east up an ancient trail called La Vereda del Aguaje, the Trail of the Spring, and was out of sight of El Carrizal ten minutes after it left the waterlot. When it reached the end of the El Carrizal home pasture after a drive of only ten miles, Paul counted it through a gate and let it go to thrive on lush foothill pasture that had been saved for fall use.

An old man and his wife lived at the spring. The crew stopped to eat lunch in the shade of their house. Mikey liked the fresh cool-ness and smell of the shade under the adobe walls. The yard was fenced in with rods of live ocotillo cactus planted side by side and was alive with green leaves. The fence was impenetrable for any-thing but a lizard. *Verdolaga*, wild parsley that grew with the sum-mer rains, was lush on the ground inside the patio of the house and was also abundant on the *verano*, the summer vegetable garden.

The old couple served coffee in china cups before the crew mounted its horses to leave. Mikey was used to people bragging about his being hand enough to ride with his father on excursions near home, but he had never been this far from home and isolated to the life of the vaquero before. That night he would not go home to his mother. He sat still and smiled while the crew and the old people bragged that he must be a good cowboy to be starting his life's work so young. In those days it was not hard on him when people bragged to make him feel proud. He was a little feller who belonged with his father and it was not wrong for him to believe that he was good at cowboy work. Later, after his father was gone, no one ever acknowledged that he was a good hand. In fact, he found himself trying to work with people who could not open the same gate for the kind of cattle that Paul and his crews could have driven up the side of a house, across the roof, down the chimney, through the front room, and out the front door without breaking a lamp. Those people tried to tell him he would never be able to believe he was any good at cowboying, because his father was a drunk and his brag about his little son could not have been true.

As the crew went back to the trail and left the valley floor behind, Paul rode up beside Mikey. "How does the verdolaga resemble a cow, son?" he asked.

"It's *gordita y delicadita*, a delicate fatty," Mikey said.

"That's true, son, but also, *tiene la semillita metida en la orquetita*. Its little bull's seed lies inside its little forked place."

"What is the bull of the verdolaga like, daddy?"

"Aw, we don't get to see him. He comes and goes on the wind in the night."

At the foot of Cerro de Los Leones, the Mountain of the Lions, the crew tied the remuda and the pack mules head-to-tail so they could be led up a narrow trail to where the first camp would be made. Paul led the mules, Gato led the horses, and they reached the crest of the mountain at midafternoon. They stopped to water the animals in a spring and have *pinole*, cornmeal mixed with *panocha*, brown cane sugar. They mixed the meal with spring water in tin cups. The vaqueros carried their cups tied to the saddle strings under the flare of their chaps. Paul carried the pinole and corn for his horse in a morral that he hung over his saddlehorn. He and Gato each also carried amphoras, slender half-pint bottles of mezcal, in their morrals. They took swallows of mezcal in the evenings when their horses got tired and their bones ached, or to ward off heatstroke, and they poured it on wounds as antiseptic.

In the late afternoon, after Paul's bones started to ache, he made Mikey ride just ahead of him so he could watch him and speak to him. He kept asking the boy how he felt because he did not want him to go to sleep and fall off Pancho. Mikey had long since discovered that complaints would not soften the trail or get him to camp any sooner. Complaints made it so Paul would think twice before he invited a kid to ride with him again. Once Paul and

Uncle Buster had left him behind in camp all day because he made the mistake of saying he was "a little" tired. This would not happen again.

Before the pack train and remuda were halfway to El Aguaje de Santa Brigida, Saint Brigit's Spring, where they would pitch camp, the sun was on the horizon and Mikey began to doze and jerk awake. He could sleep and keep his seat on Pancho on an ordinary trail, but that trail into the Sierra de San Juan was rough and steep and crossed large slabs of smooth rock. If the boy fell off, he might land on his head under his horse or a hundred feet beneath the trail.

The crew reached a cattle bed-ground and Paul told Mikey to turn Pancho off the trail and wait, then rode up beside him, took a swallow out of his amphora, and handed it to the boy. "Take a little swallow, son," he said.

Mikey swallowed about a dram without mishap, handed it back, and then felt the fumes pour out his nose and the pure spirit seep immediately into his whole spine. "That's not for you, little man," Paul said. "It's to revive Panchito, smoothen his pace, and rest him."

The vaqueros pitched their camp in an oak grove at Santa Brigida long after dark. Two ten-foot tents protected their beds and provisions and a ramada sheltered their cook fire. A stout new corral of mesquite poles lay in a draw below the campsite. A kiln had been built so that limestone could be cooked and used to mortar a rock trough inside the corral. Pipe had been packed in so the trough could be filled with water from the spring.

Mikey's camp job was to wrangle the horses in the morning, sweep and sprinkle water on the campground to settle the dust, dry dishes and put them away, carry water in buckets from the spring, and help prepare the meals. Paul made Dutch oven biscuits every other day and Gato made flour *gorda* tortillas every other day. Bull, deer, and javalina jerky was the staple meat.

Maverick bulls were often castrated, earmarked, and branded on the spot when they were caught. The nuts were hung by their cords from the vaqueros' saddle strings and eaten at the next meal. A fire was built wherever the vaqueros found themselves at noon.

Coffee was made. Bean or potato and jerky burros, the *criadillas* from the bulls, and any other fresh meat Manuel Valenzuela or Gato might catch with their .22 rifles, were cooked for *lonche*.

One evening, after the crew was all in camp, Paul came to the fire with an armload of wood. Just as he reached the campground, he cussed, dropped the wood, brushed and batted crazily at the side of his head, and scraped off a big straw scorpion that fell at Gato's feet. Mikey would not have thought Gato was afraid of anything in the world, but he jumped back as if a rattlesnake had struck him. "Ay, *me mata*. It will kill me," he cried. Later he explained that he was shy of all scorpions but deathly allergic to the sting of the straw scorpion.

"He stung me on the ear," Paul said. Then he squashed the bug under his boot heel, took out his pocketknife, sliced off a third of his ear, and handed it to Gato. Blood poured through Gato's fingers as he pressed a handkerchief against the ear. Gato pressed a wet dishtowel against the wound, sat Paul under a tree, put Paul's hand on the towel to hold it in place, then walked away from the camp with a shovel and buried the ear. Mikey sat down next to his dad. Paul turned his head until he could see the boy out of the corner of his eye and grinned.

"Daddy, why did you do that?" Mikey said.

"The scorpion stung me on my ear, son."

"But will you be able to hear out of it?"

"You're darn right I will. I didn't cut off the whole thing." Mikey was so pale from the sight of his dad's blood that his freckles turned black.

Gato came back and asked Paul how he had found the courage to cut off his own ear.

"The poison might have deafened me or poisoned my brain," Paul said.

"You certainly took no chance of that, did you?"

"I had no reason to." Paul turned back to see how Mikey was doing. Mikey had slumped headfirst in a faint to the ground.

When Mikey recovered, Paul showed him the wound so he could tell him how it looked. Mikey did not think it looked bad at all. Paul now had a devil's ear because he had sliced off the outer curve. The ear was still normal in length with a sharp top and an untouched base.

Gato made a paste from the leaves of yerba el pasimo and bandaged it on the wound. The wound did not give Paul any trouble after it stopped bleeding. It did not swell up, and he claimed it never hurt. He said it stopped hurting when he cut off the stung part. The scorpion's sting had hurt a lot more than his sharp knife. He quit bandaging it after three days.

Mikey never knew and did not care what day it was. He did not know a Sunday from a Wednesday. He knew sunup and sundown, and he knew where to look after the second sleep for the early morning *guia* star that rose in the east to tell him he could sleep a little longer.

Paul and his partners had built traps everywhere that cattle watered on the Sierra de San Juan. Each major spring had been fenced inside a lot that covered about five acres. The only entrance to the lot was through a chute, the sides of which were made of poles laid one upon the other and tied together. The sides were hung inside the corral from a large frame at the entrance and they sloped toward the ground inside the corral, but did not touch the ground. Inside the corral the ends of the poles were sharpened to points. The sides of the chute could be swung and left wide open, or closed so that the sharpened ends came together in a V. Heavy rocks were wired as anchors loosely to the bottom of the pointed ends.

When the trap was set, the thirsty cow would go through the chute and her sides would open the sharpened ends and she would see daylight to the water. She pushed the sides of the chute apart as she went in to drink, but the sharpened ends closed behind her when she stepped out of the chute. After she drank and licked salt and turned to leave the corral, she found no exit. The pointed ends could only be opened by the next cow that came through the chute.

Paul and his crew had six of these traps in rough country that were all within ten miles of the camp at Santa Brigida. The vaqueros split up and rode to check them every day. When cattle were found in a trap, the vaqueros gentled them before they tried to drive them back to camp. All the cattle were wild and were either *ladinos*, cattle that were wise to man's ways and had gone wild after they were branded and counted, or were *mostrencos*, mavericks that had never been touched by human hands, had never even seen a man on a horse.

To break the cattle so they could be driven, the vaqueros worked them horseback in a corral inside the waterlot. They penned the cattle in a small corral and let them run along one side, then stopped them and turned them back, stopped them against the fence again and again, and kept turning them back on one side and then the other. They did this by the hour until the cattle wanted to stand and rest after they were stopped. After a while they settled down and would not move unless a horseman made them move. When the cattle became that unafraid, but still respectful of a man on a horse, they were left in peace. Cattle in the trap would attract more cattle when the vaqueros were gone.

When cattle had been gentled enough so they could be controlled, they were driven to a holding pasture at Santa Brigida. If the vaqueros saw that a certain animal would give them trouble on the drive, the animal was tied neck-to-neck to another one like him, or a heavy green pole was suspended from his neck so that it dangled between his front legs. Those devices slowed the troublemakers so they could not make mad runs away from the herd.

Cattle that were found in the traps were branded, earmarked, and castrated while they were worked and gentled, and their wounds were watched for screwworms. Screwworms were doused with Peerless, a compound of chloroform, to kill the worms and their eggs. The wounds were also covered with pine tar thinned with mezcal to protect them from the flies that laid the eggs that became screwworms.

To be branded, the grown cattle were roped by the head and heels, and the little calves were caught and dragged to the fire by the heels. All the cattle had their turn being manhandled by men on foot. That treatment made them respect a man on foot or horseback so they could be managed when they were driven out into the open or moved about in alleys and corrals. Cattle got hungry while they were held in the trap, but they were all slick and shiny with good feed that fall and they would have plenty of feed ahead of them after they were driven out of the mountains. Hunger in the cattle helped the vaqueros manage them when they were let out of the traps. They were not as likely to try to run away if they had to keep their heads down to eat on the drive to Santa Brigida.

One afternoon, on their way back to camp from the traps, Gato and Mikey stopped at a seep by the side of a trail to get a drink. With his big hands Gato dug a hole in the sand the size of the crown of his hat and waited for the water to seep in so they could drink. A herd of javalina had been there before them and their neat hooves had chewed up the ground. After he drank, Mikey sat on a rock above the seep and rested while Gato drank and Pancho and Gato's horse, Saino, drank. The javalina had left the strong smell of their musk at the spring.

"The javalina stink, Gato," Mikey said.

"Which javalina do you mean, the four-legged or the two-legged?" Gato asked.

"The four-legged."

"The gentle *javali* don't smell so gentle, do they?"

"The water is sweet, though."

"I have always wondered about that," Gato said. "All my life I've waited for something bad to happen to me when I drank after the javalina. So far nothing. What do you think about that, Polito?"

Mikey laughed. "I know what would happen if I didn't drink."

"There you are. You're like me. You don't care what happens to you. When you need to drink and eat, you drink and eat."

"What's a javalina *de dos patas*, of two feet, Gato?"

"A Yaqui. Haven't you seen his track?"

Mikey looked around, but he could see no Yaqui tracks. He found a deer track on the beaten trail. "I see the print of a deer," he said.

"You think you see a *venado* track? Well, maybe not. It might be the print of a Yaqui dancer."

Mikey only looked at Gato.

"When a Yaqui eats or drinks, he feels like dancing. When he dances he turns into El Venado, the deer. When he runs for his life, he turns into El Javali."

"I don't see any people tracks except our own."

"Believe me Polito, the people tracks are ours, but the deer and javalina tracks could be Yaqui. *No lo dudes.* Don't ever doubt it."

Mikey hoped he would get to see Yaquis. The other vaqueros showed him other signs of them from time to time. The whole Yaqui nation loved Cabezon Woodell and Paul and sooner or later runaways from the reservation were bound to call on them for help. Once, a Yaqui boy had come to ground at Cabezon's camp at Santa Margarita only minutes ahead of a troop of government cavalry. Cabezon hid him and sent the troop on its way. He kept the boy, fed him, doctored him, and returned him safely to his family. Before that, the Yaqui people had been welcome to eat and rest in his camps, but he had wanted them to leave as quickly as they were able. After he had made the choice to protect the Yaqui boy against the soldiers, he made it known to the Yaqui nation that his camps would always be sanctuaries for them.

Cabezon also made the government patrols believe they were welcome. He reasoned that they would not be so apt to harm Yaquis if they left his camps with their bellies full of beef, beans, and tortillas. He had been known to hide whole families of Yaquis only a few yards away while the soldiers ate, drank, and slept in his camps.

When the crew awakened in camp at Santa Brigida the next morning, the Yaqui everybody called Agonia, Agony, was squatting under the ramada. He had already built a fire and put on the coffeepot. He served as a guide for families who fled to the north. He shook hands with the vaqueros as they arrived at the fire. He did not look into their faces. He was sunbaked to the bone, but the palm of his hand was limp and moist. Mikey stared at him.

"Are you alone this time, Agonia?" Paul asked.

"No, I'm *bien acompañado,* well accompanied."

"Do you know where the guachos are?" The soldiers were all short, squat, southern Indians that the Sonorans called guachos.

"No," Agonia said. "Where are they?"

"Didn't you know they killed a family of the *gente,* the people, at Los Molinos a few days ago?"

"Yes, a family of five. The Durazos."

"I thought the government had recalled Lieutenant Urbalejo. He is the one who does the most killing, is he not?"

"I think the generals only sent for him to promise him more bounty for our ears, then sent him back to kill more of us." Agonia looked into Paul's face and smiled. "Now it won't matter what kind of Christian he kills. He gets fifty pesos for two *orejas prietas*, dark-skinned ears, no matter who they belong to. He won't be made to distinguish a Yaqui ear from a Mexican ear. I see you are missing an ear now. Did they catch you and only get one ear, Pol? Did they stop cutting on that one ear because they thought you might be a white man? Do you know that you could pass for a white man?"

"Ah, don't you know I'm called Fast Paul?"

"Ah, *correcto*. That is correct. I forgot. I never saw them cut one ear and not get the other. Who is this little gente, who comes with you this time? How has he escaped the guachos?"

"My son."

"You better keep him close to camp. His ears are too dark. Urbalejo will think he is javali, like me. His ears are not clear like his eyes."

"His name is Miguel Pablo, but he is called Mikey and Black Man by his mother and his uncles, and Polito by these vaqueros here. So you see, he already has aliases, like you."

"I can see he is your son by the green eyes, but of what tribe is his mother?"

Paul turned to Del Mercer and Manuel and they laughed with him. "I never asked her," he said.

Agonia left the clearing and after a while came back with two Yaqui men, two women, and five children. They came slowly to spare their resources. They squatted in a close bunch underneath a white oak. The women kept looking at Mikey's face and then smiling into each other's faces when he turned toward them.

One of the men climbed a butte above the spring to watch for the soldiers. The Yaquis liked to stop at La Brigida. It was on the *cordón*, the spine of the Sierra de San Juan. A lookout on the butte could see the whole world.

The older Yaqui woman was the mother of the young one. To keep their hands free on the march, the women wore every article of clothing they owned, and some of the men's clothing. They walked in *teguas*, rawhide-soled, ankle-high moccasins. Their long hair was entwined in cloth and wrapped in great coils upon their heads. The children were also over-clothed. The older woman was gray-haired, but she was straight and lithe. The young woman's belly was as full of a baby as it could be. The hair, skin, and clothing of the women were bright with cleanliness.

The men were dark and dried, almost charred, by their efforts in the sun. The women were dark, but their russet skin glowed. The young woman's face was delicately beautiful, especially her brow. Mikey wondered at the childlike, vulnerable brow with which she headed into the world. A thick swath of her hair had strayed from a coil and been caught and held down by sparse sweat on her forehead.

Manuel, Paul, and Mikey rode into the holding pasture and brought back a fat, barren heifer. Paul caught her on his reata as she ran through the gate into the corral. The cattle that came in with the heifer streamed back out to pasture while Paul, without dismounting, snubbed her close to a post in the center of the corral.

The Yaqui men, women, and children swarmed on the heifer to hold her still and she bawled her death song. Almost gently, Agonia plunged a slim blade into her jugular, sliced her throat open, stopped the song, and emptied her life's blood in a single instant.

The women caught the blood in a five-gallon lard can as the heifer slumped to the ground at their feet. After the quick pain of the knifing, she relaxed quietly toward the ground until she went still on her side. When she stopped breathing, her head was still held halfway up the snubbing post by the reata, her body had stretched her neck as far as it would go, and the reata had disappeared under the hair of her throat.

The Yaquis skinned, dressed, and quartered the heifer on her hide. They cut the pulp of the meat into sheets for jerky and salted and peppered it with black pepper. They broke and cracked some of the bones and put them in a five-gallon can with salt and pepper to boil with beans. They broke and cut the shells off the hooves and put the knuckles in another can with more broken bones to boil. They opened up the paunch, washed it, and cut it up into squares to cook with the knuckles. They ate small slices of raw liver and bites of marrow gut as they carved the meat. They sent the loin to be broiled on the bed of coals of the cook fire under the ramada.

Gato boiled the blood, and then fried it with the brains, onions, and potatoes and the crew shared it with the Yaquis at a late *almuerzo*, lunch. For supper, the four vaqueros and the ten Yaquis finished the heart, liver, sweetbreads, and the tongue *menudos* with broiled steak. Other menudos, the hooves, paunch, and bones were eaten with boiled, parched corn the next morning for early breakfast.

The Yaquis stayed at Santa Brigida until all the fresh meat was eaten and all the pulp of the muscle had been carved into sheets and dried and cured in the sun. The jerky had been folded tightly in flour sacks and tied with string. One morning the crew rose to find the Yaquis ready for travel.

The expressions on the Yaqui faces were the same on full bellies as they had been on empty, but their eyes were more content. Agonia separated himself from his people, squatted close to Mikey, and looked into his face. With much gravity, he said to Paul, "We'll take this boy with us, if you want. *Es muy vaquero*. He is much of a cowboy, but do you know, he is *titiritero*, a shaman. Don't look into his eyes and then try to tell me he is not. We'll train him as a *curandero*, healer, and learn from him while we do."

"I know what he is." Paul laughed. "But I need him, too."

"What other thing can I do to show our gratitude?"

"You can tell the Polito why you are called Agonia. How long have we known each other, three years? Well, the boy's been asking me about your nickname and I don't know how to explain it."

"You want me to tell him the reason I am called Agonia? Ah, because when I was his age, General Álvaro Obregón killed my father and all my eight brothers and sisters. My mother and I were left destitute. The rest of our people were also pursued and driven away in different directions from our home at Santa Margarita in the Sierra Madre.

"My mother and I wandered, hid, and begged for months. One day we arrived at the edge of the town of Guaymas. The *yoris*, the ordinary Mexicans, were not our enemies. We only watched and hid from the soldiers as we skirted the town. My mother knew only one person in Guaymas who might have food. She had been told that one of her sisters lived near a cemetery and kept pigs. Her name was Eva, but she had not been called by her Christian name for many years. She had been nicknamed Cuauhtémoc because her ways were the same as that Aztec chief's.

"The journey to Guaymas had been very hard on my mother. By the time we came in sight of a cemetery, she was finished. She rested in the shade of a *brea* tree and sent me on to find her sister.

"I went to the *campo santo*, the cemetery that we had seen from far away, but found nothing but the monuments of the tombs. I went on and approached two vaqueros as they day-herded their cows.

"They did not know I was upon them until I spoke to them. '*Por favor*, can you direct me to the cemetery?' I asked. They leaped at the sound of my voice and then stared at me in astonishment.

"The drover nearest me said, 'If you did not know your way back to the cemetery, why did you leave your grave?'

"I was so desolate and hungry, I could only ask the man to pardon me for frightening him.

"'No need to ask for pardon. Now we can say we have seen someone who suffered an agony worse than Christ's. Jesus, at least, enjoyed a last supper before He was given up to die.'

"'Jesus is my name, too,' I said. 'I am a Christian like you.'

"'Well, I know why they called you Jesus,' the other drover said. 'When you were born, your mother looked down, recognized the face of agony, and was forced to say, *Jesus!*'

"The drovers were good Christians. One of them drove his horse and cart with me to get my mother. We stayed with them through *las aguas*, the rainy season, and helped them milk their cows and make cheese. They never called me by any other name except Agonia, and I have been Agonia ever since."

"And your mother's sister, the one they called Cuauhtémoc?" Gato asked.

"We found her months later, but she was too *coda y agarrada*, stingy, to be of service to anyone but her pigs. Thank God that He gave us the drovers instead."

"Why did they call the woman Cuauhtémoc?" Gato asked.

"For the reason that she was so tight," Agonia said. "She was older than my mother, a spinster, and she never gave anyone anything. As you know, Cuauhtémoc was the Aztec chief that the Spaniards burned because he refused to give them his treasure. As a spinster, people said that she treasured her virginity so much that she would have submitted her body to be burned rather than give it to someone who might have loved and cared for her. So she was called Cuauhtémoc."

Agonia led the Yaqui family in single file past Cabezon's crew so everyone could shake hands, and then led them back on the trail to the north.

FIVE

La Vaquereada

*L*a Vaquereada, *cowboy work, is the same in Sonora as it is in Arizona, and the name connotes a certain decency, responsibility, and keen skill in the vaqueros who practice it. The same kind of people do the work in both countries. Both are affected by the work, whether they know that vaquereada means to cowboy, or they speak so little Spanish that they don't know the word vaquereada from the word for beans. They are cowmen, and as such, most are decent persons. Almost everyone who occupies himself with the husbandry of livestock at least learns something about how to be decent.*

In November, Cabezon's crew moved camp across a high saddle and up Amol Mountain to El Aguaje del Encino, the Spring of the Oak Tree. Mustang cattle and ladinos that ran in that country felt safe on the edges of its cliffs and steep aprons of smooth rock where horsemen could not follow. They were in good flesh on the black grama grass and the red-stemmed *sacate de raíz*, root grass, and the short *sacate liebrero*, the grass of the hare, which had begun to cure in the fall. Those grasses would be juicier with the summer rains in July, but they were at their strongest in October and November when they dried and cured. The *juanimipili*, a sweet legume, was still lush and strong in those mountains that November.

On the last day of November the crew moved camp to El Aguaje de la Morita, named after a blue mustang filly who was seen to water there on the same day long ago that it had been discovered by some Spaniard or some vaquero. The famous *cardon* cactus grew there, the rare big brother of the saguaro that yields a white fruit and protects itself with thicker, longer spines than the saguaro.

The pack train approached the Spring of the Blue Filly. Paul was relaxed and happy as he led the remuda behind Mikey. He called his son's attention to the pretty ways the summer died in lost bloom and leaf and faded colors. All of a sudden he went silent, stopped his horse, and hissed for Mikey to stop. Gato was behind him with the pack train, but the rest of the crew had gone on to repair traps that would be worked from La Morita.

Paul sent Gato to the other side of the spring, handed the lead animals in the strings of horses and mules to Mikey, and motioned for him to hold fast behind a thicket of *tesota*. He then rode in a circle to get below the spring without being seen. Mikey had a clear view of the spring. Clear water welled up from inside a pile of granite boulders and watered a draw that was shaded by the cottonwood and willow trees that hid Paul. For a long time Mikey could not hear any sound of the horsemen. He wondered how two vaqueros riding shod horses over rock and through thick brush could be so silent.

Paul had seen a *toro lomo blanco*, a linebacked bull, slip through the brush ahead of him. He hoped the bull would stop and drink at the spring so that he and Gato could snare him. The bull was enough of a bull to be unafraid of horsemen. He was a branded ladino who had slipped away and escaped Cabezon's crew for three seasons. He had escaped the first time during a bad screwworm season before Paul had been able to castrate him. Paul already knew he would never be caught in a waterlot trap. The only way to get him into a herd and make him merchantable was to rope him and lead him in. Paul would wait until the bull filled up with more water than he could carry comfortably, then put the run on him.

Paul moved up to get a good look but the bull saw him and moved to a higher place on the spring where Mikey could see him. The white slash along his black back looked wild enough to have been scarred on by a streak of lightning. He kept drinking even after Paul moved out into plain sight. His occupation as a sire made Lomo Blanco proud of himself as a real bull, but it also made him real thirsty. He was so thirsty that nothing mattered at that moment except the water.

Paul and Gato let the bull drink until he was so full that he sloshed, and then they crowded him to make him run. Gato moved first and drove the bull downhill toward Paul and Mikey lost sight of him. Paul would try to turn him back and run him uphill to slow him down, and then catch him in an open spot in the draw.

Mikey knew the bull had flushed away from the draw when he heard the brush crash in his thicket of tesota. He looked up and Lomo Blanco broke through the thicket straight toward him with his tail in the air like a scorpion's stinger, his horns ready as a scorpion's pincers, his eye full of fight, and his black muzzle shiny wet with spinning slobbers. He had beaten Paul out of the draw, but Fast Paul was close behind him and both tore a big hole through the brush.

The bull did not consider Mikey a threat. He came at the boy as though he weren't there. The mules and horses danced and snorted and looked for room to get out of his way. Mikey wanted to delay him for Paul and Gato, but when the mules were sure that what they saw was a bull with horns that charged straight at them, they wheeled and reared and rushed aside and tangled Mikey and the horse string in the thicket. Paul and the bull burst on through the thicket into the open and Mikey was able to watch the ongoing wreck.

Paul caught the bull on his reata on a ridge where random winds from all directions clashed with a constant wind from the west. The winds whipped the animals and turned their hair and blew Paul's hat away. The bull lost control of his momentum and fell into a stand of garambullo brush and the reata scorched the rawhide on Paul's saddlehorn. Chamaco the horse could not brace his feet and slide in the garambullo as he had on the ridge. He bucked through the brush, dove and wiped his head against the ground, and lunged to get rid of Paul. The bull regained his feet and lined out in the open again, jerked Chamaco in line, and began to tow and drag him at a dead run. Paul laughed and waited for something in the flesh and blood and hide of the wreck to come apart. Finally, his reata broke and Chamaco quit bucking. The line-backed bull raced on with his head high and six feet of the reata trailed from his horns like a plume of victory.

Paul did not pull up. He tied a new honda in the end of his reata on the run while he turned the bull back toward the spring. He caught him again, but Chamaco fell and the reata broke again.

Lomo Blanco ran on with two ribbons of Paul's reata trailing from his horns, but the load of water in his belly began to weigh him down. He had jammed his muzzle into the rock when he fell and his nose was bleeding. His muscles began to cramp.

Chamaco rolled and kicked on top of Mikey's dad, then stomped him when he got up. As Paul walked up to remount, Chamaco struck him on the foot with a shod front hoof. With that, the man voiced every obscenity in English and Spanish known by vaqueros all the way to Texas, a string of words that Mikey had never heard but certainly understood.

Paul remounted, caught up with soggy Lomo Blanco in the draw, and tied on again. He turned Chamaco to the opposite side of a willow tree from the bull. He dragged the bull's head into the tree, rode around, and wrapped his reata on the trunk and held him there.

Gato came on, caught Lomo Blanco by the heels, and stretched him out until he sloshed over on his side. The two men tied his horns against the tree trunk with manila rope. They left him there and gave him time to think. Left to himself overnight, he would lunge and twist until his horns became so sore he could be led back to camp.

While Paul and Gato rode back toward Mikey, Paul looked down and saw that half his ring finger was gone. His stopped to examine his hand. He remembered that the coils of his reata had whipped up in front of his face and caught his hand against the saddlehorn just before it broke the second time. If the reata had not come apart, it probably would have cut half his fingers off. As it was, his middle and little finger were flayed from the middle knuckle to the ends, all the nails were gone, and half his ring finger was gone as though sliced off with a knife.

On the way back to camp, Gato gathered a feed bag full of *chicura*, the chicory weed that grew abundantly below the spring of La Morita. At camp he washed the broad leaves, seared them with a bundle of twigs until they oozed their sticky juice, and bandaged Paul's hand with them.

Paul laughed about his lost finger. He was not interested in looking for it, only in repairing what was left so he could work. Manuel Valenzuela and Gato knew every medicinal herb that could be found on that mountain. Manuel rode the brows of the canyons and found some yerba del pasimo to paste on Paul's hand under a new bandage of chicura. Gato went back and looked for Paul's finger that evening, found it, and buried it.

That year all the country's medicinal herbs could easily be found. Manuel found some *oja de palvia*, the leaf of a gray weed for Paul to chew to calm the pain. Paul could not get the boot off the foot that Chamaco had stomped and Gato loosened it by fractions until it came off. The knee and ribs upon which the horse had fallen were swollen and bruised.

Left alone in camp the next day, Paul hunted around the draw for other herbs to apply to his ailments. He stumbled upon *hierba la flecha*, arrow weed, an herb that could cause laughter. The herb is called arrow weed because, like laurel, it has a long leaf with a sharp end that resembles an arrow. Dip a stem in your coffee and keep the back door open. Loosened by this tea, the bowels become an open spillway.

The crew returned early to camp that day and Paul put the coffee on to boil. He poured the first coffee for himself and Mikey, then dropped a stem of hierba la flecha into the coffee water, let it boil another moment, took it out, and smiled. He winked at Mikey and put his finger to his lips.

For two hours after supper and before bedtime Paul's companions kept him laughing, first at their expressions after their first sips of coffee, then at the jerky responses of their bodies to the messages of urgency from their bowels, then at the sight of the peculiar gallop for the bushes, and finally at the return to camp of relieved carcasses.

Paul was the first man up the next morning and this time he brewed a pot of pure coffee. He was solicitous of the crew and when they all agreed that they had rested well through the night, he grinned with pleasure. He told everyone he was sorry he had laughed at them, but mirth had been fine medicine for him. The crew could not understand how everyone but Paul and Mikey had been stricken with the spurts, for everybody had eaten the same food. Mikey had not laughed at anyone when they ran for the bushes. He was still young enough to have troubles from time to time in that department even without hierba la flecha. After much discussion, the crew decided that the water from a spring beside one of the traps must have been bad, for Paul and Mikey were the only ones who had not watered there.

Paul could not work, so he and Mikey rode down to El Mesquite, the ranch of Gato's uncle Plutarco Celaya. That night Paul came down with a fever that put him to bed and he did not laugh for five days. Mikey had never seen him so sick that he was unable to laugh.

Tío Plutarco was a widower and his camp was not graced by the care of a woman. He trimmed the torn flesh and bone from Paul's hand with a sharp knife and wire cutters so Paul could use it after it healed. He dosed him with good Bacanora, the Sonorans' best mezcal, to alleviate the pain of the surgery.

After a week of rest, Paul was ready to go back to work, but his horse was gone. When he asked Tío Plutarco where his horse was, the old man handed him fifty pesos.

"¿Y esto?" Paul asked. "And what is this for?"

"El Chamaco. Lo vendí. I sold El Chamaco," Tío Plutarco said.

"But why?"

"He bucked with you and then fell on you and struck you when you needed him to be trustworthy. You were two hundred miles from a hospital. He cost you a finger. For that you will remember him the rest of your life, and that is enough to remember him by. For that experience and lesson, no one should have to pay more than the price of one bullet. I got you fifty pesos for him. Be happy."

"Where is he? I only need him a little longer."

"I know you need a horse, so I've decided to sell you my Cognac horse. Now, even more than before, you need a mount you can trust. You also need a smooth walking and generous horse. You won't have to do Cognac's thinking for him. He will do yours for you. All you will have to do is point him to the task and ride."

"I know, but he is worth more than three Chamacos. Keep the fifty pesos as my guarantee that I will buy him from you or return him in good condition. It's worth more for me, the way I feel, just to have a smooth horse to ride back to El Carrizal."

"I confess I don't want to sell him."

"Then, if I decide not to buy him, I'll rent him for the fifty pesos and call you a merciful man."

Mikey understood the reason for all the fuss over the loan of a horse. Paul and Tío Plutarco lived by the same creed. One of their main axioms was that a vaquero does not loan his horse, his pistol, or his woman. Tío Plutarco did not want to seem foolish, so he offered to sell a horse that he did not want to sell because, at that moment, his friend needed him more than Tío Plutarco did. He could allow the friend to try him out before he paid for him. Paul could give him a guarantee of fifty pesos as a down payment that he would forfeit if he returned the horse. That way, if the horse was injured while Paul used him, both men would be satisfied that Tío Plutarco had been compensated.

Now that Paul had the use of Cognac, he could return to La Morita, take the pack string back to El Carrizal, and put it out to pasture. Then he and Mikey would go home to Nogales to recuperate until after Christmas.

At La Morita, Gato and Manuel helped saddle the mules with the packsaddles. Mikey tied each rig's tarp on the crossbars of the saddle with its sling rope. The crew ate lunch together and Paul and Mikey said good-bye and left with the string. Darkness caught them before they could negotiate the trail above the San Juan Ravine, a canyon hundreds of feet deep with sheer walls.

A mentally deficient gray and white paint mule that the crew called Goo Goo was the weakest link in the string. Someone had beaten him over the head with a club before Cabezon bought him. One of the blows had crushed the bone over the top of one eye and caused the eye to bulge. The blows had also probably been the cause of his distraction. Half the time he did not know where he was or if he should walk, stand, or lie down.

Paul and Mikey needed to be careful of the length of rope with which they tied Goo Goo to the mule ahead of him, and they never tied him by the tail to a mule or horse behind him. Because of his distracted ways, he was even trouble when he was loose. The pack string was usually turned loose and driven ahead, but after dark it was tied head-to-tail and led.

Paul penned the string above the San Juan Ravine and tied it together head-to-tail. The only place for Goo Goo was last in line where he could only bother the mule ahead of him and he could be towed by the rest of the string when he forgot where he was.

Paul only had one hand to work with, so Mikey helped him tie the string. Goo Goo had been known to stray off the trail far enough to poke his head around the wrong side of a tree. This always stopped the string dead and made it strain to go on. Then someone would find Goo Goo with both eyes about to pop out while the whole string used its weight to try to pull his head through the trunk of the tree.

Paul and Mikey had been living near this trail called Camino Real for three months and knew that people used it day and night. They did not see or talk to most of the people who used it by night. The travelers who came by their camps always had a long way to travel before they reached their next food and shelter, so people did not often stop to visit. The vaqueros liked to visit with people to find out what had happened elsewhere in the world, but they only greeted the travelers and got out of their way if they did not know them. They always invited people to rest and eat with them if they stopped to talk.

Mikey rode out ahead so Paul could keep track of him as they started across the rock above the ravine in the dark. Paul bragged that the boy could see better in the dark than he could see in daylight. Mikey knew that his dad wanted him close ahead and out of danger if something went wrong with the string.

Mikey trusted Pancho to see the trail. Paul laughed and told him not to worry about bumping his head on a tree in the dark on that stretch above the San Juan Ravine. On his right was an empty chasm three hundred feet deep. On his left was the canyon's rock wall and no place for a tree.

About twenty steps before the lead mule would have been out of danger of falling and taking the whole string into the ravine, Mikey heard the string lunge, grunt, moan, squeal, and rattle rocks into the ravine. Paul cussed and told Mikey to stop. All the mules in the string were gentle except the dark brown mule named Negro, the first animal in the line, the one whose lead rope Paul held. When Negro was pulled to a stop by the mule on his tail, he bucked ahead with enough force to try every breakable fiber that held him. His shoes slipped and sparked on a slab of rock, he skated sideways toward the chasm, and almost pulled Paul off his horse when he spun to catch himself at the brink.

By the light of a sliver of moon Mikey watched Paul turn Cognac back and lunge him toward the brink, dally Negro's lead rope on his saddlehorn, and hold him before he disappeared over the edge. The mules settled down quickly, but Paul could not get loose from Negro to go back to find and remedy the trouble that had stopped the string.

"Son," Paul said quietly. "Don't try to turn your horse around. Just get off and walk back to me, please."

Mikey obeyed.

"Now, son, watch you don't goose my horse. Hold out your hand and feel for his butt. It's awful narrow here, so come along next to the wall. I want you to go back and see what stopped the string."

Cognac vibrated when Mikey touched him. He knew the tight he was in. He might have wanted to lose his head, but he knew he would probably lose his good old sensible life if he did.

Mikey tried to cram himself between the canyon wall and the horse's hips. He pushed the horse away, then moved ahead an inch. Cognac pushed back and squashed Mikey against the wall. Mikey could not get past the horse that way, so he slid to the ground between Cognac's legs and skinned out the downhill side. The horse lifted his feet and danced in place to give him room.

Mikey picked his way back between the pack string and the wall and found Goo Goo on his side on the downhill side of the trail. His hind legs kicked over the edge of the cliff in space. His lead rope was still tied fast to the tail of the mule ahead of him and that was all that kept him from slipping away into the void.

Mikey told Paul that Goo Goo had fallen and had become the anchor of the pack string. Paul wanted to know if Mikey could help Goo Goo regain his feet. Mikey told him the mule's legs were way out in thin air and darkness. Paul said for him to be ready to cut Goo Goo loose if the mule ahead of him began to struggle and lose ground.

The mule who owned the tail from which Goo Goo was about to dangle was called Sarah, after the temperamental movie actress Sarah Bernhardt. Cabezon's Sarah liked to throw temperamental fits as a regular drill. Mikey opened his knife and stood ready to cut Goo Goo's lifeline.

Boulders crowded the space between Goo Goo and Sarah. Mikey climbed inside them to examine the position of Goo Goo's head and Sarah shifted her weight and pinned him against a boulder with her butt. Goo Goo grunted with every breath and Mikey was sure Sarah would not postpone her next fit for long. If she could have taken one step backward, Goo Goo would have gone into the well. Mikey at least was sure Sarah would not kick him. Goo Goo's weight anchored her hind legs to the ground.

Mikey tried to make Sarah move so he could get out, so she oozed *caca* all over him. The stuff ran like hot gravy down his neck and the front of his shirt and the gases sputtered in his face.

Mikey knew that a little fresh manure would not kill a body, would not harm it, would not barely inconvenience it, but he had always been more or less able to control the amount he got on him. Sarah just emptied her gut hot and fresh in his face and he could not move an inch to save himself. He poked her in the flank with a thumb to see if she would move. She only shifted enough to mash all the air out of him against the boulder. With the first breath that he was able to take back he inhaled a big gulp of her stuff and almost drowned. Goo Goo slipped and Sarah stomped on Mikey's foot, which hurt so much that he jerked free of her with all his might, fell, and landed facedown over another boulder.

When Mikey recovered, Sarah's entire weight was against the back of his legs, but he was not hurt. Paul said something to him, but he could not understand him and could not answer. He could not move from the waist down, and he coughed and gagged on manure, but he could see that Goo Goo's head was still on the safe side of the cliff's edge. He rested his face on the boulder and coughed.

A shadow covered him. A heavy hand struck him on the back and pounded out all the manure and a strange voice asked, "*¿Qué te trai*, Chamaco? What's got you, boy?"

"*Esta mulada.*" Mikey said. "This whole pack of mules."

"Does it seem that the owls have flown away with you and are about to let you fall?"

Mikey could not see the man's face. He saw the moonglow on the blade of a machete in his hand.

"I can't move because Sarah is on my legs," Mikey said.

The man laughed. "Are you hurt?"

"No."

"Why were you choking? What's that below you?"

"The Goo Goo mule hangs on the edge and his weight holds Sarah on my legs." Mikey would never, never tell anyone he had inhaled fresh mule manure.

"Ah, yes, El Goo Goo, I am not surprised. I know Goo Goo. Is he the last one in the string?"

"Yes, he is always falling down, so he must have..."

"*Menos mal*," the man said. "Small loss." The moonglow on the machete sliced through Goo Goo's lead rope and he sailed away silently into the ravine.

"Goo Goo!" Mikey squalled. The man with the machete led Sarah back on the trail. Paul returned Negro to the trail with the help of other *arrieros*, drover companions of the man with the machete. The man and Mikey followed as Paul led the string away from the chasm to an open bed-ground. The arrieros built a fire and unsaddled the mules. When Mikey reached the bed-ground, Paul told him to unsaddle Pancho. Mikey took a canteen of water off a mule and went away from everyone in the dark to wash his face and the front of his shirt.

When he returned, Paul said, "We'll have a little drop of mezcal and some meat with these friends and unroll our beds here, son. They want us to stay, and where would we be if they had not come along and helped us? We sure had our tails in a crack, didn't we?"

"What about Goo Goo, daddy?" Mikey cried. "He fell into the ravine."

"To hell with Goo Goo, son. We almost lost our lives and a whole string of mules because of Goo Goo. Forget Goo Goo."

"But that man just cut him loose and let him fall."

"Son, I asked him to do what was needed to get our string moving. Let's forget it now."

Mikey helped the men gather dry cow manure chips off the bed-ground to use as fuel for the fire. The manure was easy to gather in the dark and made colorful flames and a smooth bed of coals, but Mikey was sad because Goo Goo had not made it away from the ravine with the rest of the string. One of his countless false steps had finally been the end of him.

Paul sat by the fire and grinned at the arrieros' jokes, but Mikey could tell he was in pain with the sore hand and a foot that was probably broken. The man with the machete was young, tall, redheaded, and very formal and polite. He was called *El Mochomo*. The mochomo is a large red ant that hurts farmers by colonizing the centers of crops in the fields in places that cannot be seen from the outer edges of the crops. Before they are discovered, the mochomos often eat large expanses of crops right down to the bare ground. Looters in the revolution were also called Mochomos. They could not afford firearms and they carried only machetes, but they killed, hacked, and destroyed everything they could not carry away while they laid whole regions bare.

Two of the arrieros were El Mochomo's younger brothers. Paul and Mikey were not introduced to the third companion, an uncle. The uncle stationed himself on the dark edge of the savannah with a rifle and did not go near the fire.

El Mochomo's father, a rancher named Ernesto Vigil, was a friend of Paul's and he often stopped at Cabezon's mountain camps to visit. When Paul told the story of an adventure he had shared with Ernesto, El Mochomo said, "Ah, *sí, sí, eres El Ligero, el Pablo Ligero.* Ah, yes, yes, you are the Fast One, Fast Paul. I know you. When I was a little boy you came to Caborca to buy cattle from my father. El Gato Cañez is my uncle. Gato works with you at La Morita, does he not?"

One of the brothers came to the fire with a twenty-liter barrica, a small wooden cask bound in brass hoops. Another brother lined up tin cups on the ground, broke a wax seal on the cask, opened the bung, and sloshed mezcal into the cups. The fumes of the spirit dodged the fire and played right up Mikey's nose.

The arrieros carried little in the form of camp comfort. Eleven mules carried two barricas apiece. Two mules carried blankets and provision. These men were not poor, though. They carried a lot of prosperous meat and muscle on their bones, and they were mounted on sleek horses. El Mochomo wore two coarse gold chains around his neck with golden medallions that bore the images of Jesus and Our Lady of Guadalupe. He wore gold rings on both hands and carried a gold pocket watch on a gold chain. His smile showed a gold acorn inlaid in the center of an eyetooth.

As leader, El Mochomo did not do much of the hard work. He ordered his brothers to unpack and unsaddle all the animals and to bring Paul's and Mikey's bedrolls to the fire so they could sit on them in comfort. He prepared Paul's and Mikey's plates of fried jerky and beans and brought them coffee. He treated Paul as an esteemed elder and Mikey as an honored guest. He did not allow Paul to empty the last drop out of his cup before he replenished it with mezcal. He prepared warm water so Paul could wash his sore hand, and he dressed it with the paste of yerba el pasimo that he prepared from the supply in Paul's morral.

Another twelve-mule pack string arrived led by another cousin of El Mochomo. The leader dismounted and walked straight to Paul and Mikey, nodded respectfully to them, and shook their hands. He turned back to shake El Mochomo's hand, then walked back to supervise the unpacking and unsaddling of his string and had not said a word.

Before the second string was unpacked, a third string arrived, led by El Mochomo's father, Ernesto Vigil, Paul's friend. Guards were posted and Paul and don Ernesto spent the evening telling quiet stories. Mikey usually could not get enough of the stories of Paul's life as a vaquero in Mexico, but he did not put up a fight to stay awake. Sleep dropped him before the end of the first story and his dad put him in his bedroll.

In the morning, El Mochomo made Paul and Mikey sit still and visit with don Ernesto while the arrieros saddled all the animals and lined Paul's string out on the trail for him. He ordered Paul's and Mikey's horses saddled and brought to them and stood by while they mounted. He and don Ernesto mounted their horses, ordered one of the brothers to bring up the rear, and rode with Paul and Mikey for the first half hour of the way to Carrizal. In this way, by helping with their departure and keeping them company on the first part of the trail, they sealed their friendship with Paul and Mikey. When the last bad place on the trail had been left behind, they said good-bye and went back to their own business.

"What are they going to do with all that mezcal, daddy?" Mikey asked after their escort was out of sight.

That made Paul smile. "Why, son?"

"That was an awful lot of mezcal."

"And?"

"It sure smelled good last night when we were all tired and the man opened the barrica."

Paul laughed at that until the tears came to his eyes. "Son, are you getting to like the stuff?"

"I never saw or smelled that much of anything so good before."

"I know, and those people made us feel that we could have all we wanted, didn't they?"

"El Mochomo must be awful rich, daddy. Is that what it's like to be rich?"

"He is rich, but most of all he's splendid and generous with his time and his help."

"He's like you, isn't he, daddy?"

"Son, you gotta be splendid about the way you give if you're to have any style and if it's to do you any good."

"What's he gonna do with all that mezcal?"

"I guess as long as people like the stuff the way you and I do, he won't have to worry about that. He'll just keep selling it and getting rich. He'll sell that load across the line and when he comes back his mules will be loaded with bales of American money."

"Isn't that wrong, daddy?"

"It would be wrong for you and me because we don't need money, but it might not be wrong for don Ernesto and El Mochomo. They probably have a big use for money and need to be rich."

Just then Paul and Mikey heard a lost creature gag on a desperate call to his mates. The whole train stopped and looked back. The battered carcass of a mule rounded a bend behind the string, stopped, raised his head, and choked out another pitiful, hacking cry.

"Well, I'll be damned, son, it's Goo Goo," Paul said.

The apparition did not look much like Goo Goo. He had been scraped and gouged, gashed, bashed, and bloodied from his ears to his hooves. He limped and his voice cracked, but he showed great joy at the sight of his mates. The tree of his saddle had been crushed and was held together only by shreds of the wood in one crossbar. Twenty feet of lash rope dragged behind him.

Paul had a tear in his eye when he dismounted and walked up to Goo Goo. He praised him and patted him, removed the shreds of the saddle, then tied him back in his place on the end of the string. Goo Goo did not stray off the trail again.

At dark Paul and Mikey did not stop at the old folks' house at El Aguaje de la Vereda because the lamps were out. When they topped the last hill above El Carrizal, the sight of Balbaneda's lighted kitchen freshened the trail for them and they forgot their tiredness as they rode off the hill. As they unsaddled the horses and mules in the corral, the girl called from the house and told them their supper was ready.

The next day Paul and Mikey started back to Nogales in the ranch truck. At the line, Paul asked El Cabo to tell him what day it was. El Cabo told him happily that the date was December twenty-third and tomorrow was *Noche Buena*, Christmas Eve.

Paul asked El Cabo if the police had caught Kelly, the gangster who had robbed the bank at the time he and Mikey crossed into Sonora in October.

"Yes they did, but he was not the famous one with the *ametral-ladora*, the Machine Gun Kelly."

"He wasn't?" Paul asked.

El Cabo laughed. "No, this one was only a local single shot from Douglas, a *pillito*, a would-be thug of no importance."

"I bet he was important to the widow of the man he killed in the bank," Paul said.

The day was cold. Paul and Mikey drove through the Altar Valley to Tucson and stopped at a bar by the rodeo grounds to warm up. Mikey listened for a while as Paul made friends with other cowboys, and then passed out in a booth. About dark Paul carried him out to the truck and he woke up as they headed into a cold wind toward Nogales.

Halfway home, Paul stopped at a wide spot in the road to sleep off the whiskey and Mikey stepped out of the truck to throw rocks at cans. A big, new Studebaker loaded with three merry couples stopped nearby and woke Paul up with their laughter and shouts. The driver was a pretty blonde in nothing but her petticoat. She fell out of the car, stood barefooted on tiptoes, reached for the sky, and stretched. Mikey could see that she was very drunk, but her balance was good. Her calves and toes were pink and pretty. She arched her back and stretched again. At that moment she must have decided that she no longer enjoyed the gladsome time that she had been having with her companions. She proclaimed to them that she was angry and did not want to be drunk anymore. Her companion in the front seat threw open the door and shouted for her to shut up and get back in the car before she caught pneumonia.

Paul started the truck and drove by the Studebaker to get back on the road. A man leaned across the front seat and grabbed at the woman through the open door. He glanced up at Mikey with his hair in his eyes.

Fifteen minutes later, on a long, narrow bridge, the left front tire of the truck went flat. Paul drove on to get off the bridge, and then turned off the road to fix the flat. The two spare tires had been unloaded at El Carrizal to make room for a load of hay, but the hay haulers had not loaded them back on the truck. Paul and Mikey did not have a spare. They stood and looked at the flat tire. The Studebaker stopped on the highway above the truck.

Mikey thought that even though his dad's hand had been maimed, their luck had been good as far as getting help was concerned. El Mochomo had come up the trail at the right time and now a pretty woman with a carload of decent people had stopped to help them only minutes after they found more trouble. Paul would make best friends of this bunch with his first smile.

The blonde lady unloaded herself out of the driver's side of the car, rushed around the front, and scolded Paul. "Are you and that brat so stupid you can't tell when a tire goes flat? Goddammit, do you have to look at it like idiots before you can tell it's flat?"

"Shoot, Dick Tracy, is that what's wrong with it? We would never have known! We were waiting for someone like you to come along and tell us," Paul said.

A cold wind swelled the woman's petticoat and she hugged herself and pranced back into the driver's seat in the car. The man in front laughed at her. Paul thanked the man for stopping. Mikey saw that he was shamefully drunk, but appreciated that at least it had not kept him from being concerned for a man and his boy who were stranded on the highway.

Paul stepped up on the pavement in front of the car and told Mikey to come on so they could go with the people to get help. The car's rear wheels squealed and it almost reared up as it roared straight at Paul. Paul threw himself backward and slid upside down into the barpit. Mikey saw the woman cover her eyes with both hands and twist away from the steering wheel when she thought the car would hit Paul. The man's hands were on the wheel, so Mikey figured his foot was probably the one on the accelerator as the car roared away toward Nogales.

Paul got up off the ground. "Well, I'll be damned," he said. "I thought that lady wanted to help us, but I think she lured me up there so she could run me over."

Soon after that, a wood hauler friend of Paul's named Gabriel Amado came by in his loaded truck and stopped. When Gabriel drove into Nogales to make deliveries, he always slowed down when he saw Mikey and Billy Shane in front of their houses and invited them to hop on the back of his truck. He knew they liked run and overtake him, hop on the tailgate, ride to the Nogales curve with their feet dangling above the highway, then drop off and wave him on.

Gabriel jacked up Paul's truck and pulled off the tire, loaded it on top of the wood, and took Paul and Mikey to Carmen Unincorporated to fix it. Paul produced his amphora of El Mochomo's mezcal and shared a few nips with Gabriel and Abe Fernandez while they helped each other fix the flat. Then Gabriel took Paul and Mikey back and bolted the tire on the truck.

Paul and Mikey did not get home until midnight. All the lights were out in the house. Granny's porch light went on, but she did not come out. Baxter met Mikey at the door, showed that he was happy, but made no sound. Mikey hugged him and became a five-year-old boy again. Paul switched on the kitchen light and began to fix supper. He knew all the ways to make a hand in a kitchen and he was quicker, cleaner, and more efficient at it than a lot of women.

After a while Maggie came to the kitchen in her nightgown and negligee. She looked rested. Every hair was in place, but she did not wear makeup. Paul and Mikey could tell that she did not look upon them as friends. Mikey did not go up to give her a kiss, because the look on her face made it clear that she did not want any darned kisses.

"Hi, honey," Paul said. "You look goooood."

"What are you doing here?" Maggie asked. "You're supposed to be way down in the Big Germ country."

"Well, no, we're back. Aren't you glad to see us?" Paul could only hold half a grin when he asked that. Anybody could see the woman was still as mad as she had been when they left home in October.

"I'm not."

Paul poured himself a drink from his amphora and went on fixing supper. Maggie walked over to the sink, arched one eyebrow at him, and took a big swallow out of his glass. "Well, what brought you home?"

"Mama," Mikey said, to remind her that she was his mother and he was her son. "Daddy lost a finger in the dallies." He thought, "Oh, my Lord, what will she do when she sees his ear?"

Maggie picked up Paul's bandaged hand. "Did you try to rope with your left hand? Idiot. No wonder you lost a finger."

"I don't know how it happened except I tied on to a bull in rough country and my ring finger came apart."

"Well, you don't like to wear a ring, anyway."

"Hell, a cowboy can't wear a ring. Sooner or later he's bound to snag it."

"That's right, there's lots of wedding ring snags down in the Big Germ."

"Aw, Maggie, don't be mean."

"I'm not mean. I'm just not surprised that you're out of work again as the result of another wreck that was probably all your own fault."

"I won't argue with you about that, honey."

"Did you perchance bring home some money?"

"No, I haven't seen Cabezon to get my pay."

"That's just great. Did you know that a few days after you left I went flat broke? The bills came and I couldn't pay them. I've never been broke before. Before you, the men in my family protected me from that. Now, since there's not enough money coming into this house to suit me, I've had to find new ways to get along."

"As soon as I can find Cabezon I'll get you some money."

"Oh, I'm not broke anymore. I sold Little Buck and the milk cow."

"Awww, honey, you didn't need to do that. The cow was getting old, but I know how much you loved Little Buck."

"I needed money; I sold a cow. I sold our whole herd of one milk cow, by God. I'm sure not ever going to milk a cow. And why do I need a horse? I have another kid on the way."

Maggie's tone did not get any nicer when she turned her attention to Mikey. He got, "Hurry up and finish your supper. You're going to bed right after you eat and take a bath, so hurry up. Don't drink so much water. I don't want you having to get up to go to the bathroom all night."

Mikey's folks argued on after he went to bed. Paul finally got mad enough to raise his voice, but Maggie reminded him that Mikey would hear him and would not approve of his father talking mean to his mother and he shut up.

Mikey was on the sleeping porch and Maggie came periodically to spy on him through a window in the door. Then it was, "Quit wiggling. Lie still. Why did you sneeze? Why are you awake?" and "go...to...sleep," in a low growl. Mikey wondered how in the world he was able to make her growl even as he lay as quiet as any boy could lie in his own bed.

He was at least not worried that his parents would come to blows. When he was hardest pressed, Paul only made exaggerated accusations that were not meant to be believed. Maggie would then pounce on him with taunts and insults that she wanted them both to believe. Most of the time, Paul only made wisecracks that were intended to be enjoyed by them both. They were even attempts to make Maggie laugh. Maggie's cracks always sounded full of hate.

Maggie finally caused Paul to raise his voice again by striking at his parenthood. He had been able to give reasonable answers to the insults she made about his drinking and his staying away and his not bringing enough money home to suit her, but she finally made him angry when she told him that because he was not enough of a father and husband to bring in the money she needed, she would have to get it from Mikey. She told him that she liked the money she got for Little Buck so much, he was going to have to sell his paint horse and Pancho because she could use that money, too.

"There I can't help you, madam, for I don't own the paint," Paul said.

"Then you'll have to talk to your son about selling Pancho."

"There you are. Pancho's safe in Mexico and I don't know how you'll get him out."

"You want me to believe you've worked for Cabezon all this time and you don't have a horse of your own? You've risked your life a hundred times training horses for Cabezon Woodell, but you haven't made one good horse for yourself?"

"That's right, lady."

"What about that Chamaco horse you're always bragging about?"

"He was mine to ride, but he belonged to Cabezon and he's been sold." Maggie's tirade needed another breath. When she found it, she said, "Well, Pancho isn't Cabezon's."

"No, by God," Paul roared. "And he's not yours either. He's my little son's and you can't make me sell him."

Mikey's chest had begun to hurt when he heard his mother decide that she was willing to sell out her son and his horse because she wanted money, but he was almost sure she was only threatening it to hurt Paul. Now he felt a great, loving gratitude for his dad. The whole family would fall apart if he weakened. If Paul had said he would give in and let Maggie sell Pancho, Mikey would not have wanted to belong to that family anymore.

Then Maggie said, "I want that Pancho sold and the money brought to me and that's that. If you're too weak to do it, bring him home and I'll do it. I know a man who wants to buy a gentle horse to ride in his orchard."

"God have mercy," Paul moaned. "But why do I have to fight for my life every time I come back to my own home? I must have been born under a dark star."

"I don't know if it was dark, but it was darned sure weak. You're so weak, you're almost not even here when you do come home."

Maggie and Paul went to their bedroom and quieted down and Mikey went to sleep. Then a primal scream pierced his slumber and sat him straight up in bed. The sound had come from Maggie as from a wounded mother elephant. After the scream died, she shrieked, "For the love of God and his Blessed Mother in heaven, Paul Summers, where in the hell is your ear?"

SIX

FATHERS AND MOTHERS

*P*art *of the expertise of men and women who raise cattle is a knowledge of the bloodlines of their stock. They are so practiced, they can look at a calf and tell who his sire is and which cow is his mother. They do the same with people. The DNA of the stock is in the shape of the nose, the sound of the voice, the lift of the chin, and forty or fifty other characteristics plain to see by a practiced stockman.*

Maudy Marie, Mikey's little sister, was born in March and Maggie divorced Paul that summer. Mikey was six and had started first grade when Paul came by one day and asked Maggie if he could have his son for a week at Thanksgiving. Maggie said yes, so he promised to come and get the boy the next day. He was in his cups and bragged that he would buy Mikey a new pocketknife and a pair of boots. Mikey did not want him to think he had to sweeten his visit that way. He was drunk, but Mikey did not care about having those things and Paul's drunkenness did not bother Mikey. It bothered him that he never got to see his dad.

Mikey dressed and went outside long before daylight the next morning so he would not miss his dad. He thought that the earlier he made himself available to go, the earlier Paul would come. He climbed into his elderberry tree to wait. The elderberry's perches were close to the ground and he could drop out of the tree when he saw Paul coming, load his warbag, bed, and saddle, and jump into the car. That way his parents would not have to talk to one another. He knew how much they dreaded seeing each other's faces and having to be nice to each other.

From the elderberry tree he could see all the way to the Nogales curve. He watched every car from the moment it came around the curve until it went by. His butt got tired on the perch, but he was afraid that if he did not watch every car come by, he would miss his dad. Baxter waited under the tree. Mikey talked to him about what they would do when Paul arrived. He promised Baxter he would come and get him after he and his dad had some private time to themselves. Baxter was the only one to whom Mikey could talk about Paul. Nobody else wanted to hear how much he loved his dad.

At sunup Mr. Wingo, Granny's next-door neighbor, pulled out of the driveway in his car and stopped at the highway. He was the district forest ranger and a real gentleman. He was neat and stocky and his gray hair was always combed. He wore steel-rimmed spectacles. His daughter Nita was Mikey's buddy. She was tall and red headed, two years older than he, and a gentle pal. She had taught Mikey how to ride her bike. Mikey dropped out of his tree and caught Mr. Wingo before he drove onto the highway. He said he knew where he could find his dad if Mr. Wingo would give him a ride to town. Mr. Wingo told him to get in the car. The man did not pretend to know where to find Paul, but he lived close enough as a neighbor to respect the boy's mission. Mr. Wingo would never even think of going to the places the cowboys did. Mikey knew where to go because he had been there himself when he cowboyed with Paul.

Mikey asked Mr. Wingo to take him to the Morley Avenue garita and when he arrived there he saw Paul in the door of the

International Bar with Cabezon Woodell, Roy Adams, and Herb Cunningham. He jumped out of the car, ran through the customs stations, tackled his dad's leg, and held on.

Paul was only ordinarily glad to see his son, and he dutifully bragged to his cronies that Mikey showed a lot of style in the way he had tracked him down before the rooster even crowed. He looked over his shoulder to see if he could find out how Mikey got there. Mr. Wingo waited by the Mexican garita to see if the boy would be all right.

Mr. Wingo might have been out of place, but that did not bother him. He probably never went across the line even for a cheap haircut, but Mikey could see he did not feel right about leaving a six-year-old boy with that wild bunch in Mexico, even if one of them was the father. Paul sure had not wanted to be caught in his disreputable haunt at that hour by that neat old man who never in a hundred years would have followed anyone but Mikey across the line.

Paul said that Mikey should go on back home with Mr. Wingo and wait for him a while longer because he still had business to attend to. He tried to get his cronies to affirm that they would make sure he went to pick up Mikey after their business was done. They turned away and did not lie, so he took Mikey by the hand and gave him back to Mr. Wingo and did not make any more promises.

Mikey did not say a word on the way home. Mr. Wingo was not one to stick his nose in other people's business, so he did not say anything either. That day Mikey began to appreciate the truly decent fathers like Mr. Wingo and Uncle Bill Shane who helped him when he was in trouble for a father. He began to learn how lucky he was that those two men lived on both sides of him and did not mind showing how a good father handled himself without saying a word against Paul Summers.

Mikey climbed up to wait in his elderberry tree again when he got home and Maggie did not know he had even been gone. When he did not come down at noon, instead of fighting him to make him come in for his lunch and nap, Maggie took him a peanut butter sandwich and a glass of milk. He did not come down all afternoon.

She was only able to get him out of the tree that evening after he could see for himself that it was so dark even an owl could not see Paul coming. Paul never came, anyway.

After his banishment, Paul missed many chances to see Mikey. He was invited to all of the boy's family fiestas and he always promised to come. That was when Mikey learned the expression "showed up." Paul Summers almost never showed up.

A few months after the time Mikey involved Mr. Wingo in his troubles, Paul came by again and told him he would pick him up at school the next day. This time they would be headed for his camp in the Magdalena Mountains *sin falta*, without fail. Maggie asked Miss Lewis the principal to let Paul take the boy out of school early, because he had to drive sixty miles back to his camp over dirt roads before dark. She drove Mikey and his gear to school in her car that day.

When Paul had not come for him after noon recess, Mikey ran away to the arroyo bridge to watch for him. One more minute of waiting in school was more than he could stand. Paul would have to cross the arroyo bridge if he came to the school from any direction except from Patagonia. If he tried to come to town or leave town, Mikey would see him. He was supposed to be coming out of Mexico, so he had to cross that bridge over the arroyo or drive by close on the other side. Mikey watched for him in every face in every car that went by. After a while, he began to fear that Paul might have gone to Patagonia early in the day and might have come back to the school from that direction while Mikey was at the bridge. He went back to Miss Lewis's office and asked her if his dad had come.

Miss Lewis was a stocky little woman, very compact, who always wore a blue dress. Mikey thought she was a lot like Madam Katzenjammer, only small. He never saw her smile. She wore the same steely, blue-eyed, poker-faced look of his family's women, probably because she was a cousin through the Parkers. She usually spoke in a loud voice, but when he went in to ask about his dad, she took off her glasses, rubbed the bun on the back of her head round and round to ease its tightness, and answered quietly. Paul had not come yet. Maggie had notified her that he would come and she had been watching for him. She knew Mikey would be no good for the rest of the afternoon in school, so he could go back to the bridge if he wanted to watch for his dad. She promised to keep Paul there and send for Mikey when he came.

School let out while Mikey was still in Miss Lewis's office, so he ran to the bridge to wait again. He watched each car come and go and still no Paul. Then Mr. Clark drove by in the bus on the way home with Mikey's schoolmates. He looked Mikey's way but did not recognize him, and then he thought about what he had seen and looked back and saw that he was Mikey. He had to turn the bus onto the bridge before he could stop. Mikey was sitting on a wall in front of someone's home. He jumped down and hid behind the wall. Mr. Clark waited on the bridge for a long, long time, but Mikey did not show himself and Mr. Clark finally drove away.

Mikey had been feeling worthless. Hiding from Mr. Clark made him feel even more worthless. Mr. Clark's strictest rule was that he never waited for anybody at a stop and he would not stop anyplace except at a designated bus stop. He broke two of his rules for Mikey and the boy had hid from him. Mikey knew he had not put anything over on Mr. Clark, and their friendship would never be the same again because the man's rules were his rules. He always remembered Mr. Clark's friendship as the first one he ever sacrificed to an obsession.

After dark Maggie drove up and stopped her car in front of Mikey and he was caught. Mr. Clark had stopped and told her that he saw her boy waiting for his dad by the arroyo bridge. He knew, everybody knew, that Paul was supposed to come for Mikey that day.

Maggie did not scold Mikey because she knew his heart was broken. Mother and son always managed to keep each other from perishing by showing respect when one of their hearts was broken. Sometimes Maggie knew what was right to say and do. They both knew she could not help him with a big show of sympathy. She could not say out loud, "Poor, poor Mikey, you poor little old kid." That would have meant she did not want him to have courage and hope that the situation would get right tomorrow or at least sooner or later.

Maggie made no disparaging remarks about Paul, either. Mikey could not have listened to her run down his dad. He said, "Maybe he came to school, missed me, and went back to Magdalena disgusted. Maybe he thought I hid from him so I would not have to go. Maybe he went by when I was down behind the wall hiding from Mr. Clark or when I left the bridge and went back to talk to Miss Lewis." He could not face it that Paul had broken his word.

"No, Mikey," Maggie said. "If he'd missed you at school, he would have called me. He would have gone to Miss Lewis's office. Miss Lewis even waited for him after school let out. He might only be late. Everybody is late from time to time. He could have been held up with his cattle, or maybe his road washed out. He might be waiting for you at home when we get back. At any rate, he'll probably call you tonight. Honestly, how could I have ever expected you two to make contact unless I sent you out with a police escort to meet him? You're so alike you were bound to mess it up."

Mikey was not sure that he was the one who had messed up. The only way to have a reunion with Paul was to go and find him where he worked or played. When he came out of Mexico he always drank whiskey before he did anything else and he had a lot of friends who liked for him to do that. Mikey loved him more than those friends did, but Paul did not consider anything else when it was time for whiskey.

That same year Paul ran out of work in Mexico for a while and took a job as a jailer in the county courthouse. Even though he was in charge of the jail, he became as much an inmate as the prisoners. His time as a jailer became the only time in his life that Maggie and Mikey could get hold of him when they wanted to. They might not ever be able to get him to help them, but at least they could worry him about it.

Paul's being at the jail was hard on Mikey because he was supposed to catch Mr. Clark's bus and go home every day after school, but the county courthouse was only a fifteen-minute sashay from school. Mikey could do it on one leg and skip every other step.

Mr. Clark the bus driver was the grandfather of Sonny Clark, the boy who was Mikey's best friend when he was not with Billy

Shane. Mr. Clark was a good friend of Paul's, even though he did not drink whiskey for fun as much as Paul. Even so, he warned Mikey that he would not support him if he missed the bus to steal a visit with Paul. If Mikey was the last person to get on the bus, a worried Mr. Clark gave him a scolding. He wanted to be able to find Mikey when it was time to haul him home from school, no ifs, ands, or buts. That was the first time Mikey ever heard about no ifs, ands, or buts, and that convinced him that Mr. Clark was adamant. Mr. Clark did not make rules that he did not mean to enforce. At the same time, both Mr. Clark and Mikey were absolutely sure that Mikey would skip the bus sooner or later because he knew where he could find his dad.

Mikey considered skipping the bus every single day. What was the use of having his dad where he wanted him if he could not visit him? Time with his dad should not count against him. He knew, however, that any unscheduled visit he made would get him in trouble, and maybe even get Mr. Clark in trouble.

Time went by and Mikey decided he had the right to visit his father and still be able to take the bus home like everybody else. Nobody got mad when other kids spent time with their dads. Kids got to see their dads every day without landing in trouble. Mikey's uncles were as hard on their wives as Paul had been on his, but their wives did not get divorces. Mikey was learning that in 1936 nobody else in his world got divorced.

He was learning that if a kid's folks divorced, the folks might be happy because they got their rights back, but the kid lost almost every one of his rights for the rest of his life as a kid.

One day when school let out, knowing that he would thereafter be looked upon as an outlaw by people he respected, Mikey headed straight for the courthouse without even a glance toward the school bus. He made such a beeline for his dad that he left his pencil box and tablet somewhere in the school building and never recovered them.

Later, Maggie reminded him that he had showed that he could be as irresponsible and ungrateful as Paul. He had seen fit to chuck everything she had worked hard to get for him, had disregarded the feelings of everyone who cared about him, and had run off to "God knows where." No matter how large the sacrifice, even though Maggie was short of money all the time, she always made sure that Mikey had "first-class things." However, like Paul, he was just not one for "things." He could not understand how anybody could worry about the things a kid lost when he had a chance to sell out everything to go see his dad.

Mikey found Paul in the sheriff's office by himself. Fast Paul's wings had been clipped. He did not grin when he saw his son. His nice smile made an appearance and then quickly disappeared. Mikey read that to mean that he knew the boy would be in Dutch for running away to see him and if Mikey was in Dutch, so was he.

Mikey could smell whiskey on Paul's breath under the odor of the Lysol used in the sheriff's office, but that made Mikey the outlaw glad. At least the man's life had not gone completely sour for being in jail.

The sheriff's office looked like a place where whiskey was not so far out of place. Nothing would have seemed out of place in there, especially anything a man ought not to have. Besides, anywhere Paul settled would have to be a good place for whiskey, or he would not stay. He might be down, but he would never be so down he would give up his whiskey.

Paul, however, had become spiritless. His eyes swam in tears. He had given up being slim, brown, smiling Fast Paul while he was a jailer. He was having to plod and his coat was dull.

He sat Mikey down in the sheriff's office and introduced him to everybody who came in, including the trustee. Paul ushered Mikey to the main door of the jail and showed him the bullpen and the individual cells for the permanent inmates. Paul had made friends with all the prisoners who were there for long terms, so he introduced Mikey to them and they smiled and waved to him. He ignored four shambling males who were loose in the bullpen. He said that they were only there because they had been drunk, vagrant, disturbing of the peace, or had done something sneaky. Those transients clustered together and smoked jealously clutched cigarettes, made sidelong glances at Mikey, and spoke in low, sinister voices. With them in sight, Mikey felt clean and innocent and no kind of an outlaw.

The long-term inmates braided horsehair, painted pictures, or played cards outside the doors of their cells. They looked freshly showered and shaved. Their undershirts and overalls were clean, their brogans were shined, and their faces were open. Paul laughed and said that they were happy because they stayed busy and kept the devil away. The overnighters and short-timers did not do anything except give everybody fearful, dirty looks.

Panfilo was in the cluster of short-timers that day. Mikey was not surprised to see him there. He believed that someday no one would be able to find Panfilo anywhere unless it was in jail or under a rock. Mikey often saw him with his family at Sunday Mass at Sacred Heart Cathedral. At Mass he looked dumb and mindless. In the bullpen he looked cunning, crafty, and completely at home. Paul let him out while Mikey was there and he made a mark in the place where he was supposed to sign for his wallet and comb. His eyes went blank and he swung his head from side to side to make Paul think he was crazy. Then, when he turned to leave and he thought no one was looking, his eyes found some old misery inside himself to look at.

Paul did not ask Mikey if he planned to stay at the jail, or how he would make it the four miles home before dark. Paul was there *de planta*, planted by the powers that paid his wages, and he did not seem to have solutions or considerations for life in the outside world. He took the same meals as the prisoners and slept on a cot so close to the bullpen door that he breathed the same air, made the same sounds, and saw only the same walls day and night.

When Mikey decided that he had better head for home, a young Mexican cowboy trustee named Bonifacio Santa Cruz walked for a way with him. Bonifacio had come in from the ranch for a night in town and had been in a fight over a girl. He stopped and turned back before he was out of sight of the jail because he was forbidden to go any farther. As he walked back to jail, he turned often and waved to Mikey.

Mikey went back to see if he could still catch the bus, but the school was empty inside and out. The door on the side of the main building was open, so he went in and walked down the center of the main hallway. The corridors were dark. He decided all of a sudden that he needed to get outside as fast as he could. He ran, turned a corner, and collided with Panfilo.

Mikey tried to get around him, but he blocked the way. His black eyes glittered in the dark hallway. "Ah hah, I followed you," he said in Spanish. "You are not supposed to be here."

He seized Mikey's shoulder in one hand and held him at arm's length, probably because he remembered the poke in the nose Mikey had given him. Being boxed in by cattle and horses had taught Mikey not to waste time squirming or whining. He also had developed a habit of kicking rocks, so Maggie had taken his shoes to a cobbler to have brass tips put on the toes so he would not wear them out. He kicked Panfilo in the shin twice before the man could draw a breath. The first kick made him howl. The second made him turn loose the kid.

Mikey ran out of the building and headed for home. He crossed the grounds in front of the school building and saw a person hiding behind the hedge that bordered the grounds. He saw that the person was a girl and he stopped beside her. Lorraine Knox's white face turned to him and she started to cry. Her cheek was cut. Mikey held his handkerchief against it to stop it from bleeding. He asked Lorraine if the bus was coming back.

"No."

"How come you missed it? What're you doing here?"

"I followed you to the courthouse and a man chased me back here," she said.

Mikey knew it must have been Panfilo.

"How'd you cut your cheek?"

She smiled. "I stuck my head up in the hedge to hide until the man went inside."

"Why did you follow me?"

"I saw you skin away to go see your dad and I wanted to bring you back so you wouldn't miss the bus. Then that man came out of the courthouse and when I asked him about you, he scared me so bad I ran and he chased me all the way back here."

"He scared the darned peewadding out of me inside the school when I came around the corner of the corridor."

"I got ahead of him and hid, but he walked right by the hedge where I was and it was dark enough that he didn't see me. Boy was I scared."

"Well, now, we've both missed the bus, haven't we?"

Mikey looked up and saw Panfilo hurry through the light of the front window of a house up the street. His head was drawn down into his shoulders like a turtle's, as though he was afraid someone would see his face. Anybody in town could recognize Panfilo Gandara without even looking at his face.

"Panfilo, I know what you did," Mikey yelled in Spanish. Panfilo hurried on.

Right then Mikey's mom and Nina drove up in Maggie's car. Mr. Clark had called and told Maggie that Mikey missed the bus. She loaded Mikey and Lorraine in the backseat and headed for home.

Maggie went into a tirade about the reasons she should not be mad at Mikey for wanting to see his father. Worthless as Paul was, he was still the boy's father. Worthless as he was, Paul might someday reform and she did not want him to be able to say that she had kept his son away. Then she made a lot of talk about his drinking, and some talk about his good points, and after all, who could blame the boy for taking it upon himself to visit his father? Oh, but she prayed that was the worst thing he would ever do.

At the Knoxes', Mikey could see lamplight between the boards of the house's walls. Nobody came out, so Maggie went to the door with Lorraine and knocked. Mrs. Knox opened the door and Mikey heard her call Maggie "Miz Summers" in a low, respectful voice. He could see Bill crouched over a bowl with a spoon in one hand and a piece of bread in the other. Bugs flew around a kerosene lamp in the middle of the table. As Maggie visited with Mrs. Knox, she smoothed Lorraine's hair with one hand and held on to her hand, as though she did not want to let her go.

When she came back to the car, Maggie paused and looked back at the closed door. Mikey could hear Bill Knox's quiet voice.

"Mikey, what were you kids doing?" Maggie asked. "Why is that girl's little face scratched?" She switched on the light inside the car. "Let me look at you."

"I'm not scratched, mama."

"How did your little friend get scratched, Mikey?" Nina asked.

"She crawled up inside the hedge in front of the school."

"Why did she do that?" Maggie asked.

"She said somebody chased her."

"Who was that?"

"I think it was that crazy Panfilo."

Nina laughed. "Panfilo's a character in the Mexican funnies. That isn't anybody real, Mikey. You sure have a great imagination for stories when you're in trouble."

"You know, Nina. Panfilo Gandara."

"Gandara? Oh, yes, you mean Ruben Gandara. I guess the kids do call him Panfilo."

"Am I going to get a whipping?"

Nina laughed again. "Ay, *muchachito*," she said.

"We'll see," Maggie said.

Mikey knew then that he would be spared. Maggie did not waste time waiting or talking when she had spanking on her mind.

The next day Mikey examined Lorraine's face at recess. She was always one to lead in the games and play hard, but not that day. She lifted the bandage so Mikey could see the cut on her cheek. It was not deep and she said it did not hurt.

Lorraine and Mikey had been fast friends since the day she mesmerized him at her house when he was three. Her power to mesmerize him was the only reason he had time for her. She seldom laughed or acted happy, but as far as he could tell, that was not because she was unhappy. She seemed to love fun as much as other kids as long as she could be the one who led the fun. He did not worry that she did not smile; he figured that she was probably too pretty, mysterious, and wise to give in to silly mirth. Most of the time when Mikey laughed he went absolutely silly and every decent thought in his head went away and left him blank as a post.

At first recess Lorraine walked away by herself and Mikey was kind of glad. Ordinarily she wanted too much attention from him and he would rather play sports with the other boys. At lunch she came and sat with him, so he tried to get her to tell him what was bothering her. She only said that she could not tell anyone, so he knew she was just trying to act mysterious after all. During last recess all she did was watch the street in front of the school, so he went over and asked her what she was worried about, because he knew that was what she wanted him to do.

"You'll see after school, maybe," she said.

"You still afraid of Panfilo?"

"No, Mikey, 'twas Frankenstein who chased me all the way down from the courthouse."

"Well, you don't have to be afraid of Panfilo," he said. "He can be killed with one kick in the shin."

"Do you still want my pocketknife, Mikey?"

"Sure."

Lorraine took a pocketknife with a red and yellow handle out of her pencil box. "I'll give you this knife if you'll walk me to the bus and get on with me and sit with me every day until I say to stop."

"How long will that be?"

"Maybe not too long."

"Give me the knife now."

"No, not until I don't need you to walk me to the bus and sit with me anymore."

Mikey thought it over. Walking a girl to the bus every day would put an awful cramp in his style. Everybody in school knew that he had the guts to skip the bus and visit his dad; had become the only kid in Nogales with free access to the sheriff's office and jail; was good friends with a trustee; had watched the convicts in the jail; prowled the school alone at night; and put Panfilo, the spookiest person any kid in Nogales had ever known, in the breeze. He did not want to give up all that glory to become a kept escort for a girl, but he would have to do it. He would do anything Lorraine asked him to do and he would do it for nothing. Lorraine had already bribed him more than once with the promise of that knife, and then reneged when it came time to pay off.

Mikey said, "Lorraine, you've already given me that knife. When can I have it?"

"This time I'll give it to you."

"You know that I'll walk you to the bus and sit with you, don't you?"

"Yes."

"Then give me the knife now."

"No."

"Why not?"

"You'll take it and forget your promise."

"I don't do people that way. You do."

Lorraine smiled into his eyes. "I have to be sure you'll stay with me after school."

"The best way to be sure of that is to give me the knife."

She said, "Hah!" and almost laughed.

After school, when Mikey walked out to see if the bus had arrived, Panfilo was standing in the middle of the street selling rocks to himself. He walked along, stopped, picked a rock off the ground, held it up, sold himself on its merits, pocketed it, then snapped his head around to see if anyone was looking. "Panfilo," Mikey said. "*Se lo que hiciste.* I know what you did." Panfilo wore his street veneer that afternoon, so he was able to ignore Mikey and did not even glance his way. Mikey was at least glad that the nut did not give him his menacing stare.

He went back into the building and told Lorraine that Panfilo was busy as a vendor and would not bother them. She held onto his arm and only glanced once at Panfilo as she walked to the bus.

When they boarded, Mr. Clark said, "You two sit in the back and stay put because I don't want to have to explain to your folks that you got away from everybody again." He watched them in the rearview mirror all the way back to their seats, then periodically glanced at them to make sure they stayed put until all the other children boarded. He did not stop watching them until after he shut the door, started the bus, and drove it away from the school.

Two blocks later the bus passed Panfilo and he looked up past Lorraine straight into Mikey's eyes with the most evil menace the boy had ever seen. Mikey did not know one other kid in Nogales who was so hated by that man. He knew that Panfilo entertained inordinate affections for all kinds of odd pastimes, but he had not expected to be singled out for a lifetime of his hate. Mikey wanted everybody to like him. What had he done to deserve that kind of look, except punch Panfilo a little in the eye and nose and give him a little brass-tipped kick on the shin?

One evening after supper, Mikey perched in the thickest foliage of his elderberry tree to watch the cars go by. He liked to watch the people's faces flash by, catch their expressions, then shut his eyes and imagine what they were like. Most of the faces seemed content, but sometimes they would act mean to one another as they went by and the meanest face was usually on the driver, maybe the father. When the father's face was mean, the faces of the mother and the kids showed that it made them suffer, so Mikey found that he was not the only one who had trouble at home.

The difference was that Paul was never mean. Maggie was the only one who put on the mean face in Mikey's family. However, she was not often mean when Paul was gone and never as mean about anything the way she was about Paul.

Mikey's trouble did not seem as bad as some of the trouble that went by in the cars. Mikey was not afraid of Paul and neither was Maggie. Mikey saw fear in the faces of some of those mothers and kids that went by. Most of them were happy, though, even when the father's face was fixed on the road and his own thoughts. Once in a while the mother's face would be mean. Then, usually, the father's face was fixed expressionlessly on the road, unless he was giving as much as he got.

In the 1930s people often went out for drives on warm nights for pleasure. A drive on a warm evening with all the windows rolled down cooled the passengers. People did not drive so fast that they did not have time to recognize their friends and wave to them. They even waved to people who were not their friends. Some people even waved to cars before they saw the faces inside. Mikey's uncles Buster and Fred did that.

On that spring night, Mikey watched the people go by for the simple pleasure of it. Baxter lay quietly under the tree and only raised his head when the Horrells' half-breed Boston bulldog came marching stiff-legged up the highway to taunt him.

The Horrells' dog hated Baxter, Mikey, and Billy Shane. His body was white with black spots, and his head was black with a white diamond on top. His tail was bobbed too long and was clubby. He owned the angry disposition and the stringy build of a grouch who could not enjoy anything long enough to gain any meat on his bones. The dog was called Popie, as in Little Pope. Carmen spoke with a thick Mexican accent and for "puppy" she said "Popie." Billy called him "the Pope."

Before Mikey or Billy tried to cross the dog's backyard, they always had to scout his whereabouts. Sometimes they could make it across without being terrorized by him if he was on the other side of the house or inside. He enjoyed a terrible advantage over the boys because the Horrells' storeroom and garage was only a few feet from their back door and the yard was fenced all around. If the dog caught them in that lane between the back door and the storeroom and the two closed gates, he could, as Billy said, "Trashmash a *bato*." A bato was kind of a Mexican fellow. Kids were all batos to each other.

Sometimes the dog would be inside the house and see the boys coming. He would lie quietly in ambush in a dark corner of a hallway until the moment they passed the back door and had almost made it safely across his yard. Then he would erupt with a fierce *grashing* noise that was a cross between a growl and the gnashing of teeth, and he would throw himself against the inside of the screened back door with such savagery that the boys would feel instantly trapped inside the very breath of hell.

One night the dog waited for Billy behind a bush outside his door and bit him on the bare heel and put him in bed with an infection for a week. That taught Mikey to worry about hydrophobia, or rabies. For the two weeks that the dog was in quarantine, Billy and Mikey were afraid that the dog's madness might have been caused by the rabies.

Because Mikey was dangerously dreamy, every now and then he wandered through the Horrells' yard in a trance and exposed himself to the lurking dog. One winter day, Mikey jumped right out of both shoes when the dog charged him from around the corner of the house. For the next three or four seconds that he used to effect his escape the loss of his shoes presented no problem. Without shoes he could outrun Beelzebub himself. However, the dog stood guard over his shoes and chewed on them for the rest of the day and nobody came out of the house to call him off. When Mikey finally told Maggie about it, she had to call Carmen Horrell and ask her to take hold of her dog so Mikey could get his shoes. Not much was left for him to take home and he got a spanking.

On the evening that Mikey was in his tree watching the cars go by, Baxter sat up on his haunches and growled at Popie. Popie did not see Mikey in the tree because he was too much of a coward to take his attention off Baxter. In a whisper, Mikey ordered Baxter not to even think of attacking the dog on the highway where he might get run over. Baxter did not look up at Mikey and Popie cocked his head as though he thought Baxter was the one who had whispered. He pranced stiff-leggedly toward Baxter with his head up and eyes bulging, scared to death. Baxter collapsed under the tree and sighed. Popie strutted closer to see if he could make Baxter run out on the highway after him.

Baxter sat up on his haunches again and Popie ran backward as though he had been nipped on the nose. A car came by and braked and honked to keep from hitting Popie and that was enough to make him scurry home.

Mikey wondered why the only two cowards he knew in the world had come to hate him and Baxter. He didn't know anybody else who was hated at all. He didn't know any cowards except Panfilo and Popie, either. He guessed it was just his bad luck that the two nuts who had been born with the worst dispositions in Arizona happened to have their eyes on his and Baxter's territory.

SEVEN

THE DARING YOUNG MEN

The headlong stunts cowboys pull off during their day's work opens their graves. They take mortal risks to make a wage and keep their charges prosperous. They don't risk the trust that has been put in them. They are trusted to take risks with their carcasses. The daring that goes with being a cowboy has to be born in a boy or a girl and exhibited early, and they have to like it. Later, after a boy starts to shave his whiskers and a girl has to put on her face to go out the door, it's too late to learn it.

An earache began to plague Mikey as he started the second grade at Lincoln School. At first, Granny was able to alleviate it with treatments of warm olive oil, but the pain always came back. Maggie and Granny did not give him anything else to stop it from hurting, so Mikey could only hope that he would wake up some morning and be well. He could have endured the ache better if his imagination had not made him believe that something evil grew inside his ear. He did not want it to take him over, so when Granny's remedy did not work, he stopped complaining.

Every day after school he climbed into his alamo tree to watch for Paul. In earache time it was not hard for him to sit still. His alamo was immense and a main branch stretched over the highway. If he climbed out on the end of that branch into its leafiest part, he could sit over the center of the highway with an unobstructed view of the road all the way up to the Nogales curve.

After these vigils began, Mikey never saw anything but empty hours in his tree. He was able to endure empty hours when he waited for his dad. He was good at standing vigil because waiting and watching was a duty that he had learned to perform as soon as he learned to ride.

Now that he was seven and had been given additional catechism instruction and had received the Sacrament of Confirmation, he believed in purgatory. After he thought about what purgatory would mean for him, he figured it was a place where God punished cowboys so they could atone for the sins that did not warrant eternal damnation but still carried an unpaid debt. When he decided on the worst punishment God could give a cowboy without killing him off and handing him over to the devil, he was sure it would be "holding herd." In Mikey's experience, cowboys were usually good enough persons to eventually be forgiven their sins, but Mikey believed that all of them, after facing God's judgment at their time of death, would be sent to purgatory and given one minute to saddle a horse and then minimum sentences of 250 years to maximum sentences of 16 trillion years holding herd. They would not be able to graduate to heaven until their sentences had been served. They would not be allowed a change of horses for their entire sentences. Every cowboy would be sentenced to hold herd in purgatory on one tired horse that nobody had ever loved. And to that, in Mikey's case, God probably would add an earache.

To Mikey, holding herd was the purest form of punishment for any cowboy. A cowboy's job holding herd was to turn back the cattle on his side when they tried to leave the herd. He stopped them and turned them back into the herd when they tried to leave. This was done best when it was done slowly, easily, and without fuss. A cowboy could not hold herd on a fresh horse, either, because a horse tired of it even faster than a cowboy did. For hours a cowboy did this slowly and carefully and made it look so easy that the cattle were bluffed into thinking that they could not all jump and run and leave together in different directions any time they wanted. Even the first minute on a fresh horse was not easy. After a very short while a cowboy began to wish for a cow to make a wild dash for the wide open spaces so he could swing out ahead of her at a dead run, risk his neck to beat her to a thicket or some other kind of cover, then run her straight back into the herd and a standstill. But no, a cowboy spent days and days, hours and hours, step by slow step, sitting his horse and only moving three or four slow steps at a time to turn thousands and thousands of cattle back one at a time over and over and over again until a herd was finally worked and turned loose. In purgatory that herd might not be turned loose for 16 trillion years. One *hour* excruciated a body.

What sins could a cowboy commit to have to hold herd for 250 years? Everything that was fun, short of willful blasphemy; anything to keep from working; being unfaithful to his family and friends so that he might indulge himself with cowboy work; and working himself and his friends and family until everybody died unhappy and broke were a few such sins. Another sin that might warrant only 250 years would be waking up too late to feed the horses, then hurrying back to the comforts of camp and forgetting to close the gate so the horses strayed out onto the highway.

A sin a cowboy might commit that would deserve 16 trillion years might be to stay away from his wife and children so he could run and play with a neighbor's sister, then not go home until all his wages were spent, then confess the sin to his wife for everybody's own good and to show his extreme honesty, then to beat his wife to within an inch of her life when she became righteously angry, then to forget to feed the horses, then to bawl great tears because he was sorry about the mess he had caused.

Holding herd is a cowboy stationed at a dam to plug a hole with his finger. The hole is of a size, location, and height that preclude him from lying down, sitting still, or standing up straight to rest. He can't go to sleep, but his body stops functioning, as his blood stops flowing because he and his horse are forced to remain at a standstill and once in a while are allowed only a walkstill three yards long.

An ordinary cowboy holding herd does not get to ride into the herd and do what the bosses do. The bosses and top hands get to work inside the herd in cowboy glory. They rope calves and drag them out to the branding fire. They cut the bulls away from the heifers, or the heifers from the steers, or the culls from the keepers. Their horses perform at their peaks. The bosses get to show verve and style and expertise. The waddy, the cowboy who stops a hole on the edge of a herd, gets to watch and wait and hope that just before he falls off his tired horse from paralysis of the joints, some boss will agitate a steer so much that he will try to get away from the herd. A cowboy who has been paying for his sins would not be able to do anything but ache and watch the work until his eyes burned and would have to go on holding herd while other cowboys with lesser sins got to run after that steer and bring him back.

Because Mikey had held herd a lot, he knew the travail of sitting still for long hours. It was something he could do with a throbbing earache in an alamo tree because of the hunger and thirst and aching bones he knew from holding herd.

That earache was so bad at times that Granny put Mikey in Uncle Joe's bed in her house and Dr. Gonzales came out from Nogales to see what he could do. He always only instructed Granny to pour more warm olive oil into Mikey's ear.

While he was in bed, his Nina came to see him every day. Art Robinson, his Nina's younger brother, also came by to see him. He was a cowboy too and he told Mikey he knew how much an earache hurt. He had gone through it once after a tick crawled in and camped on his eardrum. After the tick was discovered and plucked out, his earache got worse and he had to go back to Dr. Gonzales to find out that the tick had left its head imbedded in his eardrum. That story made Mikey feel a little better. At least he could be pretty sure that he did not have a tick in his ear.

Mikey's uncles and his dad's cowboy partners, whom he also called his uncles, heard that he was sick in bed and came by to sit with him and tell stories. He guessed they were afraid he was going to die and needed to check on him for his dad, because his dad was never able to come. The uncles made Mikey realize that it was good for a man to be tough when something hurt a lot. He suffered a lot when he thought about his dad not coming to see how tough he was. He suffered when he heard the bootsteps and low voices of cowboys coming through his Granny's house and then his dad was not with them. His uncles did not bring him candy or play pretties. They did not expect that he needed presents for being a man. They came to make sure he was man enough to get well as all men were required to do. They showed that they approved of him and that came close to making Mikey feel good until they were gone again, but he still did not seem to get well.

He felt good enough to go back to school some days, but he missed a lot and his teachers told Maggie that he would not pass second grade. Dr. Gonzales told her she ought to keep Mikey out until he got well. His ear would swell up and get real hot, then go down for a short while, but it always throbbed and rang. He imagined that he might have a colony of ants in there, or a den of poisonous worms with fangs, or a hairy tarantula's lair. He would climb into his tree and press his ear into his hand on the limb and watch the road for Paul. He did not have to go to school, but he was getting desperate to be useful again and would have done anything to stop his ear from aching.

Then Uncle Bill Shane gave Billy a red and white Schwinn bicycle. That machine made Billy proud and Mikey proud of Billy. Uncle Bill was a stern, hardworking man who came home every single day of his life to be with his family. Through the years he rose from the lowest position of customs inspector, who worked all day afoot on the line, to chief inspector with authority over the whole port of entry.

Billy's little sister Bea had been born six months before Mikey's little sister Maudy, so both boys now had sisters. A baby daughter the Shanes called The Flapper had been born before Billy. The Flapper and Bea were both pretty little blondes, but Mikey never knew anything but a picture of The Flapper. She had died of pneumonia when she was only two.

Uncle Bill liked to grow vegetables and every minute he was awake he worked, either at his duties in the customs service, or in an acre of truck garden on his property. That's how Billy got his bicycle. Uncle Bill bought it brand new for twenty-five dollars that he made on his vegetables.

For a time after Billy got his bicycle, Mikey did not have to walk to Billy's house. Instead of stepping out onto the highway and hollering and then reaching for the sky with a broad wave for Mikey to come on over, he would come get him and transport him back to his house on the handlebars of his bike.

Billy always went as fast as he could pump the pedals at first, then he and Mikey coasted in their own wind while he rested. The dashes that the two made on the highway with humming tires and flashing spokes on the bright, new, solid, shiny, red and white bike made Mikey love bicycles forever and made him realize again how much his Uncle Bill loved him.

Uncle Bill was absolutely a real man. Mikey believed that anybody who thought he wanted to be a father and husband ought not to even try unless he could be like Uncle Bill. Of course, the bike was Billy's, but it brought great joy into Mikey's life with its rubber-scented tread and winking spokes, its own headlight that was shaped like a comet for the dark, the way it smoothly chained he and Billy on their way in time with the pumping of Billy's legs, the engine of Billy's breath, and the grip of Billy's freckled hands. All Mikey could do while he took all this in was sit still, watch, listen, and ride.

Billy led Mikey into some precarious situations, but he was never overbearing and he never used force against Mikey, even in fun. He was not one ounce a bully, but he was tough and brave and to Mikey he was 100 percent hero. Other kids lived on the Tucson highway and all of them except Skippy Swikert were closer to Billy's age, but Mikey was Billy Shane's best friend and he was Mikey's and everybody else was a sissy.

Maggie loved Billy too and usually gave her son over freely into his charge, but she gave him hell and Nina gave him absolute hell when something went wrong with his and Mikey's ventures and they became casualties.

Once the boys found an old rope and Billy knew immediately what to do with it. They hiked up to the Devil's Cliff above Indian Springs and Billy climbed out onto a black oak limb and tied the rope to it so it hung out over the cliff. The boys took turns swinging out over the cliff. That was daredevil stuff. The cliff was forty feet of sheer rock above a solid mesquite thicket, which allowed the boys to swing out a long way over the canopy of the trees. In the summer, when the mesquites were in full leaf, those treetops looked like a soft green carpet far below and the boys could not see the hard, old ground beneath them.

Each time Mikey and Billy arrived at the Devil's Cliff swing they warmed to the thrill of it little by little. To build their nerve, because the cliff was so high, the boys first swung only five or six feet out into space without looking down. Then they swung out and made themselves look down. Then they backed off to the end of the rope and took a run at it, sprang off the edge of the cliff, swung out, turned, and looked down all the way back. They usually did not go home until darkness made it hard for them to see the cow trail that led them off the hill.

Mikey always followed Billy's lead. Billy thought up the variations of stunts they dared to do and was first to perform them. Mikey did them the way Billy did. The drill made Mikey as fearless as the second lamb who follows the first to slaughter. Sometimes Billy's feats caused Mikey to think and look before he leaped, but not often and not for long. New feats waited to be performed and Billy did not like for Mikey to stall.

Neither of the boys ever worried about the wear they put on the rope over the Devil's Cliff. Billy always leaned back and put all his weight on it before they started swinging. Mikey thought he was thirty or forty pounds lighter than anything, so after Billy swung on the rope, he knew it would hold him. Then after a summer or two that their rope had hung over the Devil's Cliff, they went back one dry, windy, spring day to swing again.

They tried the rope and their courage with short swings, then with wider, longer ones, then after a running start. Then they returned one-handed. They swung out holding on with both hands, turned when they reached the outer limit of the swing, let one hand go, and returned one-handed. They could just barely hold on that way long enough to get their feet back on the ground.

They tired of that and Billy decided there was one thing they had not tried and that was to both swing at once. They tied a foot loop in the bottom end for safety. Swinging with one foot in the loop was not their idea of a stylish way to do it, but it was the only way they figured Billy could hold on safely with Mikey on his back. Mikey got on Billy piggyback and they swung.

They were clumsy the first time, but they kept trying until they warmed to it and by the fifth try Mikey was less a part of Billy's performance and more on his own. Instead of being like a monkey on Billy's back, Mikey was more like a flag or a scarf waving from his neck. They suspended use of the foot loop and made a run for the edge of the cliff with Mikey running behind Billy. At the edge, Mikey sprang onto Billy's back and wrapped his arms around his neck and his momentum shoved Billy out over the chasm. They often slipped down the rope before they made it back, but they always made it because Billy was too tough and brave to let go. The rope creaked on the limb and stretched. They finally stopped when they suspected that the rope or the limb was about to come apart. Besides that, Billy's neck felt like it had already come apart.

Before they left the place, while Billy rested, Mikey decided that one more stunt on his own would be safe. He climbed with the end of the rope to a place on top of a rock that was level with the limb on which the rope was tied, dropped into space off the rock, hit the end of the rope, swung away from the edge of the cliff, and returned to the ground on Billy's side of the tree.

Billy's eyes got big and he forgot how much Mikey had tired him by hanging on his neck. He grabbed the rope, ran to the top of the rock, and sailed out over the void with such wild banshee verve that he scared Mikey.

To get even, Mikey took the rope and ran back to the top of the rock, grabbed the bottom loop in both hands, kept the rope taut as he ran across the rock, and leaped out into space. Gravity took over that time. The rope broke just below the knot on the limb as though it had been chopped with an ax. Mikey watched himself plummet all the way down into the top of the mesquites.

Billy later said that Mikey disappeared at the point where the rope should have stopped his fall and the rope trailed away after him and not even the sound of him remained. Mikey was light as an ant and did not feel that he was in danger, though a free fall forty feet to the ground through a big tree was not his usual way of getting off a swing. He had always trusted that the canopy of the mesquite thicket below the Devil's Cliff would be a safe cushion. He was surprised when it did not gently stop him, but he was taken into one tree's embrace, grabbed from all sides all the way down, and caught short of the ground in a bottom fork.

The tree only scratched Mikey in the places it grabbed him on the way down. He owned one little gash at the base of his skull, a badge wound that bled enough to give evidence of derring-do, but not enough to hurt and not deep enough for stitches.

Billy risked more in his hurry to get down off the cliff to Mikey's side with no tree to take him into its embrace. Mikey was already safe on the ground when Billy reached him. When he heard the exciting story of what Billy had seen, and saw Billy's concern for the bloody gash, Mikey thought it best to at least give out a sob, because that was what a little kid was supposed to do. He was only able to summon it up from his heart and get a real tear for it because of the awful worry on Billy's face. Not only was he unhurt, but he was happily satisfied and thrilled by what he considered to be a great achievement.

Mikey had pulled off the last stunt that had been offered to him by the black oak tree, the cliff, and the old rope. He had performed the ultimate stunt that Billy and he had risked death time after time to achieve, and he had been the first to do it, and the last. This ultimate stunt would never have been accomplished if he had swung back safely to the ground. Billy Shane, the inventor and leader in their partnership, had not been the first to perform that stunt. Mikey had done it first. If anybody wanted to achieve what Mikey had accomplished, he would have to find another old rope that only had one stunt left in it.

That was not the only stunt Mikey pulled that made him proud, but, not counting his cowboying, it was the best that he had achieved up until that day because everything had come apart and sure death had opened its mouth to receive him. That was what he and Billy always looked for and hoped to accomplish. They pushed a stunt to its limits to see if anything would come apart, waited without hoping for that to happen, and trusted that their guardian angels would keep them from being killed. When the stunt came apart, they wanted to ride the torn and broken remnants of it all the way to a standstill and then enjoy the thrill itself as it subsided and their lives lapsed into peace again. After that, they would have the delicious memory of it.

Of course, Mikey did not analyze his reasons for doing stunts. People who like that sort of adventure only begin to analyze why they pull stunts after about the five-thousandth one and they find themselves in their sixties still pulling stunts. Mikey knew the satisfaction of achievement only after everything came apart. The victory was no good unless he had tried the limits of his luck. He took the risks necessary to make things happen that he had not known would happen, and then he realized the victory of standing unbroken among the broken fragments of everything that had gone through the disaster with him.

Mikey knew well what the residuals of the Devil's Cliff venture would be: the soreness of body and head, a disgusted examination of the gash on his head by his Nina on the way home, banished by his Nina while his bosom pal got a whipping, met and scolded in his backyard by Maggie, examined under Maggie's hard touch, bawled out for getting bloody and tearing his clothes, and then finally not whipped so that all would not be forgotten quickly. Granny's love touch was as hard as Maggie's. These two women of Mikey's had in common a disapproval of all his stunts, anger when they had to nurse him, and hard handling of his wounds. They never kissed anything to make it better in their entire lives.

Granny was only different in that she soon completely forgot his stunts. She examined the gash on Mikey's head and treated it once and Mikey never heard anything more about the Devil's Cliff from her. Maggie took a look at it while Granny doctored it and never said a word, but she got after him so much about the clothes that had been torn and bloodied that he learned to hate the sight of them. If he complained about having to wear them when it was their turn to be worn again, she made him put them on anyway.

Billy's little sister Bea and Mikey's little sister Maudy were helpless and could not be counted on for anything. Maggie and Nina made darned sure the little sisters did not share in any of Billy and Mikey's adventures that took them out of the yard, or up a tree, or on a horse.

Bica watched Maudy so well that she could not be lured into any kind of trouble, even if Mikey had been the kind who would try to enlist her cooperation in trouble. Maudy became stubborn about staying out of danger just so she could stay on the good side of Maggie, Granny, Nina, and Bica. All she had to do was curl an eyebrow and say, "No, I have to stay here because you go too far," and Mikey knew that she would squeal on him for what he was about to do and he would get the same spanking he would have been given if he had succeeded in taking her along.

Mikey had kidnapped Bea when he was five and she was an infant. Paul had been off cavorting with a bunch of charros down in Mexico and he brought Mikey back a charro suit. The suit was black, so Mikey figured he would be a bandit when he wore it. He might grow up to be a bandit, a fact that was often pointed out to him. Bea was tiny and helpless, so one day he put on the charro suit and stole her out of her crib and took her back to his house. He barely got past Popie's house with her when he heard his Nina howl. Nina loved Mikey completely, so he figured she would be greatly amused and relieved when she found out Bea was with him. His poor Granny was so innocent of the caper, and she thought they looked so cute together, she sat them on her back steps and took a picture of Mikey with Bea on his lap.

The kidnapping of Bea was a mistake. Bica understood what Mikey had done and let him know that Nina was suffering, so he got a little worried and headed back with Bea. He figured he could get her back inside the house without being discovered because he could tell where Nina was as she yelled for Uncle Bill and Billy from one side of the house to the other. All Mikey had to do was get across Nina's backyard and through the back door to redeposit Bea in her crib without being seen.

He paused at Uncle Bill's pump house to listen to his Nina, heard the front door slam, and hurried across the backyard with Bea cooing in his arms. She loved Mikey and he loved her, so she was no trouble to carry. As he reached the back door, Nina came around the corner of the house like a mother cow on the fight with her head up and a mean, hot wind smoking out her nostrils.

"¡Tú, muchacho!" she yelled. "You, boy, give me that child." As she came on stepping real high, Mikey realized it might be that she thought he was somebody else. He sure did want to be recognized before he was killed. She was angrier than he had ever seen anybody in his life. When she was excited like that, with the prospect of having to kill a kid, or rescue one, or run off a mean dog or a bandit, her clothes would slide away and reveal large expanses of clean, bare leg or bosom or shoulder, as though she were coming right out of them and would leave them behind if they got in her way. Now the perspiration stood out on her upper lip and her eyes were hot and a wet, steamy mist seemed to envelop her as she set upon the one who had taken her baby.

Just before she laid hands on Mikey, he saw that her eye was so hot that she did not recognize him at all. She did not know he was Mikey, the boy she bragged would someday marry that same little daughter.

Nina swept Bea up high in her arms and slapped at Mikey with the back of her hand and knocked off his charro hat. "Mikey!" she yelled, and in her thick Mexican accent she said, "what are you doing? How long have I been calling? Do you realize what you have done? You have finally driven me *insane*."

Well, Mikey really bawled after that banishment. He would have tried to kill anyone who scared his Nina like that. He felt worse when he remembered how she had looked at him before she recognized him. He would never have believed the time would come when his Nina did not know him. Maggie would have known him in a bearskin, in knickers, with a bowtie, and a Frankenstein mask. He never wore the charro suit again.

Mikey stayed home the next day until Nina called up and said it was all right for him to come over and play with Billy. She said for him not to think she was mad anymore. When he was back in her house again, she even joked that he should have kept Bea at his house because her temper had been bad ever since he brought her back. Then, to make him smile and feel better, she asked him when he thought he could kidnap her again.

Mikey's Nina did not mention the kidnapping again except jokingly. Mikey believed she only joked about it to make up to him for that instant of rage when she did not know him. He had lived every day of his life convinced that she knew and loved him as well as her own kids. Later, after Billy's little brother Spike was born, Billy once seriously accused her of loving Mikey more than either of her own sons. She was capable of a most extreme kind of rage, and many times Mikey had seen her look straight at Billy as though he were a bank robber and not her son. She only looked at Mikey that way once, and that was enough. When Spike grew up big enough to get into mischief, he never made her as angry as Billy and Mikey had, but he was a much nicer, gentler kid than those two.

Billy had a lot of style and never got mad at Mikey for any reason. He was serious about staying outdoors where he could best enjoy every minute that he walked the earth. He was another one like Lorraine whose enjoyment kept him serious most of the time. Not Mikey. Mikey was a giggler and Billy's seriousness made him giggle a lot.

Billy's bicycle made him more mobile on the highway, but he was not a boy to confine himself only to a road and a machine. He found much more wonder in the arroyo and the three rows of trees one hundred feet tall along the front of his and Mikey's houses and the steep hills behind them. The boys hung Granny's lariat rope in an alamo that spanned the arroyo and they could swing all the way from the railroad tracks on one side to a pasture fence on the opposite bank. They swooped down from a height of about twenty feet on the banks to within three feet of the arroyo bed. They enjoyed knowing that if anything went wrong they would fall into deep sand, unless the arroyo was in flood. Granny made them bring her lariat back every evening because it had belonged to Mikey's Grandaddy Bert.

The boys were not brave enough to use the swing when the arroyo was in flood. Heavy rains south of Nogales, Sonora, made floodwater roar down from Mexico. The boys could hear it coming, often before a drop of rain had fallen on their neighborhood, often in full sunshine with no sign of a cloud. They could even smell the brown wall of the flood as they ran to watch it come crashing down the wash around the Nogales curve.

The arroyo in flood became a place for violent, sure death. If the boys heard the torrent coming in time they would lie in the middle of the warm sand bed and watch the head of the flood get fooled at the bend in the arroyo beside the Nogales curve. At the curve, it would stride on and reach blindly straight ahead toward the Baffert cow pasture because the wash curved out from under its momentum. Then it would be rudely shouldered away from the pasture by the bank and back into the channel toward the boys.

The head of water would roil and scoop up sand and dislodge and roll new boulders and trees to make itself huskier while it spewed geysers of chocolate colored water into the air. It careened from bank to bank for fifty yards after it left the curve, and then it settled down to a straight dash for the last one hundred yards before it reached the boys. It came on faster and faster and its roar drowned all other sound in that stretch where nothing turned it or stood in its way.

The sight of the head of a flood from ground level was a look at a running catastrophe that was as real as a tornado or a tidal wave that had been forced into a channel only thirty yards wide. The flood was of a lot more than water. Rocks and sand and tree trunks and dead carcasses came with it. It resembled the headlong stampede of a herd of tusky wild boars in a panic that trampled and leveled everything in the way, rabid boars that came on shoulder to shoulder through a narrow alley faster than any boy could imagine, tearing chunks out of each other as they came.

Just before the front wall of the flood reached the boys, they jumped up and ran up the bank to the railroad tracks. They always lay side by side and faced the flood and waited to run until they could barely make it out of danger. Billy could run only as fast as Mikey could. Mikey was faster than boys his own age and Billy was short-legged. Mikey was able to outrun him by the time he was seven.

The boys liked to climb in an old three-story iron mill above the Nogales curve that had been gutted by fire. They could climb the scorched beams to a platform under the roof, then jump out over space about two feet to catch the edge of a hatch and pull themselves onto the roof. The perch on top the burnt roof was rickety, high, and spooky, but the boys could be on top of their world and see a long way. That jump to the hatch meant sure death if they missed, but any kid could do it a hundred times out of a hundred and to be on top of the roof was worth the risk. The cement floor three stories down awaited the kid who could not jump out and up two feet and catch the sill of the hatch with both hands, swing with the momentum, hang, then pull himself onto the roof. Billy and Mikey were the only kids they knew who ever did it. To get back they grabbed the sill on the edge of the hatch that was closest to their platform, swung back over the platform, and dropped.

Mikey and Billy never told their folks about that stunt in the mill. They kept a vow of silence about stunts they pulled that were done out of sight of their mothers. They got in enough trouble without bragging about what they did when they were out of their mothers' sight. Their mothers' punishments were stunts in themselves, for the boys were never sure that they would come out of them alive.

Mikey and Billy could not stand anybody who bragged. They believed that anybody who bragged about doing things that nobody saw them perform were liars. Mikey and Billy believed that they performed the very most dangerous stunts anybody, kid or grown-up, ever performed without an audience. That was the cowboy way, too. Cowboys pulled off risky stunts horseback way out where no one could see them.

Billy's bike was too tall for Mikey to ride by himself, so he could not learn on it, but Nita Wingo had a girl's bike that was easy for Mikey to handle. He could straddle it in the girl's well, get it rolling, then stand up on the pedals and pump. Nita was the same age as Billy and a good friend to Mikey, but she never left her yard to go with the boys and never felt she had to make excuses for it. She watched Mikey trail along on foot after Billy a few times when Billy forgot to load him on the handlebars, and she decided to take a risk and teach him how to ride her bike. After he learned to ride in her yard, she let him borrow the bike from time to time so he could keep up with Billy.

The kids in that neighborhood were taught to be careful about the traffic, but the only locals who raced their motors up and down that part of the highway were would-be swains who drove out to look at Maggie. They liked to come swerving around the Nogales curve, spin their tires, race their motors, honk their horns, and scowl at Mikey from behind their windshields when he was standing out in front of the house instead of Maggie. Families still drove wagons and teams on that highway. Men and women still rode to town horseback. Automobile traffic was light.

Billy and Mikey would pump the bikes up the hill of the Nogales curve, rest a minute, then pump back down the hill and around the curve as fast as they could on the outside lane, gain speed as they freewheeled down the hill, veer to the safe left lane, then coast down past Billy's house with their tires humming.

Mikey would take the lead in front of his house so he could show off in case Bica, Maudy, Maggie, or Granny were looking. Then Billy would take the lead when they zipped by his house.

One June evening when Billy was ten and Mikey was seven, Billy came by on his bike, so Mikey went over and asked Nita for her bike. The boys raced out of the Wingos' yard side by side. Mikey looked left and shouted, "Clear," and Billy looked right and shouted, "Clear!" They swerved onto the highway and headed toward Nogales on the left side, single file, with Billy in front.

The passenger train from Tucson came up behind them as they pumped hard to make the hill on the curve. The engineer waved at them and blew his whistle to warn traffic that was out of sight at the mill crossing around the curve. The boys pumped hard to see if they could stay ahead of the train, but eased off when the train passed them and Billy waved to the engineer.

Billy's hearing was sensitive and both boys hated noise. Mikey's hearing had not been as sensitive as Billy's since the earaches started. The train with its charged-up steam engine ran by them only thirty yards away and absolutely deafened the whole world. Mikey did not know what possessed Billy to cross the highway right then, unless it was the noise of the train, but he veered to cross to the other side. Mikey took his right hand off the handlebar to wave at the passengers and his bike swerved left and caught the dirt shoulder of the road. At that moment, he felt a heavy rush of hot wind as a black car passed him on the wrong side of the road. The car hurtled by so close that it ticked the fingernail of the little finger on Mikey's right hand as he reached for the handlebar. He realized later that if he had not waved at the train, he would not have veered off the pavement and the car would have hit him.

The blare of the car's horn was muted by the rattle and whistle of the train. The car headed for the right side of the road but did not slow down. Billy never saw it coming. Mikey screamed to warn him, but his voice was nothing in the din of the train. Billy and his bike separated and blew up into the air above the hood of the car. His face was turned away from Mikey. His limbs remained stunned and stiff with the shock of impact and the momentum of his flight. His hair stood on end. He and his bike tumbled over the car, skipped off the roof, bounced onto the highway, and lay still. The black car sped around the curve and was gone.

Mikey looked back and saw that the people on the train had seen the car hit Billy. Their faces were as still as snapshots as they went out of sight around the curve. Then the train and all the noise were gone. Mikey abandoned Nita's bike and ran to Billy. Mr. Wingo ran across his lawn toward him with his pipe clenched in his mouth. A heavy shock of his gray hair tumbled down over his forehead. The doors of his house burst open with frantic limbs and flying red hair and wan white faces as his daughters and Mrs. Wingo yelled and ran to find each other.

. Billy lay flat and still. The bike was rumpled and broken, ruined and still. Both were ugly and wasted. Mikey's life was over. An instant ago, he and Billy had leaned with verve as they turned onto the highway in a concert of pounding hearts, their hair full of the wind they made, their lungs full of sweetness. In the next, their lives stopped. Mikey became a small wad of broken bone, bleeding flesh, and hair that stuck out everywhere, like Billy.

A hairy, bloody patch of hide lay on the pavement apart from Billy. In his confusion, grief, and shock, Mikey could not imagine that it was a piece of Billy's scalp. Mr. Wingo knelt beside Billy with his teeth making snipping sounds on the pipe. Mikey watched his face because he needed the man to look at him so he could know what had become of Billy. Mr. Wingo looked toward his house to compose himself. Then he brushed his hair off his forehead and turned to Mikey. "Go home, Mikey," he said softly. Then he picked up the scrap of scalp and tried to put it back where it belonged.

EIGHT

GRACE

Horses have made their way in this world for at least forty million years with nothing but their grace and speed. Their grace of movement and form lasts only for a limited time. The good ones are also gracefully innocent and they keep this all their lives. One of the great joys of a husbandman is knowing this and seeing it in his own offspring. One of his great sorrows is to watch it die in his sons.

On a Sunday morning in May, Mikey found himself kneeling on a red velvet prie-dieu at the foot of the altar in Sacred Heart Cathedral. The light was so bright from all sides that nothing on the altar cast a shadow. Mikey was dressed in a white suit, white shoes, red necktie, and his tough feet were in thin, white socks. He held in front of his nose a fat, lighted candle that was half as long as he and adorned with golden flowers. He held a white prayer book with golden letters engraved on the front and white rosary beads. Father Duval was celebrating High Mass for the First Holy Communions of Mikey and three other children.

This was what came from doing right. Mikey always tried to make an effort to do right and this was the way a boy was rewarded when he succeeded. He had risen to a victorious height. The months of lessons with Sister Clara in Sacred Heart School were over and he had been given a place up front in the light, one of four personages for whom hundreds of people had come to celebrate Mass.

Mikey thought, "I am probably not the person who kneels here for everybody to see in the state of grace. I am a much shabbier person than this ceremony and attention make me out to be. I have been ambushed. I was given no idea that such grandeur would be prepared for me, or that I would be shown off with such magnitude."

Mikey's catechism instruction for his First Communion had started when Sister Clara asked him in Spanish, "Who is God?" Then, after he gave her the best answer he knew, she told him who God was. She asked him other questions about his faith and morals every day for a month, told him the answers, then answered his questions. She then asked him to repeat the answers and explain them to her. He also memorized them from his catechism book at home to prepare for the next session.

Learning his catechism was as easy as standing still for a caress on the cheek because his Nina godmothered him through it. She seemed to love him a lot more during the time of his instructions for doing right. She picked him up after his classes at Lincoln School, left him alone with the nun in the classroom at Sacred Heart School, visited the altar in the church until his session was over, and then took him home. On the way home she helped him memorize his prayers from Sister Clara's Spanish into English.

Every time he said the Apostle's Creed for the rest of his life he remembered his Nina's voice as she recited in her Mexican accent, "I behlieb en Goth, theh Fathair Almighty..." and knew again the deep, calm love with which she said it. Her faith in God and His angels and saints immediately became Mikey's. He absorbed his faith through his Nina in the same way his heart had begun to beat through Maggie. His faith did not ever come with the ceremonies of churchmen, the pulpit preaching, the churchgoing, the dictated prayers, or the wordy dedication to the performance of good deeds.

How could he ever go to hell? He knew his *madrina*, his Nina, would forgive him no matter what he did, and if she would forgive him, God would too. God would never deny anything to Natalia Shane, and she would never let Him send her godson to hell. Woe be to *anybody* who tried to do that. Mikey bet that God had long since decided that anyone Nina loved had better be loved by Him, no matter what He thought, and that was all there was to it.

Mikey had gone to his first confession in the dark church Saturday evening to give Father Duval a true account of all his sins. Now, after his First Communion, he would make a clean start to do right. He was now inside the light of complete approval of people and God and would probably hear the songs of angels any minute.

After Mass, Father Duval herded the communicants and their families to his quarters for breakfast. Sister Clara was at work in the kitchen and Mikey grinned and waved to her. She gave back an impersonal smile as though she only knew him as a presence she was there to serve. That was when he found out that Sister Clara would not talk to him when other people were around. Before that morning, he thought he knew her, owned her as the special friend who had showed him how to finally do right. She had given him his entire catechism instruction in Spanish. Now she did not know him. She made it clear to him that nobody owned her but God.

Mikey spilled cocoa on the lapel of his white suit before everyone even sat down for breakfast, and Maggie took him to the kitchen sink to clean him up. Sheriff Brown came in and told him Paul was outside and wanted to congratulate him. Mikey ran outside to the sheriff's car.

Paul laughed when he saw Mikey, and then picked him up in a hug. He was saturated with whiskey. His eyes swam in a glaze of green water, but his hands were gentle and his laugh was happy. He was at the very peak of celebration for being in town, and Mikey knew he was as clean hearted as anybody else in the world even though he never seemed to do right or put himself where he might hear angel music.

Mikey sat with Paul in the back of the sheriff's car. Sheriff Brown sat in the front and watched Mikey's eyes. A shotgun was cradled in a bracket on the back of the front seat. Handcuffs and a blackjack lay in the seat between Mikey and Paul. The car smelled like the bullpen in the sheriff's jail.

Paul handed the blackjack and handcuffs to the sheriff. "Sheriff Brown wants to talk to us, son," he said.

"Michael Paul, tell me what you saw when Billy Shane got hit by the car," Sheriff Brown said.

Mikey did not feel that he was in much of a state of grace anymore.

"It's okay, son," Paul said. "You're not in trouble. It's just that you were the one closest to Billy when he got hit. You could have been hit, too."

"What side of the road were you on when Billy got hit, Mikey?" the sheriff asked.

"On the left side," Mikey said.

"You were on the safe side, then?" the sheriff said.

"Yes, sir," Mikey said. "Uncle Bill made us promise to ride our bikes on the left so we would see the cars come on our side and so we would be on the other side of the road from the cars that came up behind us."

"Were you side by side?"

"No, sir, Billy was in front of me."

"Where was Billy when the car hit him?"

"In the middle of the highway."

"Was he crossing to the other side?"

"Yes, sir."

"Why would he do that if he'd promised his dad that he would ride on the left?"

"I think it was because of the train."

"The train was going by?"

"Yes, sir."

"That's the first time I heard that a train was there. Why would the train make Billy cross to the other side?"

"It rattled awful loud and whistled for the crossing."

"What else happened?"

"The car came up behind me and went by so close it hit my little finger."

"How was that? I thought you said you were on the left side of the road."

"I was. I waved at the people on the train and my bike turned off the pavement and right then the car came by and nicked my finger."

"You were clear off the road on the left side and it hit you?"

"Yes, but it didn't hit me; it just ticked me."

"But how? You're telling me the same car that hit Billy almost hit you?"

"Almost did."

"If it was on the left side of the road and hit you, how did it hit Billy?"

"After it passed me, Billy was right in front of him."

The sheriff thought a minute, then said, "You know, Paul, that driver must have gone to sleep, veered over to the left, woke up when he almost hit Mikey, then overcompensated for his mistake, and hit the other boy. He didn't see Billy in time."

Mikey was silent about that.

"Did he honk at Billy or anything?" the sheriff asked.

"I didn't hear anything, and I don't think Billy did because of the train."

The sheriff thought another minute. "Tell me what you remember about the car, son."

"It didn't stop after it hit Billy."

"What color was it?"

"Black."

"Old or new?"

"Brand new."

"How do you know?"

"It was real shiny and smelled new."

"Had you ever seen it before? Do you know who it belongs to?"

"No."

"Try to remember the car. Did it have a license plate?"

"I don't remember. The back was all black, except the bumper."

"What color was the driver's hair?"

"I didn't see a driver."

"How could the car hit your hand and you not see the driver?"

"It went by before I could see who was driving."

"Did you see the back of his head or anything?"

"No. All I could do was yell at Billy when I saw the car was going to hit him."

"What make of car was it? A Ford? A Chevy? A Studebaker? What kind?"

"I don't know."

"Would you know it if you saw it again? What else do you remember?"

"It was a new black car."

"What else?"

"It was going fast and I couldn't hear it," Mikey said.

A lady named Mary Bell came around the corner of the church carrying her Sunday hat and gloves. She was the aunt of one of Mikey's best friends in school. She lived on a ranch near Ruby where Paul had worked for the highway department. Paul had stayed with her family while he was on that job.

Paul and Mikey got out of the sheriff's car and Mary walked right up and smiled into Paul's eyes. "I bet you haven't even been to bed yet," she said.

"Michael Paul made his First Holy Communion this morning," Paul said.

"I was there. Congratulations," Mary Bell sang. She took Mikey's hand in both of hers and smiled sugar all over him. She was a good-looking woman, tall and brunette. She wore her hair in the same style as Maggie's, parted in the middle and wavy to her shoulders.

"You look so *handsome*, Michael Paul. Can I take you home with me?"

Mikey looked away and saw Maggie come out of Father Duval's residence. She beckoned and he headed back to her. As she waited for him, Maggie narrowed her eyes for a complete study of Paul and Mary, then turned and went into Father Duval's ahead of Mikey. In the vestibule she said under her breath, "My Lord, now he's with Mary Bell."

As soon as Maggie stopped the car back in Mikey's yard, he jumped out and ran to Billy's house. Maggie yelled at him to expect a whipping if he got his suit dirty, but she did not make him come back. She knew he wanted to show off the suit and tell Billy about his first confession and First Communion, if he was awake.

Billy had been taken straight home from the accident, but he was in a coma and had not even moved an arm in the two weeks since he was hit. Mikey ran to Billy's every day but was not allowed in the house. On the Sunday of his First Holy Communion he knocked and waited at the back door. A terrible silence smothered the Shanes'. The birds did not sing there. Uncle Bill's hens did not cluck and his roosters did not crow. Nina's flowers were dead in the sun. Mikey never went to the front door because Billy's bed was in the living room and most of the time the doctor was there. Nurses were stationed by his bed day and night. The cars on the highway even seemed to slip by and make no sound as they passed the Shanes'.

Nina was busier than usual with meals, laundry, and housework, but she was kinder than usual to Mikey and she had seen that he did not miss his final catechism instruction. He expected that he would get to see Billy that day because Nina had seen him through his communion ceremony and Father Duval's breakfast and did not seem worried about Billy. Billy seemed to be doing all right for a boy who broke almost every bone in his body.

He had suffered a fractured skull and broken his collarbone, ribs, arm, pelvis, leg, ankle, foot, and toes, all on the right side. He had not moved or made a sound since he was picked up off the pavement. Nina said that one tear formed in the corner of his eye when he was first brought into the house and she called his name and kissed him.

Mikey did not believe that Billy would die. Uncle Bill said that a coma was like a deep sleep. Nothing bad should come from it. The deeper the sleep, the better the waking. Billy would get well. Mikey did not even think to pray that he would come out of the coma, because none of the grown-ups told him the doctors worried that the coma was a sign that Billy's brain was dead.

More visitors than usual were in the house that day, but nobody came to the back door when Mikey knocked. Empty cars filled the driveway, but Mikey could not hear the voices of the people inside the house. He sat on the back step and listened to the ringing in his ears. After a while he felt that he was about to have another earache and went home.

Baxter came across the yard to meet Mikey in his humble little way. Maggie came out and herded Mikey and Baxter into the house. She doctored Mikey's ear with warm olive oil and put him down on her own bed with Maudy Marie for a nap. She sat at her kitchen table with a cup of coffee.

Dr. Gonzales advised Maggie that Mikey needed to be taken to a specialist in Tucson for better treatment on his ear. Maggie decided to ask for a leave of absence from the assessor's office. She would leave Maudy with Bica and Granny, take Mikey to Tucson, enroll in a six-week stenography course, and see that Mikey was cured of the ear trouble once and for all.

Mikey woke up from his nap with a full-fledged earache. Bica gave him peanut butter, melted butter, and honey on a hot flour tortilla and Maggie gave him eggnog with nutmeg on top and put him back to bed. He slept until midmorning on Monday when his little sister Maudy came to his bed, spoke his name softly, and took hold of his hand. He awakened and smiled.

"Hello, sister."

"*Maikeh, los angelitos llevaron a Beely,*" Maudy said. "The angels took Billy."

"No, Maudy, it was probably only the ambulance. Did the ambulance come while I was asleep?" Mikey spoke to her in Spanish. Maudy refused to understand English most of the time.

Maudy pulled Mikey out of bed and led him to the kitchen. Bica was crying so hard at the kitchen table that her nose ran and tears dripped off her chin. Maggie was washing pots and pans in the kitchen sink. She turned to Mikey and the corners of her mouth drooped in a small, quick spasm. She kept her hands in the water. "Well, Mikey, your best little friend died," she said.

Mikey went to stand at the picture window in the front room. Maudy still held his hand. Baxter lay under the elderberry tree and watched the highway. Bees hummed thickly in the tree and on Maggie's flowers. She had already watered the lawn and flowers and Mikey could smell their perfume. The heavy front door stood open. Maggie opened all the doors and windows every morning so the house would fill with cool air, then closed them before the sun took its grip on the yard and house. Mikey's throat swelled and hurt with sadness.

Car tires hummed quietly by on the highway, slowed, and turned in at the Shanes'. Mikey saw Uncle Bill Robinson and his wife Lydia go by. Uncle Art Robinson, the cowboy who had told Mikey about the tick in his ear, was in the backseat with them. They were Nina's brothers and sister-in-law. Uncle Art cowboyed near Patagonia. Uncle Bill owned a mercantile store in Nogales, Sonora, where a rancher could buy anything he needed. Aunt Lydia was beautiful and kind and could stop Mikey's heart with a look. He would get to see his Robinson uncles and Lydia now. The Carroon Mortuary hearse tooled by and turned into the Shanes' driveway and did not make enough sound to even drown the hum of the bees.

Mikey detached himself from Maudy, jumped into his overalls, and ran to the Shanes'. He stood behind Uncle Bill's hedge and watched a thick crowd of grown-ups mill in the Shanes' house and yard. Uncle Art watered Nina's wilted flowers. Uncle Bill Robinson fixed a piece of hardware that was needed in the house and carried it in. Doctors and nurses loaded cars with the para- phernalia that had been used in Billy's care. Men in suits clumsily bumped a stretcher as they carried it through the front door. Mikey ran to the back door and went in. The front room was packed with men. Uncle Bill lifted Billy off his bed and laid him on the stretcher.

Mikey could only see the top of Billy's head. Under the covers, he was as small and crumpled as he had been the day he was dashed to the pavement by the black car. His hair stuck out at dif- ferent angles through a bandage. After he was laid on the stretcher to be taken away, his hand dropped outside the covers as though it had come alive and wanted to stay behind. Nina's soft, clear *Aiii* was the only sound anyone made. Nobody else seemed to notice that Billy's hand had fallen out from under the covers.

The dead hand seemed smaller than Billy's everyday hand had been. Mikey could not see Billy's freckles on it. Billy's lines were all there in the hand. It made Mikey remember the essence of Billy. Billy's hands had grabbed a lot of boy business when they were alive; they had always been too busy to represent an ordinary boy's loveliness. Now that the hand had retired from Billy's business, it showed all the beauty Mikey remembered of his friend.

Neither boy had thought their boy-time adventures could get them killed. They played at being killed because play was not supposed to really get them killed. The hand belied the exploits of a wild person who took big risks with life and death. Being dead made it as small and hapless as a little kid's again.

A man in a dark suit placed Billy's hand on his chest, spread another blanket over him, and the stretcher men carried him out to the hearse. Some of the people boarded their cars to follow the hearse to Nogales. Mikey watched from Nina's dining room window. Aunt Lydia and Nina's sister Bea came in with Little Bea. Aunt Bea drew a glass of water and began to curl Little Bea's blond hair. Aunt Bea was nineteen, tiny and pretty with curly brown hair. She was another who could stop Mikey's heart with a look, but she did not leave him for dead the way Aunt Lydia did. He understood why Aunt Lydia could not stop for him and give him attention. Her three children were as full of mischief as Mikey. Bea was quick to smile and play with Mikey to keep him from crystallizing with admiration, and because of that they were pals. Bea was engaged to a man named Angel and she would go to live with him in Monterrey, Mexico. Mikey did not like it when Nina reminded him and teased him about that. She teased him because Mikey's hopes and yearnings always showed on his face.

Maggie put Maudy's shiny hair up in Shirley Temple curls every morning the way Aunt Bea did little Bea's. Mikey appreciated it when Maggie, Bica, or Granny gave his little sister attention. He thought she was the prettiest human on earth and he loved the way she looked at the world. She was never at odds with him, but she had more sense about stunts than he. She was brave enough to say that she was afraid if she did not want to take a risk. She also knew that being afraid was an acceptable excuse for a little girl to give in order to stay out of trouble.

Mikey sat on the couch with Billy's little brother Spike. Spike was a serious child and no crybaby. He was like Maudy, too smart to risk killing himself for a stunt, but fearless when he needed to do right. Even at the age of three, when he grew big enough to keep up with Mikey and Billy, he was strong enough to fend off criticism and stay out of the risk business. He could not be convinced that he should join in foolishness and would not be bullied. That day in Nina's front room Mikey realized that Spike already knew how to do right. He would never get himself run over by a car. Uncle Bill said that he would grow up to be an insurance man and be paid a lot of money by other people who did right and kept themselves away from accidents.

Uncle Bill was right about everything. He had predicted that although Africa was not nearby, Billy and Mikey would someday be trampled by elephants. He knew they would have done anything to go to Africa to swing in those trees and then the very worst finally happened only twenty bicycle lengths away from home. One of them finally got killed.

Mikey felt guilty to be alive and waited for his punishment. He and Billy had partnered in every adventure and every punishment that went with it. Now Billy had gone on to new adventures and Mikey was left alone to take the punishment. Any minute, some grown-up would turn to him and say, "Well, you were there and guilty of the same stunt. Billy is gone and we can't give him his whipping, but you are not. We held off because of your sorrow and ours, but we've had time enough for that. You, Michael Paul Summers, *are gonna get a whipping.*"

The Summers and Shane families were probably surprised that Mikey had not been killed, too. Now they could be certain he would be killed if he went on taking risks, so they probably intended to prevent it by warming his butt so it would not cool for the rest of his natural life.

The alternative to a whipping was too awful for Mikey to con-
template. What if they hated him for being the one still alive, or
did not care enough about him to tell Maggie to give him a loving
beating? What if they never looked at him again?

"*Ahijado*, godson, you have to go home now," Nina said. Her
face and hands were wet with tears. Mikey went home.

After Billy's rosary, wake, funeral Mass, and burial, Maggie
packed a suitcase, told Mikey to say good-bye to Granny, Bica,
Maudy, Baxter, and Pancho, loaded him in the car, and drove to
Tucson. They unloaded the suitcase and Maggie's potted plant at
the Kentucky Heights Boarding House at midnight and went to
bed. Maggie walked Mikey two blocks to a street corner the next
morning and put him on the bus for school. He was enrolled in
Saint Peter and Saint Paul's summer school because he had missed
so many classes that he had not passed second grade. She warned
him that he needed to remember the way to the corner because she
would not walk to the bus with him again.

Mikey had never even heard of Saint Peter and Saint Paul's
School. He got off the bus when it arrived on the playground, followed the other kids into the main building, and presented
Maggie's note to the first nun he saw. He was escorted to the
principal nun's office, questioned, escorted to the homeroom of
the second grade, deposited in a desk, and left for dead. He never
talked to another nun as long as he was there. He followed his
classmates outside at recess and back to class when recess was
over. He made friends with two tough Mexican *cuates*, twin boys,
and played with them at recess. He caught his bus after class and
found his way back to Kentucky Heights. He discovered the routine and began to learn. His classroom was half empty and most
of the other kids were there to have their rowdiness quelled by
the nuns. Nobody at Saint Peter and Paul's had ever heard of
Billy Shane.

After about a week Maggie took Mikey to see Dr. Smith, an
eye, ear, nose, and throat specialist. The doctor was dressed to the
floor in a stiff white gown, wore a round mirror on his forehead,
and eyeglasses with a magnifying scope attached. He did not say
more than "do this" and "do that" to Mikey and his magnified eye

was as cold as an aggie shooter. He made Mikey come back three times for examinations and his medicine did not ease the earaches. Each time he made an examination he poked a metal probe into Mikey's ear and scratched the sorest place. Finally, he told Maggie that Mikey had abscesses on his eardrum and they would have to be lanced. When Mikey heard that, he worried that an abscess must be some kind of fangy worm that was trying to eat into his brain and its ugly head with the fangs would have to be cut off. All doctors' treatments had only seemed to make the parasitical beast grind its teeth and chew on Mikey's eardrum more.

The next time Mikey went to the office, the doctor wore rubber gloves and a mask over his mouth. He motioned for the boy to sit, gripped the top of his skull, stuck a cold, metal blade into his ear, sliced, and then quickly turned Mikey's head so the ear could drain into a basin. Mikey's ear belched stuff into the basin and the inside of his head roared like the Nogales train. Maggie took one look and fainted against the wall. The doctor held him over the basin until clean blood came out, then turned his head up, swabbed out the ear, stuck him with the razor tool again, and the ear belched out more stuff. After a while, the doctor swabbed the inside of his ear with iodine.

A nurse revived Maggie with smelling salts and she stood up and took Mikey's hand to steady herself. The doctor told her to bring him back the next day and turned them both loose so they could lead each other by the hand and wobble home. They could do nothing but hold their heads the rest of the day.

During the next week the lanced abscesses dried up and disappeared, but the doctor squeezed Mikey into the chair again and lanced another abscess that had been hiding underneath them. This time Maggie went away to the Santa Rita Hotel for a cup of coffee so she would not faint in the doctor's office. When she came back, the doctor said that Mikey would probably not have to come back. Right then, Maggie decided to forfeit the money she had paid for the stenographer's classes and Mikey's summer school and take them both straight home to Nogales.

When Maggie and Mikey stepped out onto the hot pavement in front of the doctor's office, Maggie told him that she had a surprise for him. If he did not mind a little walk, he would get to see some people who would make him happy. She led him into the cool lobby of the Santa Rita Hotel.

Mikey was no stranger to that swanky place for cowboys. The Santa Rita was the meeting place in Tucson for cattlemen who bought and sold thousands of steers from the easy chairs in the lobby, and cowboys who were ripe for a bath, a soft bed, and a good time. When Mikey and Maggie walked in, his uncles Fred and Buster, and Joe and Roy Adams and his wife Helen were sitting in the lobby with tall, iced drinks in their hands. During a drinking party the week before, they had discussed the trouble Mikey suffered, had called Maggie at Kentucky Heights during the week, and had come to Tucson to see him. Roy and Helen had also arranged another large surprise.

Mikey's ear stopped hurting the minute he saw his illustrious uncles. The only remnant of the ear trouble that ever remained was a bright, pleasant ring in the ear that did not go away. He shook hands with his grinning uncles and withstood a big, lush hug to soft titties and a kiss that tasted of whiskey and lipstick from Helen.

"Well, the little old kid didn't even beller the first time that doctor lanced him in the ear, but I fainted," Maggie told them. "Let me tell you, if a doctor ever lanced that close to my brain, they'd hear my squall all the way to Yuma."

Mikey realized that he had not enjoyed a happy moment since he and Billy last wheeled their bikes out of Mr. Wingo's yard. Then the actor Tom Mix walked up and shook his hand. "Mikey," he said. "I've heard a lot about you and always wanted to meet you. I've been a friend of your dad and your uncles for a long time, and Roy and Helen told me that I would have a chance to meet you here today. I've heard you're the bravest and toughest of all the cowboys." He carried a box wrapped in string.

Mikey was surprised the actor was not pasty-faced the way he looked on the screen. His complexion was ruddy and healthy and his hair was as black as that of Mikey's Indian-looking uncles. He wore the same high-crowned Stetson, three-piece western suit, and tiny, polished boots as Mikey's uncles did. He sat next to

Mikey on a couch and asked about Pancho. He already knew stories about Mikey and Pancho in Mexico. He told Mikey that his horse Tony knew more about the movie business than he did. Tony knew that when the director shouted "action" it usually meant for him to go, and when he shouted "cut" it meant for him to stop. After a while the man untied the string on the box and brought out a new pair of fringed buckskin chaps. "Let's see how they fit you, cowboy," he said.

Mikey buckled them on and they fit down over his heel and instep as they should if he was to wear them on a horse. A wide cuff was sewn on the bottom so they could be let out when Mikey's legs grew longer. Mikey looked around and the whole family grinned at him.

"What do you say, son?" Maggie said.

"Thank you, Mr. Mix," Mikey said, and he shook hands with the man again. He hoped this did not mean that he would have to give away the pair of old chaps his Uncle Herb had given him when he was born. Uncle Herb's chaps were bull hide strong enough to turn away a herd of horns. Tom Mix's chaps were thin and soft as cotton and would not fend off a calf's kick, but his autograph was branded across one pocket.

"Call me Tom, Mikey. I want you to know, I wish that I was the one who first had the idea to give you those chaps, but I wasn't. Your Uncle Roy and Aunt Helen called me in Los Angeles last week when they found out I was on my way to Arizona and told me you'd been sick and asked if I could find you something from my studio's wardrobe. I think I was lucky to find a present you could use. Smell them."

They smelled of campfire smoke.

"The buckskin was cured, tanned, and sewn by an Apache Indian lady friend of mine who works in the wardrobe department at the studio."

"They're awful nice," was all that Mikey could say. His Uncle Joe stuck his hand out for Mikey to shake so he would know what to do. Mikey shook hands with everybody again.

He realized then that his uncles had known how downcast he had been from missing his dad, having the earache, and losing the bosom pal of his life. His uncles had arranged the meeting with Tom Mix so he would know a victory. Nobody but a bunch of cowboys would have known how lonesome he was. Paul Summers was the only one missing.

The meeting with Tom Mix might have been the greatest event in the life of any kid in the 1930s. Mikey told people about it from time to time, but he decided that Paul, Roy Adams, his uncles Buster, Fred, and Joe had every bit as much style as Tom Mix. They were all as tall or taller than the actor. Roy was a world champion calf roper. Mikey's uncles and Paul found more to laugh about in their own exploits than anybody else could find in a thousand jokes or a hundred movies. Mikey was absolutely sure that his dad could ride the hide off any bronc and rope and tie down any animal alive because he had seen him do it with one hand and a laugh.

Tom Mix was a nice man, but he was only important because he did a good job as a make-believe player of men like Mikey's dad and uncles. Even though Tom Mix started out as a real cowboy, he did not mature in those skills and now was given importance and a lot of money to act like a cowboy. Mikey did not think anybody in the world was more important than a real cowboy. Paul and Uncle Buster had an uncanny talent for getting cattle to do what they wanted them to do when the cattle thought they were sure to get away. That was cowboy. Tom Mix even wore his hats and boots like Mikey's dad and uncles; only they were handsomer and more stalwart than he. Even so, after that day, Tom Mix held an esteemed place in Mikey's heart because his gift was generous and cowboy splendid. He might have made a living in make-believe, but his heart seemed to be true cowboy. He certainly had become a good representative of the cowboy in the movies.

That evening, after a steak supper and many drinks, Tom Mix walked everybody out to the street to board their cars. Mikey and Maggie loaded in her car and she was the last to leave the curb. Tom Mix stood by himself in front of the Santa Rita. Mikey looked him in the eye and waved to him.

"So long, cowboy," the man said and waved back.

Mikey returned to his routine, but Billy was gone. Granny and Maggie had kept him on a routine since the day he was born, so he was comfortable with it. He hid in the routine from the specter of Billy's accident and did not cry for him. The load was too big to let go that way. He wanted help when he cried but was under orders not to cry. He had never grieved before, but he knew if he cried with the magnitude of his grief, he might not ever stop. This time, if he cried and was told to shut up, he would not make it.

Maggie was hired full-time as a clerk in the country assessor's office. All her money was gone, but Granny bought her a new Studebaker to drive to work. Mikey went back to school in the second grade at Lincoln. He was only there a week when Miss Lewis came for him and escorted him into third grade, which was taught by the beautiful Miss Ruth Gatlin.

Miss Gatlin was the sweetheart of another of Mikey's uncles, a cowboy named George Kimbrough, called El Zurdo, Lefty, by the Mexicans. Mikey was slow with arithmetic and Miss Gatlin often tutored him after school. George came on those days and took Miss Gatlin for a ride after he took Mikey home. George was a favorite of Granny's and often boarded with her. He was another cowboy who had been raised by Granny and Bert Sorrells. They had kept George with their own children since he was newborn.

Once Mikey asked Granny why George needed her to raise him and she said he was an orphan. That was when Mikey learned what an orphan was. Later, someone else in the family told him that George's mother was not dead; she had gone off and left him. Granny told that whole story in a way that did not sound true to Mikey. He knew that Granny did not want him to believe it, but she could not tell him the truth about it. Mikey's greatest fear was that someday his parents would go off and leave him. He felt a kinship with George because of that. Besides, George looked so much like his real uncles that he could have been their brother. Even the sound of his voice was the same. The shape of his nose and even the color of his eyes, the length of his legs, and the shape of his hands were the same as Maggie's brothers. He could have not been more like Mikey's uncles if he had been their twin.

Mikey was sad that whole year of third grade. Paul was in Mexico and Mikey knew better than anyone how absolutely lost to the world that could be. Maggie suffered from boils, one after another, under one arm and then the other, and she worked five days a week. Pancho was in Mexico with Paul.

Mikey did have his home and at least still owned his and Billy's haunts in which to roam, but he roamed little. Nina's house was wrapped in grief. His sweetheart Lorraine was gone and nobody would tell him where. Sweethearts were out of his life for no telling how long, maybe forever, now that Lorraine was gone, so he dismissed all sweethearts from his dreams. Now that he was in school and Maggie worked, he did not get to ride to town and sit in the car and watch the people go by. He was too big for that, anyway. He climbed his alamo, but he enjoyed no high, wild times up there anymore. He only climbed to its highest fork that would support his weight to be alone, secure, and undiscoverable. He did not look for faces and forms in the clouds anymore. He did not swing down from the top, either. Billy was not there to set the example and talk him into it, then appreciate his daring. Mikey waited to get some kind of hold on life again.

He did go to the shows with Granny on the weekends, played hard at school, and daydreamed. He was no great student, but he was clever enough to pass his tests. At home after school, he needed to daydream more. The Saturday and Sunday movies with Granny made daydreams better, especially the make-believe cowboy shows.

After the double feature on Saturdays, Granny would take Mikey to Walgreens or the Owl Drugstore for hamburgers and milkshakes. Then they would load back into the Pontiac and drive to the middle of Arroyo Street so Granny could hail the paperboys without getting out of her car. She made the boys run to her with the *Nogales Herald* and the *Nogales International* newspapers. She dug nickels and pennies out of her coin purse, snapped the purse shut, and paid them with penny tips. Granny's jewel-like little car tooled home at twenty miles per hour without a sound. The only place it ever went its entire life was three miles to Nogales and back. Granny would not even drive it the fifteen miles to Patagonia.

Mikey usually could not speak to anybody when he first came out of a movie. After a cowboy movie or a sentimental one about city people, he could not say a word for an hour. He savored what he had seen and heard in the theater of fathers, mothers, horses, dirt, dogs, cows, trees, grass, bosom pals, sweethearts, hats, boots, dust clouds, guns and gunfire, silver-mounted spurs, buckles, and saddles so much that afterward Granny sometimes watched him closely to see if he was all right.

He stopped using the elderberry tree for prayer and meditation. That tree made him sad. He had waited, yearned, and hoped in the elderberry too long for nothing. In spite of all the hours he perched there, his dad never came to get him and Billy never came out of his coma. Mikey cried too much on that perch, or he cried inside the house at the front window with his eyes on that tree with Baxter under it. In the year after Billy was killed, he climbed almost every day into the alamo as high as the limbs would hold him, lay in the fork with his back to the ground, and daydreamed.

He dreamed that he was a silver-mounted cowboy on his top horse Pancho with big silver buckles and conchos on his belts and spur straps. Even the bridle and reins on his horse were silver-mounted. The silver on his trappings made a rich buffing sound that silver only makes on silver when he buckled it on—a sound that only he knew. When he ran the silver tip of his belt through the buckle and then through the twin silver keepers, it released a spray of rich, sparky dust that only he could hear and see. His father and mother turned him loose but longed for his return. He was covered with dust from the work he did with large herds of cattle and horses. Baxter backed him up and licked his wounds when some cutthroat shot or stabbed him. In his favorite daydream, he watched himself brush and groom Pancho to a shiny blue, then he saddled him with a silver-mounted saddle and rode into the brush by the arroyo. He waited patiently in ambush for the school bus. When it came, Mr. Clark saw that Mikey was not at his place beside the road, so he drove on. Mikey spurred Pancho into a run out of the brush, fell in behind the bus, and boarded through the back door. He was so tall that he ducked his head inside to keep from denting the crown of his hat. Lorraine gave him the old I'm-your-only-woman look, so he leaned over and kissed Enriqueta on the mouth. That was so Lorraine would know he did not need her darned I'm-your-only-woman looks anymore. Well, he could still daydream sweethearts, but he was now only a make-believe cowboy with only Tom Mix, Hopalong Cassidy, Buck Jones, Ken Maynard, Johnny Mack Brown, and Roy Rogers to admire. Except for George Kimbrough, those were the only kind he ever saw anymore. Then Viv O'Brien came to call on Maggie.

NINE

ONE GILLETTE

A cowboy's job is to see that his charges "do good." He wants to see herds of "good doers." When an animal has been left to rest and recuperate on his own all night after a day of being driven or ridden hard and a cowboy finds him full bellied, rested, and ready to go to work the next morning, he is a good doer. When a cowboy can work all day on one can of tomatoes and no water and no salt, he is known as a good doer. In praise of a cowboy who is a good doer, it will also be said that he can go all day on one Gillette.

Viv O'Brien was taken with Mikey's little sister Maudy Marie. He liked to stop by on his way to someplace else to see his "Curly Girl." Maggie did not like for him to come to her house with no warning, so he was told that he had better call so she and Maudy could make themselves presentable before he arrived. After that he came regularly. He was plainly lonesome, infatuated with Maudy Marie, and seemed to enjoy visiting with Maggie and Mikey.

Mikey and Viv got along well after Viv reminded him that he was raised with Paul Summers in Pecos, Texas, and considered Paul to be the best cowboy who ever buckled on a pair of chaps. He also said that his partners Roy Adams and Herb Cunningham bragged all the time that Mikey was as good a cowboy as any grown man they ever hired. He began to stop by the Lincoln School from time to time to eat lunch with Mikey and he sometimes picked him up after school and took him home. He said he would soon have a bunch of cowboying for Mikey to do. As an advance against his wages, one afternoon he took Mikey to Brackers Department Store and outfitted him with a new hat, boots, Levi's, and a blue shirt. He wanted to be sure he could depend on Mikey's help. He intended to cross several thousand steers out of Mexico, and he wanted Mikey to help drive them from Nogales, Sonora, to the Baca Float Ranch outside Nogales, Arizona.

One Saturday, Granny and Mikey came home from a double feature and found Pancho back in his pasture. He had grown into much of a horse while he made a hand for Paul in the Sierra de San Juan. To Mikey, this meant that Paul would come for him any day. Viv O'Brien would have to wait. Mikey had not worn the outfit Viv bought him since he tried it on in the store. He fed and exercised Pancho to keep him in condition for the day that Paul would come for him with work to do. Pancho needed to be calmed down. His new way was to show the whites of his eyes when he looked at people, as though he were anxious about the burden someone might load on him.

One day, as Mikey filled Pancho's tub with water from the hose, he looked up and saw the faces and horns of a big herd come around the Nogales curve. Boy, he could not let anything like that go by. He bridled Pancho, jumped barefoot on his back, and rode him out to the front of Granny's house to protect her lawn and flowers.

Roy Adams and Viv O'Brien came along in a pickup behind the drags. Felix Johnson, Manuel Valenzuela, Uncle Buster Sorrells, Grover Kane, Bud Parker, and George Kimbrough were horseback with a herd of eighteen hundred Mexican steers that belonged to Adams, Cunningham, and O'Brien.

As the herd passed, Mikey fell in behind it to help in the drags and look for Paul. When he did not see him, he asked Roy where he was, but Roy said Paul had stayed in Mexico with Cabezon Woodell and Del Mercer. Roy and Viv had bought the herd from Cabezon. Mikey did not know it, but the Adams, Cunningham, and O'Brien Cattle Company owned Pancho. Paul had been with Cabezon's crew at the stockyards in Magdalena when the cattle were delivered and had sold Pancho and Cognac to Roy, and then went straight to the cantina with the money. Uncle Buster had met the herd in Nogales and hauled Pancho with a supply of hay and grain for his keep to Maggie's. Pancho was at Maggie's for Mikey to ride, but he was not Mikey's anymore.

Viv and Roy stopped the pickup in the shade of a big tree and began to call the cowboys for lunch. Mikey saw that the pickup was the old one that belonged to Paul, the one he had driven for years, the same pickup Mikey had hoped to see when he waited at the arroyo bridge all day, the truck Paul owned when he worked as a jailer in the courthouse.

Roy called Mikey for lunch.

"Where's Paul?" Viv asked and feigned an abrupt and unsmiling way. Mikey knew this was a sham. Viv knew where Paul could be found a whole lot better than Mikey. He asked for Paul in that way because he knew Mikey liked to have his father's name brought up.

"I don't know," Mikey said. "When I saw you in his pickup, I thought you would know where he was."

"Paul brought this herd down out of the Sierra and delivered it to Roy, but he sold his truck to me and went back." Viv said. "We need him here, don't you think?"

Mikey sat his horse and nodded. Viv pointed to a pile of bread, jam, cheese, open cans of sardines and Vienna sausages and said, "What do you crave, boy? Eat your lunch."

Mikey jumped down and took an open can of tomatoes, a spoon, and some crackers and squatted underneath Pancho to eat. Canned tomatoes could be both meat and drink to a cowboy when nothing else was handy. Pancho stood over him and dozed. His whiskers poked Mikey on the back of the neck. One hour with Mikey on a herd and he was gentle as a kid horse again.

Mikey figured Paul was probably down in Mexico craving a drink, now that he'd sold his pickup. Later, he found out that every cowboy on the drive had seen Paul when he delivered the herd at Magdalena.

Mikey remembered when he learned what "crave" meant. He had asked Paul why he drank so much even though he knew it caused so much hurt. Paul looked him in the eye and said, "I crave it, son. It's a craving I have." Mikey understood the word without explanation because he recognized the famished edge in his father's look.

Mikey knew a craving or two himself. He already knew how much a person could crave a drink of mezcal for his tired body and mind as he rode the trail home in the evening. He craved the risk of his life when he launched himself into space on a swing. He craved to be close inside his father's reach, close enough to smell his whiskey breath. That sure would be sweet to know again.

Mikey loved canned tomatoes but did not crave them. He loved pan de huevo with café con leche with his Nina after Sunday Mass, but they did not stretch the cords of his being to satisfy a craving. He loved his Granny's bland mashed potatoes and gravy and bland boiled carrots served on her blue china with Chinese birds above Chinese trees; albóndiga soup; fried steak; potatoes and gravy and sweet peas; horseshoe-sized pancakes with molasses and bacon; a glass of cold, raw milk; eggnog; and peanut butter sandwiches with jam or honey or mayonnaise, but he craved to ride Pancho and cowboy with Paul Summers and did not think of meat or drink when he could do it.

Mikey was given plenty to eat because Maggie was a good provider. Last Thanksgiving she was broke but able to provide a fat hen for their dinner. Granny would have provided a turkey, but she went off to California to be with her brother Fred and his family. Maggie headed home Wednesday night after work without a bird for Thanksgiving. She always drove too fast. As she passed the Morales's Mariposa Dairy a rooster chased a plump little hen up out of the bushes by the side of the road. The hen came out looking back at the rooster, and when she saw the car she did not change course, but widened her eyes at Maggie and flew up as high as she could. Maggie said that she could tell by the look in the hen's eyes that she would rather take her chances at overflying Maggie's hurtling car than turn back and be caught by the rooster.

Maggie did not have time to stop or swerve. The hen whacked against the top of the car's grill, stretched her wings straight out in front of her to break her fall like a diver who at the top of her dive discovered no water in the pool, folded into a bunched mass as she struck the windshield, and rolled over the top of the car. Maggie stopped to pick her off the highway and to see if she was still alive. Maggie saw that she was cow-killed and felt the warm, clean tallow of the leg under her thumb, got in her car quickly, dropped the hen on the floorboard, looked straight ahead, and drove home. She got out of the car with the hen at the woodpile, saw her blink an eye, chopped off her head, was glad to see she bled well, then held her away so she would not bleed on her new high-heeled pumps and silk stockings.

Maggie's story of the Mariposa Dairy hen that she stole for Thanksgiving dinner got funnier every time she told it, and she could always bring it up as a remedy for desperation in the family. Everybody had been feeling desperate lately except Maudy Marie. Maudy was like Granny; she figured life could only stay good as long as she did not have to work desperately to make it so.

After lunch Viv and Roy drove up close behind the herd and Roy told Mikey to give him his horse and board the truck with Viv. Roy then swung up on Pancho's bare back and rode into the drags. His legs were so long, his feet almost dragged the ground.

Mikey climbed in beside Viv and smelled his father's sweat again. He watched Roy laugh and joke with Felix Johnson as though he enjoyed being down close to a herd in the dust again.

"Now, highpockets, do you want to work for me?" Viv asked.

"Yes, I do," Mikey said.

"What kind of wages do you get?"

"I don't often get paid wages."

"No? Wouldn't you rather be paid? You're too good a hand to work for nothing. You work for me, I want to pay you. How would that be?"

"All right."

"Oh, that'd be all right. Well, I'm glad that'd be all right. What kind of money are we talking about?"

"I don't know."

"How old are you, Mikey, eight? How come you don't know how much you're worth?"

"I just don't."

"And what? Don't care?"

"I care, but I haven't thought about it."

"Well, think about it. What are you worth?"

Mikey wanted to cowboy, but he would not argue about pay. "You don't have to pay me," he said. "I'll work as a favor to you. I've always done it that way."

"Well, son, I admit you're awful young to hold down a paying job and somebody else might not want to pay you because you're little, but not me. You're as good a hand horseback as any man who works for me, even better than some, so I'm going to pay you ten dollars a drive. You can help drive the saddlehorses from the Baca Float to the pens across the line the day before every drive, then make each cattle drive back to the Baca Float. How does that sound?"

"Fine."

"Okay, and as a bonus, you'll own Pancho after ten drives."

Money talk perplexed Mikey and ownership did not concern him because he owned so little, but he knew he already owned Pancho and Baxter. He did not imagine how anyone could be so mistaken as to try to lay claim to Pancho.

Viv must have read the look on his face because he said, "What are you thinking, that Pancho is already yours?"

"No, you just probably didn't know that he's always been my horse," Mikey said.

"You're wrong, Black Man. Pancho belongs to Adams, Cunningham, and O'Brien. Roy bought Pancho from Paul at the same time that I bought the truck in Magdalena."

Mikey was silent for a long time. Viv did not press the subject or say anything against Paul. Mikey was to learn that Viv always handled a situation that involved the boy's hurt feelings by giving a practical solution to it, or he would bring up another problem that needed to be solved. He liked to bring a problem out in the open, solve it quickly and frankly, write it off, and go on to new business. He did not consider feelings to be an obstacle that should slow a man from doing his day's work.

"Now," Viv said, "we need to get a few things straight before you come to work for this outfit, is that all right?"

"Sure," Mikey said.

"Let me ask you this. How do you recognize someone who might be a cowboy when you first lay eyes on him?"

"I guess, by his hat and boots."

"Would you know a cowboy just by the way he wears his hat?"

"I think I would."

"How about the way you're dressed? If boots and a hat made a cowboy you'd sure come up short today. Where's the outfit I bought so you'd be ready to go to work when the outfit needed you?"

"I didn't even know the herd was on the way until it came around the Nogales curve. Nobody told me anything. I couldn't have made you a hand if I'd waited to saddle my horse and put on my cowboy outfit."

"What were you doing bareheaded and barefooted? Were you playing in the trees again like a monkey?"

"No, when the herd came around the curve, I was watering my horse."

"Well, doesn't this help you understand something about people?"

"Yes."

"I don't think you do, so, to be sure, let me tell you what I think. Not everybody who dresses like a cowboy is one. Not everybody who doesn't dress like a cowboy isn't one. Not everything a man says he owns is always his.

"Be that as it may, if you want to be a cowboy and do the work, you better wear the outfit. If you're going to do a man's work, you have to wear the boots so you can at least get down off your horse and open a wire gate in a hurry if you have to. You have to wear a man's hat so the sun won't cook your brain before the day's work is done. You need to wear a long-sleeved shirt so all the hide won't sunburn off your arms. You understand what I'm telling you? If you got sunstroke or the hide sunburned off your arms and face, I'd have to leave the job and take you home to your mama. Our crew would lose its two best men because you didn't wear your long-sleeved shirt and hat and boots. Understand?"

"Yes," Mikey said. He figured Viv must not know about all the cowboy work he had already done on Pancho in Santa Cruz County and the Sierra de San Juan. All Viv could see was a bareheaded kid who liked to play. Mikey had thought he would only take a few minutes to help with the herd. He only considered himself provisional help for an hour or two that day. By trying to make a hand and plugging a hole when he saw he was needed, he had only made himself look bad.

"Good. I'll say one thing," Viv went on. "You're damned tough to ride all day barefooted and bareheaded on one can of tomatoes and six saltine crackers. When you grow up you'll be one of those guys they say can go all day on one Gillette," meaning he'd been given about as much as one razor blade's shave to sustain him, yet he'd been called upon for a month's energy. One Gillette blade was only good for so long, then it was only good to throw away.

Mikey smiled and Viv patted him roughly on the shoulder. The boy liked Viv O'Brien a whole lot better now that he could be certain the hats and boots that Viv had bought him were not a bribe so the man could get close to Maggie. Every cattle human in Santa Cruz County knew that Mikey wanted to cowboy, so people were always telling him they would come and get him and give him a job with their cattle for one reason or another. Mikey would never in a hundred years have believed that Viv would keep his promise and give him all this good work.

Now Mikey believed he was finally on his own with the right outfit. Roy Adams and his Uncle Buster had probably promised Paul they would put Mikey to work to keep him busy in the family where he could be watched and trained. Uncle Buster was up ahead pointing the herd away from the houses and yards. He was sober that day and not clowning as he did when he worked with Paul. He seemed to be there for the pure joy of doing his job. He was a good clown but a better cowboy any day.

Mikey appreciated all the good people on the drive. Manuel Valenzuela was on point across the herd from Uncle Buster. Everything from the spurs on his heels to the jacket on his shoulders was scuffed, fit him as well as his old hat, and it all fit well on his horse. Manuel was always glad to see Mikey and Pancho, but the containment of eighteen hundred cattle as they tromped past houses and lawns and barking dogs did not give him much time to grin and say hello. Only the cowboys in the drags were able to visit with each other.

Grover Kane, Jim Kane's son, was there. Mikey hung close to Grover any time he could be with him. He was fifteen and already made a living as a cowboy. He would go to Wyoming to work on a wagon for a big outfit that summer. He would leave home with his bed and saddle and live outside until the outfit's cattle were branded, weaned, and shipped in the fall.

George Kimbrough was there and when he rode up and fell in step beside Uncle Buster, Mikey could not tell them apart. Bud and Dink Parker were two more of Paul's best friends that Mikey called "Uncle."

Viv O'Brien was the only one on the drive who was not an absolute bosom pal of Paul's. He liked to talk about how he knew Paul when they were kids in Pecos, but he did not love Paul the way the other cowboys in the crew did. Paul's buddies told stories about Paul Summers all the time and when it was Viv's turn he could only say that Paul was a year older, had been in a lot of mischief as a child in Texas, and had boarded a trainload of cattle for Arizona when he was twelve.

Mikey understood from the way Viv talked that he was from a better class of Irish than Paul. His people had come from the same part of Northern Ireland as Paul's, but Paul was from shanty Irish poor people. Viv's people had never been poor.

Mikey only knew that Paul's grandparents came from Ireland, and his father was an Irishman. His mother was an Adams, sister to Roy Adams's father. Paul was Irish from his mother because her mother was a Coyle, but he was Irish and Comanche from his grandfather's side. Maggie would not listen when Paul and Roy talked about their Comanche blood.

In those days, only people as reckless and don't-give-a-damn as Paul and Roy ever admitted their Indian blood. The Sorrells never did. The Sorrells were from Ireland too, but down the line they moved West and married Cherokees. They did not admit it for 150 years. Admitting their Indian blood was something Americans who lived in Apache country did not do. How could they admit they owned the blood of the murdering enemy Apache? When other Sorrellses from Houston contacted Maggie and told her they owned head rights on the Cherokee nation, Maggie asked Grandma Melvina about it. Grandma said, "Oh, those Texans are other Sorrellses." Grandma Melvina and Maggie looked more Indian than Irish. All of Grandma Melvina's Parker family showed their Indian blood but would not admit it either.

"Black Man, you savage little shit," Roy Adams once said when Mikey made a run so reckless that both his and Pancho's eyes watered. "You got to be more careful. People will be able to tell you're *Comanch* and find us all out."

Mikey did not like to be called an Indian, so he answered, "I'm not a Comanch, Uncle Roy. My mama says that Paul's a flannel-mouth Irishman and she's quality French and Irish."

Roy laughed. "Yeah, I'll tell that to your Granny Summers and her father the chief. I'll tell your Granny Summers's blanketass brother that he can't braid his hair anymore."

A few weeks later, Mikey was alone with Roy in the pickup behind another herd and asked, "Are you my blood kin, Uncle Roy?"

Roy Adams was as honest a man as Mikey would ever know. He said, "Black Man, I'm your daddy's *primo hermano*. That means to the Mexicans that I'm a first cousin brother of your father, because my father and your daddy's mother were brother and sister. In Mexico I would be your uncle. If we lived in Boston, I'd be your second cousin."

"You're my own flesh and blood, then and we've always been family, haven't we, Uncle Roy?"

"We sure have, Black Man."

Mikey decided he'd better get one more fact cleared up about Uncle Roy. "Is it true you robbed a bank back there in Texas where you and my daddy are from?"

"Who told you that, Black Man?"

Mikey's Nina had heard it from Uncle Bill Shane, who was customs service but also Texan. Mikey was listening when Nina told Maggie. Mikey always eavesdropped when Maggie and Nina talked. Ninety percent of their private conversations were about him, anyway.

"Nobody told me. I heard my mama talking."

"Well, young sir, I hope you don't go around telling people everything your mama says."

"Did you rob a bank, Uncle Roy?"

"If I'd done anything like that, don't you think I'd have to hide?"

"Would the rangers come after you if you did?"

"They sure would. The worst kind of rangers, the damned *Texis* Rangers."

"I guess you would have to hide."

"You don't see me hide during the day and come out to water at night, do you?"

"No."

"Then don't worry about that and don't carry tales. Somebody might believe you and cause trouble."

"I won't."

"I mean, you sure ought not to tell that story about me robbing a bank to anyone anymore."

"I think I'd like it if you robbed a bank."

"Well, I don't want you or anybody else to believe I'm a bank robber because a robber is a criminal. If I get that reputation, I won't be able to do business in these steers, or have any fun, or anything."

"But you were a world champion calf roper, weren't you?"

"You're darned tootin' I was."

"And you won it on your old horse Clabber who is down in the pasture at the Baca Float?"

"You double-barreled darned tootin'."

"I know because I saw that picture on Aunt Helen's fireplace mantle that was taken of you when you won the world champion calf roping at Cheyenne."

"Why do you say it's Aunt Helen's fireplace? I live there, too."

"You do?"

"Of course I do. Your Aunt Helen is my wife; that's why you call her Aunt Helen."

"Well, that's not what Aunt Helen says."

Roy laughed. "What does she say?"

"She says you don't live there. Everything in that house is hers, and she's gonna sell it and move to New York because you won't bother her in New York."

"Why does she say that?"

"She said you wouldn't ever go to New York unless to rodeo in a garden and she darned sure wouldn't have a garden."

Roy really laughed at that. "No, Mikey, that rodeo in the garden she told you about is in Madison Square Garden, a big indoor arena where cowboys rodeo in the wintertime."

"Oh."

"Your Aunt Helen lied if she said she'd never go to the Garden for a rodeo. She would no more be able to stay away from a rodeo that I was in than you would be able to stay away from old Pancho."

"She sounds like she doesn't love you anymore."

"Well, she does, but she gets perturbed at me from time to time."

"She won't divorce you like Maggie divorced my dad?"

"Naw, your Aunt Helen likes to brag that she's going to divorce me so your mama won't feel so bad about divorcing your dad."

"Does Maggie feel bad about divorcing my dad?"

"I bet she does, or she wouldn't complain about him to Helen all the time."

"I wish she'd let him come home. This is getting to be too much."

Mikey believed that everybody wanted Maggie to take Paul back. Why else would she tell Mikey to ask his friends to come visit? Why did she want Mikey to hang out with Paul's cowpuncher friends? Why did she ask Mikey if he had seen his dad every time he came home from a drive?

Mikey watched for his dad. Maggie could not take him back if he never came home. Mikey looked for him in every car that carried big hats. He never knew what kind of hat to look for because

Paul was hard on hats. He bought a new one to wear in town at the end of a season and wore it into complete disrepair the next season.

Mikey's world almost collapsed one day when he found out that Grover Kane went out drinking with Paul in Nogales, Sonora, the night after that first drive when Mikey rode bareback on Pancho. Not only was Grover so privileged, but also Roy, Uncle Buster, and the rest of the crew had all gone back to meet Paul in Nogales, Sonora, after the drive.

Grover had enjoyed a high old time with Paul but did not have the guts to tell Mikey about it. Mikey learned it from Manuel Valenzuela. Manuel was devoted to his family and did not go to cowboy parties across the line. Mikey decided he was glad he had bawled so long and so loud at Grover's dad's funeral.

Every once in a while somebody would come up to Mikey and say, "Well, well, look at you, Michael Paul. Boy, you sure have grown. I remember how you bawled at Jim Kane's funeral. Started bawling before the preacher got up to talk and drowned out the whole testimonial. I left early and the town was empty because everyone was in the church, but I could hear you bawl all the way out of town. Usually a body laid out for his funeral could expect to hear his mourners sing 'Red River Valley,' or 'Home on the Range,' or 'La Golondrina,' but all Jim Kane must have heard was Michael Paul Summers bawl 'til he slobbered."

Mikey was only about a year old when Jim Kane died. It seemed to Mikey that everybody who was at that funeral and some who were not even there told the same story. They all had left early and heard Mikey bawl all the way out of town. Mikey figured he must finally have been the only one left in the church to mourn because every other son of a gun left early.

Then one day, after the herd was delivered to the Baca Float, Viv O'Brien sent Mikey home with Grover. Mikey had not talked to Grover since he found out Paul had partied with him in the Sonora bars.

"Where did you go on that *parranda* with my dad?" Mikey asked Grover.

"Mikey, we were in and out of every bar in Nogales, Sonora," Grover said.

"How did my dad look?"

"Like a happy cowboy."

"Did he sing songs?"

"He sang 'Panchita' and he got the mariachis to play 'Cuatro Milpas.'"

Those were Paul's favorite songs, those and "La Potranca."

"What other songs?"

"He had them play 'La Potranca' three or four times."

Paul's betrayal of his family was true, then. Maggie was La Potranca to everybody in Santa Cruz County. So Paul Summers was now so lowdown that he could spend Maggie's support money on mariachis and bawl out her song in the gutter, but he could not spare an hour to visit his family. Paul's favorite father-like statement to Mikey was, "I've never let you down, son. That's one thing I'll never do."

"Who else was there?" Mikey asked.

When Grover answered, every name that fell out of his mouth became Mikey's enemy for life. He would make his uncles sorry they thought they could run and play with Paul Summers and keep him away from his family.

Then one day, after the herd was delivered at the Baca Float, Roy Adams dropped Mikey and his outfit off at his house and Viv's car was in Maggie's driveway. Viv came out the back door when Mikey laid an armload of his gear on the stoop. Mikey went back to the highway to carry in the rest of his outfit and Viv went with him to help. He said he admired Mikey's bed and saddle, chaps and spurs, but advised him to get rid of that reata and tie a manila rope hard and fast to his saddle horn to save his fingers. Mikey had never roped with anything but a reata.

Viv said Maggie and Maudy had gone away to take Bica across the line to visit her folks. Granny had gone to town to play the slot machine at the Elks Lodge. Viv helped Mikey stow his outfit on the back porch, then dished him up a bowl of albóndigas from a pot on the stove. He could not be still. After Mikey was finished eating, he asked him to come into the front room to talk.

Viv sat down and opened his arms to give Mikey a hug and then just sat him on his knee. Mikey was not used to that. Not that he did not like Viv's show of affection, but the man ordinarily kept Mikey at arm's length and the boy was not one to sit on anyone's knee. He did not remember *ever* sitting on anyone's knee except Nina's. He had been known to sit on his Nina's lap because there was just no denying her when she decided to give affection. She was a lavisher, a splasher-on of love, a grabbing hugger and a smoochy kisser with plenty of wet, but Mikey was not a sitter for anybody else's knee. He decided he could remain there a moment for Viv, but he did not like it.

"Michael Paul, you and I have become good friends, don't you think?" Viv asked.

Well, that could be true, so Mikey said yes.

"And of course you know that I love your little sister as though she was my own child."

Mikey looked way off.

"Because of that and because your mother and I care a whole lot for one another, well, son, we drove to Lordsburg last week and got married."

All Mikey understood from this was that Viv would not be one to help Maggie and Paul get back together, after all. Viv had not been coming around to help Paul. Instead, Mikey would have to live with this man and that would make it hard for him to see his dad. Viv was as different from Paul as a draft horse was from a bronky cowhorse, as different as any cattleman, businessman, trader, or speculator was from a reckless cowboy who did not care about anything in God's world except how he could use his life to see if it would come apart.

Mikey did not think Paul did right with his life, but he wanted to grow up to be a Paul Summers with the styles of Roy Adams, Buster Sorrells, and Viv O'Brien all thrown in. One of the qualities he liked about Viv was that he could show open admiration for another man like Paul who was so different from him. Another of his good traits was that he was a high-dollar speculator on cattle, but he also was compassionate with the thousands of animals under his charge, and he did not skimp on their care. He was not one to pet his horses or give names to his cows, but he made sure animals did not know cruelty after he became their owner. However, he wasn't don't-give-a-damn enough for Mikey.

Mikey kept a seat on Viv O'Brien's knee, but this was too much of a difference in the way the man usually treated him for him to like it as, he guessed, he was supposed to like it. Mikey knew Viv's real love was for Maudy. He had never shown that he loved Maggie enough to want to marry her. He did not hold Maggie on his knee, so that knee was the last place on earth Mikey thought he should be.

Then the man said, "Mikey, you need a father and I need a son, so from now on I'm going to be your dad."

Mikey stepped down off the knee and faced him.

"No, you're not," he said. "Paul Summers is my dad."

A kind of tender, hopeful light went out of Viv O'Brien's eye and never came back for Mikey again.

TEN

EXILE

When a cowman ships the yearly increase of his cattle, he feels relief that the load on the feed in his pastures has been lightened, a crop has been harvested, and his herd and family have been preserved. Even so, he hates to see his charges go. He has taken care of them for a lot more than the money. When the loaded trucks leave his pens, he almost always takes one more look to see if he can recognize a face in the bunch and wish it good-bye.

The decision to send Mikey to Saint Michael's College in Santa Fe was made long before he ever heard of the place. He thought he would go back to Lincoln School. A week before classes started at Lincoln, Maggie drove him to Nogales in Viv's new blue car and bought him school clothes.

Mikey wondered at the quantity and quality of the clothes. For Lincoln School, he never started the year with more than one new pair of Levi's, one pair of corduroys, three dress shirts, one sweater, one pair of everyday shoes, and a jacket. This time,

Maggie bought him a half dozen of almost everything plus a warm cap, mittens, earmuffs, towels, washrags, toilet articles, two neckties, and a three-piece suit. The earmuffs gave off a highly expensive new smell that made Mikey think that Fast Paul's family had sure found prosperous new management.

Mikey and Maggie returned home with two new suitcases full of clothes. The suitcases were not explained, but Mikey knew that things like that were used to ship people away from home. He got real quiet, could not look at Maggie or speak to her, and began to look at everything else as though it might be for the last time. He had been condemned and he did not know why he deserved it.

He tried on all the new clothes to be sure they fit and did not let himself wonder why Maggie folded them and put them back in the suitcases. He went outside and climbed up on the fence to sit with Pancho at the corner post. Granny opened her back door and gave him a solicitous look. Maggie asked Granny if she wanted to come over and see Mikey's new clothes and luggage.

"No, I won't go over there, for I don't want my grandson to think that I've had a part in your dirty tricks," Granny said. "I bet you still haven't told him what you plan to do with him."

Maggie glanced quickly at Mikey to see if he understood, but Mikey looked away and pretended that he had not heard his Granny. Saint Michael's had been mentioned plenty during the past few days, but only as a place of exile. Maggie had used Saint Michael's as a threat to keep him in line, but he did not want to believe that she truly meant to send him there. He stayed in line to be sure that she knew he did not want to be sent away, but now he felt that he would have to go anyway. He asked himself how Maggie could do something that would make him realize his worst fear. He had not been surprised when she threatened him with Saint Michael's because she was always mean enough to make big threats and knew how much he feared being sent away. Could she send him clear out of sight as she had done Paul for being a drunk? No....Yes, the suitcases and new clothes were proof that she was mean enough for that.

When Mikey realized that he would probably be sent up to Saint Michael's he decided to pull off the one great stunt that he and Billy had always wanted to pull: to plummet out of the alamo and swing over the highway and terrorize an enemy so badly he would wreck his car. He and Billy had imagined ways to perform the stunt but had been thwarted by its magnitude. Mikey would have to do it now, or it would probably never be done. Since he had lost Viv's friendship and backing, his whole world might be lost.

Before he died, Billy had confided to Mikey that he wanted to get even with one person by scaring him so badly he would have a wreck. Mr. Karns who owned and managed the Karns Swimming Pool had banned Billy for life for running recklessly on the wet cement that surrounded the pool and for bouncing on the high diving board in a suicidal manner. Mr. Karns also owned an orchard only a quarter mile down the road from Billy's house. He visited his orchard every evening at five o'clock and he sicced his dogs on Billy every time he came near the ripening fruit in his trees.

Mr. Karns sicced the dogs on Mikey, too, but Mikey did not hold it against him. Billy had hated Mr. Karns so much he wanted to scare him into having a stroke or heart attack. Billy had thought if he swooped down out of a tree on him as he drove peacefully down the road, he might at least *crystallize* him so he would lose control of his car.

Mikey decided that as the surviving daredevil he was honor-bound to perform his and Billy's dream stunt on Mr. Karns. In order for the stunt to work, Mikey needed to tie the swing rope to a slender limb fifty feet above the highway. For Mr. Karns to suffer substantial fright, he would have to come driving down the highway with his thoughts on the sweet fruits of his orchard and all of a sudden look up and see Mikey fall from a great height straight into his face.

On the day after Maggie bought Mikey the two suitcases and extra school clothes, at about four thirty in the afternoon, he climbed with the end of the rope to the highest branch that would hold him. He had rehearsed the details of the stunt in his mind but had not imagined the awful height and distance he would have to command. The branch from which he needed to tie his grandfather's manila rope was only as big around as his arm. The rope was forty feet long and its end dangled ten feet above the ground. He hauled up the rope and tied a knot in the bottom end. He held it and climbed down to a limb in the center of the tree, sat down, and looked at the several feet of slack on the end and waited for the nerve to do the stunt. He and Billy had thought about using this starting point before, but it was so high and in a part of the tree so unknown that they had both been afraid to try it.

Now that he was in position and had taken the steps to accomplish the stunt, his legs were so shaky that he knew he would not be able to stand until the stunt was over. He might not even be able to push his butt off the limb. Even the fabric of his trousers seemed to take a death grip on the limb. He was so scared his spit dried up. The theory and planning stage was over. Performance was imminent. His bowels turned cold. He looked down at the ground, tried his grip with both hands around the rope above the knot, saw how far he would drop before he took up the slack, and was almost sure that if the fall did not tear the rope from his grasp, the green limb that anchored the rope in the top of the tree would bow with his weight and break.

Then, all of a sudden, terrified as he was, he knew he would do it. A breeze moved the whole tree around him. A thrill went through his gizzards. He could not back down. Billy Shane watched. Mr. Karns was due any minute. If Michael Paul Summers sat there like a coward and watched him go on by, his courageous friend Billy Shane would look down from heaven and call him a chickenshit, something he had never done when he was alive.

Bica came out the back door with clothes to hang on the line and this almost spurred Mikey off the limb to show off. All he needed to do was holler for her to watch and he would have to go, but he did not do it. Bica would be dealt such a fright that she would tell on him and put an end to the whole sashay.

Then, Lord of all Lords, Mr. Karns's new Studebaker tooled around the Nogales curve toward him. It was about the same color as Maggie's car, but Mikey imagined that Maggie's was a year or two older.

The sight of the car sent a thrill from Mikey's toes to the roots of his hair. Nothing, not fear, not conscience, threats of Saint

Michael's, or the anger and disapproval of Viv and Maggie could stop him from piling his and Billy's enemy into the ditch below the tree. The ghost of Billy Shane sat on the limb beside him and strengthened his hold on the rope.

"Bica, watch," Mikey shouted just before the car came into range. He kicked off and fell into the wind, bounced at the end of the slack, felt the high limb bend and straighten like a bow with his weight, saw that he would intercept the car at the very bottom of his arc, and tucked up his legs so he could skim over the car an inch above the windshield. The light of the setting sun glanced off the windshield into his eyes. Mr. Karns's pasty face was a blur in the sun's reflection as it turned to look at him. The car's horn blared and tires shrieked. The reflection of the sun on the windshield dimmed and Mikey looked straight into Maggie Sorrells Summers O'Brien's startled eyes.

Mikey wanted to stop right there, but he flew on to the top of his swing. As he returned to his landing, he saw his mom crash into the ditch beside the road. The car lurched, scraped, and banged to a stop and its front wheel spun in the space over the ditch. His mom did not move to get out of the car. Her door was over the mouth of a culvert. Mikey let go the rope, fell to the ground, and ran to the passenger door. Maggie stared straight ahead.

"Mom, I'm sorry," Mikey cried.

After a while Maggie slowly turned her head toward him and said, "Well, this time you almost killed us both. Do you realize, if you keep this up, you will cause both our deaths?"

"Mom . . . "

"Get in and sit down."

Mikey quickly placed his butt in the seat beside her. He did not have to worry about being hit or slapped if his butt was in the seat. Nobody in his family struck a kid or a horse on the head for fear they would make him head shy. The butt was the only place anybody ever got hit.

"Mom, I'm sorry. I thought you were somebody else."

"Oh, you wouldn't mind if you scared somebody else to death?"

"Well, yes, but I didn't want to scare you. I only wanted to see if I could do the stunt."

"Mikey, this decides me. You want adventure? I'm going to send you on an adventure that will mean something, an adventure in the education that you sorely lack."

Mikey kept quiet. After this largest of all the scares he had given her, he was ready to give up his life. He could not blame her. He was lost and as good as gone and it was all his own fault. The worst fear of his life would finally be realized. Everybody he loved would live on in his home without him, not because he had been killed or was dangerous to himself or because his parents had forgotten him somewhere and lost him, but because they could not live with him. Maggie was finally justified to ship him clear out of sight and be rid of him.

"Mikey, you're going to Saint Michael's."

"Oh," Mikey muttered softly. That time he was hit in the heart.

Maggie glanced quickly into his eyes because he had made the kind of sound she hoped he would not make. His eyes filled with water because his banishment was finally real. He looked up and saw his Nina hurry up the road toward them. The sight of Maggie's car hanging awry and astraddle of the ditch had put her in a frenzy. The buttons were popping open on her dress, which clung to her as though to keep from being shed as her shoulders and thighs bared themselves.

"Now, be a man," Maggie said. "I don't want to have to take a lot of lip from my *comadre*."

Nina ran up on Mikey's side of the car and shrilled, "*Apaga el motor*, comadre. Shut off the motor, comadre. Turn off the motor. The *motor*."

Maggie shut it off. Nina looked into Mikey's face. "Are you hurt, *mi hijo*?"

Mikey shook his head.

"No, only your feelings. What are you two *doing* in a car that is about to fall into a ditch? Get *out* of there. Why is this boy *crying*?"

Mikey wiped his eye with the heel of his hand. "I'm not crying," he said.

"You are crying, and why not, you've been betrayed by your own mother. Isn't it true, comadre? You're finally really going to send your son away? Have you even told him?"

"I just told him and he's all right, aren't you, son?"

"Yes."

"Huh, it's yes, is it?" Nina said. "Those religious will make a *priest* of him. Is that what you want, comadre?"

"No, comadre," Maggie said. "I only want him to be what he wants to be."

"So he can be anything as long as he becomes a priest or brother or some other kind of prisoner? Shame on you, comadre."

Nina took three steps toward her house and turned back to Maggie again. "Don't send him away without letting me see him again. I will pack a suitcase for him myself."

"We've decided to drive him to Santa Fe."

"Are you sure he needs that much mothering? Any nine-year-old ought to be able to pack himself away to a boarding school. Why not just set his suitcase out on the highway and let him flag down a bus? Wouldn't that be better than driving him all the way to Santa Fe?"

"Viv and I want to see Santa Fe and the school."

"Lucky for your kid, comadre. Ay, comadre," Nina cried. She turned and walked home.

Mikey and Maggie sat in the stranded car and did not speak until Nina turned into her driveway and disappeared.

Maggie sighed. "Well, son, you don't have to go if you don't want to. I thought you'd be pleased. Doesn't this go along with the plan we made a long time ago? We've talked about getting you a good education ever since I taught you how to read *Dick Tracy*."

"I know."

"Sooner or later every little boy becomes a man, son. This starts you on that journey."

"I know."

"We'll take you to Santa Fe and stay right with you until you're settled."

"When do we have to go?"

"Your classes start next Monday, so we have to be there Saturday."

"When will we leave?"

"Friday."

That was when Mikey began to count the days that remained for him to be at home, a sorrowful accounting that he would do the rest of his life. He would have Monday night, then Tuesday, then Wednesday, then Thursday. Three more days and four more nights. Time to go was not here, yet. Not too close, yet. The joy he anticipated with the accomplishment of his feat on the swing had definitely not been realized. He climbed to the top of the tree, took down his grandfather's lariat, coiled it up carefully, stored it in his Granny's closet, and forgot it.

Billy Shane was gone. Mikey would be gone. Spike Shane, Little Bea, his Nina, and Uncle Bill would still be at home every day. Maggie, Bica, Maudy Marie, Baxter, and Pancho would get to stay home. His Granny's place would be absolutely unchanged. He would be a stranger who might be allowed to visit from time to time.

Still, the realization of his banishment was not as bad as he thought it would be. He did not drop dead from sorrow. The shade under his alamo was still sweet when he climbed down with the lariat. Bica called to Maggie that supper was ready and Maggie's answer was cheerful. Not many cars ventured by on the highway. The ones that did timidly passed his house on tiptoes for fear that Tarzan would fall on them. Nothing was wrong at home because of Maggie and Viv's decision to send him away to school. Nina and Maggie threw fits of frenzy over him at least once a week, so this last one would not have extraordinary consequences.

Mikey climbed to the top of the corral post that evening to rub the adobes out of the corners of Pancho's eyes. The horse stood so close that he impaled Mikey's belly with his chin whiskers.

"Well, Panchito, you've gone away from time to time to become a horse and now I have to go away to become a man," Mikey said. "We've never been able to stay together long because you had to be a good horse. Now I have to go. I'll send you my thoughts and you send me yours like horses do. I hope you get mine because I'll be clear over in New Mexico.

"I might come home for Christmas, but you'll probably be at work with the remuda at the Baca Float. You'll have to pay for your feed that way because I won't earn money while I'm gone.

Maggie won't pay for your feed and Paul will probably stay down in Mexico."

Mikey looked into Pancho's eye and started to bawl, but he kept talking to get through it. "Anyway," he squeaked, "I'm just glad that you're such a good horse and I'm grateful for every cow you turned back for me. I know which of us was the one who did it and which one of us got to look good."

Mikey stopped there. He loved Pancho, but he had never said anything like that to him. He was not dumb enough to believe that Pancho loved anybody but another horse. Nobody else was good enough to be loved. He fed Pancho his grain and hay and the horse forgot him. Mikey figured that Pancho liked to be petted, but only if it kept the flies off. He was all business and did not look around to be loved or petted when he was at work because that was the way he made his living. He was in his own world now with his supper because that was his pay for being Pancho.

At the supper table, Viv asked Mikey if he would be ready to cowboy on a drive from Nogales the next day. Mikey looked away from him and said he would not help because he needed to pack and say good-bye to people. Viv then decided that if Mikey was not going to work anymore, Pancho could be turned out to pasture on the Baca Float to save his feed bill.

The next day when the Adams, Cunningham, and O'Brien herd came by, Manuel Valenzuela rode into the yard without looking to the right or to the left, caught Pancho, and led him away. As Pancho lined out to leave the yard, Mikey saw that his eye was on business and he did not look back for Mikey or anything else.

The three days went fast and Mikey did not have time for sentiment. Uncle Joe came by with a new football for him. Uncle Fred stopped by, sat, and visited with him in his car and then drove away. Mikey did not expect attention from his other uncles because the cattle needed them.

Nina came in and out of Maggie's with pan de huevo, care, and advice. Bea and Spike came with her at times, but Mikey did not notice them. Maudy Marie was away with Viv all the time. He went over to say good-bye to the Wingos. They were nice, stiff, cool, impersonal, and polite and wished him luck, as always.

He went over to say good-bye to Uncle Bill and caught him as he backed out of his driveway on his way to work. Uncle Bill always kept himself stern, untouchable, and crusty if he thought Mikey was about to bawl. Mikey knew he would bawl if he smelled his Prince Albert tobacco, so he stood away from the car window. Uncle Bill kept his hands on the steering wheel, but he looked into Mikey's eyes. He told Mikey to write to his Nina and be a good boy, then backed out and left for work.

Mikey decided that driveways were the saddest places on earth. The Shanes' driveway was where he and Billy were playing the day Billy's favorite little dog Gypsy dragged in her broken body after a car hit her. That first sight of Gypsy made Billy go mad with grief. Mikey had not seen that kind of grief again until the cars and people gathered there to take Billy's body away for burial. Uncle Bill had treated Mikey like a man so he could go off to school without more pain than necessary.

The grief that he knew from the driveways was not the kind that made him bawl. They were much worse and much more painful. Driveway grief was dry, a drought-stricken grief that tapped everybody's deepest well, the dark well with a bottom that could not be seen or even guessed. A lot of water welled up somewhere inside Mikey at that moment, but he could not tap it. The water was there, but he dare not stop and draw on it.

On the night before they were to leave for Santa Fe, Viv and his partners were tied up with cattle, so Maggie decided to drive Mikey to Phoenix and put him on the train. Mikey was relieved. He and Maggie both knew that two days cooped up in a car on a trip all the way to Santa Fe would probably cause them psychological damage. A drive to Phoenix was just right. He did not want to leave Maggie, but at least he would have a last ride alone with her when he left home. A drive to Phoenix was also short enough so he might not get on her nerves.

The Cunninghams owned a home in Phoenix, and Frankie had driven down to visit Herb. When she heard that Mikey needed a ride to Phoenix, Frankie offered to take him and save Maggie the drive. Maggie did not consider taking him herself for another minute.

Mikey loaded his suitcases into Frankie's car. Nina brought him a shiny new cardboard valise, but her eyes filled with tears and she would not answer when he asked what was in it. Mikey climbed Granny's stoop for a hug and a kiss. He was sure that she would still be right there behind her screen door with her sweet no-lipped kiss if he ever came back. She inverted her little lips when she kissed him. He was lucky. Uncle Buster was the only other one she ever kissed. Something could happen to the whole world, but Granny did not allow anything to happen to her. A hug and a kiss was all he got with the usual "be a good boy," but that was all he wanted.

Baxter climbed the stoop to smile and beat Mikey's leg with his tail. Mikey gave him his hug when he turned away from Granny. He did not love any of his family more than usual that day, but he wanted them all to show it back. Only Nina and Baxter seemed compelled to show anything extra. His mom showed the semblance of a tear, but he knew from experience he could be mistaken about that.

He did right for his mothers when he took his leave. He wanted to bawl, but not from being banished. This was not his first exile, so he would survive, but he had gone away on the other banishments in the company of people he loved. He was not afraid to be alone under the care of people he did not know, either. He felt like bawling because the one he loved most took his going away the way Pancho did. His mothers would go on after he was gone as though he was no longer part of their lives, but Maggie would be the least affected.

Nina smooched him a shrill good-bye, hugged him until his ribs popped, and went home. Maggie kissed him with her straight, full, cool lips. Frankie backed her car out of the driveway and headed down the road to Phoenix. Mikey did not see his Nina when they passed her house.

After that, he looked miserably out his window and did not see or think for a long time. The telephone poles were appropriately bare, weathered, and unaffected by his sorrow as they stuttered by. The railroad rails looked as dirty on their smelly ties as he knew them to be. He did not like to be around railroad ties, except the one that had been used all his life as a corner post on Pancho's corral.

Slowly he began to breathe the load off his chest because he owned a spirit that could not stay sad. Before he reached Tucson he and Frankie laughed hard about the way Uncle Herb sat his horse when he was drunk.

Mikey realized that he was seldom free of sadness over Maggie anyway. He knew that he needed to be able to laugh in spite of being exiled, or he would never know any fun at all.

Frankie stood by him, fed him supper, and put him to bed in Uncle Herb's sister Tootie's bed that night in Phoenix. She woke him up, gave him breakfast, took him to the station, and gave him to the train conductor the next morning. She stood outside the window by his seat and waved when she saw him on his way and never once commented about how awful a turn poor Mikey's life had taken.

Because of Frankie's friendship, Mikey did not dwell on the awful turn in his life. Frankie told him how much she loved train depots and trains, so for the rest of his life Mikey saw what she saw about train depots. He sat comfortably in his own seat by his own window and set out to see the world the way adventurers did. The lady who sat across from him cried into her handkerchief and would not look at him, so he did not have to talk to anyone.

Mikey felt a glimmer of happiness when he first realized that he was alone in the world with his first look at new country with no grown-up commentary, opinion, or judgment to influence him. He saw a lot of cow country that turned green as soon as the train crossed the Arizona-New Mexico border. He saw sheep, cattle, and horses of the Indian country with people traveling horseback and in buckboards. He stepped off the train for a thirty-minute rest stop in Albuquerque and squatted to visit with a Pueblo Indian in the shade of the El Tovar Harvey House. The Indian said he lived in a pueblo between Albuquerque and Gallup. He told Mikey that he had competed in football, basketball, track, and boxing on Albuquerque Indian School teams against the Saint Michael's Horsemen when he was in school. He said everybody in New Mexico respected the Horsemen. After Mikey told him he wanted to be an athlete at Saint Michael's, the Indian asked him his name because he said he wanted to be able to tell his friends that he knew him when he became a star.

Mikey told him his name and the Indian said, "That's a good Indian name, Michael Summers. What tribe?"

"I'm not Indian," Mikey said.

"Don't be ashamed of it," the Indian said. "Indians and Mexicans are all we have in New Mexico. You fit in here with us."

"Okay, I'll admit it to you, I'm Yaqui."

"Ah ha and you speak Spanish like me."

"*Como que no.*" Mikey smiled happily and went on in Spanish, "How could I not speak Spanish?"

Then the conductor said, "All aboard," and Mikey stood up to leave.

"How did you know I was Indian?" he asked.

"Your accent," the Indian said. "You are freckle-faced and green-eyed, but your eyes are slanted, your hair is black as mine, and you have the accent and skin of a Yaqui or Apache. I've met those people at our ceremonials. I also know that you are titiritero, shaman. Tell me you have not been told you are titiritero."

"That's what a Yaqui headman told me."

"See, I knew it when you came off the train and looked at me."

Mikey went back to his seat on the train. He did not think he wanted to be an Indian shaman. He had not minded it in Cabezon's camp, but after he came out of the mountains he was somebody else. Nobody in his family except Paul would like it that an Indian saw kinship with him or that he owned some kind of Indian magic. If he ever said he had Indian blood everybody else in his family would throw in with Maggie and Viv and he would be exiled forever.

Then, because he was alone and did not have to answer to anybody else, he decided he could enjoy being recognized as an Indian as long as it was kept between he and the Indian and not broadcast to the whites of his family. This trip on the train had become as good an adventure as Maggie said it would be. He figured an adventure *should* help a person find out who he was.

Mikey was let off the train at Lamy, New Mexico, in the early evening. An old Mexican met him there in a wood-paneled station wagon with *La Fonda Hotel* painted on the door. Lamy consisted of a station house and platform in the middle of a forest of the squat juniper trees that people in the cow country called cedars. The country was one cedar tree after another all the way to the outskirts of the dark, Mexican town of Santa Fe. Mikey was to find out that nobody in Santa Fe wanted their town or themselves to be called Mexican. Mexican was in fact a dirty word. Santa Fe and its people were first-class "Spanish" and to be called Mexican was an insult.

The driver did not say a word from the time he left Lamy until he stopped in front of the La Fonda Hotel. Mikey stepped out of the station wagon and asked him in Spanish where he should go from there. The man placed Mikey's bags on the sidewalk, looked down the street, and pointed with his lips at a heavy figure in a black suit who hurried toward them at the military pace of 120 steps per minute.

The man in black stopped in front of Mikey, gazed into his face, picked up the two suiter suitcase and its mate, executed an about-face, and headed back the way he had come at 120 per. After ten steps, he looked back over his shoulder to make sure Mikey knew he was supposed to follow, tucked his chin to his chest, and disappeared around a corner of the hotel. Mikey picked up Nina's small bag and ran to catch up, fell in behind the man, and hit a high trot to keep up.

The only light on the street was from *luminarios*, candles inside paper bags that lined the edges of the roof of the pueblo-style La Fonda building. The rest of the narrow street on the way to Saint Michael's was lined with high adobe tapia walls that were not lighted.

Mikey began to sweat healthily and enjoy the trot in the warm evening. He switched Nina's valise from one hand to the other as he trotted. The street crossed a creek that was lined with willows and cottonwoods in full leaf. The stream ran fast and gave off a sharp, pure smell of green cottonwood and clean water. The climb from the river to the gates of the school was steep and Mikey felt the labor of his lungs at seven thousand feet. Nogales was almost five thousand feet, but Santa Fe was a headier place in a lot of ways besides the altitude. To him it was entirely old, beautiful wrought-iron and adobe colonial Mexican. A place on the final climb to the school smelled as Mexican as Nogales, Sonora, with its red and green chile, garlic, and broiled meat.

The trees and buildings on the campus were enormous. Mikey followed the stocky man through an iron gate between brick pillars, through a narrow passageway between tall buildings, and along a veranda to a washroom. Two rows of washbasins with mirrors above them were placed down the center of the room and the walls were lined with steel lockers. The man came to a halt in another room that was lined with larger, wooden lockers. He unlocked locker number thirty, gave Mikey the key, and ordered him to unpack his suitcases and put his clothing inside.

An enormous man came into the room. He wore a floor-length black robe with a square, starched, white bib under his chin that was split down the middle. A small, black beanie sat on the back of his head. He addressed the stocky man as "Prosper" and spoke to him in French, then turned unsmilingly to Mikey. "I am Brother Benildus. Your name, please, young man."

"Michael Paul Summers Sorrells," Mikey said, adding his mother's maiden name, as was the custom in Sonora.

"Hereafter and until you return to Mexico, you will drop the Sorrells in your name. We won't use it here. Here you are Michael Paul Summers and will be called Summers." Because he was so stout, the man grunted with every word.

"I'm the principal of this school and this is Saint Michael's College, also called Saint Mike's and SMC." With only a glint in his eye that might have been good humor, he then said, "We are the scourge of the Santa Fe High School Demons and all other lesser and ordinary devils from hell. You will be happy here. We will give you work, study, sports, and play. If you need soap, toothbrush, or a comb, Brother Prosper will give it to you and charge it to your account. You will also give him all your dirty clothes to be laundered. I have been instructed by your parents to give you an allowance of twenty-five cents per week.

Allowance is handed out every Saturday. Today is Saturday, so here is your quarter."

Mikey took his quarter.

"Now, Brother Prosper will give you clean sheets and a pillowcase, take you to your cot in the dormitory, and show you how to make your bed. After that, he'll take you to the refectory and Brother Anect will give you supper. You are to be assigned to the Little Boys. Brother Louis will be your prefect, your immediate superior.

"Now, go with Brother Prosper. After you are given supper Brother Louis will take you to join the rest of the Little Boys for a visit to the fiesta and the burning of Zozobra."

Mikey wanted to ask who Zozobra was, but Brother Prosper carried his sheets and pillowcase out the door and Mikey ran after him. Two rows of beds lined the walls in the dormitory. Tall windows with spacious sills aired and lighted the place. The windows were set deep inside plastered adobe walls. Mikey's dormitory room of twenty-four beds shared a bathroom with another room of twenty-four beds. A narrow carpet was spread down the center of the room between the two rows of beds.

Brother Prosper chose a bed in a corner of the room, manhandled a cover over the mattress, flapped the clean sheets on it, tucked them under the mattress, dropped the mattress on the springs, spread two army blankets over the sheets and tucked them under the foot of the mattress, slithered the pillow into its crisp case and dropped it in its place, folded the top of the sheet over the blankets, and headed out the door before all the air had a chance to breathe out of the pillow. He did it all so quickly, simply, and effortlessly that Mikey never needed to be told how to make a bed again.

The dormitory was not only a room. It was a hall with an immense, scrolled ceiling. It smelled of calcimine and clean bedding and was airy and cool. Heavy curtains hung beside every window. The lower halves of the windows were covered with old, scrolled paper. Mikey did not know one bit of the history of the place, but he sensed that it was very old and had been used a long time by persons of dignity.

Mikey followed Brother Prosper to the dining hall in the basement of another old building and there another French Brother named Brother Anect served him a bowl of red chile and beans, a quarter loaf of fresh bread with butter, and two glasses of rich, cold milk. The chile was the best Mikey had ever tasted and so hot it curled the roots of his hair and made his mouth feel raw, but was so delicious that he could not stop until he ate it all. Brother Anect watched Mikey out of the corner of his eye and when he was finished with the chile he served him a large bowl of tapioca pudding and poured canned milk over it, exactly the way Mikey ate it and liked it in cow camp.

Brother Louis came to get him while he ate his tapioca. Brother Louis was small, quick, and black-haired with a short, sharp little beak and a ruddy face. He was also courteous and friendly.

The Brothers treated Mikey the same way cowboys treated him. He might be one of the Little Boys, but he was treated with respect and reserve. Mikey never felt that Brother Prosper was unkind when he used the pace of a French foreign legionnaire and did not look back for casualties in his wake. The man was a teacher and only wanted Mikey to learn to move on down the road and not let walking distance stand in the way of progress.

The Brothers were kind to him because they figured he was probably homesick, so in respect for his feelings, they used an impersonal tone. What he liked most was the way they looked him in the eye to see how he was holding up while they gave him orders and made sure he had everything he needed. A kid in Mikey's position might bawl when he saw that a grown-up was trying to look after him, and he could bawl for being deprived. Anything could make a kid bawl when he was seven hundred miles away from his fathers, mothers, horses, dirt, dogs, cows, and trees. Cowboys and vaqueros knew how to treat Mikey when it looked like he was about to cry. His uncles and the cowpunchers he knew looked him in the eye and used that same impersonal tone when they suspected his feelings were hurt. They would not direct one word at his feelings, but watched to see if they could help him keep from clouding up and blubbering. If he did emote because he could not help it, they looked away but kept on talking about some prospect at hand. They talked about something impersonal to help him get past the emotion that bothered him and bothered them. That way they kept the everyday world going so it would be there when Mikey recovered from the crisis.

Brother Anect did not say a word to him, but he kept a kindly eye on him. As long as Mikey knew Brother Anect he never heard him speak to a student. He was in charge of the Brothers' refectory. He also received visitors in the chapel of San Miguel and told them its history. The church was the oldest in the United States and he told visitors about the priests and Brothers who were buried under the altar, martyrs who had been killed in an Indian mutiny against the missions. He showed visitors the arrow holes in the walls and a spear hole in one of the paintings. He showed them the beams that had been charred but survived after most of the church was burned. His deep voice with its thick French accent droned and droned. His drone was famous among the boys of Saint Michael's and probably unforgettable to the tourists.

Mikey found out about Brother Anect's drone the next day. Nina had made him promise that he would say a prayer of thanksgiving as soon as he arrived at school, if he did not perish on the train. He forgot to say the prayer at early Mass, so he went back to the chapel at midmorning. While he prayed, tourists rang the bell and were admitted through the front door by Brother Anect. The people went silent when they entered the cool hush of the chapel. Brother Anect turned on the lights over the altar. To Mikey, that altar looked like a place prepared for worship by savages. Smudges of the blood that was spilled in the mutiny were still there. The same savages who had killed the priests and Brothers and burned the chapel had repainted and readorned it. The natives who had worshipped savagely at the altar had also savagely killed and burned there, and then fixed it up again because they never lost their faith in Christ or the saints, only postponed it a little to settle a grievance. A lot of blood was on that altar, real blood from the martyrs and probably their slayers and painted blood that welled from deep wounds in the hands, feet, hearts, and brows of the figures of Christ, His Blessed Mother, and the saints.

That chapel became the house of Mikey's secret best friends. He never talked to the Brothers when his heart was heavy, but he knew good spirits in that chapel listened to him. His friends the saints had seen hundreds of years of every kind of trouble.

That first evening, Brother Louis led Mikey out of the basement dining room and up to the second-floor study hall of the Little Boys. Twenty boys Mikey's age stood by their desks reciting evening prayer as he walked in. After the prayer Brother Louis introduced him to the boys and told them to get ready to go to the fiesta and the burning of Zozobra.

Mikey shook hands with a gang of thugs that were just like he and Billy Shane. Not one seemed unhappy to be away from home. Several were from families in Mexico that sent their boys to Saint Michael's to learn English. The first boy Mikey met was Manuel Enriquez. Manuel could not speak a word of English, but he walked up to Mikey and started talking to him in Spanish as though he knew Mikey would understand him. "¿De dónde eres tú? Where are you from?" Manuel asked.

"Nogales," Mikey said. "And you?"

"Chihuahua."

"What's your name?"

"Manuel Enriquez, and you?"

"Miguel Pablo Veranos."

"Stay with me. My brothers are in the Big Boys and they'll take us out for steak."

Manuel's brothers Carlos and Ignacio were in the eleventh grade. They had been at SMC four years and were varsity athletes. They took Mikey in when Manuel introduced him and they called him *Becerro*, or Calf. Carlos and Ignacio fed their little brother a steak, but Mikey was too full of chile to eat with them.

The Enriquez brothers were formal and reserved, as Mikey knew people of Chihuahua to be. Manuel was even more serious than his big brothers. He seldom smiled and he never giggled. The older brothers joked with him all the time to get him to laugh, with little success. Manuel reminded Mikey of Billy Shane. Billy had been serious and no giggler. Manuel combed his hair straight back without parting it as Billy had done.

Zozobra was a giant made of tinder, the biggest and most fearsome figure of a man Mikey had ever seen. He was the symbol of evil to the faithful Indians of the City of the Holy Faith, so they set him afire and burned him down to have done with him for another year. He sent sparks high into the clear darkness and the heat of the burning effigy was welcome when the night turned cool.

Mikey entered into the Saint Michael's routine that night when he and his companions knelt by their beds to recite prayers in unison. Sunday morning everybody was allowed to sleep until seven, then they awakened to the prefect's whistle and got up to dress and wash for eight o'clock Mass. At eight thirty everybody went to the dormitory and made their beds. Sunday breakfast was always cold cereal, bacon and eggs, and a sweet roll. Recreation time began after breakfast and the boys did as they pleased until noon. Dinner at noon. At 1 PM the Little Boys formed up with Brother Louis and filed downtown. On Saturdays they went to the Paris Theater for a double feature that consisted of one cowboy movie, one detective movie, an episode of an action serial, and a cartoon. On Sundays they went to a feature motion picture, a newsreel, a cartoon, and a short subject at the Lensic Theater. The Little Boys sat in a group with Brother Louis during the movie and marched home with him like chicks after a mother hen when they came out.

The Big Boys were allowed to walk to the movies on their own, take dates, hang out at the soda fountains, and do as they pleased until 5 PM. The movie theaters were the terrain of Saint Michael's and Loretto on weekend afternoons and the Santa Fe public school boys and girls entertained themselves elsewhere. The rivalry between the parochial schools and the public schools was so strong that the public school kids stayed away from the theaters on weekend afternoons and went in the evenings. That fact about territory never occurred to Mikey because he was obliged to stay close to Brother Louis outside the walls of Saint Michael's. The boarders fell back into their routine on Sunday evening with benediction in the chapel and study hall after supper.

On school days Mikey was up at six, washed and at Mass at six thirty, breakfast at seven thirty, and classroom formation outside the main building at eight thirty. Every session of study hall, formation, class, and activity was preceded and ended by prayer. Classes ended at three thirty and the boys who did not go to practice in team sports could do anything they wanted until five when athletes and nonathletes were called to study hall for an hour. Benediction in the chapel was at six, supper at six thirty, recreation until study hall at eight, and bed at nine.

That was the schedule of an ordinary day without extracurricular business. Extracurricular business was football, basketball, boxing, softball, track, tennis, hiking, handball, archery, band, drama, the writing and makeup of the yearbook and monthly *San Miguel News*, choir, altar boy service, and anything else that might occur to the Brothers that kept boys busy. The boys involuntarily abstained from the Saturday and Sunday movies during the forty days of Lent. They made the sacrifice because they were confined to the campus except to take group hikes. They could make the voluntary sacrifice to abstain from candy if they wished, but on Saturdays they hiked back and forth to the mountains until their tongues hung out. Lenten sacrifice was relaxed on Sundays, so they studied, read, played games, and listened to the radio.

Mikey did not think of his fathers, mothers, horses, dirt, dogs, cows, and trees for at least one month after he started school at Saint Michael's. After that he remembered them only fleetingly. He did not miss them because he did not have one minute for them. He still only applied himself to his studies enough to pass. He loved all activities outside the classroom. He was not one to lounge with the other kids in the recreation room with its Ping-Pong and pool tables, punching bags, card games, Monopoly, checkers, chess, and weights.

He hung out on the football field so faithfully that the Horsemen made El Becerro their mascot. He kicked with the punters and field-goal kickers, passed with the passers, centered with the centers, tackled with the linemen, and ran laps before and after practice. He could think of nothing but football and the big game that was the reason and goal of the season, the most important goal of the whole school year: the defeat on Thanksgiving Day by the Horsemen of the Santa Fe High School Demons.

Athletics became Mikey's passion. He performed adequately as a student, but that was only a duty to fulfill. Athletics brought out a bloom in a boy like Mikey who loved adventure, contact, exertion, and competition. He could find no end to the athletic trials that were available to him at St. Mike's. He caught on quickly, improved fast, and excelled in everything from kick the can to boxing.

As he excelled, he made enemies. Because they were part of the busy community of Saint Michael's, only he and they were ever aware of the enmity. Not the Brothers, not his classmates, not even his best friends knew the enmity that boiled between Mikey and three other boys in his class.

The enemies were three day-scholar bullies in his class who lived in a section of Santa Fe called La Cañada and bragged about being members of the Cañada Street Gang. One was a freckle-faced, redheaded boy named Jimmy Rojas. The other two, Skinny and Porky Franklin, were first cousins. The three had been companions since babyhood.

They tried to bully Mikey by acting as though they owned him after the first time he played in an organized tackle football game. He caught the ball on the kickoff and ran it all the way back for a touchdown and made them jealous. As he ran he saw Rojas and the Franklins drop softly to the ground one by one and cover their heads with their arms to protect themselves before anyone hurt them.

As long as Mikey played football with the three Cañada bullies he never saw one of them make a clean, hard block or a brave tackle, but they were always nearby to criticize Mikey if he tried one and missed. Usually, when Mikey hit somebody, he became airborne and there was no doubt about who had made the tackle. The only time he ever saw the Cañada Gang go in for a tackle was after somebody else hit the runner and stopped him and gave them a chance to pile on from behind.

The bullying began after that first game. The three smiled a lot in Mikey's face and patted him on the back. At first they invited him to hang around with them at recess, then they demanded that he meet them at recess. If he did not show up, they demanded to know where he had been. To stay away from them was to grant them an opportunity to backbite him to his classmates.

As a nine-year-old seven hundred miles away from his folks, he was vulnerable in a lot of ways, but he was sure the football field was not one of them. There did not seem to be any dark corners where cowards could hide on the athletic fields of Saint Michael's, but Mikey found out there were plenty of mean political corners everywhere else in that society.

ELEVEN

THE STAKES

A *cattleman sits in a poker game with God to serve Him. God has unlimited stakes and has dealt himself all the winning cards. The man's stakes are the land and livestock he has worked to obtain. The man is dealt cards that are the sum of the talents he needs to win enough prosperity for his livestock so that he can stay in the game for another hand. God's hand is always flush with drought, disease, accidental catastrophe, and the wild dispositions of animals and men. The man cannot hope to win temporal prosperity without end; he can only hope to stay in the game for the love of the game and of God. If the man loses too many hands in a row, God takes his land and livestock and the man is left with nothing more to ante, so he goes away with his heart broken to find something else that God might want him to do.*

At first Mikey liked all the Brothers who taught at Saint Michael's. The look of cowmen was in their eyes. As the school year progressed, he learned to dislike some of them, but the ones he met that first night always remained his favorites.

Some of the Brothers showed their anger more than others. Brother Louis put up with a lot of mischief and rowdiness from the Little Boys. A flare of anger reddened his face from time to time and Mikey knew he was angriest when his nostrils pinched in and turned white. He recovered from anger quickly and never held a grudge. He always knew what a boy needed. He made it his most important business to know every boy's aspirations. He found out that Mikey was born on August twenty-fifth, the feast day of Saint Louis King of France, the saint whose name he assumed when he became a Brother. When Mikey felt low in his first days at Saint Michael's, Brother Louis cheered him with examples of Saint Louis's fortitude. When he ran out of Saint Louis stories, he bolstered Mikey with stories about Saint Michael the Archangel and the sinful life of blustery old Saint Paul. Brother Louis was a bolsterer. He knew boys would always have reasons for gloom, but gloom must be put down and did not deserve discussion.

The Brothers would not tell the boys anything about themselves. They did not have personal lives. Asked what they wanted from life, they answered, "For you to learn everything you need to be a good man." They all had taken aliases when they joined the order of the Christian Brothers of Saint John Baptist de la Salle. They called themselves "the religious" because they were members of a religious teaching order of the Catholic Church.

Brother Louis told Mikey that when the Brothers joined the order they gave away their identities and birthrights. They would not tell the boys their family names, no matter how the boys pleaded, cajoled, or kidded them. The boys kidded them a lot, because they liked them and the Brothers liked it. The Brothers kept straight faces, took the cajoling, remained reserved, and never gave back more than a twinkle in their eyes, which was all the boys looked for.

Brother Prosper was in charge of the infirmary and became angry at boys who malingered. If a boy showed up at the infirmary with a complaint, he had better be telling the truth. If he was faking, Brother Prosper put him straight back out into the breeze. The boys did learn something about Brother Prosper's former life. At a meeting soon after all the boys arrived for the school year,

Brother Louis told them that nobody had better get caught stealing from the lockers or fake an illness to get out of classes because Brother Prosper had served as a medical corpsman in the French Foreign Legion. No thief alive could fool him and a faker was a fool to lie to him.

The Brothers' reserve did not hide their affection for the boys. In fact, they had to care a lot for the boys. They did not have any other reason to be there, as they were not paid. None of them believed they were guaranteed to go to heaven. They admitted it. Yet, to care for every need of all those boys required the patience, generosity, and fortitude of the saints. Their reserve was one of their defenses, but their candor also often saved them. Anytime one of those big men admitted in one way or another that he was not perfect and not sure he would get to heaven, it made a boy think better of him. Even the most rowdy boys soon approved of the Brothers as friends.

Too many youngster feelings were hurt every day, too many reckless kids were bruised and bloodied on the playground. The Brothers were everywhere. They could not let any one boy's problems bog them down, but they could make moving targets that any boy could find.

The boys always managed to revive and recuperate from heartbreak, physical harm, humiliation, and other drastic afflictions of boarding school. To help them recover from the tragedies of the day, the Brothers simply found work and other activities that kept them busy long enough for nature to heal them.

Midway through the first semester Brother Damian replaced Brother Louis as prefect of the Little Boys. Brother Louis became prefect of the Big Boys for a while and then was made special assistant to Brother Benildus.

Brother Damian did not have the look of the husbandman in his eyes. He was an overseer. He was tall and portly, narrow of shoulder, broad of beam, and ponderous in his every movement except in his long, delicate, white hands. He took over Brother Louis's alcove in Mikey's dormitory and spent his nights there. Though always reserved, the other Brothers' eyes showed kind regard for the boys. Brother Damian's reserve was heads-up and haughty and he never looked a boy in the eye.

When the senior prefect blew his whistle at 6 AM Brother Damian turned on the lights in the dormitory and led the boys in prayer as they fell out of bed onto their knees. Brother Louis had awakened the boys good-naturedly and even helped the littlest boys dress. Mikey was one of the littlest boys and he could dress himself, but he appreciated it when Brother Louis helped the two boys who were smaller than he. Brother Louis's voice was high pitched and raucous and he scolded and taunted the boys good-naturedly to help them get started. All his boys filed out of the dormitory in a good mood and ready to go to work.

Brother Damian's voice purred the morning prayer, but he might as well have been saying, "I love to see your little bodies scramble at the sound of me, no matter how nicely I purr. I will make life miserable for you while I purr to you. What do you think I will do if you make me raise my voice?" The sound and sight of him made Mikey feel like a complete orphan.

Mikey knew what it was to have control of herds of cattle and horses, so he knew how a voice inflection, a gesture, or a look could move an individual in a well-broken herd if the herder wanted his status to change. A good husbandman accustomed his herd to his subtle signals and he controlled it with as few threats and as little force as possible.

Brother Damian purred, but Mikey could tell by the look in his eye that he did not know kindness. That scared Mikey into trying to stay out of his way, but the man was always too close, always hovering too big and near the Little Boys. The worst part was that most of the time he was the only grown-up to whom a boy could turn with a problem.

One way that he exerted power was to call a boy out of a group at play or study hall to purr a disciplinary admonition into his ear. He especially liked to do it when he knew another Brother was watching. Brother Benildus would walk by a group of Little Boys on the playground and Brother Damian would call a boy out and purr in his ear whether he had done anything wrong or not. Every Little Boy came to attention when he spoke to them in the same way milk pen calves pay attention to the milkman who steals their mothers' milk. The hungry milk pen calf watches the milkman for the moment he will be released from his pen for breakfast at his mama's titties. The boys were more comfortable when they could work and play in the close safety of their herd of boys and Brother Damian used that to control them. They did not like to be called singly away from the herd. They did not go to Brother Damian happily, because they knew he was not their friend and did not care about their welfare.

If Brother Louis and Brother Benildus wanted to speak to a boy, they walked in and separated him from the bunch in a way that did not intimidate him. The boys trusted them as big friends in a community of big and little brothers.

Brother Damian was intimidating even when he was not disciplining the boys. He could not just hand Mikey his allowance and be done with him. He had to put his hand on the back of Mikey's neck or around his waist and play keep-away with the quarter for a while before he gave it up. He could not hand Mikey his quarter at arm's length in a decent, manly way. Mikey felt that if a boy had his pay coming, the man should hand it over the instant he came within reach to get it.

Brother Damian tried to harm Mikey in a sinful way. Halfway through football season when Mikey was in a glory of activity, Brother Damian stopped by his bed in the middle of the night and reached under his covers inside his pajamas to fondle his tally-wagger round and round. When Mikey opened his eyes he was under the great, black hulk of a man that blocked the light from the golden bulb of the ceiling nightlight. When Mikey realized what Brother Damian was doing, he scooted down out of his reach and the hand retreated.

Later, Mikey tried to think of a reason the man needed to do a thing like that. During the fondling, his tallywagger had not tallied even one wag of its own. It just rolled with the wagging and took it until Mikey realized what was happening and fled to the bottom of his bed.

Mikey did not even know the word "pervert," but he was canny enough to figure the man had done wrong. He hoped Damian was the only Brother who did things like that.

Mikey did not know what to do about Damian. He sure did not want to be fondled again. He only knew the fondling was not good like a caress on the ear by his daddy. His daddy had not caressed him anywhere on his entire carcass more than five times in his whole life and never, never reached for his tallywagger. His Nina gave him a lot of *caricias*, caresses, but not on the tallywagger. His mom offered big kisses when she felt like it without other hugs or touching, and his Granny offered little dry kisses and light pats only. His Uncle Buster liked to rub his back under his shirt with an old, hard hand when he asked Mikey to give him a report on his adventures. Mikey knew few caresses from his women and fewer from his daddy and uncles. He had always found it difficult to hold still long enough for that kind of foolishness, anyway.

He knew Brother Damian's fumblings were not caresses by someone who loved him. "Thank God," Mikey thought, "he did not try to kiss me." Then he began to wake Mikey up with his hand inside his pajamas almost every night. All Mikey had to do was scoot down to the bottom of his bed and Brother Damian would give up and go away. He could not arouse Mikey. Loathsome assaults by huge specters in the dormitory dark scared the pee-wadding out of Mikey. The man was spooky enough in the daylight as he hovered about with his pasty face and hands and black skull-cap and robe. At night in the dormitory, the white split bib of his collar and his pasty face and hands were all Mikey could see of him. The head floated in the darkness. When he stopped at Mikey's bed, the white hands fluttered nervously at his bedclothes a moment before the boy could wake up and escape to the foot of the bed.

Mikey could only lie awake for so long. He always went to sleep while he watched for the black shadow of Brother Damian to turn away from his patrol on the center carpet and go to his own bed. Mikey learned to sleep with one eye open so he could awaken as the man's hands settled toward him like big, white moths.

What the man did accomplish after a while was to cause Mikey to wet the bed every night. The peeing made the monster quit fooling around because Mikey's bed smelled like a skunk, and the boy stank like stale urine all the time except on Wednesdays and Saturdays when the Little Boys took their showers.

Stinking like pee all the time changed Mikey's status on the campus, but it did not make him miserable, afraid, or ashamed. He slept well and sometimes did not even wake up when he peed the bed. Every morning after Mass he hung his bedclothes and mattress outside so all the world could read the map of his battleground. Every night his bedding was fresh again when he brought it in, but it stunk again as soon as he climbed in and warmed it up. The boys were allowed to change their sheets and pillowcases every two weeks, but the legend of the Damian war was etched on his mattress forever.

Because Mikey was afraid of Damian and because the man was afraid of having his sin discovered, he had little to do with Mikey in the daylight. The closest he came to touching Mikey after he began to stink like pee was on Saturday when he stuck his hand way out from his body and dropped the quarter allowance into Mikey's hand.

Mikey's wetting the bed brought him a lot of conversation and communication of a kind he did not want with the other members of the community, but he did not know how to stop it. After all, he was not the only Little Boy who wet the bed. Little Forbes from Nogales was another one.

Damian presided over the Little Boys' study hall by sitting at a big desk on a raised platform in front of the boys. When a boy raised his hand for help with homework, he was told to come up close and whisper his problem so as not to disturb the other boys. His custom was to reach under a boy's shirt and massage his back while he helped solve a problem. The other Brothers who were not perverts also massaged the boy's backs and necks from time to time. Uncle Buster did that, so Mikey did not worry about Damian until after he turned into a pervert. Before Damian showed his unnatural tendencies, Mikey had put up with the massage because he was little, it was not unpleasant, and he needed answers for his studies. He went up to the man because he needed his help and having his back rubbed was better than being stupid the next day in class.

Then one evening Damian was helping Forbes in study hall with his hand under his shirt when Ignacio and Carlos Enriquez looked in the door to wave at Manuel. When they saw what Damian was doing they gave him such a wild, passionately savage, mean Mexican look that he snatched his hand out from under Forbes's shirt as though he had grabbed a buzz saw.

After that the Enriquezes spent more time with Manuel and Mikey. Mikey was now not only called El Becerro; he was also called Summers Valdez. He could not only be Summers, a gringo, so he was given a Mexican name.

Mikey quit going to Damian for help after Damian let it be known in front of everyone in study hall that he could not stand Mikey's bad smell. Mikey already had a whole corner of the room to himself. He did not mind being a stink. He was darned afraid of Damian's purring ways and fluttering moth hands and was glad to stay away from him. Brother Louis did not mind helping him, and he was Mikey's fourth grade homeroom teacher. Brother Louis did not seem to notice how bad he smelled. That was odd, because even Mikey could not stand his stink in a closed room.

About a week after the Enriquezes gave Damian the dirty looks, he was transferred away from Saint Michael's. The expulsion happened so quietly, no one knew he was leaving until he was gone. One morning he was there to awaken the boys and usher them to wash hall, Mass, and classes, and that evening Brother Louis presided over the Little Boys' study hall. The Brothers offered no information about his leaving and nobody asked about him. Mikey forgot about him immediately and probably would never have given him another thought, except one day the Enriquez brothers said that they had helped Damian carry his satchel downtown to the La Fonda station wagon. After that, Mikey quit wetting the bed.

Six weeks later Damian returned to the school and was assigned as assistant to Brother George in the manual training shop. He helped teach shop, carpentry, and other manual arts and crafts. The recreation room shared space with the shop. The punching bags, the weights, and the Ping-Pong and pool tables were in the same big room with the planers and squares and stacks of lumber.

Brother Damian slept in a loft in the shop. Mikey wondered about that. All the other Brothers except the prefects who slept in alcoves in the dormitories slept on the second floor of the main school building. Brother Prosper lived in the infirmary in case somebody needed doctoring in the night. Nobody needed Damian to be in the loft of the shop and recreation building, but Mikey did not know any boarder who was surprised that he roomed in a whole building by himself away from the community. Mikey guessed that he was not wanted in the Brothers' community, either. He wore civilian clothes most of the time. Brother George, the senior shop teacher, wore his black robe everywhere with sawdust all over the front of it. Brother Damian wore his black robe for formal school ceremonies and daily Mass and benediction, but the rest of the time he was in khaki.

Mikey did not need to have anything to do with Brother Damian and neither did any other Little Boy, or any boy who did not take shop classes. That was the way Mikey liked it. He was in the recreation and shop room one day playing doubles in Ping-Pong with the Enriquezes when a long-awaited electric saw was delivered to the shop. The day was cold and a wind was blowing, so all the boarders were inside during the period between the last class of the school day and first hour of study hall. Everybody was supposed to be glad the saw had arrived, and Damian purred as he set it up in the middle of the shop. He balanced it, fired it up, and sawed the length of a plank in half, then another and another. He took out the circular saw he had been using and installed a cylindrical planer. He shaved the bottom off a short board, then another. On the third board he shaved the ends of the fingers off his right hand.

So Mikey saw him get his punishment. He had watched the demonstration with everybody else in the room; only he stayed farther away than anybody else. He always tried to keep a roomful of other boys between himself and Damian. Now the very fingers Damian loved the most had been shaved down to nubbins.

Mikey watched Damian roll on the floor, howling like an animal and trying to stop the blood from spurting out of the stumps of his fingers and he thought, "See what you get for trying to play with my tallywagger?" He was sure the man had done the same thing to other boys and maybe was still doing it, so he got what he gave. Mikey's sense of dread that the monster would surprise him again had been bad, but the score was even now and Mikey could forgive him. He could not watch him roll and listen to him howl and not feel sorry for him.

Damian became custodian of the music room after that. The destruction of those fingers proved Mikey's faith in his Nina's God. Nobody had better try to commit a sin with an innocent boy because, Lord, look what surely would happen to him. The hand of God would saw off the most sensitive parts that he needed in the performance of his sinful deeds because innocence would be protected.

Tommy Franklin of the fifth grade was a tough athlete from La Cañada street. He was a cousin of Skinny and Porky. The fifth grade was Mikey's fourth-grade team's toughest competitor. Tommy and Mikey liked each other because of this competition, as did other Cañada Street boys from the public schools who played against Mikey. Mikey's bad luck was to always have the three worst weasels from Cañada Street on his team.

One Saturday afternoon Tommy was batting flies to the three Cañada bullies on the playground. Mikey had never played the flies game. After a fielder caught three flies or six grounders, he took his turn at bat.

Mikey stopped to watch and said, "Hit it hard, Tommy."

Tommy took a full swing, batted Mikey over the left eye in the follow-through, and knocked him down with his blood pouring on the ground.

Mikey was wide awake when he hit the ground and he looked up for help. Tommy turned his back, joined the three bullies, and ran away to Cañada Street.

The Enriquez brothers were nearby and saw the accident. Ignacio wrapped his shirt around Mikey's head and knotted it tightly. He and Carlos picked Mikey up by the feet and shoulders and ran to Brother Prosper's infirmary. Brother Prosper stopped the bleeding and taped the cut, then marched Mikey to Saint Joseph's hospital downtown at 120 per where a doctor put seven stitches above his eye cold turkey.

Mikey never held the accident against Tommy Franklin, even though he was disappointed by his cowardice. He realized that Tommy acted naturally in the way of the other Franklins, as a wild goat would act in a crisis, a way that Mikey had never seen except in animals. He guessed that way of acting was a trait of cowards who were ashamed of who they were. They ran and hid in their holes when they were faced with trouble and might have to give their names.

Tommy transferred to a public school where he did not compete in athletics against Saint Michael's. Toward the end of the year he came back, but he avoided Mikey and never looked him in the eye again. He did not compete in athletics again.

The Cañada bullies only smirked and turned away when Mikey asked why they ran away like cowards. He knew the reason. They would rather slink away and hide than be asked to help anyone who was bleeding. They never tried to hide the satisfaction they had enjoyed when they abandoned Mikey in trouble.

Mikey knew personal victories in the individual sports of boxing and track. He did not have to worry about competition from the Cañada Gang in boxing because a boy could get a bloody nose learning to box. He was a catcher in baseball and his foes certainly did not covet that position. Not one of them had the guts to be a catcher, especially after they all saw what an errant hardball tipped by a batter did to Mikey's face. Mikey kept the catcher's position, but he found a catcher's mask to wear after that.

During boxing season Mikey did not see the bullies at all. They disappeared so completely that Mikey was not even aware they were in his classroom. They only reappeared after boxing was over.

The Christian Brothers were fair, so no one could pass his classes as a gift. The weasels made their grades in class but did not put out any work anywhere else that anyone but the Brothers saw them do.

Mikey threw in with the Brothers and took part in every activity they offered. Brother Louis said Mikey could be proud of the cut over his eye because its seven stitches were a school record. As far as Brother Louis knew, no varsity football player or boxer had ever needed more than three stitches to close a cut. Mikey had been so happy since Damian cut off his fingers that not even being laid low with a baseball bat could ruin his good humor. He did not miss an hour of his classes because of it.

He had not been homesick or sorry for himself one minute since he arrived at Saint Michael's. He knew why Pancho turned away from him and was totally concerned with his own business when he was led away to work. Mikey was a colt in training like Pancho. He had been saddled, ridden, raced, worked, and taught on schedule continuously since the first day he arrived at Saint Michael's. He conceded that Maggie did right by putting him there. This was the kind of training he needed to be a good cowman.

The Horsemen won the Thanksgiving Day football game against the Santa Fe High School Demons and that put a satisfying end to that year's football exertions of every boy at Saint Michael's. The victory gave Mikey proof of the existence of God and the power of prayer. If the Horsemen had lost that game it would have meant that God could turn his back on every Brother and boy at Saint Michael's, every nun and girl at Loretto, and all their alumni for all time. He hated to think about the sense of banishment they would all suffer if they ever lost a Thanksgiving Day football game to the Demons. He understood that the Horsemen had lost in other years, but he believed that was only because Mikey Summers was not there to bolster the team with his powerful prayers.

The Day Shift basketball team was made up of little boarders from Mexico. Manuel Enriquez of Chihuahua and the Sonorans Michael Paul Summers, Rene Salido, Eugenio Sterling, and the Oviedo brothers made up the first team. Their only substitute was the little sissy boy named Forbes from Nogales, Sonora. He was two years older than Mikey, but only one grade ahead of him. This was his first year at Saint Michael's also. He was no athlete. He applied himself full-time to his studies, but he did not excel as a student. He wore glasses and was blonde, pretty, pink, and delicate as a girl. Mikey felt protective of him because he turned to Mikey when bigger boys picked on him, and Mikey liked Forbes because he could talk in Spanish about home and friends on both sides of the Nogales line with him. Mikey, Forbes, and Manuel understood each other perfectly in Spanish, which they called "the Christian language."

One Friday evening at the beginning of basketball season, the Day Shift played one fifteen-minute quarter against Harvey

Grammar School before the varsity game. Rene Salido of the Horsemen Day Shift made the only basket scored by either team. The Brothers had issued purple bloomers and white undershirts to the Day Shift and the boys took such a razzing from their schoolmates about the way their bloomers sagged that none of them wanted to play another preliminary basketball game. They had dreaded that they would have to play practically naked in front of the crowd, but when they were accused of wearing girls' bloomers, it was almost enough to make them quit basketball for life.

Mikey bit his tongue and cut it during the game and Forbes substituted for him. At the infirmary, Brother Prosper sprayed the gash with Mercurochrome and turned him out.

Forbes played the clarinet in the band, so he had gone to the music room for his instrument after the preliminary game. When Mikey came out of the infirmary, he heard someone call Forbes's name from the direction of the music room. Mikey thought everybody in the school except Brother Prosper and Brother Anect were in the gym for the game. All the buildings from the infirmary back to the dormitories were completely dark. The dim light over the door of the infirmary was enough so that Mikey could see the outline of a black robe with the white bibbed collar of a Brother at the door of the music room. Forbes was running toward Mikey as though the owls were after him.

"Come back, Forbes! It's no sin, it's no sin," the voice called, but Forbes kept running.

"What's the matter, Forbes?" Mikey shouted when he recognized his friend.

Forbes ran right by him toward the gym.

Mikey saw the black robe go back inside the music room, then he ran and caught Forbes at the back door of the gym. He was crying.

"What's the matter?" Mikey asked.

"Nooo," Forbes said and jerked his arm away.

Mikey grabbed him by both shoulders. "Tell me what's the matter, Forbes. I know what's the matter. Brother Damian tried to play with your thing, didn't he?"

"Yes, Mikey, but don't say anything."

"Don't worry. It wasn't the first time, was it?"

"Don't say anything. I don't want anybody to know."

"Don't worry about it. He won't do it anymore."

The next day after their 10 AM shower and after they had dressed to go downtown to the show, Mikey took Forbes to Brother Benildus's office in the main building. No one was in the office, but the door was open. Mikey left Forbes inside, went to the Brothers' quarters on the second floor, and knocked on the door.

Brother Adrian, another of Mikey's favorites, answered the door. "Well, hi, Summers," Brother Adrian said. "Whatchoo need?"

Mikey's mouth turned down and gave him up by trembling at the corners, but he braced and said, "Brother, I have to talk to Brother Benildus."

Brother Adrian looked closely into Mikey's face and said, "What's wrong, Michael Paul? Just one minute. Now, stay right there. Will you stay right there?" He closed the door and was gone. A few minutes later he came back, put his hand on Mikey's shoulder, and walked him back to the office.

"Do you both want to talk to Brother Benildus?" Brother Adrian asked when he saw Forbes.

Forbes only waited for Mikey to answer. "Yes, Brother," Mikey said.

"You guys sit right there and Brother will be with you in one minute."

Brother Adrian went out into the hall to watch for Brother Benildus and after a while he turned to the boys. "Here he comes," he said and walked away.

The boys already knew Brother Benildus was coming. The brick building shook and he grunted, chugged, and huffed like a train. A great, fresh wind accompanied his arrival in the office. The boys stood up for him. He put his big hands on their shoulders, walked them to chairs in front of his desk, shut the door, sat at his desk, and looked Mikey in the eye.

"Tell me," he said.

Mikey was not one bit afraid or intimidated because he loved and trusted Brother Benildus.

"Brother Damian has been bothering Forbes the way he bothered me when I first came here by trying to play with his parts."

Brother Benildus was a dark-skinned Cajun. If a man could mirror a thunderstorm, Brother Benildus became the picture of a thunderhead at twenty thousand feet split by lightning. He waited a full minute for the storm to wane, and then said, "Thank you for coming to me. Go back to your group."

He stood up, put his hands on the boys' shoulders again, ushered them out into the hall, and walked away toward the Brothers' quarters without looking back.

That evening after Mikey returned from the show and before he was to go to evening study hall, he went to the main building to get a book from his locker. As he climbed the stairs to a side door of the building he saw Damian arrive on the other side of the door with his suitcase. Mikey opened the door for him.

"Oh, good, thank you, Summers," Damian said. He was dressed in his black dress suit, black overcoat, and hat.

"Where you going, Brother Damian?" Mikey asked.

"Oh, I've been transferred again." The man sighed. "I love Saint Michael's, but we religious have to be prepared for a transfer at any time, you know. I'm needed at a new station."

Mikey did not want to be a hypocrite, but he did feel sorry for the darned pervert.

"I'm sorry you're leaving," he said, only because he thought the man might want to hear it.

"Well, that's, as I say, the life of a religious. Good-bye and good luck to you." He went down the stairs and toward the front gate with his suitcase in his good hand. Mikey went inside, stopped in the hall, and sighed.

Brother Louis took over as custodian and director of the music room and he drafted Mikey for *Long John Silver*, an operetta for the Christmas program. Mikey had a good voice, so he was to play Long John himself with a pirate's black eye patch and a wooden parrot perched on his shoulder. He made it to the first dress rehearsal a week before the main performance, came down with the mumps, and was interned in Brother Prosper's infirmary. Forbes was given the role of Long John.

The weather was stormy for the next ten days. Mikey did not cope well with cold weather. He had only seen snow once in his life in Nogales and it melted after one day. A week after he had arrived at Saint Michael's he stepped out of the dormitory in the morning and found the whole world covered by two feet of snow. New snow fell every three weeks after that.

Most of the boarders' recreation was outdoors. The Brothers thought like Maggie: if a boy did not have a good reason to be inside, he was expected to stay out in the fresh air. The Brothers spent all their own free time outside. On Sunday mornings and afternoons they played a game they called "bool" that was like snooker pool on the ground with small, heavy, wooden balls. They threw out a small ball and then took turns lagging larger balls as close as they could to the little one. They spoke French in low voices throughout their serious game. They celebrated or mourned their shots modestly. They did not shout in triumph, moan in defeat, or jump up and down, but the boys knew they enjoyed the game. All of them played and were passionate about the outcome, only quiet and dignified.

After supper, the Brothers often walked in a black-robed horde around the football field to talk and say their rosaries. Inclement weather seldom kept them from it. Once in a while a Brother would join the boys in a touch football game or a game of five steps football, but he only stayed in the game for a few plays, then smiled, thanked the boys, and left.

One day Mikey, Forbes, and Manuel were playing five steps in front of the study hall building and the ball stuttered out of bounds near Brother Benildus. The big man wore sturdy slippers with elastic sides. To the boys' surprise, he turned and caught the ball on the first bounce. Mikey was only thirty yards away from him, so he thought Brother Benildus would only throw it back or kick it softly. He took three steps with expert form and punted the ball straight up with all his might. The ball spiraled almost out of sight above a hundred-foot cottonwood tree as though it would just keep on going and Brother Benildus's slipper spiraled right after it. Then the slipper spiraled down into Mikey's hands. The ball returned to earth later and bounced so high Mikey was glad he had not tried to catch it.

Mikey took a long time learning to protect himself against the cold. He could not keep his feet dry. He did not own a pair of overshoes or rubbers. He lost his cap, his mittens, his earmuffs, his jacket, and both his sweaters early in that first year and went on freezing at play. One day, Brother Prosper saw him playing outside in a foot of snow bareheaded, with sopping feet, and in his shirt-sleeves and ordered him to report immediately to the locker room. He then borrowed a jacket for Mikey and took him on a forced march all the way downtown to be reoutfitted with warm clothing. Mikey balked at the purchase of overshoes or rubbers. He was too vain about his fleet-footedness to harness his feet with galoshes. After that he kept a better eye on his winter clothes, but he still could not learn to keep his feet dry.

After his mumps cleared up, Brother Prosper released Mikey from the infirmary in time to go home the first day of Christmas vacation. The time in the infirmary had given him a chance to think about home because the radio was full of Christmas music and he was completely idle while his mumps went away. The Christmas music and programs on the infirmary radio made all sick boys think of their moms again. Mikey could not wait to see Maggie, Nina, Maudy, and Baxter. He would be glad to see everybody else, but he did not miss them. He supposed he had missed his mothers, sister, and dog before this, but not consciously. Now, he wanted to laugh and have fun with Maggie, Nina, Granny, Maudy Marie, and Baxter. He had learned a lot of new ways to laugh at Saint Michael's.

Forbes traveled to Lamy with Mikey in the La Fonda station wagon to board the train. Mikey helped him on the train with his big suitcase and looked after him. Forbes's father would meet him in Phoenix and Frankie Cunningham would meet Mikey and drive him to Nogales.

On the train Mikey fell into a conversation with a rancher from Las Vegas, New Mexico, named Albert Mitchell who knew Viv O'Brien and the Sorrellses. They talked about ranches, rain, cattle, and horses, but when Mikey asked the man if he knew Paul Summers, he said he did not. The boy was disappointed. He thought that everybody who knew his uncles knew Paul. His uncles' reputations had all been made in company with Paul. Mikey suspected that Mr. Mitchell knew his dad, but did not want to talk about him. Some people hated drunkards worse than any other kind of sinner, and cattlemen like Mr. Mitchell did not allow themselves to talk about people whose habits were bad, so they just would not admit that they knew them.

That day the man was worried about more than acquaintances who drank too much. He had shipped two thousand weaner calves to irrigated pasture near Phoenix by rail that morning. He would arrive only a few hours ahead of them. He said the calves and their mothers had spent a summer with no rain, and the calves were a hundred pounds too light to sell. He hoped they would bloom on good alfalfa and barley pasture near Phoenix.

"That's always the story, isn't it, Mr. Mitchell," Mikey said. "Everything might have been all right if you could have had one more rain. We always need just one more rain."

"Aw, youngster, it's a darned poker game and the cards we're dealt and the stakes we gamble are never enough," Mr. Mitchell said. "All we do is try to stay in the game from one year to the next."

Later, Mr. Mitchell said that he had been up since two thirty that morning and laid his head back and closed his eyes. Mikey turned toward the window to think. He thought about Viv and vowed to be good to him. Ever since he told Viv that he could not be his dad, their friendship had been strained. Mikey worried about that a lot. If he had only used a little of Paul Summers's blarney, only enough to grin at Viv and say, "Heck yes, you can be my pappy and I'll be your kid," even if he did not mean it, their friendship would have grown. Mikey still worshipped Paul Summers but did not have much hope that he would ever see much of him anymore. He was able to be with Paul less than anyone else he loved. He wanted to have a great friendship with Viv and he knew that if he did not watch out, he would lose him too.

Mikey was confident that Viv O'Brien wanted him to cowboy and he would be used as a cowboy no matter what other training he was given. He felt lucky and grateful to Viv for that. The way he looked at it, he might not be raised by the best cowboy in the world, but he would be raised by one of the best cattleman in the country who was admired by other cattlemen like Albert Mitchell and he would never be denied the chance to pursue his rightful calling.

When Mikey and Forbes got off the train, Forbes's Anglo father was waiting on the platform. He walked right past Mikey, picked up Forbes's suitcase, and headed for his automobile. Then Mikey saw Frankie Cunningham smile and wave at him from down the platform. Mr. Mitchell stopped to say hello to Frankie and told her he and Herb planned to meet at the Adams Hotel in Phoenix the day after New Year's.

The drive to Nogales with Frankie was a long trek for Mikey because he wanted his house to be around every curve of the road. He and Frankie would ordinarily have laughed and talked all the way, but he was anxious to be home and that was all he wanted to think about. He sat up with his nose against the windshield when Frankie finally turned into his yard.

Baxter came around the back of the house, saw Mikey's face, wagged his tail, and gave a joyous bark. The whole yard came to life. Mikey's heart jumped and then his mom came in sight, then Bica, Maudy Marie, and Granny. Mikey squeaked with pleasure. Then the Horrells' skinny, cranky Popie dog crossed in front of Frankie's car, intent on harming Baxter while his attention was on Mikey. Baxter was unaware of him. Popie pranced with stiff legs up behind Baxter.

Baxter smiled and barked and wagged his tail in a blur for Mikey. Mikey shrilled Baxter's name with the greatest joy he had known in a long, long time and right then Popie charged and nipped Baxter. Baxter was so surprised, he tucked his tail and darted aside, looked back at Popie, disappeared under Frankie's car, and screamed.

"Oh, Lord, Mikey, I killed your dog," Frankie cried.

Mikey had not heard the thump that usually happened when he was in a car that ran over an animal. He jumped out and ran back to his little dog. Nothing was left of Baxter except a small patch of mangled hair. His white coat was recognizable, but it was stained with the car's black grease. Leonard Wingo from next door, who never came over to Mikey's house, appeared, picked Baxter up with a shovel, and buried him at the foot of the hill behind the house.

Baxter's terrible death at the very instant that he and Mikey recognized each other and his being carried away as a mangled mass at the end of a shovel the next instant broke Mikey's heart. His grief warped the shape and sound of every object and every person in his world. He cried with the most terrible sorrow that he would ever know and he did not want to stop. He stumbled into the house ahead of Maggie as she and Frankie talked about the trip and he did not know how he would keep his feet moving from one step to the next. He stopped when he bumped into a corner of the front room by the picture window. He faced the world and his elderberry tree and cried. His front yard and trees, the highway, railroad tracks, and arroyo were there in front of him again. He had longed for them during his months away without knowing it, but he did not care about them now and did not want to stop crying.

Maggie and Frankie came in to sit and talk and Maggie ordered him to stop. He could not even attempt it. After a while, she ordered him to stop again and he tried and got scared that he might not ever be able to stop. After her third and most stern order to stop, he was able to curb his crying enough to satisfy her, but he could not leave the corner by the window.

Baxter had always been careful not to go out onto the highway where he could be run over. It took the very car he most wanted to see, at the most joyous moment of his reunion with his oldest, closest friend, to kill him in his own driveway. Mikey believed that nothing in the world could have hurt him more than the way he lost Baxter that day. He was never cured of his grief for Baxter. He would be stricken with that grief until the day he died.

TWELVE

COMEBACK

The Mexican vaquero says, if during a difficult journey you want to know if your horse is finished, dismount and pull his tail. If he resists, you can count on him to go on.

Mikey did not look up to face the world until spring. He had not known a victory for so long that he walked around school with his gaze on his feet. Before Saint Michael's he had set his own goals and realized personal victories. At Saint Michael's he did not seem to have time for personal goals, but he won small victories with his team in football, in other games, and in class. He had seen Brother Damian's perversity beaten but felt no sense of personal victory in the man's downfall.

He had returned to Saint Michael's after Christmas a ruined boy who believed that he would never recover. He had not been well, either. When he did not have a bad sore throat, a boil erupted somewhere on his carcass.

Then, on Ash Wednesday, the first day of Lent, he looked up and did not have a boil or a sore throat. His feet were dry, his keys were all in his pocket, his clothes were folded and clean in his locker, his bedclothes smelled good, he knew how to keep his schedule without being prodded, his books were all in his desk and he was in possession of enough pens, pencils, paper, and ink to finish out the year. All of a sudden he felt personally victorious, not the kind he knew after a stunt or a touchdown, but the kind that was won by perseverance, modesty, and courage inside a community effort.

The whole school fasted and abstained during the forty days of Lent. The boarders did not go to the movies. Saturdays were spent on all-day hikes. The boarders carried an orange apiece and hiked to Little Tesuque or Sun Mountain and returned to supper on empty, or as Cabezon and Paul would have said, they "went all day on one Gillette." Friday afternoons after class and before supper were spent in celebration of the Way of the Cross. Mikey's downtrodden mood had been well suited to forty days and forty nights of Lenten sacrifice. He was ready to deprive himself of his comforts as gifts to God because he did not see any other good reason for them and the Brothers taught that it might be appreciated. Now that he felt victorious, he could be magnanimous by giving all his downtroddenness to God.

His sense of well-being was short lived because that Ash Wednesday morning during class the La Cañada bullies decided to make a target of Mikey. He looked up from his desk and Skinny, the one he thought of as The Skull, made a fist at him from across the room. Skinny, Porky, and Rojas sat in the last three seats in the corner by the door. The other two turned their faces toward Mikey when Skinny made the fist. Then Porky made a fist at him and Rojas laughed. Rojas's seat was the last in the row. All three could mug at Mikey's side of the room without being seen by Brother Louis.

To make a fist at another kid at Saint Michael's was an invitation to Fist City. The bullies made fists at smaller, gentler kids to show that they intended to beat them up. Mikey figured the Cañada kids must have decided not to make Lenten sacrifice themselves. Instead they would make Mikey bleed for Christ.

Mikey decided to call them on it. He was through with being tormented. Their constant enmity bothered him as much as the boils and sore throats. He at least could defend himself against these three pus heads. They were not on the back of his neck; they were in a place where he could reach them and squeeze. This might be a good way to clean out all the poisons that bothered his system. He had suffered the torment of Job since he left home. The three sneaks would have been in absolute glory if they had known about Baxter and Mikey's sore throats. They enjoyed it plenty when they could see he had a boil. Today he did not suffer from even one affliction and felt altogether sound and whole for a fight.

He reminded himself of the advice Maggie gave him the first time he came home after a confrontation with a bully at Lincoln School.

"Listen, Mikey," she said, "when somebody tries to bully you, just punch him on the end of the nose the way you did old Panfilo. He might be bigger than you and he might think he's meaner, but you be just as mean as you want to be and at least give him his money's worth. A Sunday punch on the end of a bully's nose will probably give him all the trouble he'll ever want from you."

So Mikey vowed to give the bullies their money's worth. When the buzzer sounded for recess he headed straight for them. They stood up, smirked at one another, and huddled beside the door to let him pass. He stopped and made them shuffle out ahead of him. In the hall they separated and sauntered out to the playground. Several of Mikey's classmates joined him because everybody in class had seen Skinny make the fist at him.

Outside, Mikey stepped up behind Skinny and turned him around. Skinny affected a surprised look, then smiled. Porky and Rojas kept going. Skinny was just Mikey's size.

"Now, Skinny, tell me why you showed me that bony little fist," Mikey said. "Most of the time you only wipe your *mocos*, snots, off your mean little *mocoso* face with that hand."

Mikey figured that Skinny was the meanest of the three bullies because he was the ugliest. He had to know he was the ugliest kid in school unless he was a complete moron. Mikey always made sure that he knew he was ugly by the way he looked at him. Porky was not as ugly and he tried to be everybody's friend when Skinny was not around. Mikey was small for his age, but Porky was such a half-pint that his posture as a bully was pathetic. Rojas would not even have anything to do with Porky when Skinny wasn't around. Rojas did not bully Mikey, but he let it be known that he would back up the other two. Well, he would miss his chance if he kept making tracks away from them.

"No, I don't want anything with you, Summers," Skinny said.

"You think you can beat me up? Now's your chance."

"No, you're wrong, Summers. I don't want trouble with you." He did not act weepy or cowardly. He was on his dignity and gave Mikey a dead Indian eye.

Then Rojas walked up on Mikey's blind side and slapped him full in the face with both hands. Mikey was stunned, so Rojas boxed both Mikey's ears. Mikey swung a fist at Rojas's head, but he dodged it easily and slapped Mikey on both eyes. Mikey's classmates grabbed Mikey around the arms to keep him from fighting, so Rojas smacked his cheeks and ears again.

Brother Adrian stepped in and stopped it. The Brothers rarely interrupted a playground fight, but Brother Adrian must have seen this was too much a one-sided massacre. Mikey walked away to the wash hall and bathed his face and ears in cold water. His ears and both sides of his face throbbed and glowed as red as stoplights.

At the end of the last classroom session before noon, Mikey headed for the Cañada bullies again. He did not want his ears boxed, but he wanted to see if Rojas could hit him when he was not being held. The bullies left the school ground as fast as they did the day Tommy Franklin hit Mikey with the bat.

Mikey realized that he had postponed his boxing instruction too long. Sometimes he practiced on the light bag in the boarders' recreation room and put the gloves on to play with Manuel, but he did not know any way to protect himself against somebody like Rojas who really knew how to hurt him.

Every Thursday night the Brothers rented the school's gym to a promoter who put on professional wrestling matches. A twenty-foot square regulation ring was set up in the center of the gym and a heavy punching bag hung as a fixture in a corner. After school on the day Rojas almost slapped his face off, Mikey headed for the gym to see if he could teach himself to strike a moving target with his fists.

Paul Garcia, a high school student, was at work on the heavy bag. He asked Mikey to get behind it and hold it for him so it would not swing away from his hooks. Paul was an experienced amateur boxer and was training for a tournament. Mikey asked him if he could train with him.

"Polito, you've come to the right man," Paul said. "You keep me company here every day and I'll make you a champion."

After that, every day it was jab, jab, jab with the left until the lines and extension of Mikey's jab pleased Paul. Then, it was jab, jab, jab with a right lead until Mikey's right jab made Paul smile. Then, Paul coached him on how to jab with the left and move, move and jab, then cross with a right hand behind another jab. In that way, Mikey learned to punch straight with both hands and make a moving target. He worked on it until his punches did not stray or waver off a straight path to the target and his body launched his punches through the target.

After two weeks Paul decided to invite the whole school to come to the gym to learn to box. He gave all the boxers two weeks' training and then held a tournament in the gym during recesses and after school. Mikey won his sixty-five-pound class and the La Cañada bullies never bothered him again. He was too busy learning to box to worry about revenge against them, anyway. Paul convinced him that a boxer must also be a gentleman. A person who worked hard to master the manly art of self-defense had no business squaring off with anybody who was not a boxer, not even in play, not even as a joke. A gentleman did not raise his hands to strike anyone outside the ring. He took off all his clothes and performed in the ring in front of the whole world with discipline for himself and respect for his opponent. All those guys who picked fistfights had no class. After Mikey won his weight class in the school tournament, he forgot about challenging anyone to a playground fight. His enemies would have been the last ones in school to try to beat him in a fair fight, anyway.

Mikey learned his shortcomings in that first tournament. His classmate Joe McGrath owned a right hand punch that even a high school boy could respect. Mikey had sparred with Joe a lot in preparation for Paul's tournament. He and Joe were the same height, but Mikey had not been matched against him in the school tournament because Joe was heavier. Joe won the seventy-pound division. No boxer in the tournament could have escaped Joe's mighty right hand for three rounds. Joe had stopped two of his opponents in the second round with that right hand.

During Lent, the Brothers set up a projector and showed movies on Friday and Saturday evenings. The main movie was always a musical, a comedy, or a drama, but they also showed sports reels of Notre Dame football and professional boxing. The Brothers owned a library of the most famous fights ever filmed. The boys greatly admired the old champions and the fight reels were their favorites. Mikey studied form and style and began to develop his own. He read everything he could find about it. He dreamed that he would be a great world's champion. The dream helped lift him out of the loneliness and despair that Baxter's death had caused.

He did not like boxing as much as football because he was afraid before every contest, but he became obsessed by it and he had never been obsessed by football. He had been nervous before football games but never afraid. He was so afraid during the hour before he climbed into the ring with an opponent that he peed every ten minutes and turned as pale as any complete coward.

Fear fell away and was replaced by a lust for combat after the first punch was thrown. Boxing and football were alike that way, but he was naked and alone in the ring. He trembled when he had to march half-naked into the lights in front of scores of people, but when the fight started, he knew being vulnerable and alone was the only way men should fight, if they were brave.

Mikey and Brother Adrian became good friends and often held philosophical discussions. One day Mikey confided in him that he did not know why he liked boxing, as his fear gave him an awful time and experience did not seem to make him any braver. The next day, Brother Adrian loaned Mikey a book called

Boxing in Art and Literature and turned the pages to Aristotle's *Nicomachean Ethics*.

"Read that and you'll know that your fear before a fight is good," Brother Adrian said.

"How can it be good for me to be so scared?" Mikey asked.

"You have to be afraid or you can't be brave and bold. You cannot be brave unless you have first met and conquered your fear. A person who is not afraid before he puts himself in danger of being hurt is not brave. He is a stupid brute."

After that, Mikey was not troubled by his fear. He did not mind it anymore because it was only a high limb from which to launch himself. He boxed so that he could have peace and quiet. Now that he did not worry about his fear, he not only had peace and quiet, but he also had the admiration of his schoolmates. Those who did not admire him at least left him alone.

Gradually, the ethics and discipline of boxing became guidelines for Mikey's manners and conduct. He did not raise his hands to strike another boy outside the ring, not even in fun. He did not make excuses when another boxer made him look foolish or beat him in a contest. Conditioning was the foundation of a master. The better his condition, the quicker he would learn good form and technique.

Every aspect of the sport could be summed up by the four Ps that Mikey compiled as guidelines for himself at Brother Adrian's suggestion. Poise, Patience, and Pace gave a boxer Power. A fighter could lose a bout if his opponent made him look bad and if he lost his poise. A fighter could win if he was hurt by keeping his poise as his pace slowed. A fighter could win if he patiently concentrated on form and technique from the beginning to the end of a bout and did not try to stop his opponent by knockout with every punch. A fighter must know his condition and pace himself accordingly. If he kept his pace, poise, and patience, his opponent would become convinced that he would be as strong at the end of the fight as he had been in the beginning.

Paul Garcia advised him that good form and a good appearance would win fights when the give and take of blows failed. He should always remember that a boxer had to look good.

Mikey boxed in a pair of light moccasins that he polished to a mirror shine and laced with clean, white strings. His purple bloomers were freshly laundered and ironed. His clean sweat socks were pulled up and his hair was combed, and when he climbed into the ring he respectfully turned to face everybody on every side who had come to watch, and that meant no smile.

Paul also said that Mikey must remember to move gracefully and make a good picture for the judges. When Mikey asked him if good looks would help him win a fight, Paul laughed and said, "Sure it will, if you can fight."

One evening just before first study hall, a strange boy named Freddie Cline told Mikey he wanted to fight him during the recreation period between supper and last study hall. The surprise challenge struck fear in Mikey. He only accepted it because every boy within earshot stopped to see if he would turn chicken.

Freddie Cline was another Arizona boy from a cattle ranch. Mikey knew little about him. He was Mikey's age, in the fifth grade, slept in Mikey's dormitory, was a loner and a misfit, and did not care one bit about looking good. Mikey had never seen him with his hair combed or his face and hands washed clean. He had not spoken three words to Mikey since the beginning of the school year and now he wanted to see if he could whip him.

The two boys squared off in the rec room after supper. Mikey did not have the reach on Freddie and he did not have room on the wooden floor to keep away from him. Freddie's style was to rush Mikey and windmill his fists. Instead of the ropes of a ring, the boundaries were lined with boys. When the fighters pressed the boundaries, the spectators pushed them back into the fray.

Mikey was able to land punches at will as Freddie rushed him. Freddie came at him with his head up and made an easy target. His own weight gave force to Mikey's fists, but when Mikey was not able to move out of his way, he got his head tattooed with the red dye in Freddie's gloves.

Mikey and Freddie Cline fought fifteen one-minute rounds with one minute of rest between rounds. They fought until the whistle blew for study hall. Mikey bloodied Freddie's nose in the first round and Freddie bloodied Mikey's in the fourteenth. Mikey did not feel victorious, but he knew that he had not lost. His friends lifted his hand as though they believed he had won. Freddie did not have any friends, so he did not get any votes except Mikey's. Mikey congratulated him on a good fight. Freddie gave him a cowboy's iceberg look, shook his hand, and went on about his business.

A week later, Mikey and his classmate David Koury were passing a football on the playground when a fight broke out. They ran to the huddle of boys that surrounded the combatants and saw that Freddie Cline was in a fight with Joe Shirley. Shirley was quiet, serious and no bully, so Mikey wondered how enough bad communication could have passed between the two boys to spark a battle.

Freddie and Shirley were thrashing on the ground with headlocks on one another when Brother Manuel, the prefect of the Big Boys, showed up with a set of sixteen-ounce gloves. Everybody was cheering for Joe Shirley, so Mikey stepped in to lace and tie Freddie's gloves. Freddie was not one who needed encouragement, so Mikey patted him on the back and shoved him into the fray.

Now, that was a fight. Those two quiet boys landed clean punches on each other's heads and bodies for a solid fifteen minutes with no rest until the bell rang for class. The fight over, Brother Manuel made them shake hands. Freddie stood still as Mikey unlaced his gloves, but he did not speak to Mikey or even look at him. Joe Shirley had knocked a great big flake of a green booger out of his nose, and it hung on a shred of blood on his cheek, so Mikey grabbed him by the wrist and wiped it off with his sleeve.

Freddie was still not at Saint Michael's with everybody else. He did not know that Mikey wished him well, did not know who unlaced his gloves, did not care. The boy had covered himself with glory that day, but he just melted into the calcimine of the old Saint Michael's walls and did not step out into the open again for the rest of the year. No one knew when he left school for summer vacation, and he never came back.

The Optimist Club of Santa Fe held a boxing tournament for the northern region of New Mexico every year, and Paul Garcia entered a team of his school's finalists in that tournament. Mikey's first opponent was Johnny Martinez from Taos.

Paul Garcia had taught Mikey his range. The boy knew the exact distance from which he could throw a punch and land it. He could stand outside the arm's reach of an opponent and hit him by sliding in with a long left step behind the straight pole of his arm. He jabbed Martinez the instant he came in range and then stepped back out of range. At the end of the second round, he began to reach Martinez with a straight right hand behind his jab, but Martinez stunned him with both hands on the top of his head in each of the three rounds. Mikey kept his eyes open and his legs moving each time until his eyes uncrossed and his head cleared. He won a split decision.

Mikey's second opponent was Johnny Apodaca from Harvey Grammar School. He was two years older than Mikey and much feared as a tough fighter from La Cañada Street, which had earned him the nickname of Cañada Mauler. Worse than that, he was another of Paul Garcia's protégés.

While Mikey fought his fear, he thought about how he might defend himself. Everybody thought he would be slaughtered, so he did not have anything to lose. He talked it over with Paul and decided to gamble on a way to make Apodaca look bad to his hundreds of friends who would be there to watch him fight. Mikey had learned that sometimes even the craftiest and most talented boxer could be beaten if he could be made to look bad. Some fighters were unbeatable until they were made to back down, even a step or two. Sometimes, after Mikey punched his way under his opponents' veneer, they lost their poise and fell apart.

Mikey and Apodaca walked to the ring and arrived on opposite sides at the same time. Apodaca seemed to know everybody in the audience. The bullies sat with their neighbors in the La Cañada section and cheered for him. They had not made themselves so evident to Mikey in weeks. Mikey walked slowly, climbed into the ring slowly, turned, and looked into all the faces and sat right down. Apodaca glided through the ropes, danced in a pirouette, smiled and waved all around, and put on a show as if to say, "Here

I am. Ain't you glad to see me? Came to see me win a fight? Well, you done just right."

Only Paul Garcia knew Mikey that night. Only Manuel Enriquez and his brothers had come to wish Mikey luck that day. Everybody else stayed away from Mikey. The word around the school was that Apodaca had whipped so many kids like Mikey in his career that this bout was only another drill. Apodaca smiled happily through the referee's instructions.

The ten-second whistle was blown to warn the handlers to clear the ring. Paul climbed out, but Mikey remained seated on his stool. Paul reached in and held one leg of the stool with one hand and placed the other hand on the small of Mikey's back. Apodaca stood in his corner with his back to Mikey, facing his handlers and his public.

When the bell rang, Paul pushed Mikey across the ring with one hand and pulled the stool out with the other. Mikey hit the center of the ring running. Apodaca smiled all around, turned, and Mikey was upon him. Mikey kicked his left foot high, launched his straight left jab at Apodaca's smile, and fell on him. Apodaca spun with the blow. Mikey jabbed him again and he turned his back as though he wished to flee. Mikey stepped around in front of him and bounced a hard right hand off his head. Apodaca ducked and swung two hooks that swished in Mikey's direction, but Mikey had already stepped out of range. Apodaca raised his head to locate him and Mikey fell on him with another jab and buried a right hand in his bread basket.

"The *right*, again! Throw the *right*, to the head, Polito!" Paul shouted, so Mikey stepped in and hit Apodaca on the end of his nose with a right hand straight from the shoulder.

Those first big punches won him the fight. Apodaca did not smile again until after the bell ended the third round. Every time he came in range, Mikey landed a left and a right. He even began to lead with his right, because when he landed it he was a stronger boy than even the great Cañada Mauler.

After the fight was over Apodaca's smile was genuine, friendly, and rueful.

"You did it, Summers," Apodaca said. "Did I even land one punch?"

"You punch hard," Mikey said. Apodaca had landed a left and a right to his ribs midway through the first round with a lot of style that knocked all the air out of him. The first time that had happened was when Joe McGrath punched the air out of him in training. He had thought he ought to thrash on the floor until his breath came back, but Paul ordered him to keep his feet, keep his poise, and move away until he recovered. When Johnny Apodaca punched his air out, Mikey had been able to hide it from him, as he was sure Apodaca had hidden his pain when Mikey landed that good right hand in his breadbasket.

Now he would have to fight Joe McGrath in the finals. On the afternoon before the fight the boarder boxers rested in their dormitories. Joe and Mikey slept in the same dormitory and were sparring partners, but they were not close friends yet. Joe chummed around with his older brother Herbert the way Manuel Enriquez hung around his own brothers. That afternoon, while they rested in the dormitory, Mikey found out that Joe's father, Shorty McGrath from Silver City, was a friend of Viv O'Brien, Roy Adams, and Herb Cunningham. Joe and Herbert lived on a cow ranch, so Mikey and Joe spent the afternoon talking about horses and cattle and became good friends.

Mikey had already been hit hard right in the stomach and in the head by Joe and he respected him more than he had respected Martinez and Apodaca before he fought them. Joe had clear, agate gray eyes. He was never frivolous or giggly, so his eyes always seemed hard as ice, but that afternoon Mikey found out that he was warm-hearted and generous. That gave Mikey hope that he might have a chance to win the fight. He knew Joe would fight hard and could hit hard, but Mikey did not fear him after he found out that he was kind-hearted. Mikey respected him but only feared his big right hand. He thought that he could keep that hand from hitting him, so he was confident that he would make a good showing in the fight.

Besides that, Joe confessed that he thought Mikey was the best boxer in the tournament. He believed no other Saint Michael's boxer could have beaten tough opponents like Martinez and Apodaca two nights in a row. Mikey knew Joe could be the best boxer in any tournament if he landed just one right hand on each of his opponents, but he did not say a word of reciprocal praise. If Joe wanted to believe Mikey was the best, Mikey wanted him to keep on believing it.

Mikey knew he could not win if Joe hit him, so he jabbed and moved away from the awful right hand. Then, in the middle of the third round, he got careless and Joe caught him in the stomach with a hook and stopped him on his feet with a straight right hand between the eyes. For a moment Mikey was out. A whole moment went by that was nothing but a dream. He dreamed he was back on the gym floor sparring with Joe after school and Joe landed that left to the belly and right to the head and it was that time, not this time.

Joe's warm heart saved Mikey because he stepped back and waited for Mikey to recover. Mikey moved and jabbed for the rest of the round and he did not venture inside the range of Joe's punches for the rest of the fight.

Mikey won that fight by decision and his hand was raised as champion of his division. He was awarded a star-shaped medal on a red, white, and blue ribbon with the image of a bare-knuckle boxer in the center. Joe was awarded a small golden glove that he could hang on the chain around his neck with his scapular medal.

Brother Manuel presided over the boxers' banquet the following evening. The Saint Michael's boxers had won the team trophy for the tournament, which was placed at the head of the table. Brother Manuel stood up to lead everybody in the prayer before supper, but before he made the sign of the cross, he said, "We are grateful to our fifteen boxers for the outstanding manner in which they represented Saint Michael's in the Optimist Boxing Tournament. Our team was the best of eleven other teams in northern New Mexico, our fifteen boxers the best of more than 120 other boxers who competed." He lifted the trophy and said, "This boxer on this trophy represents our outstanding boxer, Michael Paul Summers."

Victory. This was victory. Mikey had not known that an outstanding boxer would be elected. Joe McGrath lifted Mikey's hand and Mikey lifted Joe's. They remained bosom pals for as long as they were at Saint Michael's.

The next day Mikey came down with the three-day measles. Brother Prosper kept him in bed in the infirmary until they cleared up. Every kid who was sick in Brother Prosper's infirmary was made to take a hot bath in an old-fashioned tub with brass feet before he was released. Brother Prosper brought Mikey clean clothes from his locker, filled the tub with water hot enough to scald the feathers off a rooster, then stood right there while the boy climbed in. The water was so hot that Mikey's flesh curled up just short of permanent scarring. Brother Prosper did not leave until he saw that Mikey was used to the water and would not jump out when he turned his back. Exactly twenty minutes later he was back with a bottle of alcohol and a towel. He supervised while Mikey dried himself, then made him rub alcohol all over himself, even between his toes.

Mikey walked out of the infirmary on Monday morning, the first day of Easter vacation and ran into Forbes and a pretty woman. The woman was Mikey's friend Queta. Now he knew why Forbes had always looked so familiar. Queta, La Prieta, the dark beauty, was little Forbes's mother. Forbes resembled his Anglo father in complexion, the color of his hair, and his build, but he resembled his mother in the eyes, nose, and mouth.

Mikey had never forgotten the night he ran away from the Cavern in Nogales, Sonora, ended up in the nightclub in the Zone of Tolerance, and saw a man beat up Queta. He remembered that the women who helped Queta thought Mikey was someone called "Forvehs." Forbes.

Queta took Mikey's hand and looked seriously into his eyes. "So, my little cowboy hero has been here all this time."

"Yes."

She wore a new scar under her eyebrow and Mikey bet he knew how she got it.

"Why was I not informed?"

"I don't know."

"I searched for you. I asked all the cowboys for news of you."

"Anybody could have told you where I was."

"Every time I was given *razón de ti*, word of you, you went away again."

"I'm glad to see you, Queta. Forbes didn't tell me you were his mother."

"¡*Válgame*! Bless me! Yes, this little blond is my son. Can you believe it?"

"Yes, I could see you in his face, but I didn't know it was you until now."

"You think he looks like me?"

"He's a blond Queta prieta."

Queta laughed. "Did you imagine a dusky gypsy like me could have a son so blond?"

"No." Mikey smiled.

"Well, look at him."

"I look at him every day. He's my friend," Mikey said.

"That's what he tells me. Now you can help your friend Forvehs show me around the school. Where are we going next, Little Man?"

"The grotto," Forbes said.

"I have an errand to run," Mikey said. "Can I see you later?" He did not want to spoil Forbes's time with his mom. If he went to the grotto, Forbes would only follow along and expect Mikey to take over the tour.

Forbes led Queta away to see the school's replica of the grotto of Our Lady of Lourdes. Queta was a mom, a person most respected at Saint Michael's. This was a victory if there ever was one because Forbes and Queta were his loyal friends.

Queta stayed for the entire week of Easter vacation. She and Forbes took Mikey out to eat twice during the week and again to dinner at the La Fonda after Easter Sunday Mass. Forbes bought his mom a corsage for Mass and he cried when Queta drove him and Mikey back to school and said good-bye at the front gate. Mikey put an arm around his shoulders and walked him to the recreation room when she was gone.

THIRTEEN

APACHELAND

A vaquero who rides the string of rough broncs on a ranch uses a
tapojo on his bridle. A tapojo is a wide leather band that lies across
*a bronc's forehead and is slipped down over his eyes as a blindfold so he will
stand still while he is mounted or dismounted. Some broncs will hurt a
rider any time he can have him close on the ground and a rider is most vulnerable when he mounts and dismounts. When people see that a horse is
bridled with tapojo, they know to stay out of range of his hooves and teeth.*

Mikey and Forbes rode the train together to Phoenix after school
let out for the summer. In Phoenix they caught the Greyhound bus
to Tucson and then the Citizen Stage to Nogales. The "stage" was
a twenty-passenger motor bus.

Viv was in Susanville, California, pasturing a herd of steers.
Maggie planned to spend the summer with him, so she arranged
for Mikey to stay with Paul on the Apache Indian reservation. Paul
now worked as a government stockman for the Apache herd near
McNary. Mary Bell was Mikey's new stepmother.

Mikey visited his home for one evening. The next morning he, Maggie, and Nina headed for the White Mountains in Maggie's black coupe. The route was paved to Tucson but unpaved for the next two hundred miles through Florence and Globe, across the Salt River Canyon and over the Mogollon Rim to McNary. They arrived in McNary late and stayed the night in a boarding house that belonged to the Southwest Lumber Mill.

Mary Bell Summers came for Mikey the next morning. Maggie only stayed long enough after Mary arrived to see that Mikey's gear was stowed in Mary's car. She gave Mikey a peck on the cheek without looking at him, turned away, loaded Nina, and headed home. Nina did not get within fifty yards of Mary.

Mary explained that she needed to run an errand and could not take Mikey with her. She drove out of town, stopped under a pine tree, told him to get out and wait, made a U-turn, and drove away.

Mikey saw an Apache wickiup in the timber about fifty yards away. He sat and waited under the pine tree. Maggie had not wanted to eat in the boarding house that morning. In fact, she left town so quickly to get away from Mary that Mikey missed breakfast, too. Every now and then he turned toward the wickiup to see if anyone would come out. Smoke issued from its stovepipe. Finally, an Apache woman came out to sweep the space in front of the door. She wore a calico dress with a high collar. The hem was ankle-length and she wore teguas, the same kind of rawhide-soled moccasins that the Yaquis wore. Her hair was combed straight and shiny to the waist. She smiled at Mikey and said something to someone inside the wickiup. A gray-haired lady in calico came out and looked straight at Mikey. She nodded to the younger woman, shyly covered her mouth with her hand, laughed, and turned away.

The younger woman spoke to someone else inside the wickiup. A boy came out and carried a tin cup and a rolled tortilla to Mikey.

Mikey did not doubt for a moment that the boy spoke Spanish. He did not know Apache, but he did not think anyone as brown as this boy would be comfortable in English. "¿Qué hubo?" he said in Spanish. "How's it going?"

"*Quehubo*," the boy said. "*Toma*, take this." He handed Mikey the tortilla. A dollop of fried beans was wrapped inside it. The tin cup was full of sweet, hot coffee and canned milk.

"What's your name?" Mikey said.

"Juan Bueno. You?"

"Maikeh."

"Your father is El Pol, no?"

"Pol Somairs."

"He's my friend."

"How do you know him?"

"He cowboys with my father and grandfather at the Haystack. I cowboy, too, but not today. Here, you can have this." He handed Mikey a shiny steel ball bearing, a steelie. Mikey gave Juan Bueno a stick of gum. Juan Bueno peeled off the paper and chewed the gum. He took out a pocketknife with the handles broken off the frame, found a bare slash in the bark of the pine tree, and dug off a hardened drop of pine resin for Mikey. He dug out another for himself, put it in his mouth, and broke it up with his new gum.

"Chew that pine rock," Juan Bueno said.

The resin was brittle and broke up easily, then turned soft and blended with Mikey's gum. He took out the wad and looked at it. The pine drop had turned into gum. It tasted good with the spearmint and made a bigger wad to chew.

Juan Bueno led Mikey to the wickiup and told him the younger woman was his mother, Filomena, and the older was his grandmother, Nana. The women also spoke Spanish. Both gravely shook hands with Mikey and looked into his eyes. Their hands were clean and wet with water.

"How do you know Spanish, Polito?" Nana asked.

"From my parents," Mikey said.

"Are you Mexican?"

"Sonoran. And you?"

"If you want to know, I'm Sonoran, too. Did you know that?"

"No."

"I was born in the Sierra Madre near the pueblo of Mulatos."

"I don't know Mulatos, but I know the mountains of Magdalena."

"My mother was Yaqui."

"My mother was born in Patagonia. I knew Yaquis who walked through the Sierra de San Juan when I was little."

"Were those the ones who said you were titiritero?" Nana asked. "Your father told us about those Yaquis."

"They said I was a wizard." Mikey laughed self-consciously.

"Your father told us about that. I think it's true that you are titiritero. Your ojos de gato, cat eyes, help you for that. Is that how you knew to speak to us in Spanish?"

"I only thought you would understand me better."

"All Apaches do not speak Spanish. Apaches don't go to Mexico as they used to because there is a bounty on our heads as there is for the Yaquis. Few of us speak Spanish now. My mother taught me. Her mother taught her. My husband is Apache and also speaks Spanish. My son-in-law, Juan Bueno's father, is Apache and speaks Spanish. They were both with Jeronimo. Do you know who Jeronimo is?" The woman smiled.

"No. Did he run from the soldiers through the Sierra de San Juan with the Yaquis?"

Both women laughed. "No," Filomena said. "Maybe, but not when you were there. He was an *anciano*, an ancient one of my husband's and my father's time. The Americans pronounce his name Geronimo."

"Juan Bueno's father lived with Geronimo?"

"Yes, he did, and his father did and his father before him." Filomena laughed again. "But Juan Bueno's father is also anciano. More ancient than *los cerros*, the hills."

The women promised Mikey that he would meet Juan Bueno's father and grandfather at the Haystack Ranch where they worked with Paul. Mikey had heard of Geronimo, but he thought he was only a fictitious character, a make-believe movie opponent of Roy Rogers, Tom Mix, and Gene Autry.

Mary showed up and Juan Bueno told Mikey to give back the steelie, because he thought it would be safer with him. Mikey was positive it would be safer with him. After one school year at Saint Michael's he could not promise that he would not lose it before bedtime. He never saw it again, but he and Juan

Bueno were friends, and he could have anything Mikey owned after that.

Mary asked Mikey a lot of questions on the way out to the Haystack and told him everything he wanted to know about his father. He did not ask many questions about Paul. Usually, people who said they loved his father thought it gave them a reason to run him down about his drinking. Mikey did not know one bad thing that came from Paul's drinking. He did not even blame Maggie's divorce on it. Mikey had been with him a lot when he drank whiskey and did not know why anyone would think it was bad. He knew of men who lied and stole in the cattle business and went to Canal Street on their wives and their families did not quit them. He wondered why people thought Paul's drinking gave them the right to condemn him to his son. No matter how much a person professed to be Paul's friend, usually he found an opening to condemn him for his drinking. Mary looked happy and healthy, so Mikey did not ask her how Paul had been doing with his whiskey.

The Haystack Ranch headquarters was in an open, grassy draw. The corrals dominated the place. They were connected by alleys that made it easy for a few hands to cut and work thousands of cattle. The saddle house was made of pine logs and the main house where Paul and Mary lived was a one-room log cabin with an outhouse in the back. A veranda with a pine floor shaded the front door. The stove and kitchen sideboard were just inside the door. Paul and Mary slept in a bed near the stove. Mikey unrolled his bed on a cot at the other end of the room. A window was across the room from Mikey's bed. A costumer stood between his cot and the bed that Paul and Mary shared.

Mary told Mikey to stay outside while she prepared supper, so Mikey put his saddle, blankets, chaps, and bridle in the saddle house. A windmill pumped into a storage tank that stood on a tall stanchion near the saddle house. A nearby pump house held a large engine in its cool, dirty grease. Mikey climbed the windmill tower and looked around. Smoke rose from another camp of tents a quarter mile away, and he figured it was the camp of Juan Bueno's father, grandfather, and the other cowboys. A herd of horses grazed in the draw a half mile away. The afternoon was cool and the place was still. Thin smoke rose from Mary's stove. Meadowlarks sang in the draw. Chipmunks chattered in the timber. A flock of blue jays swooped on the corral to water in a trough. The big draw was bordered by the ponderosa pine forest. Cedar and oak also grew in that forest, but the pine trees overshadowed everything. The smell of pine was so heavy that Mikey could taste it on his tongue. He was still on the tower when Paul drove up in a pickup at sunset.

Mikey sat on the top of the tower and watched. Paul looked slim, hard-twisted, and brown. His hat was near full destruction. His boots were tiny and he walked with a lot of muscle. Mikey did not think he had ever seen his father with whiskers on his face. Every morning Paul found himself some hot water and used his shaving mug and razor. His face looked like saddle leather in color and texture, and the lines on it could have been made by the tool of a saddle maker. The lines were all caused by his smile when he played and by his squint against the sun when he worked.

Mikey was about to climb down out of the tower when he heard Mary's voice rise in anger. Mikey settled back. "Well, how long is he going to stay?" she demanded. "I suppose you think I'm going to put up with your kid all summer." She banged something on the stove. Mikey did not want to hear any more of it. He could not hear what Paul said because he was so soft-spoken, but he could not miss anything Mary said. He stayed in the tower and tried not to listen. Paul did not call him until long after dark. Mikey climbed down from the tower before he answered.

"Where were you, son?" Paul asked when he hugged him.

"Way on over there on the other side of the pump house," Mikey said.

"Well, what do you think of the place?"

"I like the smell of the pines and the green grass."

"Wait until you see some of these *cienegas*, meadows. Wait until you see the elk and the bear, son. We have a lot of good horses, too."

Mary did not speak to Mikey at the supper table; she did not even look at him. He was to find out that as soon as Paul came home she swelled up and became sullen to keep his attention. When Paul asked Mikey if he wanted more to eat, Mary gave an impatient sigh and sat back in her chair. After that, Mikey would have starved before he asked for more. When Paul asked Mary if she had bought any milk, she asked him why he thought she would do that. When Paul said that growing boys needed milk, Mikey said, "Oh, I'm used to going without milk." That was a lie. The Brothers owned a good farm in Bernalillo, New Mexico. A truckload of milk, butter, meat, vegetables, and preserves was sent to the school every week. The boys were given almost all the milk they wanted.

Mikey would have done anything to get along with Mary. He had been friends and classmates at Lincoln School with her nieces and nephews. He would not have chosen her as a stepmother, but now that she had become one, he needed to be a gentleman and her friend. After that first supper, he could tell that he had about as much a chance of love and affection, even friendship, from Mary Bell as he did from Hitler. He remembered that he had once heard Paul and Bud Parker call her Madam Hitler.

When Mikey bedded down in the quiet of the White Mountains that night, he thanked God for this chance to cowboy with Paul again. He decided that he would not worry about anything as hard to get as the love of a stepmother. He knew that he would get along with Paul's crew. Most cowboys were regular and open with each other. They did not have any conceits that way. They got along as teammates who faced the same dangers, hard work, and fun. They watched each other's backs, even when they did not like each other.

Everybody liked Paul. Most cowboys liked whiskey as much as he did, so they were not ones to hold his drinking against him. The kind of men who came to work and quickly latched on to the conviction that they were better than Paul because they did not drink as much as he did usually did not turn out to be good cowboys. A man had to be reckless to be a cowboy. He often had to throw himself away like a drunkard in order to get out in front of a cow. If he was a good cowboy who did not drink, he at least did not think he was better than anybody who did. If he drank, he was usually too wild and crabby to think he was any good at all. Paul said he knew Mormons and Texas Baptists who did not drink but who turned wilder on cowboying than any cowboy ever did on drink.

The next morning Mikey met two Apaches, Severiano and Victoriano, and Lyle Maneer and Curry Jones, two white cowboys. Uncle Art Robinson, Nina's brother, was also there. Lyle Maneer and Uncle Art resembled each other so much they could have been brothers. Both were short, wiry, hard twists. Both were as soft-spoken and serious as the two Apaches.

Severiano and Victoriano were old fellers. Curry, Lyle, and Art were only in their twenties. None of them ever made an undue sound or wasted motion. They did not have expression when they were at work horseback. Their spirits minded their big horses. All the muscle was in the horses, and at least half the spirit and brains belonged to the horses. The decisions were made by the men, but the horses deserved the victories.

The horses knew when a victory had been won in the work but showed it only in a momentary lift of their tails, a firmer step, or a haughty look. Once in a while a horse would throw up his head and nicker in triumph after he had won a hard victory. The cowboys might look at each other out of the corners of their eyes in appreciation of something they had won, but they were too modest to rave over a victory they could not have won without their horses. The cows too often won the victories. The most a cowboy would let himself do when he won was smile to himself when no one was looking. Most cowboys watched themselves closely to make sure they did not do more than that. Cows knew too many ways to bring cowboys down off high horses.

Curry Jones was born a cowboy, did everything right by instinct, and talked all the time. He could tell a long story or say the words to a long song while he did the most difficult cowboy work and never skip any of the story or stop for interruptions. He never showed unkindness to animals or persons. Impatience was not in him. He required one full minute to say good morning. He always called Mikey M-i-c-h-a-e-l P-a-u-l which he needed ten seconds to say.

Mikey found new tools at the Haystack that he had never used before. The outfit used wagons and teams of big horses. Two brown horses and two bays made up the teams and they could also be driven as a four-up. They were bred half Government Thoroughbred and half Clydesdale.

The remuda was made up of thirty-six large mountain horses that were out of Thoroughbred mares by Government studs. If Mikey could have stood Pancho beside them, the little Mexican would have looked like one of their colts. Curry told Mikey that, except for a half Shetland in Mikey's string, they all weighed more than thirteen hundred pounds. Mikey had never known a desert remuda that big. The Haystack horses were bigger because of their breeding but also because of the green grass they ate day and night, month after month, and year after year in the high country.

Paul caught the morning mount of horses in his usual way. He ran them into a rail pen along one side of the main corral, waited until they quieted with their heads over the rail, roped them with a soft loop from behind, and led them out to their riders. Mikey's top horse was a *tordillo*, a light gray horse. The horse turned, faced Paul, and walked toward him before the loop even tightened on his neck.

Mikey climbed on the rail and bridled him. He was a monument, a statue of a horse and he stood as still as a boulder for Mikey. He was the color of granite and from a distance his eyes were navy blue. His eyes were so dark, Mikey could not see the brown mud of the world inside them unless he was only six inches away.

"His name is Eagle," Paul said. "He understands Spanish. You ought to feel at home here, son. Most of the men talk Spanish and so do the horses."

After the crew saddled their horses, they harnessed the teams to the wagons. With Curry's guidance Mikey helped harness horses for the first time in his life. Curry went by steps, front to back, the way harnessing has been done forever, then showed him how to line up the horses, bridle them, take down the lines, and hitch them to the wagons. The teams were young and juicy and Paul used them every time he could invent a reason.

The crew loaded the wagons, turned the remuda out on the road, and headed for Horseshoe Meadows where they would gather and brand calves. Curry and Lyle drove the teams and the rest of the crew drove the remuda. One wagon was loaded with a chuck box and the food provision, beds, and cooking gear. The Hooligan wagon was loaded with salt and grain for the horses, a coil of rope, wire, staples, tents, and tools.

Mikey's stirrups were short. His legs were a lot longer than they had been when he put up his saddle last fall. He would have to unlace the leathers that evening and lengthen them.

The crew used the day to move to Horseshoe Meadows and make camp. A bell was belted around the neck of a bronc named Pesa and the remuda was grained and turned into a horse pasture.

Mikey helped Curry sweep and mop the cabin floor and air it out. Everybody found a place on the floor for his bed. The Apaches owned *Saltillos*, long, wide, tightly woven woolen blankets they could wear like ponchos over their shoulders. They laid on half and covered themselves with the other half. When they were asleep, their heavy hair spread out on the floor. Their eyelashes stuck out in twenty different directions and interlocked. Father and son slept silently side by side and only their black and white hair showed over their black and white Saltillos. Paul told Mikey they were better to camp with than anybody he knew. They were silent, neat, clean, and wise. Cowboys and vaqueros tried to be that way in camp but often strayed because they knew they would be forgiven as they were when they were home.

Every night, after every man was in his soogan, Curry engaged Paul in soft conversation. Curry did all the talking in a slow, deep drawl that doped Mikey off to sleep. Mikey seldom awoke in the night, but when he did, it was to be sucked into a draft of wind and sound from Lyle Maneer's and Curry Jones's snoring.

On that first night, Paul opened his bed in front of everybody, took a sack of rocks he had collected, and sprinkled them on his flannel sheets. Victoriano and Severiano smiled and said nothing. Lyle and Art grinned. Curry said, "Well, Paul's graveling his highway to heaven again." He turned to Mikey. "Did you know your dad did that, Michael Paul?"

"Yes."

"You think that makes his dreams sweet?"

Mikey kept a straight face. "No, I think it's so he won't miss Mary too much."

Even the Apaches laughed.

On the first day of work in the meadows, Mikey went out to saddle his wrangling horse. At the corner of the saddle house he ran head-on into a stocky man. The man had a cold brown cigarette in the corner of his mouth and a dusty black hat set low over his brow. He stared into Mikey's eyes and did not smile.

"And who might you be, button?" he asked.

"Michael Paul Summers Sorrells."

"Well, I'm glad to meet you, Michael Paul. I'm Gunnar Thude."

"My dad said you'd meet us here."

"Let's go see your dad. Is the coffee ready? Who does the cooking in this lash-up?"

"The coffee's ready. Lyle's cooking and I've got to wrangle the horses."

"No, you don't. They're already in the corral."

Mikey looked around the corner of the saddle house and saw that the remuda had already been corralled.

"Now that you've seen them in the corral, you've done your duty. Let's get some coffee," Gunnar said.

Mikey fell in step with him. "Thanks," he said.

"Don't mention it," Gunnar said. "I bet you and me'll get along good."

"We will if you wrangle the horses before I get up every morning." Mikey kept a straight face.

"Naw, that's a button's job. Not a chore for a top hand like me."

"But you do it so well. I think whoever's best at it ought to do it."

"You can't get good at it unless you do it all the time as a button."

The crew was in the cabin drinking coffee when Gunnar and Mikey went in. Gunnar got his coffee, then shook hands all around. "This button tells me I'd make a good horse wrangler," Gunnar said to Paul. "I think he'll do to take along. He's as good a confidence man as Buster Sorrells and he don't stutter like Buster."

"Well, Buster's his uncle. Do you think he looks like him?"

"He's as black, anyway. Is this the one they call Black Man?"

"This is the one."

"Well, put 'er there, Black Man." Gunnar shook Mikey's hand again. "Your Uncle Buster is probably the best friend I have in the whole world besides your dad. You think you'll be anything like them when you grow up?"

Mikey looked at his dad. "You never know," he said.

All the cowboys laughed at that. Mikey enjoyed another victory. His dad had been telling the cowboys stories about him and that was proof that his life had not been completely without accomplishment.

That day the crew spread out and gathered a forty-section pasture. Mikey paired off with Uncle Art.

After a while, Art asked, "Mikey, which way is camp?"

Mikey pointed back to camp.

"That's right. In this timber, you have to keep your own compass in your ears so you'll always know which side of your head our camp lies."

"I guess I do that without thinking about it, Uncle Art."

"You always have to remember to think about it when you're in the timber. You have to look for landmarks because you're not surrounded by close mountains. Cowboying is not the same in these big pines as it is down south where you have big mountains to watch and short brush to ride through. You can lose track of your landmarks, so watch out. Everything looks the same inside these pines. You know what I mean?"

"I think so, Uncle Art."

"I know you're a good cowboy, Mikey, but any of us can get lost in this country. If you stayed in the thick forest, you could probably ride all the way to the Grand Canyon and not see a landmark, so be careful. If you and I get separated for more than half an hour I want you to stop and get off old Eagle and let him rest until I find you. If something happens and I don't catch up to you in a couple of hours, you get on Eagle and give him his head. He'll take you back to camp, either to the Horseshoe or the Haystack."

Mikey thought, "God help me if I get lost like a greenhorn. Wouldn't that be something, to ride out of the trees at the Haystack and have to tell Madam Hitler I got lost? Then I'd have to ask her to take me back to the work. She can't even pass the bread without making a face."

The country Mikey had known in southern Arizona and Mexico was broken up with plenty of landmarks and trails that were always visible underfoot or over a cowboy's head. Inside that ponderosa forest, all a cowboy saw overhead were the tops of the pines and all he saw underfoot were trunks, deadfalls, and a carpet of pine needles. Every tree was a twin to millions more.

Mikey stayed on course in the trees until he found his first cattle. He threw them in with cattle that Art found and stayed and held the bunch. Art used him to hold the bunch while he found more and brought them in. When the country was clean, they started the cattle back to camp. The cows were big Herefords who were easy to handle in the trees because Paul Summers had been in charge of them. Paul and his crew rode circle every day and made sure every cow saw cowboys every week. When Art was away looking for cattle on the flanks, Mikey was able to bluff the cattle and control them, even in the trees where they could have scattered in all directions and left the country. They had been made to believe that they could be held by one man. When cattle were that easy to handle horseback, a lot of country could be covered and a lot of cattle gathered in one day.

The miracle that happened in every one of Paul's roundups also happened that day. All the cowboys arrived at the Horseshoe pens with their cattle within an hour of each other. By noon everybody was in for dinner. Manuel Chavez, a good camp cook from Saint John's, had shown up to cook sourdough biscuits, steak and gravy, spuds, canned peas, and peach cobbler.

The cattle were kept in a holding pasture and watered in the Horseshoe pens. The crew gathered the cattle in the mornings and branded calves in the afternoons. The cowboys took turns holding herd, flanking calves, branding, earmarking, castrating, and vaccinating.

The calves were roped and dragged to the fire. That was everybody's favorite part of the work, and Mikey was given a fair share of it. Paul gave him a short reata and he heeled all the calves that he could and roped the calves around the neck that were not easy to catch by the heels.

The work was hot, dry, and long, but Mikey found himself right in the middle of the best part of another great victory in his life and he did not ever want it to end. He looked up out of his blankets in the morning glad about the work at hand and he looked up at the sunset when the last calf had been branded, sorry that it was time to quit. He never felt tired and was not visited by petty thoughts.

Evenings in camp were spent washing clothes, repairing gear, and playing poker or checkers. An hour and a half of poker and checkers killed the cowboys dead. Every man was in his bedroll two hours after sunset because they would be up and out of their bedrolls two hours before sunup.

Paul was riding one bronc, a dun seven-year-old outlaw with a mean eye he called Pesa, short for Pesadilla, Nightmare. Pesa was a real haunt to look at, with a long, heavy head, shaggy fetlocks, and big feet. He owned an atrocity for an eye, for it was as yellow as a goat's and the hair did not grow around it. He only had about a sixteenth of an inch of eyelash, but the beard on his chin and muzzle was half a foot long. He did not look or act like a real horse—more like a nightmare of a horse.

Pesa was mean. He was liable to kick, bite, and strike. When he was mad he growled in a way that made Paul believe he was insane. He fought when Paul took hold of him and could be expected to hurt any person or horse who came in range of his teeth and feet at any time.

Paul caught Pesa to ride on the day the crew was to ship a herd of old culls from the Horseshoe. When the rope settled around neck, his eyes turned black and he ran at Paul to trample him.

Paul snubbed Pesa to a post, bridled him, and blindfolded him with the tapojo on his bridle, saddled him, untied him from the post, stepped on him, and pulled the blindfold off one eye and then the other. Pesa untracked and trotted away stiff-legged with his ears laid flat. He turned his head for better looks out of one eye and then the other. He made five circles of the corral and did not hump up to buck, so Gunnar opened the gate for him and Paul rode into another corral.

Pesa did not have the look of a normal warm-blooded mammal. His eye had a serpent's yellow glint. As the crew bunched around him to ride through another gate, Gunnar's horse jostled him from one side and he recoiled into Art's horse. He bolted and snapped at Gunnar's arm with his teeth and kicked Art and his horse with both hind feet. He kicked past Art's ears with both hind feet again, then snaked his head back and clamped his teeth on Gunnar's thumb when the man tried to slap him away.

Pesa growled and shook his head to clip off Gunnar's thumb. When a horse bites something he does not open his mouth to unbite it; he tears himself loose from it by sideways jerks of his head. For a mouthful of narrow blades of grass, the jerk is tiny. For a thumb with a 160-pound man on the end of it riding a thirteen-hundred-pound horse, the jerk was violent. Pesa bellowed and whipped his head from side to side with all his might until Gunnar's thumb came off.

Paul's only remedy for the situation had been to spur the horse. Later the crew thought the spurring might have been a mistake, but nobody knew what to do while Pesa had the fit. Gunnar might have saved his thumb if he could have come unhorsed, but then Pesa would have had him in a lot better place to kill him while he took off his thumb.

Paul did not know that Pesa was growling over Gunnar's thumb. He only knew the outlaw was on the fight and his official business was to fight back. When Pesa had made his first jump, Paul's limber, old hat flopped down into his eyes and he did not see anything that happened afterward. Pesa tore free from Gunnar and bucked into the cattle and so surprised the cattle that they climbed over the top of one another to get out of his way. Then he broadsided an old shelly cow, cartwheeled over the top of her, and broke his own neck. Paul was catapulted thirty feet end over end into the cattle, but he stood right up to show he was not hurt.

Gunnar's wreck was an awful disaster to happen so far away from a hospital. Dr. Disterhafft ran a clinic for Southwest Lumber in McNary, but Gunnar had to ride the eight miles back to the Haystack so he could be driven to the clinic. Art and Lyle went with him to do the driving and to wait on him if he fainted.

Forever after that, Gunnar blamed the loss of his thumb on Paul's floppy hat. He said if Paul could have seen what was happening he would have reined Pesa into Gunnar's horse instead of spurring him. He also laughed about the way a foot-long piece of his tendon had been stretched out and laid bare to the weather when the thumb came off.

FOURTEEN

THE PLAYING FIELD

In our grandfathers' time, if a boss wanted to fire a man, he caught his top horse, led him out of the remuda, and handed him over to another cowboy.

Mikey was an old witness to the changing moods of women because of Maggie. Nevertheless, he could not figure why Mary Bell Summers had been so nice to him when she picked him up in McNary and so mean when his dad came around. At supper on the day the crew returned to the Haystack, she told Paul that she was sick and tired of spending days alone in the camp. She wondered why a ten-year-old kid could ride and she could not. She would not stay in camp alone anymore. She would ride Eagle and Mikey could ride some other horse. She would not have to ride every day, but she wanted Eagle to be her horse. When she rode, she did not want Mikey to ride. He could just stay in camp and see how he liked it. That was all there was to it.

The next morning, as the crew made ready to drive a bunch of cattle to McNary, she declared that she would ride. Mikey could stay and look after the camp. She filled a canteen with water and hung it on a nail outside on the cabin wall where it would be in the sun most of the day. She did not want Mikey in the cabin while she was gone. She did not want him to water at the tank by the windmill because of germs. If he got thirsty, he could drink from the canteen. She did not explain why it had to hang where the sun would make the water hot. The whole crew, including Mary and Paul, drank nothing but the fresh water out of the well under the windmill.

Mary did not look Mikey in the eye while she gave him instructions. She stood before her mirror, arranged a white Stetson on the back of her head, and posed in her cream-colored elk hide chaps and matching gauntlets.

When she was ready to go, she ushered Mikey outside and locked the door. As she walked toward the corral, he saw that she wore a pair of spurs that had once belonged to him. He did not mind. They looked good on her, but he had thought he lost them. He knew he would never be able to claim them now.

With a good book to read, Mikey would have been just right for the day, but Granny's gift of a new Tarzan adventure was locked in the cabin. He had plenty to do outside, though. He would build muscle with the ax and split stove wood and kindling. When he wanted to rest, he would climb to the platform on top the windmill, or to the top of a pine tree. Mary forbade him to swim in the stock tank. She said he would drown. He did not want to bounce off the top of that water naked, anyway. At that altitude of seven thousand feet, it was too hard and cold.

He chopped wood until he wanted a drink and decided to tank up on the canteen water before it got hot. The Brothers at Saint Michael's taught that he should take nine swallows from the bubbler fountain several times a day. He swallowed the canteen water nine times before he took a breath and realized it had gasoline in it. A big belch of gasoline fumes issued from his gullet and his stomach swelled. Now he knew why Mary wanted him to drink only from that canteen. At midafternoon, Filomena, Nana, and Juan Bueno found Mikey lying in the shade of the cabin with a stomachache and took him back to their camp. They gave him a cup of coffee with canned milk and sugar in it, but he only swallowed one sip. They brought out a watermelon they had chilled in the horse trough, but he could not handle that, either.

Nana walked up to him with a glint in her eye. "My wrist hurts here, and my elbow hurts here, and my arm nerve hurts here," she said. "Put your hand on my wrist."

Nana's wrist glowed inside his hand.

"Now here," she said, and she put his hand on her elbow. The inside of the joint seemed hot, so he pressed his palm against it. He felt that his hand drew her pain because his own wrist, forearm, and elbow began to ache.

"There?" he asked. "Is that where it hurts?"

Nana looked way off over his head. "Now here." She put his hand on the back of her upper arm. Mikey took his hand back and shook it until the ache went out, then grasped the back of her arm and felt pain seep into his own arm again.

He held her arm tenderly at first. Filomena watched him closely but would not meet his gaze, and that made him feel that he was doing good. He tightened his hold.

After a while, Nana picked Mikey's hand off her arm and said to Filomena, "It's gone. I knew it." She turned away from him and went to the fire.

"Well?" Mikey asked. "Did I help it?"

"No!" Nana said sharply, then she turned to Filomena and laughed.

Filomena smiled at him. "What made you think you could help anything?"

"Then why did Nana want me to hold her arm? It made mine ache."

"For nothing! Forget it."

"Okay." Mikey laughed. "Next time your arm is sore, ask Mrs. Pol Somairs to take away the pain, because a pine tree will do it before I ever will again."

Nana handed Mikey an eagle's wing feather on a leather thong. "Here," she said. "Hang this around you neck."

"What will it do?" Mikey asked.

"Make you pretty," Nana said, and she and Filomena laughed. "Does your arm still ache?"

"No," Mikey said. "Why would you think my arm still ached?"

"Nothing," Nana said sharply. "You and Juan Bueno go find some pine gum to chew for your stomach and I'll make mint tea."

The gum made Mikey belch big and the tea soothed his stomach. A strange car drove up to the cabin, dropped Mary off, and left. Mikey stayed with the Apaches until after dark.

When he went back to the cabin and knocked on the door, Mary opened it and said, "Where have *you* been?"

"At the crew camp."

"What were you doing over there?"

"Waiting for everybody to come back."

"You might as well have stayed there. The crew's not coming back until tomorrow."

"My bed's here."

"I wouldn't have come back, either, except for you."

Mikey did not know what to say about that.

"You know what, kid? You might as well come in, but you're putting a cramp on my married life."

"I don't mean to."

"You don't mean to. You don't know you're doing it. Bullshit. You know. Maybe you ought to be the one to tell me. Just why do you need all this special care?"

"I don't know what you mean."

"Your dad made me come back to look after you. Why is that?"

"I don't know."

"Because he wants to go out tonight and get drunk with his other sonsabitches, that's why. So he uses you for an excuse to get rid of me. What do you think of that? Or didn't you already know he would do that?"

"No, I didn't."

"You mean this is the first time he left you at home so he could have an excuse to get rid of his wife and get drunk?"

"Mary, you're the one who wanted me to stay here, not my dad."

"Oh, *I'm* the one, am I? *I'm* the one. You might as well go to bed, because I ain't hungry and I ain't cooking anything. Go to bed."

Mikey turned back the tarp on his cot and undressed with his back to her. He used the costumer between his bed and hers as a partial blind. He belched gasoline without meaning to.

"What's the matter?" Mary said.

"Nothing."

"Why did you belch? You been drinking gasoline or something?"

Mikey got in bed with his back to the woman.

"I wondered what I smelled on your breath. Did you drink gas to get drunk like your father? Gasoline won't make you drunk. That stuff will finish you off for good."

Mikey was positive Mary had not smelled his breath. She had put gasoline in his water. He felt like bawling. He wanted to be friends with her. How could he visit his dad if this woman went on the prod every time he came to visit? Paul would have to blindfold her—use a tapojo on her—so he could see his son. That would surely never happen.

Paul and the crew rode in from McNary before sunup the next morning. He asked Mikey how he made out, so Mikey told him he had been sick from the gas in the canteen. The canteen still hung by the nail on the wall. Paul tasted its water and said, "It doesn't taste like gas to me, son."

Mikey tasted it. No gas in it, but this was a new canteen. The other one had been old and its blanket insulation had been frayed.

Mary opened the kitchen window. "Paul, we've got sweet water in here to drink. Why are you drinking that old stale canteen water?"

"Mikey said it had gas in it," Paul said.

"How could it?" Mary came outside and tasted the canteen water. "Bull! There's no gasoline in that water. How could there be? I filled it for little Mikey myself."

Now he was little Mikey. He could see the end of any chance that Mary would include him in her family. He moved his gear to the crew's camp and did not have much more to do with her for the rest of the summer. She never asked why he made that move, because that was the arrangement she wanted. He could tell that Paul liked it better, too.

Mary lost interest in Eagle after one more ride and Mikey got him back. She would not even look toward the corrals. When the crew worked in camp she took herself to town.

One day, Paul gave the crew the day off and he and Mikey rode to Blue Mountain on the Mogollon Rim. The Apaches said that maverick cattle ran there and watered in Williams Creek. Paul and Mikey rode into that country to see what they could find.

Thunderclouds formed by midmorning and a quick shower made Paul and Mikey dismount and put on their slickers. They squatted with their backs against the dry side of a pine tree and watched the rain soak their horses until their ears drooped.

Paul rolled a cigarette and gave Mikey a puff for the cold. He said tobacco was good because it was a blanket when a man was cold, a partner at work, a bite of food when he was hungry, a soother when he was nervous, a stimulant when he was tired, and a pal when he was lonesome. To Mikey, Paul and Uncle Bill Shane's cigarette smoke smelled like the toasted stuff of everything a workingman needed.

Paul had stayed sober that summer. He did not drink even a snort in the cabin after work. Mikey asked him why that was. Paul said that he had not quit; he kept a bottle in the cabin. Mary poured herself drinks every evening. From time to time she even asked Paul if he wanted one. He did not like to drink when he cowboyed. If he had been alone at camp, he might have kept a drink for company. With that crew and Mary around, he did not think he ought to drink. He would drink when the work was done in the fall. Mexico was different. Vaqueros kept mezcal all the time but did not get drunk until the work was done. Mikey remembered that.

That day in the timber Paul asked Mikey if he was afraid of the lightning and thunder, because it struck and roared around them in the storm. Mikey said he loved it. Paul said, "You must get that from me, because I do too." Mikey said the closer the lightning hit, the better he liked it. Paul said he thought it was great that nobody knew when or where lightning would strike, and wonderful that it happened at all.

A man always knew when and where the whiskey lightning would strike. All Paul said he had to do was take one drink to get struck. Natural lightning killed a feller the instant it was time for his life to be over. The old whiskey lightning killed a man a little the first time he took a swallow and a little more every time he took another. A man could be hit more than once by real lightning and be numbed and hurt by it and still live, but that was rare, and even if he survived, he would never be the same again. That was the way Paul said the whiskey lightning affected him. It killed off a big piece of him every time he took one drink because he never stopped with one. He always went on and got drunk. Now there was not much left of him for the whiskey to kill.

Mikey thought, "Well, if whiskey was that much like lightning, no wonder a man got attached to it." Just to be near it was risky. Real lightning was full of life. At Saint Michael's the Brothers taught that it put juice back in the earth so the cow and horse feed could grow. He had also seen the whiskey lightning put new spark in the eyes of his father and uncles.

He remembered the first jolt of mezcal Paul gave him in the Sierra de San Juan and knew in his heart that he would someday want to take the same risk with the whiskey that his father did. He did not know yet that it was no risk for a man to drink alcohol. It was a sure thing that the more a man drank the sooner it struck him down. He still thought a person did not have to drink more than he wanted and could stop anytime. He did not know some men would never improve their lot with alcohol like the earth was improved by real lightning. That afternoon in the rain, Mikey still had not learned that he and his father were a lot safer from the real lightning that could make a crisp out of their pine tree than they would ever be from the old whiskey lightning.

After the storm, the whole country dripped water. Paul and Mikey climbed Blue Mountain and looked around, then rode down to the rim to look for tracks. Mikey knew this was the way his dad liked to take a day off. He didn't wonder why he did not stay in camp with Mary. He always said he would rather ride out and "rim around" than stay in camp any day.

As they rode off the top of the Mogollon Rim they saw four mavericks on the meadow by Blue Lake. The breeze favored Paul and Mikey so the cattle had not discovered them. The riders rode into the brush by the creek to get closer. A ramshackle pen squatted on a pasture fence near the lake. Paul kept block salt in the pen. A long wing made of barbwire and brush gave Mikey and Paul a way to funnel the cattle into the pen. The cattle grazed inside the wing. Paul said they probably already knew the way into the pen because of the salt.

When Paul thought he had a good angle on the cattle, he and Mikey rode out into the open so the cattle could see them. The cattle bunched like deer and watched them a moment, then turned and ran. The cowboys headed them and pressed them against the wing. They were still looking back at the cowboys when they ran into the pen.

Paul and Mikey quietly worked the cattle back and forth in the pen a while to teach them respect for their horses, then left them to cool off. Paul brewed coffee in a little pot from his morral and he and Mikey ate a cup of pinole, corn flour mixed with brown sugar and water. In the afternoon after siesta, they worked the cattle again until they could be stopped, held, and separated.

One of the mavericks was a snaky, black four-year-old corriente bull with a brown stripe down his back and a shaggy brown foretop. His horns were ivory with black tips. At first, he writhed and coiled inside the bunch and darted away when the horses came near. Then he got hot and backed into a corner, pawed the ground, lowered his head, and armed himself to fight. Mikey and Paul kept driving the other cattle up and down the fence past him until he saw that nobody would accept his challenge, then he rejoined his mates to be stopped and turned and stopped some more, but he did not like it.

Mikey and Paul left the cattle in the pen for the night and rode back to the Haystack. They unsaddled their horses two hours after dark. Mary made an angry fuss at Paul for coming in late and pretended that she had been worried, but a half-empty quart of whiskey on the counter proved her insincerity.

Madam Hitler raved while Paul fixed supper. While they ate, Mary kept the bottle close and ranted on like the very Hun for whom she had been nicknamed.

The next day Paul, Mikey, Severiano, and Victoriano went back for the mavericks. They worked them back and forth in the pen for two hours before they let them out for the drive to the Haystack.

The black bull stared at the men like a thug. When Curry saw him in the pen at headquarters, he said, "He'll *look* at a feller, won't he?" That was the cowboy way of saying that a thug like the black who would turn and stare at a man instead of turning tail had made the decision that he could become a meat eater.

Paul and Curry roped the mavericks by the horns and heels and stretched them out on their sides to be branded, vaccinated, castrated, and earmarked. When the chore was done, Mikey opened the gate and let them out into an alley. They snuffed and shied as they rushed past him and ran down to the end of the alley. Paul and Curry rode their horses past Mikey to the other end and rolled cigarettes. Mikey closed the gate so the cattle would not go back into the corral. Afoot, Lyle and Art swung their ropes and followed the cattle into the end of the alley to bring them back and turn them out. Mikey crossed the alley to open a gate to the outside. The cattle crowded into the end of the alley to get away from the men on foot. The black stag turned and charged them. Art and Lyle split and climbed the fence. The stag's eye fell on Paul and Curry as they peacefully lolled in their saddles at the other end of the alley and Curry droned along on a story. A greenness pooled in the stag's eyes as he speared toward them. Mikey was between Paul and Curry and about to open the gate to a corral that led outside to the pasture where the cattle were supposed to go. The stag was only forty yards away when he picked the horsemen for a target. Mikey just had time to run behind the heavy gate and shut off the alley in front of him. The stag barreled into the gate and knocked Mikey head over heels under the horses, but the gate stopped him. He bounced back on his haunches, shook his head, trotted back toward his mates, and put Art and Lyle on the fence again. Paul's horse came awake and walked on Mikey's hand and leg. Mikey jumped up and opened the gate so the cattle could go outside.

Later, as the crew walked toward their camp for coffee, Art caught up with Mikey and whapped him softly on the butt with the coils of his rope.

"Boy, that old snuff put us grown men up the fence with no argument," Art said. "But Mikey stepped out in front of the old thing and stopped him cold."

"Lucky you thought fast, son," Paul said. "We weren't watching him anymore."

Mikey was embarrassed. "I thought I'd better not let him get by me," he said. "I didn't think about anything but that."

Paul fell in step and put his hand on Mikey's shoulder, but his eye was stern.

"I just wasn't going to let him by me, that's all," Mikey said.

"You could have been hurt, son. Then what would I do?"

"I'm sorry, daddy." The corners of Mikey's mouth drooped and his face threatened to fold.

"Aw, son, don't feel bad; I'm the one who's sorry. I only want you to know we all think you're a pretty brave partner."

That day, each man in the crew showed Mikey his appreciation and then went on about his business. That evening, Paul proudly told Mary about the escapade, so she decided it was her business to scold Mikey. In a tone that almost screeched, she told him he was stupid to think he was big enough to make a hand in an alley against a charging bull. Paul said it was a good thing Mikey was so little because he'd stopped the stag and bounced off the gate like an ant. If he had not bounced, he probably would have broken an arm, a leg, or his back. Cowboys knew that men were often seriously injured when they backed up a gate in the face of a charging animal.

Ten days later, Mikey's stay at the Haystack was over. Mary wanted to take him to McNary to meet Maggie, but Paul opposed her and did it himself. On the way, Mikey told him that he was concerned about what Mary might do when she was mad.

Paul laughed. "What makes you say a thing like that, son?" he asked.

"She's awful mad all the time," Mikey said.

"Then I bet you're glad she isn't driving you to meet your mom."

"I'm glad you and mom will get to see each other."

"I'm a sandwich. Today I get Madam Queen on one side and Madam Hitler on the other. What do you think?"

"It's my fault you're a sandwich."

"Listen, son, nothing about my married and divorced life is your fault. I'd do anything to spend more time with you. Getting to see your mom is a bonus, even though she'll probably try to make me feel bad. Getting away from Mary for a while is another bonus, no matter how bad she'll try to make me feel after your mom makes me feel bad. The good parts of it are worth a whole lot to me and the rest is funny. The main thing is that I have a son who makes me proud. How can a man complain when he is given so many bonuses in one day?"

The prospect of being separated from his dad again had made Mikey's breast ache for a week. "Dad, do you think we'll ever be able to stay together and not have to say good-bye all the time?" he asked.

"Sure, son," Paul said. He searched the boy's eyes for tears. "Anytime now. Maybe we'll start when you come home from school next year."

"We wouldn't have to do it every year, if you didn't want to." Mikey started to bawl. "Only one whole year out of maybe every ten years. I'm ten today, daddy, and I've never spent a whole year with you."

"Aw, son, I forgot your birthday, didn't I? Someday we'll be together for good, I promise."

"Yeah, when we're dead."

"Lord, son, why do you say that?"

"The Brothers say we all get separated from the ones we love in this life, but we'll be together after we die."

"That sounds like a kind of heaven. I can't imagine any place that good, can you, son?"

"I'd like it if you and me could have our own country and stock to work."

"Feel better, son?"

"Yeah."

"I think those Brothers are real good partners if they taught you how to talk yourself out of feeling bad the way you just did."

"They're okay, but they're not my dad." Mikey clouded up again.

Paul hugged him to his side and Mikey buried his face into his smoky old ribs. When he looked up, Paul's green eyes were smattered with tears, so he figured he'd better talk about something else. "I wonder where Pancho is now," he said.

"Lord, son. Roy and Viv are probably using him somewhere. He's long gone, but if we look hard enough, we'll find another horse just as good. That happens with horses. We outlive them."

Maggie and Nina were at the boardinghouse and Paul treated everybody to dinner. To Mikey's and Nina's delight Paul and Maggie laughed about other rampaging stags in their life together, about Uncle Buster and a lot of good whiskey, and about the fun they'd all had. They laughed about misfortunes they had shared and seemed glad they did not have to be angry about them anymore. Maggie asked Paul how his shoulder had healed after he hurt it the time he rode Little Buck without her permission. Then she asked him if the scar of his devil's ear and the scar he got the time his pistol went off in his hip pocket and shot half his fanny off made it hard for Mary Bell to look at his carcass. He said it sure did and Mary especially did not like to have his feet in her bed. Maggie looked him straight in the eye and said, "That sure never bothered me."

During the last week of Mikey's vacation in Nogales, Maggie took him to town almost every day to buy new clothes. This was business and he did not have time to see his other relatives and friends, except his Nina. He went over to see her every day.

Forbes's dad drove Mikey and Forbes to Phoenix and put them on the train to Lamy. All of Mikey's summer victories evaporated in that one seven-hour auto trip with Forbes and his father. Another strange man who knew nothing about cows became the captain of Mikey's ship again. Forbes's father expounded more on the responsibilities of a good son in those seven hours than Mikey heard from Paul Summers during his whole life, even though Forbes's father did not know from which end a horse shat.

Mikey wanted to be with regular cowboys, not correct, self-righteous sissies who spent more money on their raiment, hair, and manicure care than a cowboy spent on his saddle and outfit. Then he realized that the Brothers were dressed for religion and prayed a lot, but they were regular as cowboys and darned short on sermons and preaching. They were not to blame if they did not know anything about cows. They made up for that with their style and verve as mentors.

Mikey and Forbes boarded the train in Phoenix and Forbes went right to sleep. Mikey cogitated about making the best of another school year. The greatest sorrow of his life was already established in the core of his heart. He did not have a home of his own anymore. That sorrow would go away when he owned the place he had seen in Pancho's eye. Nobody, not even Mikey, could tell that he was an orphan. He did not acknowledge that because he had long since put it aside with no identification card. He looked on himself in the same way everybody else did: he was the son of Paul Summers and Maggie O'Brien, and also the stepson of Vivian D. O'Brien. How could he be an orphan? Besides that, he had a legacy and orphans did not.

Back at Saint Michael's, Mikey fell in with the routine as a fifth grader and did not have time to feel sorry for himself. No one was as much a ninny than a motherless ninny who felt sorry for himself.

Paul Garcia, Mikey's boxing coach and the star fullback on the Horsemen varsity team, coached a Day Shift football team for grades five to eight. Games were scheduled against boys of the same age in the public schools. Mikey was one of the smallest kids on the Day Shift, but Paul did not care. Everyone played. The fifth grade boys practiced against the sixth grade and the seventh grade practiced against the eighth grade. On Fridays, Paul fielded a team against one of the public schools, and everybody played.

Paul coached Mikey to play quarterback. That meant he had to hide the ball and call the plays on offense and make touchdown-saving tackles as safetyman on defense. Mikey learned that it did not matter how little he was. If he could hide the ball, he might break loose and make a gain while eleven big tacklers looked for the ball. As the last man between the opposing ball carrier and the goal line, he could be a hero every time he made a tackle, or a goat if he missed. He did not ever miss, or even believe it was possible to miss.

To Mikey, Paul Garcia was a full-fledged hero. He gave every boy in his charge a chance to have fun at the game of football. He proved by his performance on the varsity team that he was graceful, fast, courageous, and smart. He coached the Day Shift out of the purest goodness of his heart.

A year and a half later, he became a national hero for his service with the Marine Corps in the battle of Guadalcanal. He came back from the war yellow with malaria, skinny, haunted, and recovering from serious wounds, but he soon cured himself of what he called "all that war trouble" and went on with his splendid life.

Mikey became Paul Garcia's hero when he tackled John Peabody in the first game against Harrington Grade School. Peabody was a country boy from a remote New Mexico mountain range. An eighth grader, he stood a foot and a half taller than anybody else on the field that day. He was graceful, strong, and muscular, but he did not know the rules of football or how to pass, kick, or carry the ball. If he could learn to play the game, he would go straight to the Santa Fe High School varsity team his freshman year. He was already as tall as anyone on the Demon varsity team and he ran like a trampling bull. Peabody weighed 150 pounds. Nobody else on the field weighed even 120 pounds, except Saint Michael's big Taos Indian, Eligio Vigil. At eighty-five pounds and four and a half feet tall, Mikey was only a little bigger than Forbes, the waterboy.

Grade-school tackle football at Saint Michael's was played on a patch of gravel three regulation fields wide. The players wore their school clothes, their school shoes, and no helmets.

Mikey started the game as safety on the defense that day and Peabody started as fullback for Harrington. The first time Peabody was given the ball, he caught the snap from center for an off-tackle play. Peabody crammed the ball under one arm like a watermelon, straightened, waved his other arm broadly from side to side, and roared, "Get *out* of my way, *out* of my way, out of my *way*!" He then launched himself in a straight line for the goal posts. Both the offense and the defense opened a lane for him five yards wide and watched him gallop straight toward the last man on the field, Mikey. Mikey watched him kick up clods of dirt and rocks big enough to brain a boy his size and muttered to himself, "Well, you ain't going to get by *me*."

Peabody charged straight at Mikey and roared every time his feet hit the ground. Mikey stood his ground and watched him approach. He veered off course when he saw that Mikey was too dumb to get out of his way. Mikey headed him off and dove at his shoelaces with his head and shoulders. Peabody went airborne. The ground cut short his roar as he landed on the ball, fumbled it, and skidded on the side of his head. Mikey's ears rang as he sat up to see if he had stopped the bull again. Peabody lay on his face in the dust with all the air knocked out of him and whimpered. Both teams stood aghast at what Mikey had done. The ball rolled on across the goal line, forgotten. After that, Mikey ran Paul Garcia's team.

Those kinds of feats were already part of Mikey's experience with cattle and horses. He enjoyed that advantage over most other boys. He already knew how to perform with ordinary cowboy courage. Rojas, the Cañada Street bully, did not go out for the team at the start of the season. He bragged that football was not worth his effort. Paul Garcia was strict and a boy had to be tough to play for him, so Mikey figured Rojas was afraid Paul would yell at him and make him sweat, or he might skin his little freckled knees.

Halfway through the season, after Paul called him a chicken, Rojas joined the team. On his first day, Porky and Skinny ran out on the field with him. Mikey was already there. At Rojas's suggestion, Mikey went downfield to catch his punts. Skinny faded out of sight behind Mikey while Porky engaged his attention with a stream of talk. Mikey felt strong and ready to knock heads at full speed with anybody.

He waited under a high punt. As he looked up at the ball, Skinny ran at him from behind and clipped him. He threw himself in a cross-body block against the back of Mikey's knees. That was the best, most effective block he had thrown in the two football seasons Mikey had played with him. The block sprained all the toes on one of Mikey's feet, the knee and ankle of the other leg, and his back.

Mikey could not run well, but he hid his injuries from Paul Garcia and started every game until he finished the season. He could not outrun a red ant, but he hid the ball from his opponents and did not to run the ball himself except to pull the quarterback sneak. He ran one bootleg that got him out in the clear so far before anyone knew where the ball had gone, that it made him laugh. A boy nicknamed *Sapo*, Toad, Harvey Grammar School's fullback, the slowest, sloppiest boy on that team, finally saw that Mikey had the ball and headed him off on the sideline and tackled him.

Paul depended on Mikey for defense because the boy had an instinct for knowing where the ball would go. He made half of his team's tackles. He recovered from his injuries slowly, but he always made it to a tackle. He did not feel pain on the way to a tackle, only joy. He suffered silently and worried a lot, but he did not lose his position on the team. In fact, after the first few minutes that he lay injured after Skinny clipped him, he never again showed the Cañada bullies that he was hurt.

The day Mikey arrived in Nogales on his Christmas vacation, Maggie told him that she and Viv had decided to sell the house and move. He was standing at the picture window in the front room feeling bad when he saw a man ride by on a horse that looked so familiar that he ran outside for a better look. As he burst around the corner of the house, the horse turned his head and looked at him, and he recognized Pancho. He felt shocked, hurt, and jealous, then guilty because he had not tried to find the horse. He had not even asked about Pancho. The last he had known, Pancho had been with the remuda on the Baca Float.

Viv had promised to give Pancho back to Mikey if he helped on ten drives from Nogales, Sonora, to the Baca Float. He had helped on more than twenty drives, every one of them. As far as he knew, he still owned the horse, but he had been so used to grown-ups doing anything they wanted with him, he had not asked about him. Maybe he just did not want to hear that the horse had been taken back to Mexico or some other godforsaken place out of his reach again.

He went back in the house and asked Maggie why some stranger was riding his horse. "Oh, did you see Pancho?" Maggie asked. "Since we're moving and the horse was just eating and not doing anything, I sold him to Mr. Karns. You know, the man who owns the public swimming pool. The caretaker of his orchard needed him."

"You just couldn't wait to sell my horse, could you, mom? Worse than that, you sold him to Karns, who kicked Billy out of his swimming pool for life. Now the caretaker of Karns's orchard, the rat who liked to sic his dog on me and Billy, has my horse."

"Well, Mikey, you don't need him anymore. I needed to clean up our loose ends."

"Pancho wasn't yours to sell. You've always wanted to sell him, but my dad kept you from it when you could have. I had to earn him back from Viv after my own father sold him. You had no right to do anything with him anymore. Now you're going to sell the house that me and Maudy were born in. Is there anything you won't sell out from under us? You can't be doing it for the money, because you have all you need from your new husband. What's going to happen to me and Maudy next?"

"He didn't bring much money. Mr. Karns only paid thirty-five dollars for him. You can have every penny of it. No, I didn't sell him because I needed money. I sold him because we didn't have any use for him anymore, with you away all the time at school, and all...I'm sorry, son. I guess I just didn't think."

"Pancho and Baxter were my best friends. You're just like everybody else outside my world. If you'd sell my oldest living friend for thirty-five dollars, I hate to think how much you'd take for my little sister. Christmas would be the perfect time to put her up for sale. Just think, you can get top dollar for Maudy and ruin our Christmas again in one sweep. All I can say is, you'd better get rid of us quick, before our schooling starts to cost too much. Heck, we're just eating and not doing anything."

Before he could clabber up and bawl, Maggie said, "I've been saving a surprise for you, son, but I guess I'd better tell you before your heart breaks again and you fall down dead with a conniption. We're moving to a ranch. When you get out of school next spring, your home will be on the High Lonesome in northern Arizona."

"Oh, that'll be good," Mikey said. "You won't have to sell us, then. You can work us in the summer."

He saw a tear in Maggie's eye, but he went outside before she could say any more.

FIFTEEN

The High Lonesome

When a cowboy throws himself away and goes on a spree that spends all his moral, psychological, and physical resources, he is said to have gone on a High Lonesome. The High Lonesome is also a big, grassy ranch in the Arizona high country once taken from the Navajos and used by cowmen until the Navajos bought it back. Now Navajos own it again, this time forever.

At the beginning of Mikey's summer vacation, Maggie met his train in Gallup, New Mexico, and drove him fifty miles back into Arizona to the High Lonesome Ranch owned by Adams, Cunningham, and O'Brien. They arrived in the middle of the night. Their shelter was a Navajo hogan, an octagonal mud house that was pillared, shored, and roofed by cedar posts.

Maggie unrolled Mikey's bed on the floor for him and climbed into the double bed with Viv and Maudy Marie. Mikey did not suspect anything unusual until the next morning when a tall, mean-looking Navajo came in and dippered a drink for himself out of the water bucket. The Navajo looked at Maggie and Mikey out of the corner of his eye, drank another dipperful, and left without a sound. Viv and Maudy were gone.

Mikey worried that the outfit had started work without him and was anxious to catch up. Now, on his first day, he had been left in camp with his mama. Even Maudy had gone out horseback early with the crew. He dressed, washed, and went outside. A Navajo crew worked to build another hogan in the front yard. The roof of the old hogan in which Mikey had spent the night was round and covered with dirt. Weeds grew out of it.

The headman of the three-man Navajo crew was Hoskie Kronemeyer. Charlie Redhouse was the fierce-looking one who had come in for a drink of water without knocking. The other was Willie Lynch. Charlie did not speak; he communicated with dirty looks. His job was to peel the bark off a pile of cedar logs with an ax. He held the end of a log down with his foot and wielded the ax in full swing over his head toward his foot. His ax was razor-sharp and with each swing he exposed a new layer of the log's skins. With the first swing, he exposed the white skin inside the bark. With the next, he exposed the tan layer over the red core of the log. He did not leave any of the white skin. If a strip was missed, the next swing got it.

Willie Lynch said that he wanted Mikey to tell his "daddy" that he wanted work as a cowboy. He said that he was a good helper with cement and was as deft with a sharp ax as Charlie Redhouse, but he wanted to cowboy. Mikey was about to tell him that his daddy lived down in Patagonia and the man's favorite cowboys were Mexicans, but he thought better of it. Viv would have to be his daddy, if everybody at the ranch already thought he was. He wondered why they thought Viv was his daddy even after he told them his name was Michael Paul Summers. He guessed they thought those were his first three names and his last name was O'Brien. That was the first time he became aware of an awkwardness that would arise every time the kid who belonged to Maggie and Vivian O'Brien introduced himself as Michael Paul

Summers. He did not intend to change his name. He would leave it as Summers, and if he felt awkward about it, other people could feel awkward about it, too.

A very tall white man dressed in khaki and sunburned the color of cedar bark named Jim Porter introduced himself as the windmill man, engine mechanic, carpenter, builder, and maintenance man of the ranch. He worked alone. Mikey found him when he went down to look at the windmill and its storage tank. He watched the man saw planks for a new windmill tower. His sleeves were rolled up to his elbows and his long forearms were like posts with his fists as knots on the end. He wore a billed khaki cap sopped with sweat. The uncombed thatches of hair that showed outside the edges of his cap were white as cotton. The hair that showed in the V of his shirt was white against the russet sunburn of his chest, neck, and face. His great, faded eyes did not blink. Mikey imagined that Jim Porter and Charlie Redhouse's stares belonged to madmen and wondered if the High Lonesome had made them mad. He imagined that the stare was probably good to have because it came from being able to make a hand way out where nobody watched. He hoped that he would be on the High Lonesome long enough to acquire it.

Jim Porter seldom talked to anybody, but he told Mikey in very few words that he had spent all his life, except for his time in the army in World War I, on that ranch.

Mikey asked Jim where all the cowboys had gone that morning.

"Aw, they're bringing the herd on the last day's drive from the railroad."

"Tell me how to find them and I'll go help."

"Saddle that brown horse in the corral, ride west until you reach an airplane beacon on top of a bluff. From the top of the beacon hill, you'll probably see the herd in the airport pasture below."

Mikey headed for the corral and Jim said, "There might be an extra saddle in the barn, but I don't know how you'll get it on the horse. I can't drop what I'm doing, but if you can saddle the brown horse, lead him to me and I'll help you get on."

Mikey unloaded his saddle out of the trunk of Maggie's car and carried it to the barn. The corrals were made of cedar posts that stood side by side. A gentle Holstein milk cow lounged in the corral with her calf. The calf availed himself of all the milk he wanted and that told Mikey that no one had been assigned to milk the cow. He guessed he would be the one given that chore. As far as Mikey knew, nobody else in the whole family knew how to milk a cow. Maggie might know, but nobody had better expect her to milk a cow as long as she lived. She would *crystallize* before she would stoop down to grab a cow by her leaking titties. Granny was a cow milker and could do everything else that needed to be done on a ranch. Granny could chop the head off a chicken one minute and then get on a horse and turn back a steer the next. Not Maggie. Maggie could do it all, but there were chores that she would not do, not even in anyone's dreams.

Mikey caught and saddled the brown horse. He did not know the horse, but he knew the brand on his hip. He wore Uncle Herb Cunningham's flowerpot brand. He left the saddled horse tied to a corral post to soak and went back to the house to report to Maggie. He ate two big sourdough biscuits that Maggie said one of the cowboys had baked, put on his spurs, led the horse out of the corral, and boarded him. As he rode by, he told Jim Porter he would see him later.

Jim looked up with sweat dripping off him and watched Mikey a moment. He said, "Nice spurs," and went back to work.

Mikey headed west across a wide, open draw and was soon away from the sounds at headquarters. The creak of his saddle and the plod of his horse's feet were all he could hear. His horse was dark brown with a black mane, tail, and stockings. The only white mark on him was a tiny star on his forehead. His thick mane split in the middle and covered both sides of his neck. He was well broke, easy to handle, and as eager to find the herd and his companion horses as Mikey. Later, Mikey found out that Paul Summers had broken him in the Sierra de San Juan.

Mikey stopped when he heard a meadowlark sing. He had not heard that song since he left the Haystack. He liked that warbling whistle. He spied the bird on the ground beside a bush and realized that he did not know what the bush was called. Its branches held no menacing spines.

The country was drier and the air cleaner than any he had known. The sky was broader. He could see farther in every direction than he had ever been able to see. He crossed the headquarters draw and stopped on a ridge to look back. The houses, corrals, and windmill seemed a lot closer than they should. He had ridden a long way. By now, he should have been out of sight of all humans. He could be down under the brown horse in full sight of the house and a search party would only have to ride an hour to find him. The High Lonesome was big country.

Mikey had noticed that the brown horse was not shod and he worried about it, but now he saw no reason for him to be shod. The soil of the country was a fine, cushiony, sandy loam and the few rocks were round and smooth like river rock. Mikey could not see any rock formations or cliffs. The tops of the ridges were strewn with these small, gemlike rocks, as though God had come along and sprayed handfuls out of His pocket for decoration. No cattle or horses would ever be able to get away from Mikey as long as his horses enjoyed that kind of footing. Then he saw his first prairie dog town, a community of tunnel-connected burrows.

A tan rodent feller only four inches tall stood up on his hind legs on the berm of his burrow and barked at him. Another barked from another berm and another ran to the first, stood up beside him, and barked. Mikey had never seen a prairie dog and did not even know what they were called yet. He rode to their town and watched them dust the entrances of their holes with their tails in their hurry to disappear.

The airplane beacon came in sight a half mile away. The beacon tower was painted red and white, and a red-and-white striped shed housed the beacon's engine. The beacon stood on the edge of a bluff that overlooked a hundred square miles of high, flat, sagebrush and cedar tree desert. The machine that lighted the beacon and rotated its light turned itself off at dawn and back on at twilight.

When Mikey saw his first antelope, he knew the High Lonesome was a paradise. The first pronghorn buck antelope that Mikey ever saw stood in a draw beneath the beacon. The buck's black, ridged horns seemed to protrude out of his eyebrows.

He gazed haughtily down his nose at Mikey, then loped over to a nearby pair of does, moved them around behind Mikey, then back alongside him, then started to cross in front of him again. Mikey closed the distance to the beacon and pinched the antelope close against a fence below the beacon. The antelope did not have all the room they needed, so they switched to fever gear and raced past with all their might. They opened their mouths in fright, pointed their black tongues toward open country, and gave Mikey a good look at their pretty coats. When they knew they were safely out of range, they slowed and gave him a good look at their powder-puff tails as they coasted up another long draw out of sight. They had passed so close that he could still smell them.

Mikey looked down at the airport pasture from the beacon on the bluff. He sat his horse on an escarpment a hundred feet above the flat floor of the pasture. He saw the emergency landing field that the government maintained in the center of the pasture. The herd raised dust in the flat a half mile below him.

Mikey rode down to meet the herd. The drags were so obscured by dust that he could barely see the two riders in the herd's wake. The cowboy on point on Mikey's side grinned through sunburn and dust and a big mustache and said, "*Quehubole,* Miguelito."

Mikey did not think he knew any long, skinny, fair-skinned vaqueros who wore handlebar mustaches, so he said, "Who are you behind that face?"

"I'm Grover, Mikey. Your cousin Grover Kane."

Mikey shook Grover's hand and then rode toward the rear. The cowboy on the flank was Viv O'Brien on his top horse, Sorrel Top. Viv was so fair-complexioned that the sun, wind, and dust had split both his upper and lower lips. He shook hands with Mikey, but when he tried to speak or smile he pursed his lips so his face would not come apart.

Mikey went back to help in the drags. The cattle were hungry and he could see that they wanted to spread out and eat instead of slog through the dust of the drive. Maudy Marie rode in the drags on a palomino pony that Viv had brought out of Mexico for her. She wore a dilapidated Stetson hat that was so big and decrepit that it lopped her ears, and made her look like Paul Summers. She kept it on with a string under her chin.

Maudy Marie's palomino was only ten hands tall and so skinny his ribs and hipbones stuck out. Mikey asked her when she intended to feed her horse.

"He won't eat, Mikey. He's homesick."

"How do you know he's homesick?" Mikey asked. "Nobody has to get gaunt like that when they're homesick."

"He won't eat his grain or hay in the corral. When I turn him out to graze in the horse pasture, he runs to the south fence as fast as he can go, hangs his head over the wire, and nickers toward Mexico as though his heart will break."

"Will he let you catch him?"

"Yes, and he stands still to be saddled. He lets me ride him all day, but he heads for the other end of the pasture when I turn him out because he wants to go home. What am I going to do? Daddy says he'll die if he doesn't get over it. I don't want him to die. I love him."

Mikey did not pretend to know what to do. One of the truths he had learned about horses was that a body should not pretend to know the answer to a horse's yearning when sometimes not even the horse knew.

"He looks like he's pined all the meat right off his bones, sister," Mikey said.

"Mama says he'll waste away until he dies. Why won't he eat?"

"It's sure not right, because most gentle horses are gluttons. When we get back, we'll see if we can get him to swallow something to make him greedy again."

Mikey wished he had some mezcal. If he could pour some mezcal down the paisano, he might like his new life better. That was the way Paul helped sick cattle and horses snap out of despair when they quit eating and tried to die.

The little horse seemed to have plenty of energy and his eye was bright and full. Mikey would worry that he was in trouble when his eyes shrunk and the sockets turned hollow. He knew enough about dying horses and cattle to recognize a sick eye from a long way off.

He settled down to enjoy his own horse, the dust, and the smell of the herd. He found himself in Mikey Summers's heaven. He would be happy if the drive never ended. This was the reason he was on the earth. Summer had only begun. Maybe he would make himself so indispensable that Viv would forget to send him back to Santa Fe.

Another cowboy on the crew was Cap Maben. He had lived in cow camps all his life and was an artist as a camp cook. After the herd was penned at headquarters, and as the crew headed toward the hogan for dinner, Cap bragged about the tent camp he had set up for the crew. His chuck box, cook stove, table, and benches were installed in one big tent and the bedrolls in another. A tarp fly covered the entrances between the two tents and served as a shady breezeway between them.

Cap said that he did not envy Maggie her cook stove because the oven in that stove could not cook two biscuits the same shade of brown in the same pan. He cackled as he laughed and said that, at best, Maggie's cooking was only ordinary, so maybe she wouldn't notice that her stove was no good. He glanced out of the corner of his eye to get Mikey's reaction to that.

Mikey immediately felt sorry for Maggie. He had eaten two of Cap's sourdough biscuits that morning for breakfast. Any wife who called herself a cook but could not produce biscuits like Cap's ought to go into mourning for herself.

Mikey had not even been introduced to Cap, but he believed his bragging as though it were catechism doctrine. Cap finally looked him in the eye and said, "Well, either you're Mikey, or old Viv used somebody else's name on you all morning."

"I'm Michael Paul Summers," Mikey said, and shook Cap's hand.

Cap laughed again. He had laughed all morning so that everybody on all sides of the herd could hear him. He laughed at least every five minutes. His laugh was the cross between a choked wheeze and the whistle in the song of a consumptive rooster. He wore a dusty black hat and was so thin the pockets sagged in wrinkles on his khaki-covered butt.

Mikey walked into the cook tent with the crew. Everybody washed their hands at a washstand just inside the flap, so Mikey did too. The Navajos had already built a fire in the cook stove. The dirt floor had been sprinkled with water and swept. The smell of sourdough bread reminded Mikey of other camps he had known.

He sat on the end of a bench and watched the crew help Cap make dinner quickly so it could go back to work. A barren cow, remnant of the former owner's herd, had been butchered the day before. The headquarters did not have enough refrigeration to keep the meat of an entire beef. The nights were cold, so the beef was hung naked inside the pump house at night and wrapped in a tarp and stowed on the ground in the tent under Cap's bedroll during the day.

Grover sharpened a butcher knife and carved a pile of steaks off a quarter of the beef. Cap moved a two-gallon pot of beans over the hottest lids of the stove to warm. He opened the oven door to look at the three pans of biscuits that warmed there. He let down the lid of the chuck box and propped it up with its hinged leg, sprinkled flour into a clean tin tray, and rolled the steaks in the flour. Grover greased a cast-iron skillet and Cap filled it with steaks to fry on the stove. Cap opened a quart-sized can of corn and put it in a pan to warm, then took a pile of spuds that Jim Porter had peeled and sliced them up and slid them into deep, hot lard to fry in another skillet. He poured himself a cup of coffee from a pot on the stove, tasted it, gave it a big spoonful of sugar, and poured a gurgle of canned milk into it. He sipped the coffee again and told everybody that dinner would be ready in fifteen minutes.

Mikey's mouth watered, so he hit for his own dinner table. Cap gave him a pan of biscuits for Maggie "so her outfit wouldn't starve."

Maggie fed her outfit the same chuck that Cap fed his. Maggie and Paul had always served small, salted and peppered cowboy steaks rolled in flour. Mikey figured he would not like Cap's steaks as much because Maggie and Paul added an extra sprinkle of black pepper on the steaks that Cap did not. Cap's steaks looked good, but to Mikey, the stove-hot, floured meat with extra pepper his parents prepared was the best-cooked beef anybody ever ate. Viv had imported a Flamo gas-powered refrigerator, so Maggie served iced tea and homemade vanilla ice cream, which were touches to her table that Cap did not have. Maggie would have given Cap's crew all the iced stuff they wanted if he had begged in a nice way, but he scorned sweets of any kind and considered any drink except hot coffee, water, and whiskey to be poison.

Another advantage of Maggie's table was that everybody could eat as much as he wanted. After dinner, Mikey headed for the tent to join the crew again and met Charlie Redhouse and Willie Lynch as they came away from Cap's table. Both carried a handful of biscuits and an extra steak for dessert. When Mikey went into the tent he caught the tail end of a tirade that Cap gave against Indians who ate everything in sight and did not stop grabbing unless he cleared the table. Cap begrudged every bite they ate even though Mikey was to find out that the young Indians ate only a little more than he did.

After that first tirade, Mikey knew that he'd better restrict his intake at Cap's table the way Grover did if he was to get along with Cap. Grover filled the empty spaces in his growing belly with cigarettes and talk the way Jim and Cap did. Cap did not ever stop talking, except when Jim interspersed a grunt or a word that was little more than a grunt, or when it was time for Cap to croak out a laugh. Jim and Cap also kept their cigarettes lighted during meals, probably another reason they did not eat as much as everybody else.

Mikey was ready to show he could make a hand with the High Lonesome grown-ups. A good horse was the great equalizer for any boy like Mikey, or any old man like Cap, as long as he was a hand and the horse knew how to carry him to the work. Mikey had been taught that anybody who called himself a cowboy ought to be able to make a hand on a burro with a gourd vine for a lariat if he had to, so he did not doubt that he would make it on the brown horse that everybody called Negro.

The herd was penned in a large waterlot, a fire built on one end for the branding irons, and a bucket of clean water set outside the fence. Jim Porter, Viv, and the three Navajos did the work on the ground. Mikey, Grover, and Cap roped and stretched the cattle out on the ground by the fire. Maudy Marie was the tar baby in charge of a paint can full of a thick mixture of black pine tar and alcohol that she swabbed on the fresh brands and bleeding scrotums of castrated bulls. She carried the nuts to the bucket of water to be cleaned and dressed for supper. The ropers rotated at each job so their horses were given an equal share of the task.

Fifty bulls were in that herd of 750. All the rest were steers. Mikey had castrated bulls for Paul in the Sierra de San Juan and for Viv at the Baca Float, but he figured somebody on the ground would do it. However, when Grover and Cap stretched the first bull on the ground, Viv told Mikey to get off his horse, drop his reins, and come running. Mikey did as he was told. Viv opened a blade on a new stock knife for Mikey to examine.

"What do you think of this knife?" Viv asked.

"Looks like a good one," Mikey said.

"How much do you think it's worth?"

"A whole lot."

"Guess."

"A dollar?"

"You got a nickel?"

"I think so." Mikey dug six pennies out of his pocket. Viv picked five out of his hand one by one, and then handed the knife to Mikey.

"Aw, Viv, you want me to cut the bull? You don't need to give me the knife."

"No, I'm selling you the knife for five cents so I'll know you'll always keep it handy. Every cowboy needs a good knife. I'd give it to you, but some people believe it's bad luck to give away a knife. It might sever our friendship. I'm not saying I believe it, but I don't want to take the chance."

Mikey fell on the flank of the bull, sliced off half the scrotum, held one nut in his palm, and sliced it carefully so that he only cut through the thin striffing of skin that surrounded the nut and drew no blood. He peeled that striffing off the nut and pushed it up to the base of the cord as far as it would go, sliced the vein off the base of the nut, sliced the cord way up where the thinnest strand of blood ran, and did the same with the other nut. Maudy Marie stepped up and tarred the steer's brand and empty scrotum, and the Navajos let him up. He had been emasculated in less than thirty seconds and did not realize his great good fortune.

Viv went to Negro, took down Mikey's reata, coiled it, and laid it on a fence post. He picked a new manila lariat off another post and looped the running end hard and fast on Mikey's saddlehorn.

"Michael Paul, every time you catch an animal and take those wild dallies around your horn with that snake of a reata, I almost have a heart attack," Viv said. "I want you to learn to rope tied hard and fast to your saddlehorn so your fingers won't get caught in the dallies. That way I'll be sure that you keep the surgeon's touch you'll need to doctor cattle on this outfit."

Viv had become Mikey's new maestro. The boy did not consider this to be altogether good. All Mikey's cowboying had been learned from Paul Summers. Viv wanted everything done exactly his way, and he was a genius of a cattleman, but Mikey did not think he even sat a horse right.

The crew branded and vaccinated one hundred cattle, quit at sunset, and turned the herd out in the shipping pasture. Then Viv and Mikey washed, changed shirts, and sat down at Maggie's table for a big roast of beef, beans in their soup, potatoes and gravy, Cap's sourdough bread, and tapioca pudding. After that, Viv stepped outside to smoke with the crew.

Viv smoked one big cigar every evening after supper. After that he chewed PK gum. Grover, Cap, and Jim smoked Camel cigarettes and shared them with the Navajos. The Navajos could smoke or leave it alone, but Hoskie wordlessly held out a hand to Jim for a cigarette when the white men lit up. Willie and Charlie accepted cigarettes when they were offered.

The Navajos smoked their cigarettes differently than the way the white men smoked. The white men held their cigarettes between thumb and forefinger with the lighted end toward the palm of their hand, or between the forefinger and middle finger with the hot end outside. The Navajos held the hot end away from their palm between thumb and forefinger or with the hot end against their palm with the cigarette held between their forefinger and middle finger. The habitual smokers inhaled the smoke deeply and held the cigarettes in the corners of their mouths a lot. The Navajos drew small drafts of smoke into their mouths and immediately blew it out through their nostrils or their pursed lips.

The habitual smokers craved it in their lungs. The Indians tasted it on their tongues and inside their cheeks.

Mikey could not wait to be allowed to smoke. The smell of the toasted, tailor-made Camel tobacco was more delicious even than Paul's roll-your-own Bull Durham. The crew did not smoke tailor-made all the time because they smoked more than a package a day and they would run out too soon. The ranch was twenty-two miles of dirt road away from the nearest supply. Jim and Cap smoked roll-your-own Prince Albert for their workaday smokes and Grover smoked Bull Durham. Roll-your-own smokes lasted four times longer than tailor-made. The smokers' hands were too busy during the day's work for them to stop and roll cigarettes very often, and the roll-your-own tobacco and papers cost a only third as much as the tailor-made.

Maggie told Mikey to bring Viv inside and show him his boxing medals. He got them out of his suitcase and handed them to her. She handed the newest to Viv.

"How many kids did you have to whip to win this medal?" Viv asked.

"Four."

"How many black eyes and bloody noses did you get?"

Mikey laughed. "Two or three."

"They didn't change your looks much, so you must have a good left jab."

"I do."

Maggie cupped Mikey's chin in her hand and rolled his head for a better look. "Nobody better change that face." She laughed.

"What got you started boxing?" Viv asked.

"I live with 260 other boys and most of them are bigger than me. I fight in the ring so nobody will pick on me on the playground."

"Yes, but what if you lose, son?" Maggie asked. "What if you come home next summer with a broken nose? Can't you get hurt worse in the ring than on the playground?"

"Mama, the other boys respect the boxers who lose as well as the ones who win. Nobody wants to fight me because everybody knows I can fight."

"I can't understand how your letting other boxers hit you in the face will give you insurance against getting hit in the face by somebody else."

"Nobody wins a fight on the playground, mama. Even if a boy wins, he still might get a bloody nose, torn clothes, or a black eye. Some boys are cowards and will hit you with a rock or bite your finger off on the playground. I'd look a whole lot worse after one of those fights."

"Where are the Brothers while all this fighting goes on?"

"The Brothers can't stop every fight and they don't even try."

"But aren't you afraid, son? How can you put yourself through something like that? It's not fun, is it?"

"No, it's scary."

"Well, see? How can you put yourself through that?"

"I'm scared, but I'm not chicken. That's the message the bullies get. You know what scares me most? I'm scared to take off all my clothes and stand in the ring naked in front of a thousand people. That's the scariest part, getting up there naked. Then I worry I'll make a fool of myself and disappoint the ones who root for me. Most of all, I'm afraid I'll lose my courage and show everybody I'm a chickenshit."

"Michael Paul, is that a word you use often as a boxer?"

"No, mama. I'm sorry."

"Well, keep your mouth clean, or I myself will take a fist to it."

"I'm sorry; it's a habit I picked up."

"It's a darned bad one."

"Well, Maggie, Mikey's good in other ways," Viv said. "It's no wonder to me that he's no chicken. He's little, but he's got the heart of a lion."

Before he went to sleep, Mikey remembered a thought that had come to him when he explained his boxing to Maggie. For a moment he had quit being a cowboy and become a boxer again. Explanations about his reasons for boxing brought back his craving for it. For a few moments cowboying did not matter. Viv seemed to understand that.

He guessed cowboys and boxers were obsessed. Boxing was not considered fun by everybody, so why else would anyone do it?

Maybe he was a slave to it. Everybody was sure it was fun to be a cowboy until they got the chance to cowboy. After they had done it a while, even some cowboys thought it was too much hard work and could not wait to stop. Not Mikey. All cowboying, except holding herd, was a pleasure. He would even take holding herd for the rest of eternity if it ever happened that holding herd was all that was left to do.

A week later, when the herd of two thousand had been branded and turned out, Viv told Mikey that he and Grover would camp at G-Lake for the remainder of the summer. They would leave that day and be responsible for eighteen hundred cattle that had been located there earlier that month. Viv and Maggie were going down to Nogales to get the last of their furniture.

Camping with Grover would not be any different than camping with Paul. Grover and Mikey were from the same bush, *eran de la misma mata*. Grover was seven years older than Mikey and had already spent two seasons on the wagon of a big outfit in Wyoming. Mikey and Grover spoke Spanish with the same accent. The quiet tone of their voices was the same. They spoke mostly Spanish to each other, unless somebody who did not understand was around.

Mikey was never one to move fast, but on the morning that everybody left headquarters, he got himself ready and mounted so quickly that he had to wait for Grover. Grover was methodical and did everything with grace and economy. He did not make a kid's mistakes. He knew his profession, was a natural at it, and did not ever intend to do anything else. That day he did not have to wait one minute for Mikey.

Every camp on the ranch was the same: one hogan, one windmill, one reservoir tank, one pump house beside the windmill, a set of corrals, a saddle house, and a hay barn. A new chuck box was installed in each hogan. The cowboys slept on cots with springs and kept their belongings in their warbags and bedrolls. A counter and cabinet for utensils and canned goods were set up near the cook stove. A washstand with an enamel basin and two water buckets stood inside the door. A #10 washtub hung on the wall. Jim Porter had built a brand-new two-hole outhouse fifty yards away, downwind from each camp hogan. All the hogans were built the Navajo way with their doors facing east.

The sun did not ever catch Grover and Mikey in bed. They were long gone by the time the sun shone on their door. Mikey did not know what it was to be tired, but when he stretched out in his bedroll at night, he was asleep in an instant.

The routine was the same every day. Grover made biscuits after he washed his hands and shaved in the morning while Mikey wrangled and fed the horses and carried water to the hogan. When he returned to the hogan with the full buckets, Grover's biscuits were in the oven and bacon, eggs, and potatoes fried on the stove. After breakfast Mikey swept the floor. A sprinkle of water settled the dust as he swept. The dirt floor was smooth. The sprinkling made it smoother and harder every day because the dirt was *barrial*, lake-bottom soil, which could be used to make adobe.

After breakfast the cowboys rode circle on the cattle. Viv did not want his cowboys to leave camp in separate directions because someone might get hurt and be hard to find. Work usually kept cowboys busy until sunset, so a man would not know if his partner had been hurt until nightfall. Mikey and Grover stayed together all day at the risk of being accused of riding one horse, or doing the work of one horse on two horses. They separated often, covered a wide swath, but tried to keep each other in sight.

Their job was to watch for screwworms and shipping fever in the cattle. They ran Mexican corriente cattle that were most resistant to disease, so they did not have shipping fever that year. Flies laid eggs in the bloody places of the brands when they began to peel. The eggs hatched into screwworms that burrowed into the healthy flesh of the steers. A steer with worms showed great anxiety. He danced and wringed his tail, tossed his head, and licked slobbers on the brand. Adams, Cunningham, and O'Brien branded their cattle on the left shoulder. A steer could reach the brand with his slobbers, but he could not keep the flies off.

Three or four infected cattle would bunch together to fight flies. They trotted a while to see if they could outdistance them, then stopped and milled together to see if they could rub them off. If they rubbed against a tree or a post, they aggravated the wound and gave the flies new places to lay eggs. When the cattle became most aggravated by the worms, they separated from their fellows and holed up in dense brush. They were hardest to find when they were so ill that they went off alone in a state of lunacy to fight the worms. Mikey and Grover often tracked them into the cedars but could not find where they came out or find them inside the thickets.

A carrion smell characterized the ailment. The cowboys could always smell it when they were close, but sometimes they caught the stench on the wind and had to find the sufferers with their noses. Cattle that hid alone stuck their heads deep into the brush and did not move even an ear when a cowboy rode nearby. The cowboys often rode within a few feet of them without seeing them, but the stench was always there to help discover them.

The sick cattle that Grover and Mikey missed out on the range were caught when they came in to drink in the fenced waterlot at their camp and at the waterlots that held rainwater in the pasture. Some of the wormy cattle became so wild that they only watered at night. When the ailment was at its worst, Grover closed the gates to the waterlots at sunset. Often the wildest, sickest cattle were waiting at the gates when the cowboys looked out of their hogan the next morning.

The cowboys stayed in camp on Sundays, heated water on the stove, and bathed and washed their clothes with Ivory soap in the #10 washtub. Grover taught Mikey everything the boy could absorb. He was a lifelong friend of Paul Summers, Maggie, and her brothers, and he looked after Mikey as though he were his own brother. Mikey could not have invented a better partner.

Mikey and Grover rode circle every day in the forty section G-Lake pasture and only rested in their own camp. They often rode over to help with the work at headquarters but seldom had time to get off their horses and go to the house. Viv visited the G-Lake camp in the pickup once a week, but if he did not show, the cowboys did not worry. He offered to take Grover to town once a month, but Grover said he did not need to go. He was paid forty dollars a month and everything he needed, even cigarettes, was provided. He saved his money.

Walter and Darrel Lee rode to G-Lake one day on the tracks of a stray bull. Grover and Mikey had penned the bull the night before and were planning to return him that day. The Lees owned the Hardscrabble Ranch at Witch Wells, seven miles away. Mikey and Grover could do without visitors, but they loved it when they saw them coming.

Walter was Darrel's father and Darrel was Mikey's age. The Lees were redheaded. Darrel was as fair as Mikey was dark and the sun was a hardship to him. Nothing small like chronic sunburn could have kept Darrel from cowboying. He rode a sturdy saddle with a brass horn and a brown horse named Star that was much taller and sleeker than Mikey's Negro. The Lees sat their horses like centaurs and were solemn, almost grim in visage. They were serious people, but gentlemanly, soft spoken, and later quick to smile. Mikey and Darrel immediately became friends.

Maggie came out to camp once to see how Grover and Mikey were doing, but she came during daylight hours and did not catch them in camp. The plaintive note she left said that she would like to see her son once in a while.

On a Saturday a month before he was to go back to school, Mikey and Grover roped and doctored three head in the open. The last one was a stag that Mikey had castrated. Mikey roped the stag's horns and Grover caught the heels and they stretched him out on the ground. Mikey got down to doctor him with Peerless worm medicine and pine tar. He poured the red Peerless into the wormholes in the brand and scrotum and watched the worms unscrew and boil out. When he believed they were all out, he covered the wound with pine tar, mounted Negro, and rode him up to slacken the rope. He dismounted again to take the slack rope off the stag's horns. He mounted his horse before Grover gave the animal's heels slack so he could get up. Once in a while a steer came to his feet on the fight and charged the first man or horse in sight. Mikey could protect himself and his horse better if he was on him. The steer usually stood up as soon as the heeler's rope went slack.

This time, the stag lay still and rolled his eye as though he had been killed. Mikey dismounted and stomped him on the neck so he would wake up and get up. He lay moribund. Mikey twisted a half hitch in his tail, usually a sure cure for any stag who thought he was dead, but he did not even grunt. Grover dallied his rope up short and hauled the stag's hind feet up under his belly, then gave the legs slack so he would remember to use them and get up. The legs flopped back to the ground and lay still. Mikey found two cedar sticks, put one on each side of the stag's tail, stood on the end of the tail, held the ends of the sticks in both hands, squeezed them against the tail, and rubbed them up and down. Wisps of tail hair rose in the breeze. The hot bones in the tail sent up a fire alarm. The stag bawled and jumped up, whirled, and stepped out of Grover's loop, picked Mikey up on his horns, and tossed him onto his back. Mikey landed on the stinking brand and dragged the front of his shirt across it as he fell to the ground. The stag tossed him ahead and rolled him along on the points of his horns, scrambled over the top of him, stomped his head with all four feet, and headed for a high cedar ridge without looking back.

Mikey was suddenly back in the boxing ring with Joe McGrath again. Joe had just landed the punch that rang Mikey's ears and made him wonder if his eyes were open or closed.

Grover held Mikey's head off the ground so he would not inhale dirt. He brushed dirt out of Mikey's mouth and nose when Mikey sat up on his own. Mikey's hat was covered with tar, Peerless, blood, and stench. He mounted Negro by himself, but as he rode, the closer to camp he got, the more vague he got. His head grew larger and his ears rang louder with every step of his horse. Then the worm stink made him vomit. He vomited until his stomach was empty and he kept on vomiting. He did not get off his horse because each new urge to vomit came suddenly and unexpectedly and kept him too busy to dismount.

At camp Grover walked Mikey into the hogan and helped him undress. He carried Mikey's stinky clothes outside and laid them by the door. He heated water and helped Mikey bathe and take stock of his injuries.

Mikey had been punctured eight times by the horns, but the wounds were not deep and were mostly only bruises. Grover figured that he was so light that the steer had lifted him and tossed him before the horns could go deep. Mikey could move all his limbs, but he could not talk because he had bitten his tongue.

Mikey bawled when Grover went out to unsaddle their horses, mostly to rid himself of outrage. He was not afraid or sorry for himself, only sore of head and body, so he did not cry for long.

After Grover doused his wounds with Mercurochrome, he told Mikey he thought he'd better ride to headquarters to get Viv and Maggie. Mikey was about to tell him that he was all right, but he threw up again. Grover cleaned it up and brought him an outdoor bucket in case it happened again and hit for headquarters on Mae West.

Mae West was a spayed mare that Roy Adams had raised. She was the daughter of a stud named Ben Hur and granddaughter of Man O'War. Mikey's grandfather Bert Sorrells had brought Ben Hur to Arizona. Mae West covered the seven miles to headquarters like tapping for a dance and Viv and Maggie quickly went to get Mikey in the car. They loaded him up and took him eighty miles over dirt roads to the Presbyterian mission hospital on the Navajo reservation at Ganado.

The doctor opened and disinfected each of Mikey's horn punctures and put him to bed. He said that Mikey had suffered a severe concussion. He gave him a tetanus vaccination but said he was afraid that Mikey might get blood poisoning. Septicemia on the horns of bulls was known to kill bullfighters.

Before sunup, Mikey lapsed into unconsciousness. Inside his delirium he knew again and missed all the sweetness of his fathers, mothers, horses, dirt, dogs, cows, and trees. On the fifth day he embraced them and went away in peace with them.

Maggie was singing "Panchita" in Spanish at the top of her voice while she hung a fresh wash out on the line to dry by Pancho's pen in Nogales. The wind whipped her short skirt so it showed the backs of her legs above the roll of her stockings. Mikey knew again how good she was at fixing her face and then stepping out to show the world how a pretty woman walked down the street. She did a good deed every time she sallied forth that way because people liked it when they saw her coming and that helped her make up to God for her vanity. She was good at smiling and laughing, and Mikey was sure she could wither a pine tree with her frown. All pine trees should be grateful that she did not have anything against them and they did not have to grow up near her house. Oh, when she decided it was time to show her stuff, whether it be fussing or loving, everybody had better be ready to see a lot of style. She could show more style in the way she laid her hand along the back of a chair than most people could show with a gesture they taught themselves with six weeks of rehearsal. The best part of Maggie's style was that it made ordinary sons of guns wish and dream they had it, and it made them despair of ever having it even on the best day of their lives. And, boy, could she sing. And boy, did she sing in Mikey's dream. She sang better than Jeanette MacDonald because of the way she breathed her words. In his dream, Mikey loved her voice again, a voice that was prettier than any other he had ever heard, the voice with which she had breathed in his ear when she taught him to read.

He had been unconscious six days when he heard Maggie's real voice close in his ear again and he left his dream behind. "Mikey," she said. "Mikey. Mikey." He revived and improved each day after that. Maggie took him home a week later.

On the day Mikey had been hurt, his uncles Herb, Roy, and Buster had arrived at the High Lonesome with more saddle horses from the Baca Float. They had driven to the railroad phone at Sanders every evening to call the hospital and find out how Mikey was doing. When Mikey returned to the ranch from the hospital, Viv led Pancho up to the hogan and asked him to come out and see if he could tell him who the horse was. After Mikey identified him, Viv said, "Here, take him, son. Your mom bought him back."